Mother of Souls

A Novel of Alpennia

Heather Rose Jones

BELLA
BOOKS

2016

Bella Books, Inc.
P.O. Box 10543
Tallahassee, FL 32302

Printed in the United States of America on acid-free paper.

First Bella Books Edition 2016

Editor: Katherine V. Forrest
Cover Designer: Kiaro Creative

ISBN: 978-1-59493-517-6

Other Bella Books by Heather Rose Jones

Daughter of Mystery
The Mystic Marriage

Author's Note on Pronunciation

For interested readers, there are three basic rules for Alpennian pronunciation. Names are stressed on the first syllable. The letter "z" is pronounced "ts" as in German. The combination "ch" is pronounced "k." Non-Alpennian names follow the rules for their language of origin. So, for example, Antuniet Chazillen's surname is pronounced "katz-ill-en" (hence Gustav's joke about calling her Kätzlein "kitten") while Jeanne de Cherdillac's surname follows French rules and is pronouned "share-dill-ack."

About the Author

Heather Rose Jones is the author of the "Skin Singer" stories in the *Sword and Sorceress* anthology series, as well as non-fiction publications on topics ranging from biotech to historic costumes to naming practices.

Visitors to her social media will find the Lesbian Historic Motif Project she began to change the unexamined assumptions about the place and nature of lesbian-like characters in historic fact, literature, art and imaginations. She has a PhD from U.C. Berkeley in Linguistics, specializing in the semantics of Medieval Welsh prepositions, and works as an industrial discrepancy investigator for a major Bay Area pharmaceutical company.

Dedication

For the proprietor of the website People of Color in European Art History (http://medievalpoc.tumblr.com) who inspired me to ask, "Where are the people of color in Alpennia and what are their stories?"

Acknowledgments

I would like to express my gratitude and appreciation for my beta readers and subject matter experts, for their time and candid feedback: Ginger T., Irina R., Jennifer N., Julie C., Lucy, K., Mary Kay K., Sara U., Sharon K., Ursula W., Jeremy J., Elliot C., Maya C., Shira G., Carolyn C. and above all, my alpha-reader Lauri W.

PRELUDE

April, 1823

High in the mountains to the east and south of Alpennia, spring rains and warming winds wash the winter's snow from the peaks and send it tumbling down the valleys. The melt gathers in rivulets; rivulets turn to streams; streams feed rivers. The Esikon, the Tupe and the Innek swell the Rotein, which flows through the heart of the city of Rotenek. And the city flows through the Rotein: in barges bringing goods up from French ports, in riverboats rowing passengers along the banks and up the narrow chanulezes that thread through the neighborhoods of both the upper and lower town.

They celebrate floodtide in Rotenek when the waters turn muddy and rise along the steps of the Nikuleplaiz as far as the feet of the statue of Saint Nikule, who watches over the marketplace. Sometimes the floods come higher and wash through Nikule's church and along the basements of the great houses along the Vezenaf. Then the streets of the lower town merge with the chanulezes, and all the putrid mud from the banks and canals is stirred up, bringing the threat of river fever. For those who can leave the city, floodtide signals an exodus to the pleasures of country estates. Those who remain light a candle to Saint Rota against the fever.

But sometimes floodtide fails to come. When the weeks stretch out long past Easter into the rising heat of the late spring, and the falling level of the chanulezes turns the exposed banks rank and fetid, the priests at Saint Nikule's will raise a bucket of water from the river and splash it over the feet of the statue and ring the floodtide bell.

CHAPTER ONE

Luzie

May, 1823

The first notes of the clavichord were sure and clear, then Luzie winced as her student's fingers stumbled on the keys. Just let Helena get through a few measures, soon she'd forget that her mother was listening. Yes, now the music was surer and more precise. One could almost see when the music seized her and carried her along. The notes filled the corners of the parlor, softening its stiff formality until one could imagine the designs on the carpet as a bed of flowers and the fringed swags of drapery as the boughs of trees. The high part soared over it all like birdsong.

"What a charming tune!" Maisetra Zurefel leaned over and whispered. "I don't think I've heard that one before."

"It's just a little fribble called 'The Nightingale,'" Luzie whispered back. "Meant to loosen up the fingers."

She slipped a glance sideways at Maisetra Zurefel who was nodding and smiling. Good. Helena Zurefel had begun the year awkward and uncertain, able to play with careful precision but too unsure of herself to address the music with spirit and grace. And so young to be told that her hopes of a good match might rest on her accomplishments! Helena was at that awkward age: still dressed in the plain short calico gowns of girlhood but reminded at every turn to behave as a young lady.

"You've done wonders with her," Maisetra Zurefel confided. "Her governess was in despair."

Luzie kept her voice soft, though Helena was past the point of noticing their presence. "She always had the talent, I'm sure, but she has such dainty little hands. So many pieces have intervals that were beyond her. A little confidence helps. I've been writing arrangements more suited to her fingers." Helena's hands were small, but that wasn't the whole of it. Still, it was a reason that would flatter both mother and daughter.

"I didn't realize you were a composer," Maisetra Zurefel said in some surprise.

"Nothing like that, just little amusements." Luzie winced. Why did she always do that? Today was not the day to set her worth low.

Helena had finished and stood with a curtsey to her mother. "May I go now, Mama?"

"Yes, that was very nice." Maisetra Zurefel waited until the girl had left and continued, "Well, I'm quite pleased. I do hope you'll be able to continue her lessons when the season begins again in the fall."

"I would be happy to, Maisetra," Luzie replied. "And…" She steeled herself and hoped the struggle didn't show in her face. "Perhaps we should settle the fee. You know how busy everything gets around floodtide. I wouldn't want it to be one more tedious task to remember when you're trying to get the household packed up for the summer."

"Oh, yes. Yes, of course," Maisetra Zurefel said. "That would be ten marks?"

"Yes, for each quarter," Luzie emphasized. "There's still the winter quarter to cover, you remember." It seemed an outrageous sum to charge, but if she asked for less, they wouldn't value her services.

"I'm not sure I have that much in my purse at the moment. Perhaps you could return later. My husband will settle the account."

That was the same story she'd heard when the winter's fee came due and she hadn't pursued the matter. Money hadn't been tight then. Now she couldn't afford to let the matter slide. She glanced around at the lavish furnishings of the parlor, the newly upholstered chairs, the striped wallpaper in the latest fashion. If Maisetra Zurefel's purse was thin at the moment, it wasn't reflected in her house.

"You know how men hate being bothered over household expenses," Luzie said, trying for a light, conspiratorial tone. "My own Henirik—God rest his soul—could never trouble himself over pin money and butchers' bills. If I told him that wine and tea were dear, he'd think I'd been spending it all at the dressmaker. But if it's not convenient for you to pay at the moment I can stop by this evening and speak to him." From what she'd heard of certain card parties, Maisetra Zurefel's expenses would be harder to defend than new gowns—hard enough to be worth calling her bluff.

"Oh very well," the woman said. "Let me look in my desk and see what I have on hand."

She disappeared upstairs long enough for concern. But at last she returned with a discreet envelope. Luzie ran her eyes over the contents while packing up her music case. It was the full fee and a little more. A sweetener, perhaps, to forestall rumors.

A brief shiver of discomfort overtook her when the Zurefels' front door closed behind her. What would Henirik have thought? Dunning their old friends like a common tradeswoman! But if Henirik were here to see it, there would have been no need. It had been almost ten years—far more time than they'd had together. His image was blurred in her memory, replaced by the echo of his features in his eldest son's face. She still ached for his presence. For the solid comfort and reassurance it brought. For the beginnings of something else that time and custom had only just begun to kindle in her when he'd been taken from them. She shook off the mood. There was business to do.

Luzie tucked the music case more securely under her arm and glanced down to the corner to look for a waiting fiacre. A driver caught her look and swung down off his perch in readiness but in that moment she had made her calculations. It would be a long walk to Fizeir's place on the eastern edge of town, but the afternoon was still young and the weather was fair for now. Better to save every teneir to give the boys a real holiday when they came home from school. She shook her head briefly at the driver with an apologetic smile and walked on past. When her errand was done, perhaps she'd treat herself with a ride back from a riverman. They'd take a half fare if you weren't in a hurry and were traveling downstream.

* * *

The composer received her in his cluttered office. There had never been even the pretense of more than business between them, no need to waste time lingering awkwardly over tea or for her to inquire after Maisetra Fizeir's health. Once, long ago, her father had been one of Fizeir's teachers. That had given her a foot in the door. It was hard to imagine two more different people than her father, with his unruly white hair perpetually standing on end from running his large-boned fingers through it absently, and Fizeir with his neat and dapper appearance, more like a banker in his sober black suit than an artist. Her father had been Fizeir's colleague, she was a paid assistant.

Luzie set the neatly copied scores before him and ticked off the inventory of assignments on her fingers, concluding with, "I finished adding all the revisions to *The Prince in Hiding*. Will it be performed again next season?"

Fizeir only grunted in response.

The opera's debut last year had been only politely successful, but Luzie thought it much improved now. She continued, "I've copied out the parts for the three quartets. There was one place—" She hesitated to choose her words carefully. "I wasn't entirely certain about this section here. Perhaps my eyes were tired that evening. I've set out the cello as I thought you intended it, but perhaps you could look it over and check? If I've made an error, I'll re-copy that page."

It was simple tact to imply the manuscript had been unreadable. Fizeir was a busy man and he relied on her to catch such oversights. He was no Ion-Pazit to break the rules of harmony by intent.

He grunted again and set the pages aside.

"And that leaves only the violin concerto. I'll have it finished before floodtide. You'll be leaving for the holiday?"

The question was unnecessary. A composer of Fizeir's standing would have any number of invitations from his patrons. The exodus of the upper crust from Rotenek at the declaration of floodtide was as much of a sacred ritual as any feast of the Church. No matter that the Rotein remained sluggish and low so late this year.

She waited with eyes cast down while Fizeir counted out the fee for her copywork. There was never the same awkwardness that sometimes rose over her students. Business was business for the composer. That was why her heart beat faster for her next question.

"I was wondering if you'd had time to look over that piece I showed you last time." The bank notes were quickly tucked away in a pocket of her music case beside the envelope from Maisetra Zurefel.

"Ah, yes. Whatever made you think of trying to compose a motet?"

It was an innocent enough question, but Luzie shrank inside. "I…I've always wanted to try a sacred song. There was an idea—a phrase—that came to me one day. I thought…"

Fizeir waited as her words trailed off, then said gently, "Maisetra Valorin, I have a great admiration for your student études. Your talents are very well suited to the family parlor. I'm not saying that the piece you showed me does not have promise. Perhaps in other hands…"

The disappointment was sharp, but she was no judge of her own work. Back before her marriage, her father had urged her to compose, but one couldn't trust a parent's fondness. "If you think—"

Fizeir mistook her intent. "Yes, if you like, I might find some use for the motifs. I'll buy the work from you for two marks. Unless you've offered it to someone else already?"

It would be very little for a finished composition, but better than what the manuscript would bring lying in the back of a drawer with the others. She nodded and took the additional notes he offered before tying the music case closed again.

* * *

A light spring rain was beginning as she descended the steps next to the bridge to reach the public landing. The waiting riverman handed her a piece of sacking to hold over her bonnet when he saw she had no parasol. Luzie considered waiting to share the fare with a stranger, but the weather would grow worse before it was better. Thinking of what Fizeir had paid her for the motet, she gave the man two teneirs to row briskly.

At the direction she gave, he countered, "Water's low in the chanulezes. Might be mud. Better I let you off at the Nikuleplaiz where they clean the steps regular. A month past Easter and still low! Time was it always flooded before Holy Week. Late last year as well!"

Luzie interrupted him long enough to agree to his suggestion. It was only a few blocks more. "But Easter was early this year. Do you think the weather's broken at last?"

"Not likely, maisetra. The river doesn't smell like it should." He looked over his shoulder as he pulled out into the center of the current. "Rain here doesn't matter. Floodtide comes from higher up. They'll have to throw the bucket at Saint Nikule soon, mark my words."

The weather was the safest conversation anywhere in Rotenek at the moment. Everyone waited like racers at the line, listening for the sound of the flood bell at the Nikuleplaiz. That held true whether one left or stayed.

Mefro Alteburk met her at the door to take her coat and the music case. A heavenly scent beckoned toward the kitchen and she asked the housekeeper, "Have the lodgers dined yet?"

"Maisetras Halz and Lammez have eaten and left already," Alteburk answered. "And Maisetra Ponek told me she's dining from home. But Maisetra Mazzies waited on you."

Even with her stomach calling, Luzie went upstairs to change first. It was no time of year to let damp clothing give her chill and a fever. Floodtide meant the risk of river fever, whether the waters rose or not.

Her nose hadn't deceived her; Mefro Chisillic had made potenez. The rich aroma of duck and garlic and lentils brought back a flood of childhood memories. "Oh Silli, how did you know exactly what I'd be wanting today?" she said. Nostalgia brought the childish nickname easily to her lips.

"Because my bones say there's a storm brewing," Chisillic answered. "And you always did like potenez when it's wet outside. You know what they say, ducks like rain and rain likes ducks."

Silli could always take her back to her carefree girlhood when her only worry had been whether Papa thought she had practiced enough for the next concert. The cook was her only everyday reminder of those days. She had scarcely been married a year when Papa had stopped performing and her parents had left Rotenek for Iuten to live with her brother Gauterd. Gauterd's wife ruled her own kitchen and had no need of Mefro Chisillic's services. And so Silli had stayed on in Rotenek and joined the Valorin household. Her loyalty had been a rock after Henirik died.

Luzie shook off the memory. Twice in one afternoon he'd crept into her thoughts. She lifted a spoonful of the thick soup to her lips and teased, "I'm not sure there's enough for two."

"You won't think to be taking Maisetra Iustin's share," the cook scolded, reclaiming her spoon.

Silli claimed the familiarity of treating all the lodgers as if they were her mistress's daughters—even Issibet Ponek who had been sewing costumes for the opera since Luzie herself was a girl.

"Send Gerta to fetch her down then. I'm famished."

They acted out the trappings of a family—it was better than constantly being reminded that she'd turned Henirik's family home into a boarding house. Those had been desperate months after his death. Bills from the physicians and thaumaturgists had stolen all their savings. Iohen and Rikke had been too young to leave her time to earn a living even had there been work available. She'd been too numb to know where to turn.

Issibet Ponek, out of her own need, had been the first to gently suggest the idea of lodgers. Once Luzie had agreed, word of mouth and a certain sympathy had done the rest. It was all very respectable. She took in no opera dancers or acrobats. Just good, steady women of sound reputation. And if their work around the theaters meant odd schedules and quirks, they put up with her music at all hours in return.

But it wasn't a family. Her family were all far off in Iuten and she barely saw them once in two years, except when Gauterd picked up or delivered the boys for school. The lodgers might gather in the parlor, on evenings when their lives intersected, talking and sewing and listening to her play. But there was always a certain distance. In time, they would all drift out of her life. Even Issibet had talked of retiring to the country some year soon.

Her family were distant, her neighbors had become customers, and in place of friends she had paying boarders. Luzie did her best to pretend it was enough.

"Do you think floodtide's come at last?" Iustin asked as Chisillic served out the potenez, echoing the question on everyone's lips. She waved out the window where the rain was now falling in sheets.

Luzie smiled up at the cook. "Thank you, Silli." She always felt guilty to see her serving. There should be a real parlor maid, not just Gerta who kept the front rooms in order and helped all the women dress, and Mag who scrubbed pots and kept the fires, and Mefro Alteburk who kept them all in order and hired out the rest of the work. It wasn't right to have Silli wait on the table. It wasn't fair.

She returned to Iustin's question. "I hope so. The riverman who rowed me down from Fizeir's this afternoon was doubtful, though. They always know before anyone else. Do you have a floodtide invitation you're waiting on?"

Iustin nodded. "I'll be spending the summer season with the Chaluks. They asked Maistir Ion-Pazit to oversee the entertainments at Falinz and I'm to bring my violin to play in whatever entertainments he comes up with. Filip is all out of sorts because he knows they won't stand for his usual compositions. But they aren't waiting on the river. We leave next week, high water or no."

So it was Filip now, Luzie thought. She only said, "That will give me a few days to make your room up for the boys. The term is already over, but they have to wait on Gauterd to bring them." Luzie frowned. "Have you met my brother? You share an instrument, but…" No need to remind Iustin that Rotenek's fraternity of musicians had not exactly welcomed her. Only the patronage of the Vicomtesse de Cherdillac had finally opened the concert halls to her.

Iustin shook her head and turned the subject back to the boys. "Iohen must be getting tall by now. I remember last summer he was almost to your shoulder. And Rikke won't be far behind. They grow so fast!"

And so much of that growing happened out of her sight, Luzie thought with regret. She wondered if it were truly worth the cost to send them away to school—both in money and to her heart. But Henirik had made her promise. It was the academy he'd attended in his youth, and one of the best. Even more important than the studies were the friendships they made there that would serve them in good stead later.

* * *

Plans, it seemed, were made to be overturned. Two days later, the carriage that arrived just after luncheon was not Mari Orlin being delivered early for her lesson. It was a dusty traveling coach, disgorging two laughing boys and an assortment of trunks.

Rikke ran to her arms, shouting, "Mama! Mama!" while Iohen held to his fourteen-year-old dignity.

"What's all this?" she asked after kissing Iohen's forehead where the auburn curls had grown long and fallen across his eyes. "Your Uncle Gauterd was supposed to bring you next week!"

"The Perkumais offered to bring us home," Iohen said, with the air of a rehearsed speech.

"Because Efrans asked Hennik to spend the summer with him," the younger boy burst in. The interruption earned him a scowl from his brother.

Luzie's mind spun. The Perkumais! Such an opportunity, but…

One of the grooms who had been unloading the trunks into the front hall pulled an envelope from his pocket and offered it to her, saying, "It's true, Maisetra Valorin. Mesnera Perkumai asked me to give you this."

She acknowledged the man with a nod and fumbled in her reticule for a few coins to offer as a gratuity. "We'll discuss this later," she told the boys. "Now come on in. We need to figure out where to put you."

Iustin was only a little dismayed at the early invasion. "Of course I can pack up my things to make room. I'm sure I can find someone to take me in until we leave for Falinz."

"Are you sure?" Luzie was doubtful. The weeks at the end of the season left every household in an uproar, even those who remained in Rotenek. "It's only a few days. Maybe Maisetra Ponek…"

But that wouldn't do. Issibet was always jealous of her privacy and she paid extra to keep it. Charluz and Elinur were already crowded in the room they shared. On impulse she offered, "You can just share my bed. I don't mind. Better than packing twice in a week." And that was settled.

There was still the other matter. Hours later, Luzie weighed and considered and lay restless through half the night, not only for the unaccustomed presence of Iustin in the bed beside her, but running sums over and over again. The Perkumais' invitation to Iohen for a summer visit was an honor—an opportunity—but it was a burden as well.

When she broke the news to Iohen, she thought at first to spare him that calculation. "I haven't seen you since I traveled to Iuten at Christmastide. I don't want to lose a moment of my summer with you," she began.

But at his crestfallen and rebellious look, she sent Rikke away and spoke to him as a man. "It's one thing when you're at school together. There's a certain...equality between all the boys. But the Perkumais live a very different life than we do. It's a life that requires the right clothes and the right...well, everything. I haven't the money to set you up properly for a whole summer with Efrans Perkumai. And I don't want you embarrassed to look like a poor cousin or a charity boy."

She watched him turn red as he took in the implications of what she was saying.

"It's not fair," he said.

"No, it's not fair, but it's the way of the world. Be Efrans' friend, but don't try to be his equal. Not outside of school. Now let's sit down and write a letter to thank him and explain that you don't want to leave your poor Mama alone for the summer."

He loosed one last dart. "We wouldn't be poor if Papa were still here."

She'd thought the same thing too many times for it to sting. "No, we wouldn't, but the angels saw fit to take him and that isn't for you to question. And we aren't poor, we simply aren't rich. If we were poor, we wouldn't have this nice house to live in and you'd be prenticed out by now. So give your thanks to God for that." Perhaps someday it would occur to him to give thanks to her as well.

CHAPTER TWO

Barbara

June, 1823

Barbara guided her mare back onto the roadway and signaled the carriages to a halt. The crest of the Barony of Saveze gleamed, freshly painted on the door of the foremost carriage. Should she have substituted the arms of Turinz for this trip? It had seemed…premature, somehow. Receiving the title of Saveze had felt natural, comfortable. Claiming Turinz still left her uneasy. She sidled over to the open window where LeFevre's round face peered out at the same sight that had led her to stop. Her business manager much preferred the comfort of the traveling coach. She glanced back to watch her cousin urge his own mount further from the road, picking his way through the edges of the piled earth that rimmed the massive ditch beyond. Brandel's slight form had filled out under the combined forces of a year's growth and an armin's intensive training. He was not yet ready to fulfill the duties of bodyguard on his own. For all that his skill with a sword and pistol was growing, he was still too eager, too little circumspect. But the promise was there. His parents had sent him to Rotenek a boy, and in a few weeks she would return them a young man, with the shadow of a moustache on his lip and a voice that had settled to a pleasant baritone. She whistled sharply and he turned back. Brandel wasn't on duty at the moment, but Tavit would take him to task later about never letting his guard down while traveling.

Tavit circled back on the road in front of the carriage, scanning the countryside to either side, though his eyes, too, were always drawn back to the earthworks. He was the very picture of a baroness's armin, his lean body reflecting a taut alertness that was itself as much a protection over her as the sword at his side.

At the briefest of glances, Brandel and Tavit might have seemed brothers. Tavit's build was slighter and more wiry and his black hair curled more tightly. A closer look noted the darker shade of his skin. The hardness around his mouth and eyes was a surer mark of his years than his smooth cheeks. Another man might have resented Brandel as a rival for his place at her side. Tavit had accepted him with the same taciturn forbearance as the other odd requirements of his position.

Here on the lonely highway to Turinz, Tavit's sword might prove less useful in time of need than the musket in the coachman's box. Barbara expected no threat more complex than robbers. Back in Rotenek there was the more delicate dance of honor and insult and reputation. In the city, the traditional parts of an armin's training still had meaning and her duelist's skills were as indispensible as LeFevre's more staid talents.

According to LeFevre's maps, they'd crossed into the borders of Turinz some hours past. These were her lands now, though only symbolically. It would be another half-day's travel before they'd reach the title-lands she held by deed. Yet if her title as Countess Turinz were to mean anything but ceremony, the entire region fell under her concern.

LeFevre coughed softly to draw her attention and quirked a half smile at her with the ease of long acquaintance. "I don't recall Langal mentioning anything about a canal. But during the time he held the mortgages of Turinz, it's likely that nothing except the timeliness of the rents caught his interest."

Barbara nodded and looked back at the torn earth. They'd find no answers here. She called up to the coachman to move on.

LeFevre's manner rarely crossed the line to familiarity despite the long and tangled history between them. He had served the old baron since well before her birth and had stood a sympathetic watch over her childhood, when she had been something less than ward and more than servant in that household. And LeFevre had been the only person unsurprised when the baron's last papers had been unsealed, revealing and claiming her as his bastard daughter.

But this journey had nothing to do with the late Marziel Lumbeirt, Baron Saveze. This was in pursuit of the legacy of her other father—her mother's husband, Efrans Arpik, Count Turinz. The legal intricacies of debt and inheritance had given Arpik reason not to disown her. It had been a last stab at his rival. If Lumbeirt acknowledged her, then she would have been the bridge between Arpik's creditors and Lumbeirt's wealth. And then Arpik died, leaving the world in ignorance of the fate of his infant daughter—an ignorance that had continued until her twenty-first year severed all claims, both from the heritage of Arpik's crippling debts and the rights to Lumbeirt's fortune.

Barbara had considered herself well rid of Arpik's inheritance, both debts and title. The deeds and the mortgage for the Turinz title-lands had come to rest at last in the hands of Maistir Langal, the notorious debt-broker. But he, having abandoned all hope of profitable return, had offered her those deeds for a pittance—and with it, a chance to lay claim to the title rather than let it revert to the crown.

It would have shown a want of tact to tour the property before the question of the title had been settled. Only slightly less tactful that she had drawn up the purchase contract so tightly before beginning on that process. Langal was not a man to be trusted beyond the ink and paper that bound him. The legal questions around the inheritance were delicate enough that she wanted the property solidly in hand before embarking on them. To claim the title, she had needed the consent of two parties: Anna Atillet, Princess of Alpennia, and the council of titled nobility and their heirs-default.

Princess Annek had been amused when the tangled history was laid before her. "You've inherited a superfluity of titles and a scarcity of wealth," she had observed dryly. "In his enmity toward Saveze, he let the Turinz title slip away from the Arpik line entirely. What a legacy."

"He never gave any thought to legacy," Barbara had countered. "Arpik seemed to have taken no pains to get heirs of his own in all the time he was married to my mother."

The council of nobles had been harder to convince on the matter of the title. Tomos Montein, Baron Mazuk, her new neighbor, had raised many questions and doubts about the propriety of it all, and started a whispering campaign that left many willing to let the matter slide for another year. The common sessions had nothing to say in the matter, of course, but there she found some allies who wanted the question settled after two decades of uncertainty.

The more she'd learned from her own contacts and LeFevre's investigations, the more uneasy she felt about what she'd find in these lands. It had been twenty years since there had been a count in residence. Longer still since there had been one who had any care for the place and its people. Was she old-fashioned in thinking that sort of care still mattered?

It was still dizzying, when she thought of it, to have come in the space of five years from being the nameless orphan Barbara, legal property of Baron Saveze and willed with the rest of his disposable possessions to his nobody of a goddaughter, Margerit Sovitre. Dizzying to rise from there to the point of being granted not only Lumbeirt's title but Arpik's as well. That rise had made her a few enemies purely from envy, others from more personal motives. But she had emerged from those chaotic times with one thing she valued above both titles: Margerit Sovitre's heart.

A wistful smile crossed Barbara's face at the thought. Margerit would already be at Saveze for the summer, and the sooner she untangled this mess in Turinz the sooner she could join her. Her thoughts came back to the puzzle of the earthworks and the stagnant muddy ditch that lay between them.

They found answers to the puzzle in the village of Sain-Mihail, a mile farther down the road where the attractions of gossip and a comfortable inn kept them for the night. Mazuk's surveyors had thought to cut corners. The first course they'd laid for the canal had been well within Mazuk's lands, but last winter—just as she was beginning negotiations for Turinz—a violent shaking of the earth had sent a fall of boulders across its path. The easiest path around that obstacle lay just across the line in Turinz.

"Chotilek might have taken his price, low as it was, and let him dig through," the innkeeper confided, "but he thought it better to see how things settled out. Begging the mesnera's pardon, if you see what I mean." With a nod in her direction.

And she did see what he meant. These people were not her tenants. They owed her nothing, either in rents or loyalty. But it seemed they were willing to give her a chance to speak on their behalf. To see if she would throw the weight of her name behind their concerns, only for the sake of that name.

"I'll see what I can do," she promised in parting the next morning. The region was known for wine and cattle—she could bargain with Mazuk for their transport needs and leave everyone with gains.

* * *

The title-lands of Turinz lay in the low hills and fertile fields that rose to meet the Terubirk range in the far south of Alpennia. They were far enough from Rotenek for local concerns to be overlooked, and close enough to the French border to have borne some of the brunt of the war. On the other side of the Terubirks lay Baron Mazuk's hope of wealth: iron works that needed cheap transport of coal. Turinz had no share in that particular hope, but the manor had been rich enough until the more prosperous parts had been sold off. Now, even a less ambitious man than Arpik would have been hard put to support the style expected of a nobleman in Rotenek from those title-lands alone. Well, what was sold was gone and there was little chance of regaining it. Over the years, others had snapped up the most profitable lands. Mazuk himself had speculated in some of those squandered acres, though it seemed he would have done better to invest nearer to Sain-Mihail.

The village that of old had served the manor straggled in an awkward sprawl across two banks of the Trintun River, escaping the bounds of the title-lands on the far side. Barbara consulted LeFevre's maps—or rather the maps in his memory.

"Most of the other bank belongs to a family named Perkumen," he supplied.

She recognized the name from the rolls of the council of commons.

"A few smaller freeholds," LeFevre continued. "The woods there further upstream are yours, and the mill." The manor itself lay out of sight beyond the hill. They'd deal with that shortly.

No point in thinking they could enter the village unremarked. When Barbara stepped out of the carriage and shook her skirts loose—no riding breeches for this entrance—the parish church stood before her. Yes, that would be the place to start. She eyed the stone bell tower warily. One corner had crumbled. Another casualty of that unexpected earthquake, for the fallen stones were still piled at its base, waiting to be hauled away or restored. The main building seemed sound. She signaled to her retinue and they entered under a small crowd of curious eyes. She expected that crowd to grow shortly. Good. This was a time for broad gestures and that called for an audience.

At the priest's questioning welcome she said, "A prayer, Father, if you will, for the peace and prosperity of the lands of Turinz and the well-being of its people. And when there is time, a mass to be said for the souls of all who have departed since the last time any lord of Turinz set foot in this church."

At the end of the improvised service, the priest stepped away from the altar toward the gathered crowd and announced, "My friends, please welcome Mesnera Barbara Lumbeirt, Countess Turinz."

This was different from her return in triumph to Saveze several years back, where they had known her for years. She weighed the mood of the crowd and began. "I am a stranger here among you." After that, the words came more easily. "Indeed I was a stranger to myself for many years. But I know that my mother, the last Countess Turinz, lived here and some of you might have known her." They had hardly been happy years: exiled from friends and family in Rotenek, kept out of the way by a husband who had cared only for her dowry. Barbara realized she had no idea what impression her mother might have made on the older folk who did remember her.

"The late Count Turinz," she continued, then hesitated. It wasn't well to disparage one's predecessors and there might have been some reflexive loyalty to the man. "The late Count Turinz is not a man whose legacy I continue."

That was both true and safely ambiguous. There was a muffled gust of laughter in the back that might have been accompanied by a crude joke. No matter. Better to have it out in the open. Someone tried to hush the man quickly, but Barbara turned to respond.

"No, it's true what you've heard. I'm not of Arpik's blood, and yet I am his heir. And since Turinz has fallen to my hands, honor demands that I do my best by you."

There was no aclaim, no hearty cheers as there had been in Saveze, but the suspicious frowns had faded. They would give her a chance.

Her party took over the entirety of the second-best inn the village boasted. The better one lay across the river outside her bounds. It was better to show loyalty if she hoped to win it. In what was left of the daylight she rode out to the manor itself, an ancient towered hall flanked by rambling outbuildings that ranged around a space more farmyard than courtyard.

Someone had been using a few of the rooms. Langal's agent, no doubt. Most were neglected and filthy. She climbed the stairs with a lantern found in the stables, heeding Tavit's cautions about loose stones and rotted wood, but these buildings seemed to have been spared the damage that struck the church. It wouldn't be comfortable, but with a couple days' work it might be suitable for a symbolic occupation. Entertaining…that would need to wait.

Which of these had her mother inhabited? There was nothing to tell by the rubbish that remained. Anything of use or value had long since been stripped away. Was she mad to have taken on this burden? Burden it was, for the moment. But looking out the window to the fields beyond, she could tell the land was good and would be better with a careful hand. There was promise.

That promise seemed thin indeed by the time the next day had passed. Langal's agent had demanded the next quarter's rents in advance. "For the new countess," he'd said. She, of course, had seen none of it. Some had paid. The bolder or more canny had held to their rights and delayed. And some, no doubt, had done the latter and claimed the former. There was no untangling it with the account books gone.

There was worse than that: stories of lost records, extra fees. In addition to the needed work on the church, the mill had been damaged ten years past and never repaired. Since then they'd had to send everything by wagon to a mill twenty miles east.

Barbara had raised an eyebrow at that. "Over the border into Mazuk? Not down to Fentrinz?"

Langal's agent had given those instructions, like many other questionable ones. And once again Mazuk's name cropped up more often than seemed reasonable in the affairs of Turinz.

* * *

Even without the further evidence of Mazuk's meddling, the meeting with him was not one Barbara cared to put off. She had sent a politely worded letter the first day she arrived. Throughout the past spring, Baron Mazuk had maintained a brittle hostility toward her when they met in council or on the streets of Rotenek. That hostility was becoming more understandable. The empty title in Turinz had left opportunities that her presence threatened. Yet now that their future as neighbors was established, his response to her invitation was more conciliatory. Yes, he would be pleased to come to Turinz to discuss matters of mutual interest. She might expect him on Thursday next. Hoping she was in good health et cetera. A practical man, Barbara thought, if not one of firm principles.

Given the distance, Barbara had not expected him to arrive at the manor until late afternoon. But the sun had just reached its peak when she heard a shout from the first man to spot the carriage and outriders.

She broke off the sparring lesson with Brandel and swore softly as she ran a hand over her hair where it was escaping from its pins. "Damn his timing, I'd meant to be more presentable than this." She handed the practice blade to her cousin and caught up her coat. A quick wipe of her face with a handkerchief completed the hasty toilette.

Mazuk arrived in all state, with footmen in attendance in addition to an armin as outrider. The latter she could understand, given their history, but

Barbara was used to country customs that frowned on too much formality during the summer season. Her own appearance only emphasized the contrast. Where she had donned buckskin riding breeches and a dark linen coat, Mazuk was dressed like a dandy returning from a stroll in the palace gardens in pale fawn trousers and green-striped waistcoat. Although he topped her by several inches, his stout figure made him seem shorter compared to her own more athletic build. And, of course, his hair was impeccably oiled into place. A lock of her own tawny hair escaped the pins to blow across her face. Barbara let it be this time.

"Welcome to Turinz," she offered, with a bow. "I fear my hospitality will be lacking." She nodded toward the entry. "I've arranged dinner at the inn later—you'll need to rely on it for lodging too. I haven't anything suitable for guests yet, I'm afraid." She signaled to Brandel to step up for introduction. "My cousin, Eskambrend Chamering, my mother's nephew. Brandel, our neighbor Baron Mazuk."

That set him aback, having taken Brandel for a mere hireling like Tavit. Tavit himself and Mazuk's armin were performing their own silent rituals of introduction and acknowledgment.

Mazuk had been thrown off his stride. It wasn't only the clothing, Barbara realized—though to her recollection he'd never encountered her in breeches before. After all, he'd never taken her invitation to cross practice swords at Perret's fencing salle. He had come prepared to play courtly games with a lady and found none. She hid a smile and took the steps up to the front entrance with an energy that had nothing of petticoats or kid slippers. Mazuk followed more sedately.

In the entry hall, LeFevre came out of the parlor he'd commandeered as an office to say, "I've asked for tea to be brought—or perhaps you'd prefer wine?" They followed him back in and ranged themselves around the sparse furniture with the air of a battlefield treaty negotiation.

Mazuk cleared his throat. "I understand you have an interest in my canal, Baroness...well, today shall we say Countess Turinz? Or do you keep to strict precedence?" Turinz might nominally be the higher title, but Alpennia followed French customs. Saveze held greater rank by age and influence.

"Turinz will do for today," she said. She tried to guess whether his sally had been meant as flattery or insult and her heart quickened to the game.

Mazuk's disquiet made him less than articulate in his persuasions, but his project itself spoke eloquently. They agreed on the essentials. The Terubirk range had iron but it had never been worth working at any scale unless you could reliably bring coal up the river. Easier transport would benefit everyone—everyone with the right to use it. As things stood now, goods often went west over the border to France, rather than all the way to Rotenek, or even to the nearer port at Falinz. The prices for that trade were whittled away by tariffs if it were done openly, and bribes if it were not. Easier transport would address a number of problems. And if someone else had taken the risk and work to dig the canal...and there was the rub. For Mazuk made a fuss about how much work he'd done and how little a thing it was to cut through that corner of land.

"Little enough," Barbara agreed. "And yet it wasn't yours to use. And now there's the matter of trespass."

Mazuk tried to bluster. "A misunderstanding, nothing more. That quake was damned inconvenient. The surveyors—"

Barbara cut him off. "Don't try to tell me that surveyors who can lay out the course of a canal can't tell when they'd crossed a boundary line. You gambled that you'd have no neighbor of name to answer to, and you lost."

They went back and forth for hours it seemed, like market-women haggling over the price of eggs. In the end, one simple fact decided the matter: the cost of either drawing back and going the long way around or of trying to move the rockfall was far more than the value of a few barge tolls. And so it was settled: Mefro Chotilek of Sain-Mihail would trade his corner of land for toll-free use of the canal. It might seem a small thing, but Mazuk would know he could no longer treat Turinz as his personal parkland.

* * *

Local affairs were more complicated to settle. It took two full weeks even to find the shape of the gaps between Langal's accounts and the story they heard from the villagers.

"What a tangle!" Barbara said to LeFevre over dinner at the end of the day when they called a finish. She was startled to notice three empty wine bottles on the table between them. Had they been that long at work? Brandel had long since gone up to his room and even Tavit had abandoned them. "There are no records, no receipts, no rolls. I'd be within my rights to demand new rents from them all, but that's no way to begin. There's many couldn't pay a second time. And God only knows who's telling the truth!"

"Now there's a thought," LeFevre said. "Leave it to God." It might have been the wine speaking, but it had the ring of a recommendation.

She raised an eyebrow at him.

"The bell tower repairs shouldn't wait. Tell your tenants that anyone who still owes the midsummer rent should pay it to the church. That will answer your dilemma. You could hardly start work on the manor this summer whether you have the rents or not. It will take that long to determine what needs to be done."

"Yes," Barbara said slowly. Her every fiber cried out against starting with debts, but she had slowly grown easier about treating Margerit's fortune as her own. Not—as Margerit insisted—because the old baron should have left it to her by right. Only because the pledge they had made one another—one heart, one home, one purse—had never yet betrayed them. It might have been Saveze money that paid Langal for the mortgage, but it would be Margerit's funds that turned this heap of stones into something worthy of a countess again. Oh, Margerit! She yearned to be done with all this and in her arms again. She nodded at last in agreement.

LeFevre ran a hand through his thinning hair leaving an uncharacteristically unkempt look, then drew off his spectacles and closed his eyes briefly. "We'll need to find someone trustworthy to take on the management here. Someone local who knows all the secrets, and then a second clerk to keep him honest. And you should find someone in Rotenek to oversee the Turinz accounts separately."

"Separately?" Barbara was startled. "Do you expect it to be that much work?"

He shuffled the papers before him and stacked them neatly. Barbara knew it for a delaying move. It was a habit of his before opening a delicate subject.

"Barbara…?"

That caught her attention. He hadn't addressed her by her Christian name since the day Prince Aukust had set the signet of Saveze on her finger.

"Barbara, I'm not a young man. Haven't been for a very long time. With Maisetra Sovitre's properties, and your lands in Saveze…I don't think I can do justice to another entire estate."

Barbara examined him closely. Did he indeed look more tired than usual or was he only now allowing it to show? Or had she simply not been paying attention? There had been a time in her life when that inattention could have been fatal. She tried to remember LeFevre's age. Near what her father's had been. Marziel Lumbeirt had fallen before his time, but… She felt a worm of fear. In many ways, LeFevre had been more of a father to her than the old baron had been. How could she not have taken more care for him?

"Of course," she said quickly. "We'll find someone. Perhaps it might be better to appoint separate managers for all of the properties. That would leave you to review accounts and read their reports."

LeFevre let his breath out in a sigh. "I don't know. That's becoming the worst of it. The reading. My eyes. Mostly Iannipirt reads for me these days, but…"

Barbara followed his thoughts. A clerk who could no longer read was crippled indeed, even with as faithful a secretary as Iannipirt at his side. "Why didn't you ask Ianni to come with you? He would always be welcome at Saveze."

"I didn't want to say anything," LeFevre continued. "It comes and goes. And Ianni spends the summer with family. The holiday is good for both of us."

Barbara reached out and took his hand. "You should have told me. Did you think I'd turn you out into the street?"

They both laughed at that. He had enough properties and investments of his own in Rotenek to live comfortably. But most of his life had been given in service to Saveze. It must pain him to admit his growing incapacity.

Barbara took the stack of papers from in front of him. "You should have said something," she repeated. "I'll have Brandel read them to you, if that helps. I've been thinking of using Turinz to give him some experience in managing properties."

"He's too young for that," LeFevre protested.

"Oh, not for the manager's job you were thinking of," she said. "Just…" She trailed off, not yet ready to share those unfledged thoughts. The opportunity might never come, after all.

As always, LeFevre was there with her. "He can't inherit Turinz," he said gently. "There's nothing to be ashamed of in burfroi birth, but only the nobility can hold title-lands."

"No he can't, not as he is," she agreed. "But the bloodline connection is there. He's kin to the previous Countess Turinz and the Arpik side is long dispersed. That would be enough of a claim if…"

"If he were enrolled," LeFevre finished for her.

It wasn't impossible. Common-born men could be enrolled into the nobility for many reasons. Lord Albori had been rewarded for his long service as foreign minister. There might come a day when Princess Annek would owe her a favor…

"Don't set your heart on it," LeFevre cautioned. "Even if you adopted him, it would make no difference without enrollment. I know you never really meant him to become an armin, but it's a long road to go from a country squire's son, to a courtier, to a man of sufficient note to be ennobled."

Barbara shook her head to dismiss the idea. LeFevre was right. "It still wouldn't hurt to give him some experience with properties. And no, I never meant him to become an armin. But it's a path he can understand—a prize he can value. When a boy dreams of bold knights and dashing musketeers, you can't tempt him by pointing out that a courtier will go farther in finance than fencing."

She thought back to the previous summer when she had met her Chamering cousins for the first time. "I wanted to give something back. My Aunt Heniriz had her full share of the family's misfortunes. Why shouldn't her son have a share in the legacy it brought me? There's nothing she herself needs or wants from me, but Brandel was such a fish out of water. I could see he was meant for something beyond mending horse harness and bringing in the harvest."

"It's honest work, you know," LeFevre said. "Bringing in the harvest."

Barbara winced. She knew better than most how precarious the value of noble birth could be.

"Well, it's settled then," she said, ending the conversation. "Brandel can be your eyes whenever you need him. We'll find someone here in Turinz to oversee the survey before we leave and then an accountant in Rotenek. The priest was suggesting a man named Akermen. A local family but he's had some schooling at the university."

CHAPTER THREE

Serafina

Early September, 1823

The stones of the chapel held the chill close, even late into the afternoon. Serafina pleaded through her shivers, "We could try again tomorrow. Surely there's time."

Summer had passed here at Saveze, there was no denying it. Summer had passed and she was no closer to touching the divine, to reaching the ears of the saints and having them hearken. She had spoken the right words, inscribed the right names, touched the relics and lit the candles, and except for the burning of the wick, the chapel had remained dark. Except for the rustling echo of her movements, it had remained silent. When Margerit Sovitre had spoken the same words, the space flared with the bright swirling *fluctus* and echoed with whispering power in answer to her prayer. And for her…nothing.

Margerit reached out a hand to take hers and steady her as she rose from the embroidered kneeling cushion before the altar. "We're leaving tomorrow. Time enough to try something different when we return to the city."

Serafina stared at where their hands were clasped, Margerit's pale fingers against her dark ones, like an echo of the presence and absence of the mystic light. She shook her head and drew back her hand. Rotenek would drive them apart.

She'd come to Alpennia nearly a year past in search of a teacher and had been plunged unexpectedly into a labyrinth of politics. She'd told herself it was no wonder that her studies made little progress over the winter. This summer should have been different. Here at Saveze, immersed in Margerit's little community of scholars…if she could come no closer to learning how to turn her visions into truth here, what hope would there be back in the city?

"Let me try one more time," she begged.

"Serafina, this is useless. We need to find a different approach."

Useless. The word cut through her memories. Once again, Paolo's voice rang in her ears. *What did I marry you for? You're useless! Your father promised me you could see visions and work mysteries. And what do I get? You can't learn the simplest charm. Useless!*

She had married Paolo for so many reasons: to escape the constant reminder of her mother's death, to grasp a chance to see something of the world beyond her one small corner, because he was charming and witty, because even in as cosmopolitan a city as Rome, not all men would be indifferent to the color of her skin. But above all else, she had married him because he promised to teach her to work mysteries.

Useless.

She thought he'd wanted her—wanted more than the promise of her skills. He had praised her beauty teasingly and he'd brought her a gift: a book about the interpretation of visions. They'd talked late into the evening about the nature of miracles and the study of thaumaturgy. There had been a connection, she thought. A bond of passion both of mind and body. When it was time for him to leave for Naples, he'd asked Papa for her hand and she had agreed.

They'd lived an itinerant scholar's life in a series of cramped apartments that she did her best to make into a home. She learned to cook the dishes he liked, and managed the money he carelessly kept in a tin box for everyday expenses, and put his notes and papers in order. Paolo laughed at all the things she didn't know. Everyday things that her mother had never learned in all the years after she came to Rome, and that her father had never thought important. He laughed, but he never taught her better. The only thing he taught her was magic. The only thing he *tried* to teach her.

She was slow, clumsy. The lessons that had begun in such excitement became an ordeal. *You must have stumbled over a word. You haven't performed the gestures correctly. Try again.*

He had her learn the rituals as she must have learned her first prayers, back in the days before her baby-tongue had given way to Romanesco. Word by word, without sense or meaning behind them. She read through all of Paolo's most precious books, trying to understand how she was failing. It felt like the times she had looked through her father's Ge'ez prayer book. She could sense the power in the words, but they made no sense. The *fluctus* that bent ever so slightly to Paolo's rituals lay quiet and silent under her hands.

You're useless! What good are your visions if you can't get me what I need?

The first time Paolo left her, she was terrified. After two days she ventured to the library where he'd been working to ask after him. They said he was traveling to Rome. The French who occupied the city were gathering treasures for their emperor and Paolo had gone to…to what? They weren't certain. But he had gone to Rome and hadn't thought that she might like to visit her father, or even that she might want to know when he would return. Every evening she counted over the money in the strongbox, afraid of how long it would need to last. Then one evening he was there again, dusty and tired and demanding to know why there wasn't any fresh bread in the house.

She'd cried and begged him never to leave her alone again. He'd comforted her awkwardly, and the next day he'd taken her to speak to a man in an office who'd shown her columns of figures. She never before realized the sums that made possible Paolo's carelessness with money. She'd thought he was the poor scholar that his clothes and habits proclaimed him. His banker had been instructed that she was to have his authority to draw an allowance and he didn't care to be pestered in the future over expenses.

They moved to Palermo. The next time he disappeared, it was for a month. One of his colleagues came to ask about some papers. Serafina found the unfinished work, and promised its completion. This time he returned empty-handed, angry and tired. He began the lessons again, drilling her in precise repetitions of word and gesture. Again he gave up in frustration.

She knew more by then of why he wanted her skills—the skills she didn't have. Paolo hunted books: books of magic, manuscripts with bits of rituals, thaumaturgical secrets. And she was meant to have been a hound to scent them out. He had divinations to find their traces through maps and letters, charms to call power to power in libraries and archives so that he could steal a march on his rivals. And more than that, she was to have helped him unlock the rituals, once he'd found them. His own vision came in fits and hints, hers in a blaze of glory. She was to have been the means of his triumph, but it was a blaze of light with no heat. She was useless.

The curious interest he had shown in her body when they were first married had faded to something she recognized as boredom. She was too proud to beg for his touch, even as her right. If there had been other women, she would have raged at him. Perhaps there were. She didn't want to know.

Back to Rome. She was ashamed to tell her father of her failure when they met now and again. Instead they spoke of Paolo's new work. The Vatican archives stolen by the French were being returned and the work of cataloging was more than the priests and clerks could manage, and so they helped set to the work. Paolo thought it a good hunting ground and left the tedious parts to her. Years passed.

And then, in an incoming shipment of documents, she had stumbled across a bundle of colorful notes and diagrams labeled "Observations on the Tutela of Saint Mauriz, Rotenek" and seen a woman's name—Margerit Sovitre—scrawled across the bottom of each page. For the first time in all her study of mysteries, those notes gave her a glimpse of *how* they could make sense. How the pieces came together and fit each other. She saw her own visions echoed in the sketches and the hunger burned again.

Paolo would have delighted in those papers, but Paolo was gone once more, leaving her to labor in his place. This time he had gone to Paris itself. Not everything that had been taken had been returned. As more of the crates and inventories were sorted out, Paolo's mood had darkened. And then he was gone, hunting whatever it was he hadn't found in the shipments. Serafina hadn't dared ask whether he hunted it for the Pope or for himself. If the prize were easily found, he'd be gone for months. If the quest were more difficult, a year. Perhaps two, he couldn't say.

Serafina had made plans idly at first, only daydreaming. Alpennia was not an impossible distance. A ship to Marseilles, a barge following the rivers or even a public coach. The bankers never questioned when she asked for letters of introduction. Paolo wrote rarely, but a message arrived saying that he would certainly not return before the spring, perhaps longer. She set all in motion before doubt could creep in. Why shouldn't she run madly off after her own prize, as he had so often? And if he returned to find her gone, then he could know the pain of wondering when—if—she would return.

* * *

The cold of the chapel drew her back from her memories. Serafina began gathering up the apparatus from that last working. It gave her an excuse to turn her face away. Margerit wasn't fooled. She felt Margerit's hand on her arm, turning her back toward the light from the candles on the altar.

"You have a true talent, Serafina. A talent for seeing—for perceiving how the world spins. That's the first step," Margerit insisted. "Think how much harder this would be if you hadn't the skill to see the results of your efforts."

"But there are no results! Nothing I've ever worked has had any results. I can see the currents stirred up by your slightest prayer. But mine? No one hears mine." She tried not to hear pity in the younger woman's voice. Margerit, at least, was willing to keep trying. Paolo had given up ten years past.

"The saints hear your prayers, never doubt that." Margerit's voice was softly confident.

"Is that faith speaking or knowledge?" Serafina gathered the candles and parchments and all the other small objects into a writing case then genuflected to the altar as they turned to leave.

"Serafina." Margerit was more hesitant now. "Miracles aren't granted to everyone. It isn't a judgment on you."

No, miracles weren't granted to everyone. But to enough. Any parish congregation would have enough members whose prayers could turn the ears of the saints to make their mysteries true and effective. And most of them hadn't even the vision to know it, taking all on faith. That was the curse of *visio*: that—no longer needing faith—you could see the holes in the world.

Serafina held out the writing case and asked, "Do you mind taking this back? I'd...I'd like to walk by myself for a while."

Margerit's concern stayed unspoken. "Don't be too late. It's our last supper all together for now."

There was a path that led from the gates of the manor down along the riverside and Serafina followed it aimlessly. On a still, early autumn evening such as this, she could see the trace of power in the prayer a nightingale raised in the branches, singing its praise to the one who gave it wings. The whole world around her was awash with mystical currents, from the gentle flow that coiled around the village church as the bells tolled out the hours, to the soft constant glow from the Orisules' convent, bright as the white of their walls, to the cold and ominous fingers that reached down from the mountain peaks like drifts of fog-waves breaking over a jetty. Yet when she reached out to grasp that power, it was as insubstantial as mist. She could see it, but was cut off from its touch. No, not cut off. She could be transported by the miracles others worked. There had been that time in Palermo... It was only her own hands, her own mouth that had no power and no skill.

It hadn't felt like this when she was a girl. Visions had been a joy, a gift, a promise. A tiny white-walled room, with the blazing Roman sun slanting through the shutter slats to form stripes on the carpet. She sat cross-legged on a cushion, practicing her letters on a slate. Her mother sang as her dark hands lifted up another sheet of injera from the griddle. Serafina knew it was a charm-song, even without understanding the words, by the way the light danced in harmony. In memory, the visions mixed with the aroma of the spices and the sharp scent of clove and sandalwood in the oil Mama used to dress her hair. The magic seemed to dance in time with the swaying of her gauzy white shawl that somehow never slipped from her shoulders or fell into her work.

And when the dancing sun-stripes slanted just so, Papa would come through the door, looking all-important in his dark suit just like the Roman men in the world outside, with her brother Michele trailing after him, carrying his books and writing case. Papa and Mama would say the prayers together in the tongue she'd never learned, and she and Michele would repeat the Pater in Latin and the everyday prayers in Romanesco—there was no Coptic church here and she and Michele had been baptized by the Catholic priests. Then there would be the sharp sour taste of injera and the rich spiciness of the stew wrapped within it. Papa would sigh and say he could almost think himself back in Mekelle at their wedding feast. He and Mama would be sad together for a time, remembering, but it was their sadness, not hers.

In time, the magic faded from her mother's work. She stopped singing the old songs. Serafina hadn't noticed, for the visions still came in church. They would stand together in the back and Mama would say her own prayers quietly, but Serafina would drink in the way the lights of the candles and the colored windows rose up in a great symphony of movement, answering the priests as they celebrated the Mass, or flowing throughout the crowd of worshippers during the special holidays. When she gasped and exclaimed at the sight, Mama would grasp her hand and murmur, "My little angel!" and Papa would smile with pride and say, "You will become a learned woman!"

And then she was the one who carried Papa's books and writing case to the wonderful place where he translated books for the priests, for Michele was apprenticed to a carpenter. She learned languages and studied the scriptures and read whatever came to hand while Papa worked. Michele brought home a table and chairs, made with his own hands, so they didn't have to sit on cushions on the floor anymore, he said. For months Mama stood beside the table to eat, saying the chair hurt her back, but then one day, without a word, she sat.

The next time Michele brought a surprise home, it was a wife. After Giuletta took charge of the household, her mother seemed to shrink into herself, moving aimlessly through the tiny apartment, no longer setting foot outside the door. Serafina blamed herself for how her mother faded. But what could she have done? When Giuletta was overbearing, there was escape in books. And then, one day, Mama had taken to her bed and never risen again.

Mama was gone, and all the magic had left the world with her. Even the memory of her songs, her quiet movements, her scents were swept away by Giuletta's brisk changes. Papa never talked about it, only sinking deeper into his work. That was why she had grasped at what Paolo offered—the chance to work mysteries for herself. She'd never learned her mother's charm-songs, or the other rituals Mama had used to make their home a place of magic and beauty. But if she could learn, she could have it all back.

* * *

That evening was bittersweet. They had formed a little schola here in the hilly backlands of Alpennia. In these close quarters, removed from the formality of the city, some of her fears had been left behind. Yet at odd moments, she would look around and feel herself lost and alone. She had dreamed last night that she looked in her mirror and a strange pale face looked back at her. Rotenek was no Rome for variety, but it was not the relentless sameness of Saveze.

Serafina looked around the table at this last dinner together. There was Margerit, her heart-shaped face and chestnut curls making her look far too young to be presiding over them all. And Margerit's daunting baroness, blade-sharp with understated power and authority in every movement, whom Serafina still hadn't dared to address by her Christian name. Baroness Saveze presided over their gathering like a heroine out of legend, her conversation darting equally between philosophy and farming and the dreadful state of the mountain roads this summer. Next sat the red-haired Akezze who turned schoolmaster over them all so easily. When they returned to Rotenek, Akezze would return to a formal distance, no longer the admired philosopher but a struggling tutor of rhetoric to aspiring young men. The Vicomtesse de Cherdillac had long since teased her into addressing her as Jeanne, even before this shared holiday. Hers was a more comfortable and earthy presence, though even the traces of silver in her dark hair would not stretch the point as far as "motherly." And there was Jeanne de Cherdillac's lover Antuniet, whose forbidding features discouraged friendship but who had little patience with strict propriety. If Baroness Saveze gave the impression of a golden-haired knight, Antuniet matched her as a raven-haired sorceress, softening only in Jeanne's presence. In Rotenek, Antuniet and Jeanne would once again take up their precarious infamy: too open in their devotion to each other to be entirely respectable, yet brilliant enough at their chosen positions that most of society was willing to look the other way. But there they couldn't enjoy the careless affection they knew here at Saveze.

And who would she be among them back in the city? Through the past winter and spring she had watched the careful dance the others performed, where the nuance of how every name was spoken and every movement made was dictated by the relationship of the dancers. If Paolo were here, would he be Maistir or Mesner? She didn't know. Because Margerit had accepted her, Serafina had been granted that ambiguous rank as a scholar that set birth aside. She had learned the limits of how to dress and act the part. But that acceptance didn't erase all distinctions.

Akezze, too, was granted scholar's rank and Serafina had seen how little difference that made to those who knew her father had followed the plow. She and Akezze both were welcomed and celebrated at Margerit's academic lectures and in the privacy of Tiporsel House, but neither of them had been invited to the private salons and concerts the others chattered of.

It had been like this in Rome, too. The city was full of strange wonders. As a girl, she'd never considered her family to be set apart. They'd been complete within themselves. It was Giuletta who disturbed that balance and made her doubt her place. She had tried to laugh along with Paolo at her own ignorance, at all the things she'd never learned that he took for granted. But it was Costanza who taught her just how much she lacked.

Costanza had knocked on the door one day, at the second-floor rooms they'd taken near Sant' Agnese's, when Paolo was off to Ravenna. Serafina had stared at this elegantly dressed figure, as out of place in that neighborhood as a peacock among pigeons, and stammered a question.

"Pardon me, Madame, have you lost your way?"

The woman had returned her stare, at first with a frown, and then with growing amusement. "I wanted to see just why it was that my cousin Paolo felt he needed to keep you hidden away. We've all been wondering about you."

And that was how she learned that Paolo Fortese had a large and prominent family in Rome and that he'd never had any intention of introducing her to them.

"But he went so far as to marry you, my dear," Costanza had exclaimed when she said as much. "That's the wonder!"

That was their second meeting, when Costanza had directed her to knock at the back gate of a certain villa, and she'd been led to a table in the garden where wine and fruit were served by silent women whose eyes followed her every move.

Serafina had blushed hotly in confusion, realizing what Costanza meant.

"I see," she said more kindly. "You aren't that sort of woman. But my dear, Paolo isn't that sort of man. He cares for nothing but his books. He's the despair of the family. Such clothes! And he cares almost nothing for culture. Whatever did you see in him?"

Serafina found herself liking Costanza, for all her bold ways. "Paolo promised to teach me to work mysteries," she said quietly. She couldn't confess how he had failed.

Costanza had laughed, as if it were the greatest joke in the world. But it was a merry laugh. "And for that you married him. What a strange creature you are! Tell me." She leaned forward conspiratorially. "Is he a good lover? I've always wondered."

More blushes. Was this how women talked among themselves? Serafina had only known her mother and Giuletta.

"Paolo is…was…" It had been years since he had touched her.

And then Costanza had moved to sit beside her on the bench, and taken her face in her hands, and kissed her, the taste of the wine mingling on their lips and tongues.

"Paolo is a fool," she had said.

And by the time Serafina had discovered that this was not how the women of Rome usually spent their time together, she no longer cared whether it was proper.

In Rotenek, Jeanne had become her guide to what was proper—and how improper things might be safely pursued. But there were always unexpected traps. Margerit's life was full of them. These women moved so easily between worlds, each with its own rules and hazards. With the end of summer, she would be plunged into those hazards once more.

"I had a thought," Margerit said, suddenly turning toward her. "I know you'd planned to come with me to Chalanz. But I imagine there are few things more tedious than someone else's family party. Perhaps you'd rather return directly to Rotenek with Jeanne and Antuniet? They're taking Akezze as well to shorten her road. You know how she hates traveling."

"If you don't mind," Serafina said with a sigh of relief. "And then you needn't explain me to your cousins." She waved her hand to brush away Margerit's concern. "No, I would only be in the way. If there is room, I'd be glad of the ride. But I haven't a place to stay yet for this year." She had a promise of a room at Tiporsel House until arrangements could be made, but they wouldn't be opening the house until Margerit returned.

"Oh pooh!" Jeanne said quickly. "My house isn't so small we can't make room for one more!" There was a brief speaking glance between her and Antuniet.

They might as well have heard her thoughts, but it was still an uncomfortable offer. She knew she would be intruding on their privacy. She didn't belong there, in a household that—for all its eccentricity—belonged firmly to the nobility of Alpennia.

"It is very kind of you," she answered. And then, thinking ahead to the next challenge and forcing herself to a cheerful smile, "Perhaps you can do me a further kindness. Could we speak only Alpennian on the journey? Every time I try, it still comes out half French and I can't count on the luck of a landlady who can meet me halfway again." They all laughed with her, thinking on the potpourri of languages they had used to muddle through the summer. And so it was decided.

* * *

By the time they rolled slowly through the Port Ausiz into the eastern edge of the city, pushing through the stream of returning travelers and day-traffic in the narrow cobbled street, Serafina had steeled herself for the challenge of seeking new lodgings. But not three days into her stay—barely time to unpack her valise—Jeanne greeted her over breakfast with the news, "I've found you a place to live! Iustin Mazzies—Toneke, you remember Rikerd's little protégée that I made all the rage in the concert halls last spring? It seems she's married her composer."

"Now there will be a stormy household!" Antuniet said. "It seems a bit far to go just to gain a violinist who can't refuse to perform his works."

"Oh no, they're perfectly suited," Jeanne assured her. "If they can find concert in that music of his, they can live under the same roof in perfect harmony! More harmony than his compositions can boast."

Serafina laughed with them, though the substance of the joke escaped her. Inwardly she winced. How often did men marry, not for companionship, but to gain an assistant at no extra cost? "Does he feel any affection for her? Or is it only for convenience?"

Antuniet said sourly, "Most marriages are for man's convenience and woman's need."

"If we all married for love, what a mess it would make of the world!" Jeanne's tone was light, but with a brittle edge.

"You were married once," Serafina ventured. "Was it all out of need?"

A shadow passed across Jeanne's face briefly. "Oh, yes. But he was kind enough." She shook her head to dispel the memories.

Had she broken some rule again? Serafina returned to a safer topic. "But what is all this to do with my plans?"

Jeanne reached out and touched her hand reassuringly. "So Maisetra Mazzies—Maisetra Ion-Pazit I should say!—had rooms with a widow. A music teacher, she says. Very respectable. She'll be looking for a new roomer and—" Jeanne concluded triumphantly "—she speaks Italian! Iustin says she studied opera and composition as a girl. Evidently she gave it all up when she married until—"

Serafina could complete the rest. Until she needed a way to scrape together a genteel living.

"The neighborhood is quite respectable, though hardly fashionable. Out at the west edge of town near the Nikuleplaiz. I've dropped her a note to expect you; it's all arranged."

It's all arranged. That might well be Jeanne's crest and motto.

* * *

It was a cozy house—older but well cared for. Everywhere within the old city walls, the houses lay cheek by jowl, and here a profusion of styles faced each other across a narrow cobbled road. Serafina checked the note Jeanne had given her with the description. That must be it: the dark brick one with the ivy on one side. She drew a slow breath and steeled herself for the encounter. A pull at the bell was answered after some moments' wait by a girl in a maid's uniform who stared and crossed herself unthinkingly while Serafina scrambled for her bits of hard-won Alpennian.

"I'm here to see Maisetra Valorin. Is she at home?"

More staring, then the girl collected herself and answered, "Yes, Maisetra."

There was no invitation to enter so she waited on the doorstep. Through the open door she could glimpse a cluttered entryway and stairs of some dark wood leading upward.

The mistress of the house appeared and greeted her with a puzzled look. "How may I help you?"

She was younger than Serafina had expected. A widow. Women could be widowed at all ages, and Maisetra Valorin looked much the same age as she was, though perhaps more careworn. She had the pale, creamy complexion so common in Alpennia that Serafina still found oddly like a marble statue. A few strands of mouse-brown hair peeked out from under a lace-edged cap. Her smile was tentative and curious.

"I understand that you have a room to let," Serafina began.

The woman's face fell and Serafina could almost believe it was sincere. "I am so sorry. The room's already been spoken for."

Serafina stiffened. It wasn't the first time such a thing had happened. There had been more than one "misunderstanding" in arranging for lodgings among Paolo's many moves. There was no use in protesting. She nodded and stepped back, but couldn't resist a parting line, "I'm sorry to have bothered you then. I'll let the vicomtesse know that she was mistaken."

She had barely turned away when there was a clatter of shoes down the steps behind her and an urgent voice, "The vicomtesse? You were sent by Mesnera de Cherdillac? But then—"

Serafina turned.

"But then it's you—you're the one the room is promised to. But I thought...Oh dear," the woman said in confusion. "But she said you were...a scholar from Rome, she said."

Serafina replied evenly, "If to be born and bred in Rome is to be Roman, then yes, I am Roman. I will not trouble you further. Thank you for your time."

"But..." the woman protested. "But wouldn't you like to see the room?" Serafina gazed at her trying to weigh the woman's intent. Perhaps it really had been a misunderstanding after all. "Yes, if you would."

She'd never lived in a house like this: warm wood paneling and bright-upholstered furniture crowding the rooms, with the clutter of all manner of activities scattered about. Margerit's house on the Vezenaf was a different world entirely, stately and with an air of age and dignity. Jeanne's home was something alike, but sparer, more orderly. It was a house meant for more than two and echoed in quiet moments. Here, even with no one else in evidence, the place felt densely inhabited. The air smelled of beeswax and lavender. Hints of something cooking drifted down the narrow corridor from the back of the house.

As they climbed the stairs together Serafina said, "The vicomtesse said that you spoke some Italian," and switched to a more familiar tongue. "I must say it was what decided me to come."

"Oh, yes," the woman answered in return, after a confused hesitation. "I studied it when I was a girl. For the music, you know."

Indeed, her words were flavored with the Tuscan one heard on the opera stage, but even so, the familiarity made the place feel more welcoming.

"The rooms are all small," Maisetra Valorin offered. "But you needn't share unless you want to split the cost. Maisetra Ponek has a room to herself as well. You'll meet them all later. You have the use of the front parlor when I'm not giving lessons and the dining room at all times."

There was barely room to turn around, it was true. Not much but a bed, a wardrobe, a washstand and a small writing desk, all in a honey-colored wood with gracefully curved legs. The desk stood beside a window that looked out over the street and the room sat high enough that one could see down to the end of the block where the road crossed a narrow canal. The view lent the room a more spacious feel. It was more than enough for her needs. "I'd like to take it, if you please," she said.

Maisetra Valorin seemed startled by her decisiveness. "You don't need to see the rest?"

"What of meals?" Serafina asked. "I was told that board was included?"

"It's nothing fancy," the woman said apologetically. She seemed incapable of offering any answer without an apology. "A good breakfast in the morning and then there's always something for dinner, but it's mostly soups and pot-dishes I'm afraid. My boarders often keep odd hours and the cook has to make something that will keep warm on the stove. You can have company or not for meals as you choose. Mefro Chisillic will usually know when the other guests plan to eat."

They agreed quickly on the rent, a trifle more than Serafina had been hoping for, but the place was better than what she'd had last year. Cleaner, and one hoped with fewer mice, though it would be a much farther walk to Tiporsel House.

There were few things to pack. She'd scarcely unpacked from the journey back from Saveze. Jeanne insisted that she stay for one last dinner, and so it was dark before she found herself again at Maisetra Valorin's door.

There would be a key, she'd been told. Between the odd hours of the guests and the scanty staff it made no sense to keep a maid waiting on the door. This time there was no startlement when the door was opened, though it was a different woman. The housekeeper, by her looks. She would need to learn their names: cook, housekeeper and more besides the maid she had met earlier who was summoned with a sharp, "Gerta!" to fetch up her bag.

Gerta gave her curious darting looks as she laid out the towels and brought a fresh pitcher and basin while Serafina unbuttoned her coat and changed her bonnet for a frilled linen cap more suited to indoors. Serafina pretended not to notice the maid's attention until their arms crossed by accident in the unpacking and Gerta reached out and rubbed her fingers across the back of her hand.

"It doesn't come off," Serafina said sharply.

A frightened look crossed the maid's face, knowing the act for an impertinence. Serafina frowned and dismissed her. Summer had been easier. The servants at Saveze had been too proud to treat their mistress's guests with anything less than courtesy. She sighed and closed the door.

She was tired. With her things unpacked and put away, Serafina thought briefly of going down to the parlor where she could hear the strains of the fortepiano as Maisetra Valorin played, seemingly for her own enjoyment. But the bed called more strongly and it was a pleasant enough lullaby to sleep to.

Who was the composer? She could put names to some sacred music, but the rest she'd learned only in scraps. There—that was a piece Jeanne had played for them during the summer. Beethoven, she had said carelessly, assuming everyone would know. Now a more lively tune, one that Costanza had played for her once in a quiet moment, but she didn't recall who she'd said had written it.

Sleep had nearly claimed her when the music changed. No, not only the music. The walls themselves were vibrating. There was a glow like moonlight, except that moonlight didn't curl across the floor like mist, like swirling water. She could still hear the tinkling of the keys, but it flowed through her blood. In wonder, she rose and drew on her dressing gown to creep down the stairs toward the source of that music.

She stepped quietly so as not to disturb the player. Had Jeanne known? Was this one of her little jokes? There had been none of her arch humor in the suggestion of Maisetra Valorin's place. And Jeanne wasn't sensitive to this sort of working. A music teacher, she'd said, as if the woman were nothing more. But surely a talent such as this would be common knowledge?

Serafina paused in the doorway, enough in shadow so as not to attract attention. In the glow of the lamps, Maisetra Valorin sat bent over her keyboard in the same dark gray dress she had worn earlier. The room held nothing but her and the music. The lines of worry that had marked her face earlier were smoothed away and softened. Something in her expression struck Serafina like a blow. The woman didn't know. It was like the way you recognized a man was blind when you saw that he was tracking sound, not movement. Maisetra Valorin was hearing only the music itself.

The outlines of the parlor blurred in Serafina's vision and she let out a sigh that was close to a sob. With a startled exclamation, the tune stopped. Earthly sights and sounds alike faded, but the currents that underlay them still swirled around her, slowly dissipating even as she dashed the tears from her eyes.

"I'm sorry, Maisetra Talarico. Did I disturb you?" Maisetra Valorin rose from the bench before the keyboard. "What's wrong?"

Serafina shook her head. How could she explain her sudden jealousy? "It's only that the music was so beautiful," she said. And that was no lie.

"Oh, that was nothing really. Just a few scribblings."

"Your own composition?"

She saw the woman nod hesitantly.

Of course it was. There had been no magic in the more familiar works. "Do you perform your compositions?" Serafina asked.

Maisetra Valorin shook her head with a little shrug. "Just little studies for my students and my own amusement. They're not really that good."

And that would explain her obscurity. Not everyone would have the ability to discern the effects of her music, but surely in a concert hall at least a few listeners would have some sensitivity. But if she'd never performed them publicly...

"Who told you they weren't good?" Serafina wondered. Was her own judgment clouded by the visions? She knew so little about music.

Maisetra Valorin sat again on the bench and looked down at her hands. "I've shown a few pieces to Maistir Fizeir—our great composer, you know. He did me the favor to listen because I do some copywork on his scores. He said my talents are sound but I have nothing of genius."

Perhaps he was right. Or perhaps... A spark of mischief took flame as she sat down in one of the chairs beside the instrument. "Have you ever tried your hand at setting verses?" she asked. "I have a friend—" That was stretching the word considerably, but no need to frighten her with Baroness Saveze's title for the moment. "A friend who's interested in commissioning some settings of one of your poets. I think the name was Pertolf?"

"Pertulif?" Maisetra Valorin interjected. "Oh, I couldn't do that. Fizeir has already set his works."

"All of them? And no one else is allowed to touch them?" Serafina added a touch of wide-eyed surprise to soften the question. "Which one is your favorite of his poems?"

The other immediately launched into a series of couplets, too rapidly for Serafina to catch more than a word here and there of the Alpennian, but the rhythm of the poetry was clear enough and drew her in.

"That one," she urged. "Try a setting of that one. If my friend likes it, there might be a commission in it." She had seen enough of the woman's circumstances to know that money might be a draw if vanity failed.

The uncertain look on Maisetra Valorin's face turned thoughtful and she picked out the beginnings of a phrase. There were no explosions of song and color this time, just the wisps of *fluctus* weaving around her hands, fading in and out with the hesitant notes. Serafina bit her lip. To have such talent that it leaked from your very fingers, even in idle experiment! She rose, feeling the tears starting again.

"I won't disturb you?" Maisetra Valorin asked.

"No," she managed. No, it wouldn't disturb her in that way.

CHAPTER FOUR

Margerit

Mid-September, 1823

Saint Mauriz presided over the start of the Rotenek social season as the residents of the upper city returned from far-flung estates and watering places to once more inhabit the salles and ballrooms. Margerit counted the feast of the city's patron as the anniversary of her study of the mysteries. When Marziel Lumbeirt's legacy had turned her life upside down and against all expectation she found herself in Rotenek, it had been the *tutela* for Saint Mauriz that set her to questioning and studying the visions she'd learned to ignore in her youth.

Every year since then she had carefully noted and sketched the flow and swell of the *fluctus* as divine grace poured throughout the cathedral in response to the ritual. Prince Aukust, and now Princess Anna, had butted heads with Archbishop Fereir over the churchman's revision of the text, and she had traced the reflection of those changes in her visions.

But the great *tutelas* belonged to the cathedral, and Archbishop Fereir showed no interest in a young woman's opinions on their efficacy. He had respected her talents enough to accept her as Princess Annek's thaumaturgist, but no more than that. Fereir had ignored her careful analysis of the fatal flaws in the Mauriz *tutela* except for sending her notes and sketches to the Vatican for study. There they had netted only one return: the chance interest of an archivist's wife.

Serafina had come to Rotenek hungry to study thaumaturgy with someone willing to teach her. Someone whose descriptions of the mysteries echoed her own experiences. It was only for Serafina's sake that Margerit returned to the Mauriz this year with a trace of her former interest. Few people had enough sensitivity to follow the mechanics of a mystery. Antuniet could follow only the broadest outlines. Barbara was entirely blind to divine visions, though she could imagine their structures from mere descriptions and she had a sharp understanding for how the details of language could build or destroy a ritual. But in Serafina, Margerit had found her equal in perception.

Margerit had no authority to claim a better vantage for this ceremony than the pew belonging to Tiporsel House. This wasn't a ritual of the Royal Guild where she had a place and a role. For long days past, she and Serafina had pored over her notes and sketchbooks, but today those were left behind.

Even with the whole household gathered in attendance for this, the most important mystery of Rotenek's year, there was no crowding on the bench. Antuniet and Jeanne made a habit of joining them for the great services, and of course her Aunt Bertrut and Uncle Charul were there on Barbara's other side. Aunt Bertrut looked younger than she had when they first came to Rotenek. Marriage had come late into her life and she had accepted the proposal of a penniless nobleman with the understanding that convenience and affection were all that was promised on both sides. But marriage suited her, and affection was growing into something deeper.

At the far end of the bench, Barbara's cousin Brandel completed their numbers. The armins stood in the aisles to either side like bookends: Marken's stolid bulk was a well of calm at her end, while Tavit's restless attention anchored the far end. Their numbers were fewer than might be expected for the seat of an ancient household, but on feasts like this, when she gathered everyone in, she had a taste of how such a household might feel.

"And what will we see this time?" Serafina asked, her voice pitched low, so as not to disturb their neighbors. She had regained some of the eagerness that the summer's failures had worn away.

"I'd rather wait and let you tell me what you see," Margerit answered. "It won't be quite as confused now as when I first saw it in Prince Aukust's day." She leaned more closely to explain. "Then the old and new rites were jumbled together more and you could see the *fluctus* wavering between them. Now most of the language from the old Penekiz rite has been erased, though the forms still remain. You've seen some of the Lyon mysteries before. There were a couple that we saw last spring. You were telling me how different they are from the Roman rites."

Serafina was looking around with sharp curiosity. The service itself was yet to begin, but any time an entire cathedral of people waited in expectation of a Great Mystery there were wisps and eddies of worship drifting about, waiting to be gathered up into the whole. Margerit saw others looking around as well, though most for more ordinary reasons. Who had returned to town and who was still missing? Who spoke to whom and who turned pointedly away? Who had taken up the newest fashions? Margerit cared little for fashion but she noticed uncomfortably how threadbare Serafina's dark blue pelisse had grown. She tucked that thought away as Serafina turned to answer her.

"It isn't set as much by rule as all that. Of course the Vatican follows the official Latin Rite, but Rome is such a patchwork of districts. A thousand churches and almost as many traditions. San Stefano where the pilgrims' hostels are gathered had a taste of every flavor we brought to it. In private, Mama never gave up the services she knew best, though I was baptized in the Roman church. Not all of the ceremonies performed there came to life, of course." A wistful look came over Serafina, but then something caught her eye and she pointed off toward the base of the donor's windows where the seats had been placed for the royal family. "What's happening there?"

Margerit stared where she was pointing. The effects were pale and masked by the beams streaming through the colored glass. She had never noticed anything odd about the design before, but now that her attention was drawn to it, she could see a thin rain of light drifting down from the fragments of the original window where the saint's halo encircled the darker glass of his face. The newer portions of the glass only let through mortal light.

"I never noticed that before," she whispered back. "There's a legend that one of the glassmakers for the cathedral had set mysteries in the panes, but I never thought what that might mean. Or that any of them remained." Now that she was looking for it, she could see the *fluctus* drifting down to the dais where Princess Annek and her family would sit and then pooling as it faded there. Some ancient blessing? Or a protection perhaps? Or was it chance that it fell in that spot? Had all the windows trapped *fluctus* like that at one time? Most were from the renovations in Prince Filip's day.

"There's an entire section in the Vatican library on mysteries of the craft guilds," Serafina whispered. "I never had permission to explore it. A few people still study them, but they say most of the secrets have been lost or were never written down in the first place. If words and prayers can weave a mystery and art is a prayer of the hands, then why shouldn't any creation be capable of carrying the living word? I've always thought Mesnera Chazillen's alchemy to have more of mystery than science to it."

Margerit shook her head, pitching her voice even lower as a ripple of anticipation spread through the crowd. "I doubt it. I know that many alchemists combine their work with meditation, but the heart of the practice is different. It must be, for so much of alchemy was learned from unbelievers. A true mystery can only come from God through the saints."

Serafina gave her an odd sidelong glance. "If you believe that, then there must be many strange and wonderful things in the world that are not true mysteries."

Margerit shrugged. It wasn't the time or place for a theological debate. "Look, it will be starting soon." She saw the archbishop and the other priests moving toward their places and then there was a bustling in the back of the nave as the royal party entered and made their way slowly to the place reserved for them. Princess Annek led the way, her sharp glance and strong features giving her the look of an eagle among lesser birds. She would take part as speaker for the congregation. Behind her came the Dowager Princess Elisebet. She had been accounted a beauty in her youth, but now her dark-browed, florid looks were more commonly described only as pleasant. Her hand was tightly clasped with that of her son Aukustin. The gesture made him look younger than his sixteen years. He had grown visibly taller over the summer and something in his chin and nose was reminiscent of his late father. Only the last member of the royal family, Annek's son Efriturik, was absent.

Margerit relaxed into a light awareness of the entire panorama before her as the opening blessings shifted into the back and forth of responses as the celebrants laid out the markein—the definition of the scope and extent of the blessing—and then moved on into the core of the mystery. She had become accustomed to the chaotic confusion of the *fluctus* as it wavered between the contradictory demands of the ritual, but this year it felt weaker, less directed even than it had before. For hundreds of years Saint Mauriz had answered their petitions and protected the city. Did no one else feel the loss of that care?

As the ceremony rose up later toward the *missio* that was intended to send the saint's blessing and protection out into the world, she leaned more closely toward Serafina and whispered, "Watch this closely now. This is where it goes most awry."

The light and sound that had built in waves and arches throughout the ceremony now collapsed and fell in muddy eddies toward the floor by the altar. Margerit was certain that it marked the place where the saint's relic was hidden away. She saw Serafina's wondering gaze dart toward the same location before she gazed around once more, looking for remaining traces of the *fluctus*, as the priests intoned the final prayers and the congregation gave its last responses.

* * *

"Did you see what I was describing?" Margerit asked much later, when dinner was finished and they had all retired to the library at the back of the house. Barbara hadn't been able to join them until after the meal. Antuniet had stayed, but Jeanne had taken her leave, pleading that she had little to add to a philosophical analysis. So only now had Margerit let her curiosity loose. "Did you see how Saint Mauriz's protection is meant to flow out and seek the boundaries and landmarks of the city? Did you notice how instead it covers only the relics themselves?"

"But more than just the city," Serafina said. "Surely it's intended to reach the boundaries of Alpennia itself?"

Barbara frowned a little. "Saint Mauriz is patron for the land, it's true. But this *tutela* is meant only for the parish and by extension to Rotenek."

"But I thought I saw—" Serafina began.

"What? What did you see?" Antuniet asked quickly.

Serafina shifted uneasily in her chair. She had declined the offer of one of the overstuffed seats by the fireplace, and so they had all gathered around the library table instead. She looked from one to the other seeking permission to disagree.

"What did you see?" Margerit echoed. "You noticed that bit with the stained glass that I missed. Maybe I've been focusing too much on the cathedral itself."

"I could see the *fluctus* like a layer of cloud, going out across the land," Serafina began hesitantly. "Not bright, like what happened around the altar. More like that high haze you get sometimes at mid-summer. But at the edges, it was as if a storm were tearing at it." She shook her head with the faintest of jerks. "I don't know; it's so hard to describe, because I couldn't actually see it, of course. Not the part outside the cathedral. And I don't know the land the way you do."

Barbara gestured dismissively. "Don't worry about that. I've become used to people talking about things I can't see."

Serafina shrugged. "And then, at the end, it was like the sun coming out from the clouds and the mist faded away. But the sun usually symbolizes something good. This was…a destruction. I'm not describing it very well, am I?"

"No, continue," Margerit said, scribbling down a few notes to remember later. "Use whatever words work for you."

"It…it tried. I could see that. It was trying—the blessing, I mean. But it wasn't only the collapse at the *missio*. There was something out there. I could tell. Something that worried at it from the edges like…like waves eating away at the shore. And when the *fluctus* collapsed, whatever was out there followed it, like a wave reaching up the shore before retreating."

Margerit felt a chill touch her heart. When she had first noticed the warping of the mystery, she had worried that it might leave the city unprotected in some way. Was something—or someone—finally taking advantage of that weakness? She thought back to Serafina's observation of the window. "You see so much. I wish you'd said something at the time and I would have known to look for that."

Serafina's lean face twisted in an impatient scowl. "And what good is it?"

They'd been arguing over this for most of the summer. "It will come," Margerit said patiently. "I'm sure it will. I couldn't perform mysteries on my own until—" She thought back to that desperate night when Barbara had been attacked and she wanted to weave a protection for her. "Until I had a deep need."

"If need were all it took, then every child in the gutter would be a miracle worker!" Serafina's eyes flashed in scorn. "Don't think to tell me I haven't enough need. You've said yourself that neither need nor holiness seem to matter."

Antuniet chided, "She's right. Margerit, don't promise her something that may never come."

"I'm sorry," Margerit said quietly. Whatever it was that drove Serafina, it had brought her on this long journey. And she was right: when you watched carefully whose prayers were answered by the saints, there was no rhyme or reason to the response. Was it only chance that her own voice was heard? "Tell me more about this fraying at the edges. I want to know more about what's out there trying to get in." They turned again to the diagrams laid out before them.

* * *

Frances Collfield always appeared unexpectedly. The first time, Margerit had encountered her by chance in the university library. On the second occasion, the English botanist had been collecting samples along the rocky slopes of Saveze, unaware of whose lands she had stumbled into. To be sure, this time Frances was invited and expected, but not for a month or two yet. In October perhaps, she'd said. When her book would be published. Perhaps later if the printing were delayed. The years of collecting and sketching lichens throughout the western side of the Alps were at last to be preserved in print. Yet here she was, before September was quite past, her stout walking boots and heavy tweed traveling cape looking strikingly out of place against the polished wood and embroidered cushions of Tiporsel House's front parlor. As always she brought a scent of mountain hillsides, of pine and gentian and artemisia, though in fact she had traveled directly from London.

"Frances!" Margerit cried, when she saw who was waiting. "Why didn't you write to tell me your plans had changed? Has Charsintek made up a room for you yet? Where are your bags?"

"I left them at the coaching office," she said in her somewhat stiff schoolroom French. "I wasn't sure—"

"Don't be silly," Margerit interrupted. "Of course there's room for you."

She stepped back into the entry hall and found Ponivin waiting. The butler didn't need his years of experience to tell him that unexpected orders were imminent.

"Could you send someone to pick up Maisetra Collfield's luggage? Where did you say it was, Frances?"

"It's an inn at the west end of the city, where the diligence from Paris stops. I believe it's called the Concordette? The trunk is rather heavy," she added doubtfully. "That's why I left it there. The journey was dreadful. I've never had such difficulties. You'd think we were at war with France again, the way I was treated."

"I'll see to it, Maisetra," the butler said.

To the maid who had been waiting behind him, Margerit rattled off quick instructions. "Tell Charsintek to make up a guest room and have a bath drawn. And then tea if you please." And back over her shoulder, "Frances, can you wait for dinner or would you like something more than cake now?"

"Whatever's no trouble," she answered. "But tea would be lovely."

Aunt Bertrut joined them by the time the tea was served and Uncle Charul poked his head in long enough for a greeting before disappearing to his own room. So there was no chance to draw out Frances's story before a chorus of thuds and grunts heralded the arrival of the luggage. Frances took possession of a valise while two men struggled to bring a small trunk up the steps from the courtyard.

"Did you want this upstairs, Maisetra?" one of the footmen asked doubtfully.

"No, there's no need for that. Just somewhere out of the way, I suppose," Frances interjected. "I am sorry for the inconvenience." She addressed the company at large.

"But whatever is in it?" Margerit asked. It couldn't be clothing to be that heavy, though if it weren't then Frances had brought little enough to wear. She gestured them to take it into the second parlor that served as an office.

When the trunk was settled in place, Frances undid the straps and locks to raise the lid. She pulled back a fold of blanket and lifted a thin metal plate from where it rested in its swathing. At an angle to the light, the tracery of lines and markings could be seen. "It's my book," she said. "The important part, at least. The plates."

Margerit tempered her curiosity with sympathy for her travel-worn guest and waited until the evening, when hot water, fresh clothes and dinner could do their work. The Chafils and the Faikrimeks were invited to dine and there was no chance to discover whether Frances would care to tell her story before strangers. With the table cleared at last, she suggested to her aunt that their dinner guests might enjoy a hand of cards. That distraction allowed a chance to examine the contents of the trunk more closely.

"Aquatint?" Barbara asked, lifting one of the plates carefully to examine under the lamplight.

"Oh goodness, I have no idea," Frances replied. "I suppose I'll need to find out, though heaven knows when I'll be able to have it printed now."

"You promised me a book," Margerit teased lightly. "You didn't say I'd need to provide my own printshop!"

"I am sorry," Frances began. Half her sentences started that way. "I did promise. I promised so many people." The no-nonsense crispness of her voice wavered.

Barbara gently replaced the plate she'd been examining into its wrappings and crossed the room to pour brandy from a decanter into several small glasses. "I suspect this is a story that calls for something stronger than Madeira. And perhaps we'd be more comfortable in the library?"

A few sips seemed to fortify Frances for more direct answers. "It was my brother," she said. "He's been collecting the subscriptions. We've been planning it for years. But he thought…I was still writing, you see. And the plates would take some time to be engraved. And he thought it was silly for the funds just to sit in his account. He's not a gambler, you must understand that."

"An investor," Barbara said. It was clear she felt the difference was minor.

Frances nodded. "There was really no risk at all. There shouldn't have been. He told me no one could have expected…"

"And yet the money is gone," Barbara concluded.

Again she nodded, this time more miserably. "If we could only have published, I'm sure the additional sales would have made up the lack. And the plates were already finished as you see. But the publisher refused to take the risk. He was very cold about it. What could I do? He was threatening to sell this all off to a foundry." She waved back in the direction of the trunk in the next room.

"So you stole them," Barbara said.

Frances looked horrified. "Of course not! They're mine aren't they? My own work. And I left my mother's emeralds there as a pledge, so no one can say…" She trailed off in confusion. The unexpected travel, the paucity of her luggage, all that told a story of hasty departure. "I had to go somewhere and I'd promised you a visit, so here I am."

* * *

It took only one day for Frances Collfield to return to the stout cheerfulness that had always been her hallmark. The future would manage for itself. It always had. She accepted an invitation to stay through the New Year without any discussion of what would become of her afterward. And the only remaining question seemed to be how to keep her occupied in a season when tramping over mountains to collect specimens was impossible.

"You should give another lecture," Margerit told her over the breakfast table. "You were the one who inspired me to start them." She handed Frances one of the handbills listing the next two months' topics. "There's no end of interested speakers. They've become quite the thing. I think I have all of October scheduled, but that would give you time to plan."

"Good heavens!" Frances said when she looked over the list. "Every week? That's quite the accomplishment. And all this because of me?"

Would she have begun sponsoring the lectures without that first inspiration? Margerit wasn't certain, but it would have made for a duller life. The program of women scholars had become one of the joys of her life. It was her own special contribution to the Rotenek season, given that she had no interest in holding balls.

"It's finding the venue that's the difficult part," she said with a sigh. "There's a hall down in the university district that I use but it's very small. Most places available during the season are so small, and I have to change locations all the time. I've asked my business manager LeFevre to try to find some suitable building to purchase but nothing has turned up."

Frances looked startled. "You'd buy a property just for the lectures? What would you do with the place the rest of the time?"

Plans spun out in imagination. She'd asked herself the same question many times. "There are so many possibilities. The Orisules run a charity school that could use more room. The lectures need to have general interest but I'd like to start some more intensive classes—ones that the university doesn't offer. The Poor Scholars have expressed an interest, and some of the older women who come to the lectures have suggested topics. We live in a wonderful age of ideas and yet we're reduced to begging for scraps. I'd like to see every girl who's as thirsty for learning as I was have the opportunity to drink her fill."

"Why that sounds like you're planning to found a college!" Frances said.

Margerit laughed. "You aren't the first person to say that! Antuniet keeps calling me a second Fortunatus, after the man who started Rotenek University." She blushed at how much the nickname cheered her.

"Well, I think it's a brilliant idea," Frances said.

Everyone thought it was a brilliant idea, but accomplishing such a thing would be far more work than she could imagine. And overseeing a large household gave her the basis to imagine a great deal. "So shall I put you down for the first week in November?"

* * *

Akezze was the one who found a solution for Frances's publishing woes. They were sharing a late supper at the Red Oak tavern in the student quarter after Akezze's lecture. Margerit looked around at the other tables in the crowded room. Barbara was greeted as a regular, but she would never dare come here on her own. It wasn't a rough place—if it were, Marken would have stopped her with one of those meaningful armin's looks and silences. Not rough, but filled with noise and conversation. Akezze, too, was greeted as familiar here. This was a side to academic life that Margerit had never had a chance to experience.

With her bold manner and striking flame-colored hair, Akezze had become a favorite speaker. Her speeches on the history of logic and public rhetoric might have drawn crowds on their own, but some came for no other reason than to watch her talk. In one way, Margerit thought, it was a triumph to see the listeners include so many men—serious men with hopes of public careers. But it felt like an intrusion at times, as if they might crowd out the girls and women she'd meant the gatherings for.

Akezze was still flushed with excitement, the bright spots in her cheeks standing out against her pale, freckled skin. "And did you see?" she whispered in delight. "Who would have thought I'd have diplomats coming to hear me?"

"You mean Perzin?" Barbara asked. "I suppose he might be considered a coup. He's one of Albori's rising men. I hadn't realized he was back from Paris."

Oh yes, Margerit had noticed Perzin, for his wife Tionez was unaccountably one of Jeanne's bosom friends and had stuck close to Jeanne's side all evening, though Margerit had hoped for a private word. "I doubt we'll get quite that many to hear about your lichens, Frances. I can't imagine botany has an interest to diplomats and government ministers!"

"So long as it's of interest to someone," Frances said cheerfully. "I'm hoping I may find new subscribers to publish my book here."

Margerit held her tongue. She couldn't entirely like the notion of selling a duplicate set of subscriptions. If felt too close to fraud. Her heart had urged her to fund the project herself, but she could imagine LeFevre's opinion of that. *You may of course spend your funds on any extravagance you choose. But not on all of them, so choose wisely.*

At Akezze's quizzical look, Margerit added to Frances's explanation, "Her book on the lichens of the western Alps. You should see the lovely plates she has to illustrate it. Forty or fifty I believe it was. Quite luxurious!"

"Do you know?" Akezze said thoughtfully. "We have a few of our girls placed in a printing shop. Some of them are journeymen now."

By "our girls" Margerit knew she meant the Poor Scholars. Akezze still worked closely with the charity school that had provided her own start.

"They've been looking for work to bring into the shop—something to set themselves up in business. The master printer takes half of whatever they bring in, but they're trying to save enough to set up on their own. Perhaps you could try putting out a selection of the illustrations as prints. If they did well enough, that might fund the book as a whole."

"They're looking to set up their own printing house?" Margerit asked reflectively. Perhaps...it might be enough to win LeFevre over.

"It depends on the work," Akezze said. "A press of their own would be quite expensive. They'd need an assurance of steady jobs. It's not like the hand-copying and notary work that the girls do. That requires only the skill."

Margerit had made great use of the Poor Scholars to copy those sorts of thaumaturgical books that publishers avoided. A year past, their work had saved Antuniet's alchemy text from being entirely lost. The thoughts all fell together in her mind. "I could guarantee at least three or four books that stand in need of a publisher," she said. "What would you say to putting out an edition of Gaudericus?"

Akezze's jaw dropped. "The book that's so rare because no one dares touch it?"

"The book that's so rare there are a hundred scholars across Europe who would pay dearly for a copy," Margerit countered. "I doubt his work is as risky now as it was a century ago. That's the last time someone tried to publish it." Only a few copies had escaped destruction after that debacle. Margerit's thoughts spun out,. "If I added my name to the project..."

The tapster interrupted them to offer another round of drinks. Margerit could see in Barbara's frown that she was rehearsing all the risks. Gaudericus might not be a forbidden book—not like it had been when the church held greater sway—but everyone with a hand in the process would consider the risks. There were other reasons beyond the whiff of heresy that thaumaturgical texts had been tightly controlled.

Unexpectedly, Barbara raised a different objection. "Rare, yes, but is it rare enough to guarantee a large return for the press? Perhaps better to start with a text that's never been published at all. What about that earlier work of Gaudericus that I found for you," Barbara suggested. "I don't know there are any other copies of that around. And it omits some of his more controversial writings."

Margerit shook her head. "Not that one." Her reaction felt selfish but she tried to explain. "I think that was a very early draft. The ideas are only half-formed. Some of the more daring ones only appear in Tanfrit's commentaries in the margins. It's a curiosity, but I doubt it's enough of one to turn a profit."

"Who is this Tanfrit?" Frances asked, trying to follow the conversation. "I've heard of your Gaudericus—silly superstitious nonsense."

Margerit bristled. She'd encountered the Englishwoman's disdain for the saints' mysteries before and didn't care to rehearse the argument here. "She was a contemporary of his. A great correspondent, which is a good thing, as almost everything we know of her work comes from the letters she wrote to other people. My secret book-monger found Barbara a prize—an early manuscript version of Gaudericus's *De Mechanismate Miraculorum* with commentary in Tanfrit's own hand. What I wouldn't give to have been able to learn from the two of them!"

"Though it seems to me," Akezze pointed out acerbically, "that if the best ideas in that text are found in Tanfrit's hand, then perhaps they weren't his ideas alone."

Margerit had toyed with that same thought, but it felt disloyal to the man to voice it.

"And if Tanfrit's thoughts were such an influence on his work, why wouldn't he acknowledge it?" Akezze continued. "He gives credit to Chizelek and Pontis."

"It wouldn't be the first time a woman's work has been overlooked." Frances echoed what they all knew.

"True enough," Barbara added. "And that might be reason alone to make the earlier text available. It's curious. You know the legends of course, that she had an unrequited passion for Gaudericus but he vowed to be wedded only to his studies. There are darker stories as well, about a bargain he made with the devil for that knowledge. I doubt there's any truth to them. But the legend says that, in despair, Tanfrit threw herself into the Rotein in flood."

Akezze pursed her lips in thought. "Didn't Serafina say she'd found a different story? That Tanfrit was named a dozzur at Rotenek University?"

"I'm sure there are stories enough," Margerit said. "But I don't know that I'd believe either of those. The University swears they've never let a woman lecture. That's why they wouldn't let me use the Chasintalle for my talks. And the commentaries in my book—they don't sound like a woman in love or in despair."

"Despair can be a hidden thing," Frances said quietly.

The comment made Margerit wonder. Had Frances chosen her studies freely or were they consolation when other opportunities were lost? "We were speaking of your book. If we set up a printing shop, we could certainly look into publishing it." It had become "we" so quickly.

"Yes, a place to begin," Akezze suggested. "To train more girls in the print shop. They have the use of their master's press for now, but if we had a patron and equipment of our own—"

Margerit felt Akezze's expectant gaze. Did she dare? Maybe there was something in the air of a student tavern like the Red Oak—something that encouraged impossibilities. She'd never had a chance to breathe this air in her own university years. Along with the other girl-scholars, she'd been promptly escorted home after lectures. This ferment of debate and inspiration was what she hoped to provide for all of them, all the girls who dared to dream as she had.

A fierce grin spread across her face. "Perhaps," she suggested, "if I do find my lecture hall, we could combine the two." She had been thinking only about the teaching side—about classes and studies. That might be enough for those like her who needn't think about making a living. But Akezze's Poor Scholars were hoping to find a trade with better expectations than service. A trade for the mind and not just the hands. And something that combined the two: the printing of books…

Her eyes met Akezze's and beside her she heard Barbara laugh.

CHAPTER FIVE

Luzie

Early October, 1823

So many people! The open doorway was cracked open just enough to see the first few rows of chairs beyond the open space where the fortepiano stood. Even without a view of the rest of the salle, the crowd made its presence known in a hum of voices. Above the chairs, an arabesque of gilded plaster arched to define the area that served as a stage. Luzie could barely remember the first time she'd played in public, perched on a box set on top of the bench to raise her hands high enough to reach the keys. One of her brothers had played the violin—she couldn't remember now whether it had been Gauterd or the unfortunate Ianilm. Later it had been duets, side by side at the keyboard with her father. She hadn't performed since her marriage—not for more than a few friends in private or for her lodgers. And never her own compositions before. She had confidence in her hands, but this crowd!

Somehow she'd thought it would be a small affair—a parlor, or at best a private ballroom—not the Salle Chapil. In rehearsals she'd imagined a private salon with a dozen listeners. *A few friends*, the baroness had said. *Zarne will be reciting some of his new works after you play, and Hankez is showing off her portrait of Maisetra Sovitre.* Baroness Saveze's few friends seemed to include half of Rotenek society.

How had Maisetra Talarico fallen in with this crowd? She didn't pry into her tenants' lives, but one couldn't help being curious. A letter of reference from the famous Vicomtesse de Cherdillac, familiar enough with Baroness

Saveze to secure this commission for her, and yet not familiar enough to be invited to the performance? At first she had taken Serafina Talarico as what she claimed to be: a visiting scholar of modest means, no one of note. That fiction was being torn away piece by piece. They would need to have words later.

Luzie looked out again. The space glittered with the gilt carving of the chairs and the sparkle of elegant jewelry. The guests were beginning to take their places. She could see the baroness seated in the place of honor in the front row wearing a gown of peacock-blue silk. A hair ornament of feathers and sapphires nodded as her head bent in conversation with the woman seated beside her.

If only her father could see her now! He hadn't set foot in a Rotenek concert hall since his hands had grown too stiff to play, but he would have come, if only she'd known to ask. She wouldn't have dared to beg an invitation for a truly private concert, but for something like this...surely it could have been arranged. Perhaps there would be more opportunities after this one. There were a few faces in the audience she knew from her own acquaintance: the Alboris and the Silpirts. And everyone in musical circles in Rotenek knew Mesnera Arulik.

She glanced behind her to smile nervously at the singers. DaNapoli from the Royal Opera and two others no less prominent. Baroness Saveze had suggested them. She couldn't have commanded that level of talent on her own. Now the baroness was standing before the assembled company, saying something and nodding to call her forth. Luzie stepped out and curtseyed to the crowd, barely hearing what was said of her as she and the singers took their places.

The music enfolded her as it always did. Pertulif's poetry could transport the hearer even without music. They had chosen a seasonal cycle. The baroness had suggested his "Song of the Mountain," but Luzie had refused, knowing Fizeir had set it just last year. She hadn't dared to mention this commission to Fizeir at last week's delivery for fear he'd think she was trespassing in his garden.

The soprano sang lightly of how spring crept up the mountainside. She was joined by the tenor to celebrate summer's glory with a song of young love and flirtation. In a strange double-consciousness Luzie heard sighs of longing from out in the audience while all her attention remained on the page. Next, the two men sang of autumn—not truly a seasonal poem this time but a lament for young men lost to war, old men lost to the turning years. *In the autumn of a man's life, the days grow short and the leaves fall suddenly.* The mood turned tense and melancholy in anticipation of mourning. She saw her father's face before her, now lined and careworn, his once-nimble fingers knotted and swollen. All three voices joined for the concluding movement, "Storm Over the Mountains." It was triumphant, raging, powerful. One could almost hear the keening of the wind through the passes, the icy chill sweeping down the valleys. She had been right to stand firm. It was a much better choice for this suite than "Song of the Mountain," which was Pertulif's love song to the rugged peaks he'd called home.

When the last chord faded away, the music released her and Luzie sat frozen, waiting for the audience's response. A moment of hush held sway. A breath drawn before a sigh. She turned and rose as the applause swelled from a light patter to enthusiastic acclaim. She could see heads turning toward each other with excited whispers. These were connoisseurs—the people who attended every opera opening, every concert. No matter what Fizeir had said of her work, she could believe in this. She gestured to the singers to join her and looked to Baroness Saveze to see if she, too, approved.

There was an eager smile on the baroness's lean face, but it was the expression of her companion that caught the eye. The young woman's mouth hung open in rapt wonder. Only now did she seem to remember what her hands were for and added to the applause. Luzie saw her turn to the baroness and through the diminishing clamor could hear her ask, "Barbara did you know?"

She realized who this must be: Margerit Sovitre, the Royal Thaumaturgist and close companion to Baroness Saveze. She seemed so young! From within a halo of chestnut curls, her eyes shone like a girl at her first ball. Before Luzie could think to wonder at the woman's reaction, the room dissolved into the noisy chaos of the interval between performances.

There was a pattern to these affairs, as foregone as a musical score. She waited for her hostess to beckon her over to begin introductions, but instead it was Maisetra Sovitre who approached eagerly.

"I have never seen—never heard a performance like that," she began. "How did you…why haven't I…"

Maisetra Sovitre's half-formed questions demanded answers that Luzie had no idea how to frame. "You enjoyed the performance?" she asked. Surely the woman was not so unsophisticated as to be this impressed by chamber music?

"There's so much I want to know," Maisetra Sovitre continued. "Is the effect tied to particular strains of music or have you found a way to shape the verses to call the *fluctus*? Is the power in the performance or in the music itself? Do you—"

Amusement played across Baroness Saveze's face and she leaned over her companion's shoulder. "Margerit, you mustn't keep Maisetra Valorin all to yourself. My other guests would like a word."

"Mesnera Lumbeirt," Luzie said, turning to her patron with a curtsey and a touch of relief. "I hope the work met your expectations."

The baroness nodded in a crisp, businesslike manner. "I would say it more than met them, although my expectations were quite high after our first meeting. And now that you've met my friend Maisetra Sovitre, may I make a few more introductions?"

The thaumaturgist stepped back to let them pass, saying, "Maisetra Valorin, might I call on you tomorrow?"

Luzie hesitated. "I give lessons for most of the morning tomorrow, but I could move some of them later if you like." It had been ten years and more since she'd had the leisure to be at home for visitors.

"Oh, no need for that. I could come whenever it's convenient for you. Would mid-afternoon be free?"

Luzie nodded, wondering what she had stepped into.

"Expect me then." Maisetra Sovitre smiled so warmly that any concerns dissolved.

The baroness took her arm and led her slowly through the crowd, offering names at every turn. Luzie tucked them away in memory as she nodded to acknowledge the compliments. This was a different circle entirely than the comfortable burfroi families that had formed Henirik's friends and supplied her students. Though that last, it seemed, might change.

Mesnera Estapez paused in her praise to ask, "I understand that you teach. My daughter—she's learned everything her governess is capable of teaching her on the clavichord and I was hoping...Well, now is not the time but perhaps you might let me know if you would be available."

Luzie hastily assured her that something could be arranged. This was success indeed. The commission had brought a little money, but connections for students in the upper town were even more valuable.

As the crowd began returning to their seats, Luzie found herself brought to the far end of the room where the refreshments were being served. The baroness paused as a dark-haired older woman in an elegant gown of crisp striped taffeta came up to them, offering two glasses of champagne.

"You may leave her in my hands for now, Barbara," the woman said, kissing Mesnera Lumbeirt on the cheek. And to Luzie, "I can see we shall have to become very good friends." She slipped her hand familiarly in the crook of Luzie's elbow and turned back to the baroness. "Do introduce us properly so I can whisk her away."

Luzie had never met the woman in person before, but no one who moved in musical circles would fail to recognize her. "Mesnera de Cherdillac," she murmured, "I'm honored. I've heard so much about you from my friend Iustin." It had been the vicomtesse who had launched Iustin's career and introduced the violinist to her future husband. The vicomtesse, too, who had sent Maisetra Talarico her way, which led to this commission. If de Cherdillac took an interest in her...

She found herself suddenly blushing. There were sordid rumors about what de Cherdillac's interest could mean—or had meant in the past. But no one could deny that the vicomtesse had an unerring instinct for talent. And yet...Luzie carefully disengaged her arm from the woman's grasp as she led her to a row of seats and they settled in to await the next performance. Ever so carefully. One wouldn't want to give offense.

"So," the vicomtesse said. "What did you think of DaNapoli for the baritone? Barbara thought he wouldn't do, but she has a silly prejudice that no foreigner should sing Pertulif."

"I was pleased with his performance," Luzie answered. "I hadn't realized that he'd been your suggestion."

"Oh, it's what I do, you know. I put this person with that person." She moved her forefingers together and crooked them around each other. "And voila! Wondrous things happen. So when will your next performance be?"

"I…I don't know," Luzie said. Her thoughts were beginning to spin at the possibilities. Could there be another commission here? But no, she knew de Cherdillac wasn't wealthy enough to serve as a patron herself. As she'd said, she put people together and stood back to let matters progress. Putting people together. Luzie looked over to the front row of chairs where her patron had settled in once more with her friend. "Do you…Maisetra Sovitre asked me something very strange about the performance. I don't remember the word she used. Do you know what she might be talking about?"

De Cherdillac's eyes sparkled with hidden secrets. "I wondered about that. It might have been just the ordinary power of music, but—Hush now, Zarne is about to begin his recitation!"

* * *

The evening had dissolved into a blur of congratulations and a dizzying whirl of faces with no chance for a further word with Maisetra Sovitre. And now, the next morning, it might have seemed a dream except for a card, left with Gerta at the door, reminding her that the thaumaturgist would call later that day.

Maisetra Talarico knew something. Luzie was certain of it. She wanted to question her, but their paths rarely crossed, not even at meals. She fidgeted through the morning, shooed her students out promptly, and barely restrained herself from bothering Silli one more time about the refreshments. Then, just as a knock sounded at the door, Maisetra Talarico came down the stairs. It couldn't have been by chance. Had she been watching for the carriage from her window?

Luzie gave one last look around the parlor, far too late to tidy anything further. The covers were growing shabby. Could she spare enough to refinish the sofa? Why hadn't she asked Mag to give the grate an extra polish this morning? She took a deep breath, then opened the door herself to invite Maisetra Sovitre in. She didn't look as young in the daylight. A bonnet covered the tumbled curls and her dark blue merino walking dress was the sort a woman might wear to signal acknowledgement that she was nearly on the shelf. Though why an heiress as fabled as Margerit Sovitre should suffer that fate was a puzzle.

Maisetra Talarico settled herself on one of the chairs without waiting for an invitation while the tea was being poured and asked, "So Margerit, what do you think now about the place of music in the mysteries?"

It was clearly a conversation the two of them had begun some time ago, for Maisetra Sovitre frowned at her. "That was quite a trick to play on me without warning. Perhaps Barbara didn't know, but you can't say the same."

A trick. Luzie's heart sank and she said stiffly, "If I'm to be the subject of a jest, perhaps you could explain it to me."

They looked discomfited.

"Maisetra Valorin," her guest began abruptly. "Do you see visions during the mysteries of the saints?"

Luzie blinked in surprise. "Visions? No."

"Or hear…strange things? Things other people don't hear? It would be no wonder if your talent was as an auditor instead."

There was no humor in the other two women's expressions now. Both of them watched her expectantly.

"I am a faithful daughter of the church. I make my confession and go to Mass and celebrate the mysteries like any other. But I'm no mystic."

Maisetra Sovitre nodded as if a different question had been answered. "I see visions," she said simply. "It's how I became a thaumaturgist. During the mysteries, sometimes during ordinary worship, I can see whose prayers are answered and how. I can see *charis*—how divine grace is granted during services. Serafina has the same sensitivity." She nodded toward Maisetra Talarico who now sat quietly, sipping her tea. "That's why she came to study with me. And you—" She set her own cup down and began gesturing, painting images in the air. "Your music brings visions. I can see—they look much like the *fluctus* that is shaped by the mysteries, but without the divine presence."

"How do you know?" Maisetra Talarico interrupted. "They have power. I could see it blazing like a star right here in this room. Anyone with the slightest sensitivity should have felt it last night. If not divine presence, then what would you call it?"

"Power without prayer? Without ritual? I don't think so. Don't you think one of the mystery guilds would have taken note of it before this, if that were the case? I'll grant that half the room felt something. Perhaps only the power of music itself, and that's nothing to be dismissed, but—"

Luzie rose to her feet, not caring how rude she might seem. "What are you saying? What is it you think I'm doing?" She stared down at her hands. How could she do this and not know?

"Would you play for me?" Maisetra Sovitre asked.

Was she to be shown off as at a student recital? At least she would feel on solid ground with her fingers on the keys. She crossed to the fortepiano and asked, "What would you like to hear?"

Maisetra Talarico took the director's role. "Play her some Beethoven—that piece I heard the first night I was here."

She had no idea which piece it had been, but she found a score and began the familiar strains. When Maisetra Talarico touched her shoulder, she stopped in mid-phrase.

"Nothing," Maisetra Sovitre said. There was surprise, but no disappointment in her voice.

"Now something of your own," Maisetra Talarico asked. "The beginning of Pertulif's 'Spring'."

She closed her eyes. There was no need for a written score this time. The introduction poured from her fingers. There was a sharp intake of breath behind her and she stumbled on the keys before continuing.

"If you'll pardon me," Maisetra Talarico interrupted again. "Can you sing the line, without the accompaniment?"

"My voice isn't much," Luzie said doubtfully, but she found her note on the keyboard and did her best. "Dawn lights the hills, a rose blooms in the vale."

"Much fainter," came the response when she paused for breath. "Curious. And if you only recite the words?"

She turned in irritation. "Surely you've heard Pertulif recited before." Royal Thaumaturgist or not, she was growing impatient with being ordered about.

"Please?" Maisetra Talarico asked.

Luzie shrugged and declaimed the first stanza of the poem until Maisetra Sovitre shook her head.

"It's the composition," Maisetra Talarico said. "Though I don't doubt good lyrics make it stronger."

They were talking past her again. Luzie left the fortepiano and returned to her chair. Her tea was cold. She tipped it into the bowl and poured a new cup. "When you have come to some agreement about my performance, perhaps you could share it with me."

"I don't think we're likely to agree soon," Maisetra Talarico said, following her lead and accepting a fresh cup of tea. "Margerit is used to being the only person she knows who can create new mysteries. And yet here you are."

"Are you saying that I am creating miracles?" Luzie asked hesitantly.

Maisetra Talarico answered, "Yes."

At the same instant came Maisetra Sovitre's, "No."

The other two stared at each other for a long moment. Maisetra Talarico waved one long-fingered hand in surrender. "How should I know? You're the philosopher."

The rehearsal of a long-running argument spun out around her and Luzie tried to follow the talk of prayers and rituals, *charis* and something about stained glass windows.

Maisetra Sovitre threw up her hands. "I have never seen the choir or the organ raise anything more than what ordinary worship might."

"And is that the fault of the music, or only the lack of talent in the composer?" Maisetra Talarico asked sharply. "If your tradition doesn't use music, then there would be no reason to seek out composers with the proper talent. But in Palermo I felt it once. There was a service—" Her voice trailed off and she bit her lip to keep some emotion inside. "I don't know who the composer had been. No one could tell me. But he had power. The same power and talent we have here in this room."

Luzie found it frightening to hear them speak about her like that. "I have no power," she whispered. "The only power my little tunes have is to give my students the confidence to play well."

Maisetra Sovitre looked at her curiously. "What did you say?"

"It's nothing. I write little études for my students. They play better when they know it was written for them. I think they practice harder knowing that."

"Could you play one of those?"

Luzie groaned inwardly. No doubt Maisetra Sovitre would explain it all in good time. And for all the woman's youth, she mustn't forget that the Royal Thaumaturgist had connections that could serve her in good stead—though how this talk of visions and colors would attract new students escaped her at the moment. She opened her folder of music and found the manuscript for "The Nightingale." She scarcely needed the notes herself, but the ritual helped her settle her mind.

She had barely begun the opening measures when Maisetra Talarico's excited voice came, "Yes! You see how it moves? The Pertulif piece reached out to listeners, but this one—see how it enfolds the player? The intent shapes the *fluctus* just as for an effective mystery."

Maisetra Sovitre was there at her elbow. "May I? I'm not a skilled player. My Aunt Honurat gave up on my lessons when she found me with my philosophy book propped up on the clavichord while playing scales. But I can read the notes."

Luzie gave over her place at the bench and stepped back to listen. It was true: the woman would have embarrassed herself at even the most intimate family gathering.

As Maisetra Sovitre hesitantly picked out the notes, her eyes darted back and forth around her and her mouth fell open in a little "O." She paused and returned to the beginning again, this time concentrating on the page before her. She frowned slightly and began yet again, more slowly and changing a figure here and there. Luzie could tell that this time it was deliberate and not mere fumbling.

"So it *is* in the music, and not just the performer." Maisetra Talarico sounded like a teacher as she urged, "Still faint. But crisper this time. Could you bring out the...the blue waves a bit more?"

The woman at the keyboard shook her head. "I'd need to experiment further."

"Let me—" There was an odd note in Maisetra Talarico's voice, a yearning that went beyond the desire to take a turn.

Luzie watched those long dark fingers pause over the keys before beginning. She played with awkward hesitation, like someone who had never received proper lessons, pecking out the beginning of the melody line. Then she dropped her hands to the keys in a jangled cacophony. "Nothing. Nothing!" she cried. She turned a face suddenly streaked with tears.

It hadn't been that bad, Luzie thought, and she began the reassurances she would have given any student. "It only takes practice."

"You don't understand!" Maisetra Talarico said, standing abruptly and sounding even more like a frustrated schoolgirl. "You leak magic like a sieve and don't even know it! And I—" She gestured wildly to unseen things in the room. "Nothing. I have nothing."

"But we know," Maisetra Sovitre began, her voice wavering between crisp analysis and consolation. "We know that even an effective ritual depends on the celebrant. That many people never evoke a response. So this—whatever it is, is no different."

Luzie could taste the tension between the two women. It went deeper than whatever had happened just now in her parlor.

Maisetra Talarico held her hands held up before her and started at them accusingly. "And I'm not good enough. I'm never good enough." She turned suddenly and rushed up the stairs toward her room. It would have seemed less absurd if their ages had been reversed—if Maisetra Talarico had the excuse of impatient youth.

The awkward silence drew out until they heard a door close from above. Luzie could think of nothing more useful to say than, "Perhaps a fresh pot of tea?"

* * *

The visit left so much to ponder and so little to understand. Had she ever heard of such a thing before? Poets were always saying that music had the power to transform and transport the listener. She'd never thought those claims were anything more than pretty words. But Maisetra Sovitre had clearly been speaking of something more concrete, more tangible. And how could such a thing be true without her knowing it? If it had only been Maisetra Talarico, then she would have thought it no more than the woman's mercurial humor, but Sovitre did not seem one to play jokes of that sort.

The remainder of the afternoon had been scheduled for copywork and accounts, but when she settled at the mahogany secretary desk, Luzie pulled out a sheet of writing paper, trimmed her pen and began, *Dearest Papa, the most peculiar thing has happened to me today…*

Supper passed with only Charluz and Elinur as company. Issibet would be out late. First performances at the opera always meant last minute adjustments and repairs and she didn't dare leave the sewing girls unsupervised. And Maisetra Talarico was still upstairs. The others were too accustomed to concerts to be curious about last night beyond success and failure. And though Maisetra Sovitre had given no hint that their discussion was to be kept secret, Luzie was still too confused to try to explain it to others. Then Elinur was off and Charluz settled in to the parlor with her mending while Luzie sat at the fortepiano, alternately playing a few notes and scribbling changes to the score before her.

It was later, after Charluz had packed up her mending basket, that she heard footsteps coming down the stairs and passing along the corridor toward the kitchen. Luzie frowned over the music and penned a few more changes. Half an hour later, a curious stillness made her look up to see Maisetra Talarico's face barely visible in the shadows of the doorway as she looked in with a wistful expression. Well, they would need to have it out either now or later.

"I don't care to be made a figure of fun," Luzie began. It wasn't how she'd intended to begin. She sounded too waspish; Maisetra Talarico wasn't one of her students to scold.

"I never meant—"

"I thought you recommended me to Baroness Saveze because you liked my music, not because you thought it would be a clever trick." Even as she said it, Luzie knew it was unfair. The concert had been a success. She had one new student already because of it.

Maisetra Talarico's expression slipped from wistful to mournful. "I do like it. And the other…I didn't want to spoil the surprise. For Margerit—for Maisetra Sovitre."

"And for me?"

When Maisetra Talarico was silent for long moments, Luzie returned to picking out her tune on the keys. It was meant to be an exercise for the Lozerik sisters. The younger girl wouldn't be able to manage the run in the upper hand yet, but it felt a shame to simplify the tune so much. She ran through the part again in the easier version.

Maisetra Talarico stepped out of the shadow of the doorway and came to sit beside her on the bench. "Why did you change it?"

Luzie moved the page in front of her and took up the more advanced part, explaining about the sisters. "Try that. I want to see how they go together."

"I can't. I've never learned properly. A…a friend tried to teach me a little, but I was hopeless."

"I heard you this afternoon. You'll do well enough for this. Try it."

They played side by side, slowly at first, then with more confidence.

"And now the original," Luzie said. Slowly again and much more awkwardly with constant mistakes. "No, that won't do," she sighed.

"You play them both," Maisetra Talarico urged, sliding the music across to her.

Luzie felt her intense gaze as she deftly played both versions in turn. "I need to take that run out. Maybe in another year…"

"No, the music needs it. What if you—" She hesitated until Luzie nodded to continue. "What if you change the easier part like this?" She played a few notes. Just a bare sketch. "And then shift the flowing part to the other player?"

"Perhaps," Luzie said. "It would still stretch her abilities." She tried the altered version, her hands darting back and forth to play both parts.

The other woman nodded in satisfaction. "Yes, that's better."

Luzie could tell she was speaking of more than the harmony. "What do you see?"

Maisetra Talarico's gaze became unfocused. "The simple version—it stays inward." She gestured toward her heart. "The light is...too brownish, not crisp enough. When you include the run, it flows all over." Now she waved her hands along the keyboard. "There are...stems, vines that reach out for the other player. Green and gold. I think if the other player were...were someone capable, they would twine together. It's so hard to explain. There isn't really a language—at least not one I know."

"Why didn't you tell me? You saw it that first evening, didn't you?"

"Would you have believed me?" Maisetra Talarico didn't wait for an answer. "I must apologize for my behavior this afternoon. It was...can you imagine what it would be like to see—no, to hear all the most beautiful songs in the world? To hear them every moment of every day in exquisite perfection, and to be mute and never able to join in the harmony?"

She gazed up at the ceiling and Luzie could see the tears welling once more in her dark eyes.

"And can you imagine meeting someone who has the most beautiful voice you've ever heard and discovering that person was deaf, and could never hear their own song."

"Like Beethoven," Luzie said without thinking. "They say he's losing his hearing."

"And what if he had never heard any of his works, and yet been able to compose them? What if he had done all that and never known what it was he had created except from what others told him?"

That part she could understand, though she flinched to be compared to the great master. "But why does it pain you so to...to be unable to play yourself?" She couldn't think of the words for what had passed that afternoon. "Maisetra Sovitre said that many people lack the talent."

"But they don't know they lack it. It's a rare skill that I have." She said it simply, without any sense of boasting. "Much rarer than the ability to catch the ear of the saints, as Margerit puts it. To work mysteries. Most people have some very slight skill for that. Not enough to raise a miracle on their own, but that's why we come together in groups for the Great Mysteries."

Maisetra Talarico turned on the bench to face her. "It's far less common for a lone voice to invoke divine grace, the way you can. Rarest of all, to have what Maisetra Sovitre has: both the voice to speak and the ear to hear, to better shape her mysteries to be answered. If I had even a little of that talent—" She held up her hands before her though she was no longer speaking of musical skill. "Even the slightest bit and I could shape it to work miracles. But there's nothing. Nothing to work with. I open my mouth and not even a croak comes out."

And then she seemed to wrench her mood sideways and she smiled and stood up. "Now will you play for me? Something of your own?"

Luzie moved the manuscript to one side and let her fingers choose the piece. As she played, she tried to imagine what shapes and colors the music might be taking in that vision that she lacked.

CHAPTER SIX

Jeanne

Mid-October, 1823

Though morning visits were never a chore, Jeanne was glad when she was free to direct the driver of the fiacre to set her down at the north gate of the palace grounds. By custom, the gardens were open to all, but the guard on duty at the pedestrian gate was new enough to ask her name and business before his companion stepped in to admonish him, "Mesnera de Cherdillac is here to see Her Grace's alchemist. Let her through, she knows the way."

The workshop was located in the old summer kitchens on the north side of the palace grounds where they had been set apart against the risk of fire. A stretch of garden separated them from the main palace buildings. That same risk had directed the choice to build the alchemical furnace here. The suite was a change from the dark, cramped rooms on Trez Cherfis where Antuniet's work with alchemically enhanced gemstones had first found success. No, not first—that had happened in Prague and Heidelberg where Antuniet had spent her exile. Jeanne knew only bits and scraps of those years. Trez Cherfis would always hold a place in their hearts. How could it not, when it was there that love had grown, layer on layer, like one of the gems in Antuniet's furnace? But these rooms were more worthy of a royal appointee. The furnishings went beyond the merely practical and reflected Princess Annek's pride, from the tiled zodiacal motifs on the floor to the chased decorations on every shining brass surface.

Antuniet looked up briefly and smiled as she entered, but Jeanne could tell from the tenor of the work that it would be some time before a break was possible. She could wait. Goodness knew, she'd waited long enough back when they were sorting out their hearts, when Antuniet had been consumed with the thought of redeeming her family's lost honor. Love had caught her by surprise. The work was less frantic now, more thoughtful and experimental. Jeanne didn't miss the hot, grimy summer afternoons when even her own hands were needed for grinding ores and picking over the fired matrix for the stones that lay within. But she missed the close camaraderie of that summer when it was only her and Antuniet and the apprentice, Anna Monterrez.

Anna, too, had bloomed in the new setting. Her father no longer treated her as a girl to be chaperoned to and from the workshop by a cousin or by one of his servants. Now the goldsmith was content with the security of a hired fiacre that carried her across the river from the Jewish neighborhood to the palace grounds or to the evening lectures that Margerit sponsored. The work no longer held the dangers that had left the long ugly mark that crossed Anna's cheek. That hadn't come from the alchemy itself, but from the enemy that had pursued Antuniet from Heidelberg. A battle scar earned in defence of Antuniet's secrets.

When Jeanne first met her, Anna had given the illusion of maturity by a trick of her height and the sober braided crown of her sable hair. Since then, she'd grown a little into that illusion, and to that was added the confidence that came with supervising the two new assistants. Yet Jeanne knew that Antuniet still felt it as a rebuke every time she saw that marred face, or when she saw Anna arranging her shawl over her head to cover that cheek before going out in public.

Now Jeanne watched Anna instructing the new apprentices who had taken much of the hard work off her hands. There had been no formal promotion to journeyman, but she'd taken to the task of managing them like a housewife overseeing a pair of clumsy kitchen maids. Now she snapped at the younger of the two, "Marzin, what are you about?"

He jumped. "The alumina. You said to regrind it one more time."

"These aren't kitchen spices," Anna said. "Where are your instructions?"

He sheepishly picked up the slate on which he'd copied down his tasks. "Grind at the rise of Capricorn," he read.

"And when does Capricorn rise?"

"I don't know," he whispered. "The grinding takes so long, I wanted to get started."

"If you didn't know you should have asked," Anna said sharply.

Jeanne hid a smile as Anna pulled Antuniet's zodiacal watch out of her pocket and opened the case to show him.

"You see? Not for two hours yet. If you haven't the wit to know why a thing is done, at least have the wit to follow instructions."

It wasn't entirely fair to chastise him. They really should have a better system, perhaps a standing horologe. Was there anyone in Rotenek who could build one to their needs? They might have to send as far as Geneva and risk transporting the delicate mechanism over the mountains. And if that were the case, it wouldn't happen this year. Not with the unseasonable weather keeping the roads closed to carriage traffic.

Antuniet interrupted the pair of them without making it a challenge to Anna's authority. "And that means you should take the time to clean up and eat something. Marzin, put the kettle on for tea after you've washed your hands, and then you'll have at least an hour."

That was Jeanne's cue to leave her perch. She placed a chaste kiss on Antuniet's cheek in an unsmudged spot, breathing in her sharp chemical perfume. No one but Antuniet could make a trace of sulfur smell so heavenly. "Shall we go sit in the garden? It may be our last chance this year. Anna, I've done my shopping at Lenoir's patisserie so you need have no qualms about joining us." She held up a neatly-tied box brought from the bakery.

Anna frowned a little. "You didn't need to do that."

Jeanne gave an inward sigh. Anna had long since relaxed her rules about dining with them. And now it seemed she disliked having attention drawn to the matter, even when it was intended as kindness. "But they make the most delicious cakes. Even better than the ones served at the Café Chatuerd, and that's saying a great deal."

The building in which the workshop was located had been surrounded at one time by the kitchen gardens, but they had fallen into riotous chaos. Only the herb beds were still kept in order as part of the pleasure garden. Now in October the flowers were well past and the weather uncertain, but just for today the afternoon sun still warmed a few small stone benches. There remained a delicate wrought iron table and chairs, not yet taken in for the winter. They served for the moments when Antuniet was able to tear herself away from the work.

Jeanne poured the tea, saying, "Was it only last summer we'd take our picnic to the river wall down on the south bank! How much has changed."

"How much indeed," Antuniet echoed. "Have some cake." She picked up a tiny almond pastry and playfully slipped it into Jeanne's mouth.

They caught each other's eyes as she savored it, and when her mouth was free again she said softly, "I still love my bread the best." But Anna was there and serious flirtation would have to wait for later.

Their visitor's approach was heralded by Anna's quick scramble to her feet to curtsey. Jeanne rose with more dignity to greet the bright-uniformed figure who strode along the path toward them.

"Mesner Atilliet," Antuniet hailed him. "I hadn't expected you until later. Do you have time to join us or only enough to collect your talismans?"

The cavalry uniform did much to set off the person of Princess Annek's son, Jeanne thought, as he lifted the hat from his auburn locks and bowed over her hand with that charming Austrian mannerism he'd chosen not to shed. She approved of the addition of a small moustache. She was not so old or so settled that she couldn't take pleasure from the attentions of a handsome man.

"I have a little time, yes," he said.

Antuniet received the same greeting and then he turned to Anna, bowing over her hand and whispering something that sent her into blushing confusion. Really, he shouldn't tease the girl, for all that they'd spent long months working side by side last year like brother and sister.

Jeanne said, "Anna, go fetch another teacup if you would." That would allow her to regain her composure. Brief moments later she returned, unwilling to miss a word.

"Are you back to your regiment for the winter?" Antuniet asked.

"No, my mother sends me off to Paris with Albori. I'm to be apprenticed in diplomacy, it seems, though officially I'll be nothing more than an aide. Albori thinks—" He paused, though it was impossible to tell whether he'd realized he was being indiscreet or thought the topic too weighty to discuss over tea.

Antuniet didn't seem to notice the stumble. "Ah, that would explain some of the particular stones she requested."

Jeanne had been paying only slight attention to the current projects in the workshop, but there had been something about a special commission from Her Grace. The alchemical gems Antuniet created went far beyond the techniques DeBoodt had developed two centuries earlier. Careful layers of enhanced crystals magnified the natural properties of the gems, lending the wearer their strengths. No wonder at all if Annek wanted to send Efriturik off into the world as well protected and fortified as possible. Emerald to sharpen the wits and the memory, topaz to detect poison, jacinth for good fortune in traveling, carnelian against curses and spells, and so many more, all combined and layered for best efficacy, whether in a ring, or set on a sword hilt or kept even more closely about his person.

The conversation turned to lighter matters: gossip of the court, the latest sensational novel, the news from France. Jeanne handled the reins without thought, drawing him out, bringing Antuniet out of her habitual taciturnity, allowing Anna her shy silence as she watched the conversation move back and forth, like viewing a play on the stage.

And then, without giving any hint of impatience, Efriturik rose and Anna was sent off to fetch the set of gems. He tucked the case inside the breast of his waistcoat and took his leave with a broad compliment and a wink that encompassed all three of them.

It was all no more than a matter of habit for him. In the last year, the attractions that arose from being personable and well-fashioned and a likely heir to the throne had been augmented by leaving behind the brashness of youth and by the cultivation of wit and charm. Efriturik was developing quite a reputation for the careful and gentle breaking of hearts. Some day a bride would be chosen for him, but for now any girl he smiled at could dream. And even a middle-aged widow with no interest in young men could enjoy the game.

It would soon be time to clear away the remains of the tea, but they sat for a while yet after their guest had gone, enjoying the birdsong. Jeanne saw a pensive look settle over Anna's face. Something softer than the usual moodiness of youth. "What do you want to learn next?" Jeanne asked her.

The question seemed to startle her. "I want—" She glanced over at Antuniet, looking for permission.

Without need for explanation, Antuniet nodded in assent. Yes, she understood what it was to wonder if you were allowed to want things.

"Mesnera de Cherdillac, I want to learn to be like you." Into the startled silence, Anna hurried to add, "I love the alchemy. I want to master it like Mesnera Antuniet has. But I wish...you know how to talk to anyone about anything. You're always so...so graceful. That's not the right word. But you can always tie the threads together, to move from one thing to the next and weave them all into one fabric."

Like a dam breaking, Anna continued, "When Papa has visitors, I always feel so clumsy. Entertaining always seemed to come naturally to Iudiz and Lenur—my older sisters. They've tried to teach me, but..."

It was easy to guess that an older sister's guidance might not always be welcome.

"I've studied so many things," Anna continued. "Science, and what I learn at Maisetra Sovitre's lectures, even books and music. All of this." She waved her hand in a way that indicated far more than the palace grounds. "But when I try to talk to people it feels like I'm tripping over stones and...and like they're all staring at me."

Her eyes turned toward the ground and she raised a hand to brush the scar that traced from the corner of her eye toward her chin. "It's not just this. But I sometimes think, if I could just talk to people, they wouldn't notice it as much."

Jeanne pursed her lips in understanding. In the workshop, Anna had self-possession and confidence, but outside that sphere? "It is training, as for any other profession," she said gently. "A different training than you've needed. When I was a girl, I was a protégée of the famous Mesnera Esmerzul. At one time, I might have become a salonnière myself, but..." She made a dismissive gesture. Those years weren't stories for an innocent girl. "It isn't as hard as you might think. Read everything, not just what you need for alchemy. Listen to everyone. Good conversation lies more in what you draw from the other person than what you say yourself. It's simply a matter of good manners. Learn and watch and listen, that's what you do to begin. The rest is practice."

Anna shook her head. "When would I have the chance?"

It wasn't a matter of opportunity. Maistir Monterrez was well respected and his eldest daughter served ably as his hostess, though Jeanne knew that only from repute. But she could easily envision how shy Anna would be overshadowed by her married sisters. So often, girls her age were admonished to be seen and not heard until they were safely betrothed. That wouldn't do for Anna! When she forgot to be self-conscious, she was witty and brilliant.

Antuniet rose to clear away the tea things, to give them a private space to talk.

The alchemy apprenticeship had opened an unexpected path in Anna's life. Perhaps that path could be widened a little. Maistir Monterrez considered her and Antuniet to be suitable chaperones for Anna's ventures into the world. Desirable even, despite the rumor of their irregular relationship. Perhaps he could be coaxed into agreeing to a new venture.

"Perhaps—I don't promise anything—but perhaps I might begin holding a few little gatherings at my house," Jeanne began. She would need to secure Antuniet's permission. They'd begun to entertain more this autumn, finding the meeting point between her own desire for company and Antuniet's distaste for crowds.

"Just a few people," she continued. "My house isn't large enough for more than that. And no one who wouldn't be welcome in your father's house. Perhaps—" And now her imagination was spinning out threads of its own. That fascinating composer Barbara had discovered. And perhaps Mesnera Farin. Margerit had failed to entice her to give a lecture—Mesnera Farin had never been easy among crowds—but in a smaller group? It could be just the right challenge to see if Anna could draw her out. "Yes, perhaps we can see to a different side of your training."

It was a new thought: to envision Anna Monterrez as something more than Antuniet's assistant. A woman of society? No, nothing like that. She was only a girl still—barely sixteen. Not quite old enough to be out yet. And Anna could scarcely play hostess on her own until she was married.

But a salon in a private home was a different matter. It had become easy to think of Anna as something in the way of an adopted daughter. Certainly a protégée in the old sense. Jeanne cast her mind back again to her own girlhood. The family—it wouldn't be a bar for what she had in mind. She wasn't asking her friends to invite the girl to balls. The virtue of the salon had always been in how it set birth at naught. All that mattered was that a person be clever or entertaining. The fashion had faded for a time during the war, and then when Princess Elisebet had led the court. But there were signs that the power of the salons was returning. And perhaps it was time to test whether her own place in Rotenek had been completely ruined by the gossip about Antuniet. Yes, this might be just the thing.

* * *

Having made the decision, it was a matter of a few days to bring it about. Maistir Monterrez's agreement had been surprisingly prompt and he had rehearsed her own arguments before she'd needed to present them. This wasn't a grand ball that required months of planning. Anything too elaborate would give the wrong appearance. *I would enjoy your company for conversation on the evening of the fifteenth.* Nothing more than that. The guests had been carefully selected, but to indicate why would break the illusion of spontaneity.

Jeanne watched Anna run her fingers over the keys of the spinet they'd brought in for the evening. Her gown would do for now, but perhaps—

"It will only be Maisetra Valorin playing, won't it?" It was hard to tell whether she was longing or afraid to be asked to play.

"No one will play who doesn't wish to," Jeanne reassured her. "I don't think Oltir is musical, but I don't know about Farin." She paused in directing Tomric in the arrangements of the room and crossed over to give Anna a brief embrace. "Don't worry, you'll do well. Remember what I told you: listen to each person as if they were the most fascinating person in the room and they will forgive you anything you might say! And both Antuniet and I will see that all goes well."

On cue, Antuniet came down the stairs, dressed in a sober gown of wine-colored silk. She'd taken the intrusion into their home in good part. "Remind me again who you've invited tonight," she said. As their eyes met, Antuniet briefly touched the irregular red pendant at her throat. Always so circumspect! But the gesture took the place of a kiss.

Jeanne felt the familiar thread of warmth run through her from the mystic connection of the alchemical heart-stone. "Luzie Valorin, that wonderful new composer that Barbara found. I think I may make a project of her. And Maistir Oltir. He's been working on some rather interesting poetry. I was thinking on a theme of measures. And thus Mesnera Farin. There was a time when she was quite the prodigy in mathematics and I've been trying to coax her to do a lecture for Margerit. Anna, you should ask her about better ways to do astronomical calculations. Music and mathematics go well together, don't you think?"

Antuniet shrugged.

"And Ermilint Belais to bring a touch of levity. She may not be very learned but her conversation is exquisite. And then Rikerd—Anna, you haven't met Count Chanturi before—just for a touch of wit." She had settled on a total of eight as the number that would fit comfortably in the cozy parlor. Not too many for a single conversation, nor too few should they break out into smaller groups.

"Count Chanturi?" Antuniet quizzed, with a fleeting glance at Anna.

Jeanne had thought twice about Rikerd. His ideas of humor could tread on the edges of what was seemly in the presence of a young woman. But above all, he knew the game, and he would provide safe practice dealing with that sort of badinage before Anna found herself flustered in the face of someone less kind.

At the sound of a carriage pausing in the street Jeanne signaled to Tomric and they all took their seats in readiness.

Jeanne tried not to watch Anna too closely as the guests arrived. At first she had only the task of bringing drinks and refreshments as they took their places. When all had settled in, Jeanne caught Anna's eye and gave her an encouraging nod.

Anna turned to Maisetra Valorin and said, "We were wondering if you might be willing to play something for us."

The composer looked curiously in Jeanne's direction, uncertain that this followed the plan for the evening. Jeanne nodded and smiled.

After the performance there was no need to put spurs to the conversation as Antuniet began quizzing Maisetra Valorin on the relationship between music and mysticism, while the poet and mathematician debated the merits of formal structure and intuition.

Anna's shyness made it easy for her to follow instructions. Have more questions than opinions, Jeanne had advised her. Look to the balance. Being a good hostess is like arranging flowers. Not too much of any one blossom. A contrast here; an accent there. Anna had studiously read through Oltir's verses and mastered the basics of Mesnera Farin's theories and then drawn up lists of questions to have ready for any pause. She was too earnestly studied, though Antuniet was little better at times, with her sharp, probing queries and a habit of pursuing her own curiosity beyond the rules of conversation.

In a spirit of mischief, Jeanne suggested, "But surely in the realm of music, the romantic spirit must be raised above mere formalism. How can one capture the delights of Pertulif's verse unless one appeals first of all to the heart, not the head?"

"Indeed," Ermilint agreed. "Pertulif was an excellent choice for your work, Maisetra Valorin. The ancient authors evoke such feeling!"

"I'd take your praise," Maisetra Valorin said. "But that was Baroness Saveze's choice. I was only lucky that I was the one she chose to set them."

Mesnera Farin commented, "It seems odd to praise Pertulif as a rejection of formalism when his meter is flawless! Now if you were to do settings of Zarne…"

"I don't think Zarne would be in your style," Rikerd countered. "But I could see you tackling *Eskambrend's Quest*. Historic works are all the rage now. Jeanne, did I tell you about that delightful *roman gothique* that Helen Peniluk lent me? That's just what I'm thinking of: all ancient castles and mysterious secrets and missing heirs. The French wars are long enough past that deeds of arms have become romantic again, as long as there are flashing blades involved."

Antuniet gave a little laugh. "Don't let Barbara hear you say that. She thinks sword play is the least romantic thing in the world."

An amused smile played on Rikerd's lips. "No doubt she would. It's a shame, for she'd make a delightful romantic heroine herself. Perhaps she already has."

By the time the guests took their leave, Jeanne had crowned the venture a success and was planning ahead to the next gathering. Perhaps a more frivolous theme—Anna had never entirely lost her stiffness.

Count Chanturi lingered after the others had gone. Even Anna had been packed away in a fiacre for the ride home. Jeanne smiled as Rikerd lifted her hand to his lips in salute and she said to him, "I hope we didn't bore you to tears!"

"No, no, I understand your purpose. You test your little protégée on the lowest jumps before setting her on a steeplechase. I've been curious what project you would turn your hand to next. What do you intend for her, I wonder?"

"I intend nothing; this was her idea."

Rikerd raised his brows at that. She could see the doubt passing through his mind. But then he shrugged. "If you don't overmatch her at the fences she may do well. But Jeanne, I meant to remember, do you recall that new *roman gothique* I mentioned earlier?"

"I shouldn't think that sort of novel was in your style," Jeanne said.

"Oh, not in the usual way. It's well enough done, mind you, but...tongues are wagging about who lies behind it."

"Not Lady Ruten, then? She's turned out entire libraries of those stories. I don't know why she bothers to be coy about it, everyone knows she's the author."

He shook his head. "Not this time, I think. This is a different voice—fresher. But I wasn't thinking so much of the author as the subjects."

"Ah," Jeanne said. "A *roman à clef*! No wonder people are talking. Everyone loves a good puzzle. Do you have the key?"

He pressed his lips together, hesitant to say more. "Jeanne, I think perhaps you should read it for yourself."

* * *

It took no more than one chapter for Jeanne to understand Rikerd's concern. It was a wonder she hadn't heard the gossip before this. Perhaps no one had dared mention the book, knowing of her particular friendships. And if no one had thought to mention it to her yet... She read the novel through twice, to be certain, then sent a note to Tiporsel House inquiring when both Barbara and Margerit would be at home.

The tone of the missive did its work and the next morning, in the privacy of the library that Margerit preferred to the parlor, Jeanne drew out two small volumes with matching bindings, tied together with a green silk ribbon. "I know it's not the season for gift giving yet, but I think you should read this."

Margerit laughed. "You know books are always my favorite gift! What have you found for me?"

Barbara untied the ribbon and opened the cover of the first volume. She raised an eyebrow. "A novel? *The Lost Heir of Lautencourt*. It sounds a trifle frivolous for our scholar."

"Frivolous, yes," Jeanne said. "Though quite well written, I must say. But no, it's only that I think you should know it exists and that people are talking about it."

Barbara shrugged as she leafed through the first few pages. "You sound very serious."

Jeanne took the book from her hand and held it up. "The Duke of Lautencourt dies and leaves his fortune to a poor relation. A young woman. The heir to the duke's title, a scheming villain, kidnaps her for a forced marriage but she is rescued by a mysterious young man who begs to take service as her armin. She becomes the toast of society in Rotenek with the loyal and dedicated armin always at her side. But when the villain attempts to entangle her in a satanic cult, the armin reveals himself as the duke's long-lost son. He defeats the villain, claims the title and marries the young woman. They have, of course, fallen deeply in love."

A silence fell over the room. Margerit looked frightened and Barbara's lips had thinned to a grim line. Despite the outrageous flourishes, the story was close enough to their own that it was impossible to be an accident.

Barbara broke the hush at last, asking, "Who wrote it?"

Jeanne shrugged. "I honestly don't know. Chanturi brought it to my attention. No one else has said a thing."

"Who would want to stir up gossip like this about us?" Margerit asked. "Are you sure it's meant to be us? There's no mistake?"

"It isn't clumsily done," Jeanne answered. "And there seems to be no malice in it. The characters are noble and virtuous and loyal. I think you can laugh it off if you're careful. But I didn't want you to be surprised."

Margerit held out her hand for the books. "Thank you. I suppose it's best to ignore it." She gave Barbara a meaningful glance. "No hunting down the author! That would only make things worse."

CHAPTER SEVEN

Serafina

Late October, 1823

A river shaped the lives of the people around it in unexpected ways. The Tiber had been vaster and less intimate, more a presence than a person. Here, people spoke of the Rotein as they might of a beloved aunt, a wayward cousin, an estranged lover. Especially in the west and south of the city, the narrow chanulezes, like the one that passed by Maisetra Valorin's house, threaded the water and its traffic deeply into people's lives. Morning woke to the splash of an oar and the cry of a milk delivery.

Serafina found the differences in the rivers made Rotenek feel more alien than differences in the people, more than the sound of a different tongue. Rome was vaster. It felt more crowded regardless of the number of people in immediate view. The nearness of the wharf district added some variety to the faces in the neighborhood around the Nikuleplaiz, but nothing like what one saw in Rome. The curious stares that followed her as she passed down the street—those were the same. Here she always knew she didn't belong. In Rome, those stares had rubbed at her soul. In Rome, the familiarity of the streets made it easy to forget that she would always be a stranger.

Serafina ducked into the shelter of a wall as a light rain began falling and wrestled her umbrella open. Foot traffic along the road that overlooked the river took on a more hurried pace. In gaps between the houses, she could see drifts of falling water turning the smooth surface of the Rotein into crepe. In good weather, the walk from Maisetra Valorin's house up through the Nikuleplaiz and along the curve below the palace was pleasant. Modest neighborhoods and shops gave way to the venerable stone mews and courtyards along the Vezenaf where Margerit lived.

Across the far side of the river one could see like a distorted mirror the transition from the warehouse district that she'd been warned to avoid, to a squalid clutter of taverns and tenements that gave way slowly to the homes and shops of respectable merchants and craftsmen. Such a short distance and yet such a vast gulf in the rank or the wealth required to live on one side or the other.

When the weather turned sour as it did more often now, the walk was less pleasant. The steep climb of the northern bank left one exposed to winds sweeping off the river, but a more sheltered street would add many more steps. Cutting across the bend on the southern bank led through rough neighborhoods. Shelter could be had on the water itself. The rivermen plying their trade in goods and passengers rigged canvas tents against the rain but her allowance wouldn't stretch that far too often.

Paolo's bank in Rome had confirmed her funds for the quarter once more. That meant Paolo was still in France and thought her still in Rome. She closed her mind from considering what would happen when he returned and found her gone. Or when his agent wrote something that would betray her absence, thinking it no secret. If he could go haring off, then so could she. But some day that reckoning would come.

Serafina reached the warmth of Tiporsel House before the downfall began in earnest. "This storm should settle the complaints about the river," she said to the footman who took her parasol, bonnet and coat. The first few phrases she had mastered in Alpennian had included the most popular comments on the weather.

He shook his head gloomily, treating her with the familiarity of a frequent visitor. "It can rain and rain, maisetra, but why is the water so low? It's not the storm here that matters," he intoned. "It's what goes on in the mountains. And those canals. They suck the water out. Has to come from somewhere, stands to reason."

"Ah, I see," Serafina said, though she had yet to comprehend the Alpennian preoccupation with the Rotein's flow. It was not the ancient chanulezes in Rotenek he meant, but the new channels being dug out in the provinces.

The footman's voice returned to formality. "The Maisetra said to tell you that she stepped out on an errand. That if you please you could wait for her in the library. Tea will be sent in."

The library, it seemed, was already occupied. The boy, Brandel, leapt up from a book-strewn table as she entered.

"Don't let me disturb your studies, Maistir Chamering," she said.

Serafina heard a maid enter behind her with the rattle of a tray. Margerit's household was endlessly efficient. Back in Rome, Paolo had never cared to spend for more than one hard-pressed maid of all work.

There was no need to sit idle while waiting. The cases along every wall held a wealth of books. She selected a thin volume at random and settled herself in one of the overstuffed chairs by the hearth, rather than crowding the round table.

Rather than being disturbed, the boy seemed glad of the interruption. He closed the covers of the object of his study and began, "Maisetra Talarico? Might I ask you a question?"

"Hmm?" she answered.

Brandel had arrived in Rotenek much the same time she had the year before and they both were still finding their place. But though their paths crossed regularly, she had never spoken with him at length.

"I was wondering," he began. "That is…Cousin Barbara tells me I should learn everything I can about the world and the people in it. Could you tell me something about the land of your birth?"

He didn't mean Rome. She rose to cross the room and find the atlas, then spread the folio out over the top of everything else on the table.

"My parents traveled to Rome when my older brother Michele was a baby. Before I was born. They came from here," she said, tracing a finger from the tip of Italy's boot across the Mediterranean and then down along the Red Sea. Her father had shown her on a map much like this one. "Here, somewhere. I know the name, but it isn't written here. My mother was the daughter of an important man who fell from power. In the usual way of things, they would have lost their land, perhaps their freedom. But my father had made a pilgrimage to Rome in his youth, to pray and study."

Brandel seemed surprised. "They were Christians?"

Did he think them all heathens? The boy was unlikely to be familiar with the tangle of faiths and peoples that crowded the Horn of Africa. "Yes, but of a different sort. Like…like the Greeks, who don't look to Rome. But to Rome he went, as a scholar. And when trouble came, he had friends there still. And so they packed up what they could carry and paid every coin they had to the captain of a ship and traveled here to Alexandria in Egypt." She traced her finger across the map. "And from there to Rome. But I was born in Rome. I have no memory of anything else."

And then Margerit arrived, with Antuniet trailing in her wake, and Brandel was shooed away.

The last month's study had revolved entirely around Margerit's All Saints' Castellum, the complex protective ritual she had designed while still a girl. Now it was part of the ceremonies of the Royal Guild. Last year when Serafina was still so newly come to Rotenek that she didn't know up from down, mentioning the name of Margerit Sovitre to the innkeeper had brought an immediate response. If she wanted to view the Royal Thaumaturgist, she could do worse than try to find a space in the cathedral on All Saints' Day.

She had risen at dawn and waited in the Plaiz with a growing crowd until they were allowed in to bear witness. The *castellum* itself had been fascinating, with its inventive intricacies and its raw, though ragged power. But through all the patterns and movements of the *fluctus* around her, Serafina's eyes had been fixed on Margerit where she sat in a corner of the choir, a sketchbook perched on her lap, her eyes darting here and there as she scribbled notes and directions. It had taken two weeks and all her courage to find a chance to introduce herself. The concert she chose had not been a public event—not exactly—but she had imagined what Costanza would have done in the absence of an invitation, and had charmed and bluffed her way through the door. Since then, she had only needed to be swept along in Margerit's wake.

"I took our ideas to Princess Annek," Margerit said, clearing a space on the central table for her working notebooks. "The *castellum* should be protecting against things like that shaking of the earth in the south, and the plague of rats in Amituz. Those are exactly the type of hazard we designed it for. But Her Grace thinks it would be best to continue with the form we used last year for now." She made a wry face and imitated an imposing voice. "Too many changes! We can't ask the Guild to learn new lines every year!"

Antuniet made a noise halfway between a cough and a laugh. "Not everyone is an enthusiast like you!"

Margerit continued, treating it as an old joke between them. "So what we need to do is gather more observations and try to tune the ceremony more closely based on theory alone before we present the revised *expositulum*. It all takes so long!"

Now there was a frustration Serafina could understand. "Can the ritual only be performed on that specific day?"

The other two began speaking at once and Margerit waved her hand to let Antuniet continue.

"No, not entirely. When we first began drafting it, we rehearsed the individual parts regardless of time or date. Someone as perceptive as Margerit can see the echoes of the response even without the full setting. But the parts don't work together in the same way. The saints respond best when the ceremony has a...a doorway to invoke them directly. It could be a feast day, or a dedicated chapel, or the use of a relic. With so many different saints involved, it seemed best to set it on All Saints' Day. It could be worse; there's an alchemical recipe I want to try that requires a conjunction that won't happen for another five years."

"It's not the same as alchemy at all, of course," Margerit added hurriedly. "We'll do what we can. For now I'm hoping the both of you can add your vision to the analysis. Serafina, your observations will be particularly valuable. Do you know? I told Princess Annek what you said about the stained glass window and you were right. She said it came from the workshop of the great Perandulfus and there was a tradition that their glass captured mysteries, and Alpennia would stand only so long as some part of that window was in place. It's just a legend, but someone thought it important enough to keep those fragments."

Serafina thought back to the visions she'd seen playing around the light from the window. Whatever power remained was barely perceptible.

"And that reminds me," Margerit said, taking two envelopes out from between the covers of her notebook. "I was asked to give these to the two of you."

The crisp white square gave no hint of its contents except for the script "AA" on the seal. Serafina glanced over at Antuniet for a clue, but she simply nodded and tucked the envelope away among her other papers. Yet Margerit was watching her expectantly, so she slipped a finger under the seal to break it and scanned the contents, her lips moving to follow the unfamiliar Alpennian phrases. Her heart began pounding.

"No, I can't." Serafina held out the invitation with shaking fingers. "I don't belong there."

Margerit stared at her in confusion. "Don't be silly. If you've been invited, then you belong. The dinner's not just for the Royal Guild. Princess Annek has taken to inviting all the ambassadors and notable foreigners in Rotenek. And she wants to acknowledge those who make the mystery possible."

No, that was almost worse. Couldn't she see? Margerit was too polite to comment on her awkward manners, but Giuletta hadn't been. Paolo had only shown irritation; he hadn't cared enough to correct her. How Costanza had laughed the first time they had dined together! She'd turned it to an endearment, *mia cara selvaggia*—my darling savage—watching her pick over the silverware and guess at how to manage each dish. The easy informality of Margerit's table was more forgiving, but they could tell she hadn't been raised in an elegant household. She hadn't needed to refuse an invitation outright before. But a dinner at the palace…no. It was impossible. She couldn't pass her ignorance off as foreign charm in such a setting. "I can't," she repeated. "I…," she seized on a safer excuse. "I haven't anything proper to wear."

"I thought of that and—" Margerit began.

But before she could make an embarrassing offer, Antuniet shook her head sharply and an odd look passed between them.

"Let me set Jeanne on the problem," Antuniet said. "She can work miracles, and I'm sure she can find a dressmaker to set you up properly for whatever you can afford. Trust Jeanne to take care of you." The reassurance had hidden layers. "After all, she's turned me respectable and that's something my mother never managed."

* * *

Jeanne came, as promised, late the next morning, setting Gerta all aflutter when she came upstairs to announce the visitor.

"Vicomtesse de Cherdillac to see you, maisetra," she said with a touch of awe that was normally absent from her speech. "She said to tell you to bring a wrap."

They'd be going out? Serafina had thought Jeanne meant to examine her sparse wardrobe and identify which item might best be made over into something presentable. She buttoned the blue pelisse over her day dress and traded her cap for a bonnet. Gerta continued standing by. She should let the maid assist in the details of dressing. It was part of her duties. Serafina knew that, too, betrayed her origins. But she kept remembering that first encounter—the deliberate way Gerta had rubbed against her arm—and tensed every time the maid touched her.

The hesitant sound of music from beyond the closed parlor door told her that lessons were in progress and Serafina laid a finger to her lips when Jeanne greeted her.

Out on the street, Jeanne said, "I hope you don't mind walking, it looked to be fair and we aren't going very far."

"I walk most places," Serafina answered. "Antuniet told you..." It was easier talking to Jeanne than it would have been to the others. She had the knack of setting one at ease, and somehow that made it possible to confess unease. "I'm terrified," she blurted out. "I'm going to embarrass Margerit. I don't know what she was thinking asking for me to be invited."

They had crossed the little arching bridge over the chanulez and continued in the direction of the Nikuleplaiz. Jeanne took her hand and tucked it in the crook of her arm as if they were bosom friends taking the air. "I know what you're thinking," Jeanne said, "but I rather doubt Margerit did anything beyond singing your praises. She isn't in the habit of telling Princess Annek whom to invite to her own banquets! I won't tell you you're worried about nothing. You're worried, and that's enough. Would you believe me if I tell you I've never seen you be anything but charming in company?"

"It's all playacting," Serafina said quietly. "And I'm not charming, I'm impudent and ignorant and shocking. I always say and do the wrong thing. I still remember how horrified Margerit was when I was new to Rotenek and didn't know better than to speak openly of my past lovers!"

"Yes, that," Jeanne acknowledged. "But we're all playacting, you know. You only need to learn the right lines. How is dear Marianniz? I haven't seen her recently."

Serafina felt her face burning, though perhaps Jeanne wouldn't be able to notice. "I haven't seen her since before the summer. I...she gave me a nice string of pearls."

"Ah," Jeanne said.

That and no more. It had been Jeanne, after all, who had explained to her the little rituals of affairs in Rotenek. A more extravagant present would have signaled a desire to turn their pleasant interlude into a more formal arrangement, a nominal gift would have invited her to continue as they were after the summer's separation. But pearls: that acknowledged the pleasure while putting an end to it. It was a civilized system if you knew the key.

"Are you looking?" Jeanne asked casually.

Serafina shook her head. Marianniz showed a sour face to the world but she had been a kind and attentive lover. For those few months she had provided a refuge—a sheltering nest. "I'm lonely, but I'm not looking. It's all too…complicated." For a brief moment, she wondered if a long enough stay in Rotenek would lead her through every bed in Jeanne's circle.

Jeanne laughed. "Yes, indeed. Complicated. So I shall not suggest any male lovers!"

There was no need to reply. Despite Paolo's indifference, that was a betrayal she had not yet committed.

Jeanne's voice dropped conspiratorially. "There was a time I would have been happy to fill your loneliness. Instead I'm belatedly learning the joys of constancy! But this is nothing to the point. You will go to the guild banquet and you will be charmingly exotic and no one will notice if you use the wrong fork."

Serafina pulled away from her with a scowl. "I don't want to be 'charmingly exotic,' I want…"

The mask dropped briefly from Jeanne's face to reveal sympathy and understanding. "What do you want?"

"I want to be comfortable. I want to belong." There, she'd said it. She grew so tired of pretending all the time among Margerit's close circle of friends. Pretending that she had the right to address a vicomtesse by her Christian name. Pretending that she didn't see the startled change in people's faces when she was introduced to them as maisetra. Pretending that it was only chance that she wasn't hungry when Maisetra Valorin's other tenants were dining, so that she needn't test their acceptance.

She felt Jeanne's hand tuck itself through her elbow again. "That's an unlucky thing for a woman like you to want. But more of us want it than you might think." And then as they continued down the narrow cobbled street, Jeanne's voice grew brighter. "Here we are! Mefro Dominique will provide just the thing to give you confidence."

The shop had a tidy little face with a bow window on which neat gilded letters proclaimed "Madame Dominique, Modiste." The simplicity of the display was an obvious testament to the quality of the custom she expected.

Once more Serafina hung back. "Jeanne, I don't think…"

"You needn't worry too much about the price. I won't insult you by making a present of it—Antuniet scolded me on that point! But I've brought her a great deal of business and she will return me the favor by charging only what you can afford."

"No, but Jeanne…a society dressmaker! She won't want—" How tiresome to need to explain.

But Jeanne had already opened the door, setting the bell above it jangling.

The girl who came out of the back room to greet them wore the sort of neatly elegant dress that advertised the proprietor's skills in even the simplest fashion. But Serafina scarcely glanced at her clothing, instead matching gazes with the bold eyes looking out from a brown face, framed by a lace-edged linen cap.

The girl dipped a curtsey, saying, "Good day, Mesnera de Cherdillac."

"Celeste, I do hope your mother has time to do something for Maisetra Talarico," Jeanne said. "I sent a note this morning but there was no time to wait for a reply."

She disappeared with a nod.

"Her mother?" Serafina began, a different question on the tip of her tongue.

"Dominique studied dressmaking in Paris as a girl—she came here with a group of French émigrés back during the war—but I think she was born somewhere in the Antilles. I think you'll like her. She has a knack for choosing exactly the right style. God knows she's done wonders for Antuniet!"

Serafina was barely listening. A knot eased inside her when the girl returned, followed by a tall woman dressed with equally quiet elegance. She was darker than her daughter—well, that was hardly surprising if Celeste's father were Alpennian. If Paolo had given her a child, she might have looked much the same. The thought pricked like a tiny hidden thorn. Serafina found her voice at last, "Madame Dominique, I would be very grateful if you could dress me for a dinner with the Royal Mystery Guild."

It was the girl, Celeste, who took her measurements, jotting down numbers on a slate while Dominique brought forth samples of fabric and discussed the details of tucks and ruffles. Jeanne participated with a few pointed suggestions.

"Nothing too fussy, I think. There isn't time."

Tactful of her not to mention the cost.

"Perhaps something like that wine color you chose for Mesnera Chazillen's New Year's gown?"

Dominique deftly turned Jeanne's suggestions into her own, bringing out a soft red wool with a border of flower vases woven in golds and blues. "This, I think. It was meant to be cut into shawls but if we set the border design at the hem—" She held it up to fall from just under the bosom. "—and a bit more of the motif on the sleeves. No ruffles at all, just a few tucks along the edge of the corsage." She pinched the fabric between her fingers to show the effect along the collarbone and looked up at Jeanne for approval.

"Yes, you're right as always!" Jeanne laughed.

"Will you have jewelry?" Dominique asked.

Serafina started to shake her head but Jeanne suggested, "A string of pearls?"

"Perfect! Now how do you plan to wear your hair?"

By this time Serafina had abandoned the thought of having her own opinions, but they all stared at her in expectation. "I usually…" She unpinned a lock and wound it into a tight curl around her finger to hang along her cheek. "Like that."

Celeste paused over her slate to say matter-of-factly, "I wish mine would do that."

"Then I think just a small band," Dominique concluded. "To tie around in back. No feathers, no ribbons." She kissed her fingers to set the seal of approval on her own vision.

When the decisions had all been made and the samples put away, Celeste returned to help her dress while Jeanne took the dressmaker into the front room to discuss expenses. Serafina suspected that she would be presented with a bill that was oddly thin, but there was no point to protesting.

"Maisetra?" Celeste asked as she did up the last buttons.

"Yes?"

"The vicomtesse said that you work mysteries with Maisetra Sovitre?"

Serafina shook her head. "I can't work them. But I can see them. That's what they want me there for—to watch."

"Could you...?" She bit her lip, calculating the proprieties.

"Yes?" Serafina repeated encouragingly.

"Could you bring me a candle from Saint Mauriz's altar at the cathedral? One that burned during the mystery? I don't mean steal it," she added hurriedly. "But would they let you take one away?"

"I don't see why not," she answered. "If I pay for a new one to replace it. You could do the same."

Celeste frowned. "No, not from the cathedral. I asked and the sexton told me to go about my business. And it has to be from Saint Mauriz."

Serafina looked at the girl curiously. "And are you a thaumaturgist, then?"

"Oh no," Celeste said quickly. "But I do this and that. Market-charms and the like." She glanced over her shoulder toward the front room. "Maman taught me a few things, and Mefro Charl before she died. And I try to work some things out for myself."

And then the other two women returned, all smiles and agreement, and there was no chance for a further word.

* * *

Looking at the finished gown where it lay across the end of her bed, Serafina felt the illusion of confidence ebbing away. Why had she agreed to this? Because it meant so much to Margerit, of course. And Margerit had never once questioned her presence, or her desires, or her talents, for all that they might squabble over the nature of truth. The thought of disappointing Margerit and losing all that only made her heart pound harder. She set out the fillet for her hair beside her comb and the last treasured bottle of her mother's hair oil. Not the one she used for everyday, but the one saved through the years for times when she needed that presence.

Where was that girl? Serafina poked her head out into the hallway and called, "Gerta!" It would take close to an hour to do her hair properly and she needed to be laced up first. "Gerta!"

The maid arrived in a clatter of shoes on the stairs and set about fitting the corset with impatient jerks.

"Not so tightly, I have to breathe," Serafina snapped at her. As Gerta adjusted the fit, she began unpinning her hair and teasing out the unruly cloud with her fingers. They were trembling. With the laces tied off she said, "Could you bring me the comb over there on the dressing table?" A deep breath. The next part would take patience.

She heard Gerta give a sort of snort and turned to see her sniffing at the blue glass vial that had been next to the comb. "What's this?"

"Don't touch it!"

Serafina snatched at the bottle but her fingers slipped and it flew across the room to smash across the floorboards by the window. A wave of clove and sandalwood filled the room. She stared in horror and heard a frightened squeak from Gerta.

It was an omen. The night would end in ruin and disaster. She would disgrace Margerit and Jeanne and all of them.

"Get out! Get out get out get out!" Her shouts chased the girl from the room, then she knelt on the floor, picking through the fragments of blue glass, and began to weep.

"Maisetra Talarico?"

She barely heard Maisetra Valorin's voice at the open door until the landlady ordered gently, "Gerta, clean that up and then you can go."

Serafina sat back and watched mutely as the remains of the bottle were scraped into a dustpan and the spilled oil was sopped up with a towel. The room would be scented with it for weeks to come. After Gerta left, she felt Maisetra Valorin's hands on her shoulders and smoothing her hair.

"It can't be as much of a disaster as all that. How do we mend things?"

Serafina said miserably, "I can't. My mother left it to me. It was all I had." Even now the scent evoked her presence, the touch of her hands. "It came all the way from Alexandria."

"Well then, the best place to look for more is the Strangers' Market, where the sailors sell all manner of things. But for now we'll have to make do. I have some pomade that may work. One moment." Maisetra Valorin disappeared off to her own room and returned with a small jar scented with rose. "Now sit over here and show me what you want."

One lock at a time, the cloud of hair was turned into long, bouncing ringlets as Maisetra Valorin wielded the comb at her direction. With each one, Serafina's thoughts settled slowly into better order.

"It wasn't really her fault," she said at last. "I—" She raised her hands before her. They were still trembling.

"Just like any first performance," Maisetra Valorin said. "Tomorrow you'll tell me all about it and this will be forgotten. Now let's get you into this lovely dress because I think I hear your friends' carriage out in the street."

* * *

The reception before the dinner was bearable only for Antuniet sticking by her side, equally ill at ease as the confusion of voices battered at them. The arrays of candles lighting the Assembly Hall left no dim corners to hide in.

"I wish Jeanne were here," Serafina confided.

Antuniet shrugged. "She wasn't invited this time. She isn't a member of the Royal Guild and has nothing to do with affairs of state."

The guild dinner before the All Saints' Castellum had become something of an unofficial ambassadors ball, Serafina recalled. It made her a little more comfortable to see foreign faces and hear the profusion of other tongues. She would stand out less. But the mix of interests brought its own tension. Not all the guests were on speaking terms with each other.

Margerit drifted by regularly to introduce this person or that—she scarcely recalled their names. Most memorable was the sharp-faced, red-haired man that Barbara brought and introduced as Mesner Kreiser, with the Austrian embassy. Memorable because Antuniet gave him a poisonous stare and swept away without a word.

"Maisetra Talarico," he said, bowing over her hand. "I've heard some fascinating things about you." And to Barbara, "Does your cousin still hold a grudge?"

Barbara looked uneasy. "She might have forgiven you for her own sake, but not on behalf of Maisetra Monterrez."

Kreiser looked confused for a moment. "Oh, yes, the little Jewish girl. I had forgotten." He shrugged. "These things happen in war."

"Is it war?" Barbara asked lightly. Her voice sounded like the ringing tap of steel against steel when opponents were taking each other's measure. "I had thought the peace still held."

Serafina sensed there was a game being played between them that she wasn't privy to. So many mysterious currents always seemed to swirl around these people like a *fluctus* of emotions. "I'm pleased to make your acquaintance, Mesner Kreiser," she replied.

And then he had a great many questions about her studies, her work with Margerit, and what she expected to observe on the morrow. Having answered one, and then another, Serafina hardly knew how to stem the flood, until she was able to ask, "Are you a thaumaturgist, too?"

"Not a miracle-worker, no," he replied. "Simply an observer, like you." He shot a sidelong glance at Barbara. "I observe, but sometimes I try to prod others to action. Baroness Saveze has been resistant to my hints so far."

Barbara gave a faint smile. "Your hints all seem designed to inspire others to do your work for you. If you want to know so much about the state of the eastern passes, I'm sure that a journey to Geneva or Turin or points beyond would be more instructive than quizzing me. Ah, they are signaling us to go in to dinner."

They both departed, leaving her abandoned amidst the stir of activity. There was a moment of deepening panic before she saw Margerit signaling her over from the side of the room where she was in conversation with a liveried man.

"Serafina, I need to go in, but this gentleman will find your dinner partner." Margerit reached out and squeezed her hand reassuringly. "Everything will go well."

The dinner did not go well at all. The man chosen to escort her to the tables was distantly polite and spoke no more than five words to her after their introduction. The man seated to her other side was Russian, and though they both had French in common, it was not sufficient to converse beyond the formalities.

The first course offered sufficient distraction in the challenge of deciphering the dishes. After that, her appetite failed. By the third course, Serafina weighed the competing embarrassments and excused herself to her dinner partners, saying she felt unwell.

It was true enough. When she had been directed to the appropriate room, Serafina spent long moments leaning over a basin in a misery that was not relieved, but only ebbed gradually. That misery was only intensified by the presence of a maid standing silently beside her holding a towel in case of need.

And then, when that crisis was past, there was the gauntlet of returning to her seat. Only the speeches and desserts were left. She had been seated at one of the lower tables; few would notice her entrance. But she hesitated inside the doors to the grand salle, hoping that perhaps there would be some distraction to cover her movements.

That was when she noticed the plainly-dressed woman sitting against the wall, nearly hidden by a pillar among an arrangement of flowers and potted plants. The woman glanced her way, and as their eyes met she winked and jerked her head ever so slightly.

Serafina hesitated, uncertain of her meaning, then slipped over to join her. A small easel was set up, entirely hidden behind the vases, showing a rough charcoal sketch of the high table where the princess sat. Several figures not currently present in person were sketched in dramatic poses before her.

"Shh," the woman said. "I'm not really here. But it looked like you might not want to be here as well, so we can be invisible together." She picked up a sketchbook where several rough studies of heads overlapped each other on the page and added a few lines to one that was clearly meant to be Margerit. It wasn't so much in the image itself but some essential presence.

"You're the Italian thaumaturgist, aren't you?" the painter asked.

"How did you...?"

"I have a list: the primary guild members, the important ambassadors and of course Maisetra Sovitre herself. My patron thought you might add something to the composition. 'All the world comes to marvel at the Alpennian Mysteries.' But I haven't been able to catch a good likeness where you were sitting."

Serafina thought of the grinding ordeal of the dinner so far and was grateful for that.

Abruptly the woman stood and took her by the chin to turn her profile this way and that. It was a deft, professional touch that didn't startle her as much as it should have.

"Yes, I definitely must find a place for you." The woman stared at her more deeply, but it didn't feel like mere curiosity, more like recognition. "Would you...?" For the first time in their conversation she seemed hesitant. She reached down into the case that held her supplies and drew out a calling card. "Would you be willing to sit for me?"

Serafina looked at the card. Olimpia Hankez. Where had she heard that name before? She thought Maisetra Valorin might have mentioned it. "I..." she began, but there was a stir in the room as the dishes were being taken away again. "I need to go sit. Yes, I will."

* * *

The previous time Serafina had stood in the cathedral observing the All Saints' Castellum, her eyes had been entirely on Margerit. The swirling *fluctus* had been no more than backdrop. This time the mystic visions occupied all her attention. At her side, she could hear the faint scratch and whisper of the pens and brushes as Margerit sketched and Antuniet took her own notes. Serafina closed her eyes. The patterns of the mystery still came in visions but now there was no distraction from the gestures of the celebrants and the restless movements of those watching.

She tried to envision a map of Alpennia beneath the spreading lines and structures that grew as each course was laid down. There was a geography to the ritual, rooted in the evocation of the principal regions and towns. It wasn't a geography of mountains and rivers but of the mind. She was still learning enough of the history of the land to bind the two together. Margerit had said, pay attention to the markein—the words and symbols that laid out the ambit of protection being invoked. But the markein, too, was not only geography but the range of perils and ills it was meant to address: disease, disaster, danger. With every cycle of the mystery, every course in the towers and walls, the landscape of her vision shifted. Shapes moved at the edges of her awareness, ones she couldn't connect to the structure they'd studied. A blur like fingers reaching out, a touch of cold. Was that a *phantasm* or the chill of the cathedral stones? So much to comprehend! How had Margerit envisioned all this to design the ceremony?

As the mystery wound to its conclusion, as the *concrescatio* fixed the form of the petitions and the *missio* sealed their invocation, Serafina reached out to hold the structure in memory, with all its flaws, its infelicities and its gaps. It felt like an allegorical painting where every detail carried a vital piece of the story. Margerit was right: it was far from the smooth and polished effect seen with a long-established tradition. But it wasn't only the complexity, not just the stumbles and hesitations to be expected in what was still a very new rite. There were puzzles here to solve before the full potential of the *castellum* could be realized.

Serafina started composing a mental list to have ready when they all met again in two days' time to compare notes.

* * *

With the next day free of obligations, she was tempted to lay abed all morning, lulled by the lingering scent of spices to imagine herself a girl, back in that sunlit apartment in Rome once more. Back then there had been no task facing her harder than working sums and going to the market. The market. What had Maisetra Valorin suggested? The Strangers' Market. That corner of the Nikuleplaiz where crewmen from the ships and barges sold trinkets and crafts of their own, apart from the main cargos. It was said to be a chaotic place where treasures of the seven seas and frauds were in equal supply. Not a place for the innocent or unwary. But if there were any place in Rotenek where one might buy hair oil brought all the way from Alexandria, it would be there.

There was another task to complete first. Serafina dressed for walking and then wrapped up the thick waxen candle she had left sitting on the dressing table the evening before. The dressmaker's shop was shuttered…but of course, it was Sunday. The long hours in the cathedral the day before had blurred her sense of the week. Hesitantly, Serafina knocked sharply on the door, wondering whether it would be answered. Or might they be at services?

The door opened to Mefro Dominique's worried face. "Yes, Maisetra, is there some problem?"

"No," Serafina reassured her. "I only came to see your daughter, Celeste, if I may. I have something for her."

The dressmaker stepped back to let her in, calling, "Celeste! There's a lady asking for you! What have you been up to?"

Serafina held out the wrapped candle when the girl emerged from the back room. "I remembered, you see?"

She took it with a grin of triumph. "Thank you, Maisetra!" And then, somewhat more hesitantly but without a trace of shyness, "Would you like to see my erteskir?"

The word was unfamiliar but Serafina had the sense of being offered a gift. And so, especially in the face of Dominique's quelling frown, she answered, "I would love to. Could you show me?"

Celeste led the way upstairs to a small cramped bedroom that the two clearly shared. In one corner, on a small rickety table, sat a cluttered shrine of the sort often found in private houses. In pride of place where one might have expected a crucifix or a Madonna and child, there was a painted plaster figure of Saint Mauriz, with the stub of a small candle fixed before him. A printed crucifixion scene on cheap paper was pasted to the wall behind it, faded and stained, and a string of beads lay to one side. Celeste pulled out a battered chest that had been tucked under the table and opened it to store the candle away. It was filled with trays and boxes of paraphernalia that reminded Serafina of the sorts of apparatus gathered for performing mysteries: candles, scraps of paper and parchment with prayers carefully diagrammed on them, small vials of assorted liquids, bits of cloth and many things less certain in their nature.

"Is this where you perform your mysteries?" Serafina asked. Margerit had similar images in her sitting room for private prayers, but she always performed her mysteries at the cathedral, even the minor ones.

"Not the ones I do for other folk," Celeste explained. "I mostly do healing stuff—Maman doesn't like me doing the other things much—so I don't do them here."

Curiosity stirred. This seemed more like her own mother's stories of how the marvers had practiced their miracles. "I didn't think Saint Mauriz usually granted healing," Serafina observed. The soldier-saint was more often invoked as a protector.

"He does for me," Celeste said fiercely.

And it was simpler than that, she realized. This was not the Mauriz of the cathedral windows, whose pale brown face would scarcely stand out among the weathered rivermen, only his turbaned helmet marking his origins. The plaster figure standing on the erteskir was Mauriz the Moor. In his broad nose, generous lips and coal-black skin, Celeste might see her mother's ancestors: a circle connected and an anchor to this city of her birth. No wonder she had chosen him as her own personal patron.

A tapping of feet coming up the stairs interrupted them. "Celeste, you mustn't take up any more of the Maisetra's time. You already owe her what you can't repay."

Serafina knew better than to mention the price of her dress. That had been a different transaction. But, perhaps… "Celeste, I was wondering if you might be able to do me a favor. How familiar are you with the Strangers' Market?"

CHAPTER EIGHT

Barbara

Mid-November, 1823

The library of Tiporsel House was far too small to contain the growing conclave that Margerit called together to review the *castellum*. Barbara had felt distanced from the enthusiasm in the days before the ceremony. With no special sensitivity she perceived only what anyone might feel: the prickling of her neck at the *missio* of one of the great rites, or sometimes a shiver as if someone had walked over her grave. But sorting out the results of Margerit's observations was familiar ground. Now that the forces and effects had been translated to symbols on paper, she could see the architecture clearly. She traced her finger along the colorful lines Margerit had splashed across the diagram. There in the first few pages were the ragged flaws they needed to address.

"It's nothing like what Gaudericus describes," Serafina said hesitantly. "He adapts Valla in specifying that the scope—what you call the markein—of the mystery must be defined at each point by its substance, quality and action. But Valla was concerned with unities and Gaudericus with distinctions. Your pictures show the unities, but how do they distinguish?"

Serafina always had more questions than answers, yet her questions usually cut to the heart. Over the summer she had begun to master Gaudericus and was quick to find the contradictions between his work and her previous studies.

Margerit colored a little at the question. "I know I should pay more attention to formal structures. Akezze keeps scolding me for it. But this—"

She waved her hand at the sheets of colorful watercolors. "—it says what I'm thinking so much more clearly."

Antuniet gave something like a snort as she moved a small stack of books off a side table to bring it into use. "It's clear as long as one has the key to the symbols." She added, "In some ways, it's quite similar to an alchemist's notes except that there are no standard conventions yet. If I were trying to record the same thing, I might assign a certain proportion of elemental essences to each material, just as an *aide memoire*. The sign isn't the thing itself, but it must define it in some unique way."

"That's hardly the same at all," Margerit said with a frown. "For alchemy you're trying to construct…oh, I don't know…handles? For something within the formula. And like Valla's definitions, you're concerned with repeatable unities. But when we're trying to lay out the markein here, it's more a matter of trying to define the unique essence, the true nature of where we want the miracle to act. And in alchemy the materials are there in front of you. It's a physical process. But miracles are so often—" She waved her hands in the air. "—diffuse. You may not even have the beneficiary before you."

Barbara had been listening silently, but she couldn't resist the scent of theological debate. "That leaves the question of whether God knows what's in your heart before you begin. I know Fortunatus claims that's the truth behind why miracles are so elusive. That the words and the intent and God's will might not align."

"Oh pooh!" Margerit said dismissively. "That's just his way of admitting when he has no idea what's going on. Or that he was afraid to have an opinion." She laid another diagram on top of the stack. Here the washes of color were laid over a rough pen and ink map of Alpennia. "When we designed it, I had very much in mind the flaws in the Mauriz. How the symbolic language left the door open to changes that would alter the entire meaning. That's why we anchored the markein for the *castellum* so closely to geography. To the specific regions and towns that indicate the borders."

"There's still room for it to go astray," Barbara noted. "For instance here, you've laid Sain-Pol and the stone bridge over each other to indicate Nofpunt. But there are hundreds of chapels to Sain-Pol and bridges aren't precisely rare. How can you be certain it anchors the markein to that place specifically? Might that…?"

"It flows from the context," Antuniet interrupted. "You're tracing the border here to here to here." She traced a line along the pink wash of hills on the map. "That helps to fix it to something within that scope. The structure as a whole is what matters, that each part is reinforced by the others."

Serafina moved around to the other side of the table and shifted the drawings to find the part of the map where Amituz lay at the northeast corner of the boundaries. "Except that they aren't reinforced. The structures are there—the towers and walls—but they aren't forming a barrier. This is where I first saw the problem, when they began to mark the foundations here, and then continuing all along the eastern border. It was…" Her mouth twisted in thought. "Have you ever been to a seashore?"

Barbara nodded, but the others looked blank so Serafina explained. "In the wet sand, at the edge of the water, children will build walls and towers in play. But then a wave, larger than the rest, will run up the beach and wash over them, leaving only a trace. Like the remains of ancient walls that have been overgrown. It was like that: first with the markein and then as the towers were raised. The mystery would build them up, but then something would wash over and around the structure and soften the outlines. They were still there, but indistinct."

"You think something was preventing the walls from rising properly?" Margerit asked. "I saw something like what you described but I thought it was a weakness in raising them. A flaw in the ritual."

Barbara circled the table to join her as the others argued about exactly what it was that they had perceived. The map Margerit had used for her sketches was only an outline, but there was one property shared throughout the segment Serafina indicated. "Mountains," she said.

Antuniet immediately grasped her meaning. "You're right. But why should that…?"

Margerit looked chagrined. "I hadn't noticed that, only that the problem started during the last part of the markein. I thought it was part of the complexity—that the structure was trying to hold too many things together. Serafina…something you said about waves before. Not this time, but when we discussed the Mauriz."

Serafina nodded. "And not only in the mountains," she added, "but that's where it's most obvious."

And then they were bent over the map again, trying to reconstruct their observations from the Mauriz *tutela* and add them to the present discussion.

Mountains. Something present in the mountains that nibbled away at the effectiveness of both the protective mysteries. Someone else had been needling her about the mountain passes. "Kreiser knows something about this."

All eyes turned to her. Margerit's brows narrowed in concern. Serafina was baffled, Antuniet angry.

She explained further, "He's been teasing me about something going on in the mountains. I thought it was just another of his games." A year past Kreiser had tricked her into playing his go-between when he'd tried to arrange an Austrian marriage alliance. She'd been wary of his hints ever since. "Perhaps…"

Antuniet said sharply, "I don't know why you even speak to the man!"

"He isn't just a token on the game board," Barbara countered. "He's moving pieces and directing other players. If I'm to play the game, I can't afford to ignore him or shun him."

In her heart, she knew that she loved both the game of state and the more personal game of wits she played with the man. At first, it had been a reflex of her duty to the old baron, when her position as armin had demanded intimate knowledge of every player on the board. But now she had Princess Annek's tacit encouragement to pursue her instincts.

Yes, perhaps it was time to have a more pointed talk with Kreiser.

After the others had left, Barbara began collecting up all the notes and sketches as Margerit cataloged each one and wrote a summary of their discussion to accompany them, sighing as she did so. "There's just no room to work. Who would think that a mansion on the Vezenaf could feel so cramped."

Barbara passed her another sheet. "Your Aunt Bertrut wouldn't care to have to dine in the kitchen just to leave space for all this!"

The truth was that Bertrut would never complain. The arrangement was too comfortable for any of them to chafe at such minor conflicts. And for that reason Margerit wouldn't test the limits by imposing her chaos on the entire household. Bertrut and her husband provided a shield of social respectability that two unmarried women—even if one were a baroness—could not achieve on their own.

And with the question of space on their minds, Barbara asked, "Have you thought further about your school?"

"Akezze's printers are already making plans for Frances's book." It both was and wasn't an answer. "I've spoken to LeFevre, and…" Margerit bit her lip in hesitation. "Barbara, what does Fonten House mean to you?"

Barbara could guess where she was going. Fonten House in Chalanz was where they had first met, in those last weeks before the old baron's death. It was where Margerit had first spread her wings, enjoying what an inheritance could promise her. There were many memories rooted there. But…

She set down the papers she was holding and wrapped her arms around Margerit, tilting her head to rest her cheek against the soft tumble of her curls. "We scarcely spend a month out of the year there in the best of times," she murmured. And she hadn't even done that much this past year, having gone to Turinz instead. "Are you sure you wouldn't mind giving it up? I can't imagine you staying with your Uncle Fulpi when you visit Chalanz." The Fulpis were far more disapproving of Margerit's life than the more pragmatic Bertrut had been.

"No," Margerit said with a movement of her head that gently ended the embrace. "But the only reason I might return next summer would be to host Cousin Iuli's coming out ball, and I honestly think they'd rather I just spent the money to hire the public ballroom. Aunt Honurat thinks I'm a very bad influence on Iuli, and in her position I'd think so too." She laughed. "You've read the letters Iuli writes to me—full of poetry and romantic nonsense!"

"So you're going to sell?"

Margerit returned to the previous topic. "Yes, I think I must. LeFevre says I could raise the funds to buy something on the edge of Rotenek without doing so, but it would leave matters strained. And with the work needed at Turinz…"

"Turinz will stand on its own," Barbara hurried to assure her.

"Of course, but I'd rather it didn't stand so precariously. One never knows. And Chalanz is very desirable as a summer estate. LeFevre has already had several generous offers just on the rumor."

"Then do it," Barbara agreed. "And we can start hunting for a place to build your school."

* * *

It was easier for Barbara to decide to match wits with Kreiser once more than to determine where and how to do so. Leaving her card at the embassy would be too direct. It would suggest an official flavor to the conversation that she had no warrant for. He rarely attended balls or the theater and those had no guarantee of privacy. It was unthinkable to approach him openly at his private lodgings. There was a fine line between eccentricity and scandal. In some things, even Baroness Saveze could not escape the walls that surrounded an unmarried woman of a certain age.

But those walls did have cracks and some of the cracks had been left open only because it would not occur to most women to walk through them. Kreiser was known to frequent a certain club named Sainkall's on the Peretrez. A few questions to Charul Pertinek, Margerit's uncle-by-marriage, had ascertained the Austrian's habits and confirmed her understanding of the unstated rules of such an establishment. Matters would be simpler if Pertinek were a member of Sainkell's himself but she had no such luck. Now it was only a matter of choosing the correct uniform for mounting an assault through the breach in those walls.

The dressing room was littered with discarded choices, but Barbara had reached a point where Brandel might be admitted, on a hesitant knock, as Maitelen fussed over the last few details.

"What do you think?" Barbara asked him, turning before the glass.

"You look very elegant, Cousin Barbara," he said formally.

She fixed him with a critical eye. "I wasn't looking for compliments. You should know better than that. A test: seeing me like this, what do you think I'm about?"

When Brandel had first joined her household a year past, with the bait of an armin's training and the promise to make a courtier of him, he had expected to spend his time in the fencing salle and swaggering about town in her wake. Barbara hadn't the heart to put him through the same ruthless program she had known, but he'd soon learned to expect these challenges. Half an armin's duty involved observation and prediction. She waited, watching Brandel's thoughts turn over.

"You aren't going riding," he began slowly. "You're wearing your riding coat, but the breeches are wrong."

The long-skirted coat fell halfway between that of a woman's habit and a more masculine style. Her tailor had slowly adapted to her suggestions and demands.

"And besides which, I heard them bringing the light gig into the courtyard, not riding horses. You would never wear that waistcoat if you meant to be active. I've only seen you wear it before when you attended the sessions last spring. You said it made you look more serious, but that time you wore it with skirts."

Barbara nodded to encourage him.

"And it isn't ordinary visiting or you wouldn't wear breeches at all, unless you mean to shock someone." Brandel's analytical powers were reaching their limits.

"What if I specifically intend not to shock people?"

He bit his lip in thought and shook his head.

Barbara relented. "I intend to visit a man at a club."

Brandel's face brightened. "May I attend you? I've never—"

"No," she said quellingly. "This calls for a more delicate touch. Go tell Tavit to come see me. Wait."

He paused at the door.

"What was it you came to ask about? It wasn't to admire my ensemble."

"My lessons," Brandel said. "You said you'd find someone to replace my tutor, but if you haven't, I need to know what you want me to study."

Oh yes, drat the man. No, it wasn't his fault an ailing parent had called him away to the country. She hadn't forgotten, but November was a poor time for hiring scholars. Good ones, at least. "Thank you for the reminder, Brandel. Now go fetch Tavit."

Tavit was far more perceptive in the nuances of her dress. His surprise was not for the purpose of her excursion but its venue. "I thought women weren't allowed in clubs."

"It depends," Barbara said. "In most, it isn't actually forbidden, it simply isn't done. Back before the succession debates, the dowager princess was quite familiar in the Zurik and Jourdain's." It was a thin precedent, but not the only one she was relying on. "I hope not to provoke a fuss, so I will be enough of a man for their comfort and enough of a woman for my respectability."

Tavit looked puzzled but asked, "Have you any special instructions?"

Barbara picked up her gloves and hat and turned to him. "If anyone should object to my presence, don't take it as insult or threat. I have no right to entrance. And though a man without membership might visit a friend with no comment, it will spoil my purpose if too much notice is taken. This one time, resistance shall be met with retreat. I'll let you know if you need do anything beyond standing and waiting."

He nodded in acknowledgment, and then after some hesitation, "Mesnera, may I ask you something?"

The edge of tension in Tavit's voice caught Barbara's attention. Under the strict rules of her own service, she had always asked permission to speak, but she'd never demanded that of those who served her. "Yes?" she said.

The question came haltingly. "Mesnera, have you ever thought…have you ever wished you had been born a man?"

Barbara turned the idea over in her mind. She was accustomed to the awkwardness that came with playing a man's role as often as she did. So many things would have been easier, so many paths smoother, and yet...

She cast her mind back even further. If her father's bastard had been a son, would he have thought it worth the cost to acknowledge him and regularize his position? How would all their lives have changed if she had been raised as heir-default to Saveze? And yet...then there would have been no reason for the old baron to bring Margerit into his plans. They never would have met. Even as an unacknowledged son, their lives might have run more like that wretched novel that had stirred so much gossip. The lost heir of Lautencourt, indeed! What if her rise in society had given her the chance to offer Margerit, not this private promise and the risk of scandal, but marriage and the rank of baroness? And yet...

They had met and loved as women. That much was certain. Who could say what else would have changed, what would have remained?

"Forgive me, Mesnera. I should not have asked," Tavit said quietly.

Barbara shook her head. "I think...I am more than content—no, I am joyful—to be in the place I find myself. And I don't think I could have come to this place by any road but the one I've traveled. If there are limits to what this body can do—" She gestured to take it in. "—they are limits made by others, not my limits. No, I wouldn't choose to be other than what I am."

Tavit seemed disquieted by her answer, but how could he understand? It would be a strange man indeed who could accept that one might prefer to be female despite those limitations.

* * *

The doorman at Sainkall's was sufficiently overawed by her title and manner to stand aside, but the attendant who stood at the entrance to the main salle seemed ready to expect more than a vague mention of visiting a guest. Barbara hadn't wanted to offer Kreiser's name in particular for she could hardly claim that he would be expecting her.

Salvation came in an unexpected form. One of a pair of men standing by the ornate marble mantelpiece called out, "Ha! Saveze! I've been hoping to speak to you."

Baron Mazuk's greeting was the entrée needed. Barbara nodded at the attendant and passed in.

"Have you returned late to Rotenek?" Barbara asked. "I don't recall seeing you around town." Their lives fell in different orbits; it wouldn't have been odd to miss each other.

"Too much damned business back home."

Barbara counted it a victory for her stratagem that he neglected to soften his speech as he would for a lady. "Ah yes, your canal. Surely it's complete by now?"

He shook his head and descended into a torrent of complaints about delays and overruns. "The digging—that's only the first part. There's locks and bridges and all manner of things. Until that's done I can't bring in the coal, and without the coal I can't expand the ironworks. It will all pay for itself in no time once I get to that point. I don't suppose you'd be interested in investing?"

It was clear from Mazuk's hungry look that this was the matter he'd hoped to bring to her.

"Invest in your canal or your ironworks?" Barbara asked, postponing the moment of refusal.

"Comes to the same thing, doesn't it?"

Barbara shrugged. If income were all that mattered… But the canal would benefit Turinz as well, the ironworks would not. "I don't have the funds for investing at the moment. Turinz has been badly neglected and that's where every spare teneir is going."

"But Maisetra Sovitre—"

"I don't advise Margerit Sovitre on her investments. If you have a proposal to make, speak to her man of business." And if it were promising, LeFevre might even recommend it. It was tiresome that one of the few times people pointedly acknowledged her bond with Margerit was when money was involved. To soften the refusal, she added, "You might remember LeFevre from your visit in June. He's quite familiar with your projects."

"I just may do that," Mazuk said impatiently. "She owes me at least a hearing."

"Indeed?" Barbara put enough of a chill in that one word to send a warning but Mazuk failed to take the hint.

"We all know that earthquake wasn't natural. All this poking around at the mysteries. Don't think people can't tell what comes of it. The guildmasters need to take her in hand."

He wasn't speaking of the social guilds, the ones that sponsored the public celebrations. Everyone knew there were more quiet organizations that never advertised their activities. The old baron had belonged to one or two of those, though of course she'd never been a witness to their ceremonies. It was in those ranks that a thaumaturgist found training—if he were a man. Barbara had sometimes wondered what they thought of Margerit's success. Was Mazuk…? No, if he had influence in such circles he wouldn't be boasting of it here.

"If you have concerns about the activities of the Royal Guild," she said evenly, "you should take them to Her Grace."

It had been a bluff. He backed down quickly and suggested they fetch a bottle of wine to smooth over the misunderstanding. The invitation provided the opportunity to work her way unobtrusively through the public rooms. Barbara found Kreiser intently watching a game of cards. Watching seemed to be his favorite sport. He showed the slightest flicker of surprise at seeing her and then moved casually to join her and accept a glass from Mazuk.

"To what do we owe this honor?" Kreiser asked.

"In fact, I was hoping to have a word with you," she replied.

As by a conjurer's sleight of hand, Barbara found herself in a private alcove off one of the smaller salles. Mazuk had been diplomatically disposed of.

Kreiser seated himself in a facing chair and said, "I wondered when we might have this chat." There was little of the verbal fencing in his voice this time.

Barbara, too, left off her games, though not her caution. "You've been hinting about the odd weather in the mountains. And something associated with the mountains has interfered with the Mystery of Saint Mauriz, and again at the All Saints' Castellum. What do you know about it?"

His interest sharpened. "Interfered? How?"

"We may come to details later," Barbara said. "You've been teasing at me with hints for the last year. Why?"

Kreiser steepled his fingers and considered before answering, "What do you know of affairs in Spain?"

Was this more game playing or was he coming unexpectedly to the point? "What has Spain to do with Alpennia?"

He gave her the pitying look a schoolmaster bestows on a slow-witted pupil. "Everywhere has to do with everywhere. Did you learn nothing from the French Wars? I can't explain anything to you if you haven't been paying attention. If you want to know why the passes are blocked at midsummer, I suggest you look to Spain."

Now he was toying with her. "I fail to see how Spanish politics are relevant to heavy snows in the Alps that fail to thaw. Or is that not what we're speaking of?"

"Snow prevents movement, movement brings influence, influence must be balanced. Every government has reasons to want certain movements to be harder than others. The spine of Europe is currently a locked gate to anyone traveling between north and south. Had you noticed that? Or are you still thinking only of the revenues of the innkeeper at Atefels? My own government is not entirely unhappy with the current state of things, but they are suspicious of the means. You're still fumbling at *why* when you should be asking *how*. Alpennia stands at the edge of the effect and Alpennia has a long tradition of powerful thaumaturgy. Are you so certain that the strange behavior of your mysteries is an effect and not a cause?"

The accusation under his words sank in. "You think…" Barbara felt out of her depth. Had Alpennia had a hand in the matter? The Royal Guild was only the public face of Alpennian thaumaturgy. There were those other guilds…

"It doesn't matter what I think," Kreiser said mildly. "There are those who do. The Swiss might be suspect if anyone thought them capable of it. The French—well, the French would be the obvious answer, wouldn't they? But I've never heard of anyone working at that distance in unfamiliar territory. They say there are a few people in England who might be capable of such a thing, but they're even more secretive than the Venetians. Blocking travel is only a small part of the matter. What else have your fraying mysteries revealed?"

"Nothing we can interpret. Maisetra Talarico says—" She stopped. Kreiser had told her nothing yet. Nothing of real value. Why should she give him that for free? "What exactly is your position with the Austrian embassy? I know you first came to Alpennia on the track of my cousin's alchemy, but I can't believe you stayed only to meddle in marriage alliances."

Kreiser gave a little half salute to acknowledge the substance of it. "One must keep busy, after all."

Barbara ventured a direct feint. "Was this your assignment from the beginning? To investigate the source of this unusual weather? Or is that only one more way to keep busy?"

"You still think this is about snow. And here I thought we might have useful information to exchange. I gave you the mountain passes over a year ago. Have you gone no further than that?"

He eyed her expectantly, but Barbara had fallen into confused caution again. Was he, too, thinking of matters such as Mazuk's earthquake? Was everything deeper than she thought or was this only his counter-feint? She rose. "This has been a fascinating conversation. I regret that there's nothing further I can tell you."

Kreiser smiled. "Oh, you've told me a great deal already."

* * *

Barbara knew better than to think that there was anything Kreiser had said that was not already well known at the palace. But the conversation itself— that was something she didn't care to keep to herself. Reporting it didn't seem crucial enough for haste, and this time of the year was busy for both high and low. A delay meant that Margerit could add her own theories and conclusions. Even so it was nearly the end of November before she could make arrangements for an appointment. She usually dealt with Albori himself but he was off to Paris, and not until packets had been sent there and back was an assistant minister instructed to take her report.

"And you think this…this storm is interfering with the mysteries?" the man asked.

"I'm not sure," Margerit said carefully. "The flaws in the Mauriz existed well before this past winter and we know their sources."

He waved his hand to dismiss that point. Princess Annek had chosen not to challenge Archbishop Fereir over the revisions to the ceremony. The *tutela* belonged to the church's mysteries, not those of state. It was outside his remit.

"If someone has been dabbling in weather mysteries, we don't know when it began," Barbara added. "Nothing this powerful could be achieved at the first attempt. Except for strength and duration, one winter storm looks much like another. The Austrians seem to be convinced this disturbance isn't natural. Kreiser hinted it had something to do with Spain."

The assistant minister shifted uncomfortably. Barbara suspected that he was unaccustomed to discussing politics with women. With the sole exception of Princess Annek, of course.

"That's nothing to concern you," he concluded. "The matter of the Spanish succession is long settled. We've had some difficulties with trade but I think we can weather a few hard snows." He laughed at his own joke. "Saveze, if you want to help this fellow poke around after secret thaumaturgists, you have Her Grace's leave. I'll file your report. Just let me know before you start naming names."

"He's as bad as the archbishop," Margerit grumbled afterward as their little company navigated through the maze of palace corridors. "Sometimes I don't think any of them believe in miracles."

Barbara squeezed her hand. "Sometimes I think we need a different word than 'miracle.' Unless you want to call Kreiser's blizzard a miracle. You can't blame a bureaucrat for concentrating on the problems he can touch. How does it change the tariffs on cheese or the peace with France if you see some strange lights when you're praying in the cathedral?"

"Don't you start—" Margerit began.

"You know I'm not mocking! But people believe in little miracles—the ones that touch them directly." She waved her hand to take in the city at large. "They don't believe in the Great Mysteries the same way as they do if their child is cured of the pox or their son comes safe home from war. It's what Gaudericus says: how can truth prevail when a charlatan's trick is more often believed than a true miracle? But I wish we could have talked to Albori directly. He of all people should know better. He wears one of Antuniet's alchemical gems."

A slight cough from Margerit's armin, Marken, drew their attention to an approaching figure.

"Who...?" Margerit whispered, frowning.

Barbara took on the introductions. "Maistir Chautovil, I hope you are well? And that your pupil is the same? Margerit, this is Aukustin's tutor. Chautovil, you know Maisetra Sovitre?"

"Of course," he replied, greeting them with a bow. He was young for the position of tutoring one of the potential heirs to the throne. His haphazard brown curls made him look more the student than the teacher, but the dowager princess had preferred a more sympathetic figure to the dry old schoolmaster who had been his predecessor. "Indeed," Chautovil continued, "it was seeing Maisetra Sovitre that reminded me of an errand I'd like your help with. I believe you know the scholar, Akezze Mainus?"

"Very well," Margerit said warmly, always eager to promote her friends.

"I was hoping you might be willing to put in a word. She's been praised to the heavens as a teacher of logic and rhetoric, but when I inquired, she returned a note saying she wasn't taking on more students at the moment. I wouldn't want her to think it was an official request..."

"Ah, for Aukustin, you mean," Margerit said. "No, Maisetra Mainus hasn't much use for rank, I'm afraid. But I could put in a word as a friend."

"And now you remind *me* of an unfinished errand," Barbara said. "Do you recall my cousin? You recommended his last tutor, but the man's been taken away by family business. I've had no luck finding a replacement. I don't suppose you know anyone?"

A curious look came over Chautovil's face. "Strange that you should ask. As it happens...hmm. There are inquiries I would need to make first. Might I call in a few days time to discuss the matter?"

* * *

Barbara nearly forgot the appointment with Chautovil that morning in the face of the news brought to the breakfast table.

"It's from LeFevre," Margerit said, waving the unfolded note that Ponivin had just presented to her. "Fonten House has sold."

"So soon?" Barbara said. LeFevre had mentioned interest, but who was in a hurry to purchase a summer property at the beginning of December?

Bertrut gave a quiet sigh. "So it's done. I know it was for the best, but it was such a lovely place." She still had strong ties in Chalanz. Stronger than those Margerit had left.

Charul Pertinek reached over to pat his wife's hand. "We'll still have our summer visit there. We can rent some rooms and you won't have all the fuss of a large household."

The first of the day's visitors interrupted the making of plans to begin viewing properties. Margerit often found an excuse to avoid the parlor when it was filled with Bertrut's friends, but Barbara found she had no similar escape while awaiting Chautovil. She perched on a damask-covered chair, summoned up a gracious smile, and pretended interest in what the Chafils planned to serve at their next dinner party. Relief came in the guise of a footman announcing the tutor's arrival and Barbara met him in the foyer, suggesting that they might talk more easily in the library.

Chautovil glanced into the occupied parlor uncertainly and said, "Perhaps that might...no, it wouldn't do, I'm afraid. Mesnera Lumbeirt, forgive me for allowing you no notice, but I'm afraid she insisted on coming personally." He glanced back over his shoulder at the door. "I only came ahead to avoid surprising you entirely."

Barbara's imagination jumped to the only possible conclusion and went out to meet the carriage that stood waiting in the narrow yard. Chautovil would not have bothered with a carriage if he'd come alone.

A footman handed the stately woman down the carriage steps as Barbara sank into a welcoming curtsey. The Dowager Princess Elisebet still had traces of the famed beauty of her youth. But time had coarsened her features and worry had given her once-sparkling eyes a furtive and haunted look. Less haunted now than a year past when she saw conspiracies against her son in every shadow.

"Mesnera Atilliet," Barbara said. "This is an unexpected honor. Please, won't you come in?" And for God's sake will someone please warn Bertrut! she thought.

Introductions threw a pall of silence over the parlor, leavened only by the hurried appearance of a plate of cakes offered with stiff pleasantries. Bertrut Pertinek had survived the ordeal of being presented at court as the price of having married a man of noble rank, but it was utterly unfair to ask her to entertain royalty in her own parlor. Barbara took pity and reminded her of an entirely fictional appointment.

In the wake of the relieved departures of Bertrut and her friends, Barbara turned to business. "Mesnera Atilliet, your son's tutor had consented to advise me on a small domestic matter, but I believe you have come on a different errand entirely?" She exchanged quick glances with Chautovil who looked somewhat embarrassed but at ease.

Princess Elisebet leaned back against the settee as if it were a throne. "I should like to meet this cousin of yours."

"Brandel?" Barbara asked in surprise. He was at home at the moment—or he should be. One could never be entirely certain unless he'd been given specific orders. She rang for a maid and gave hurried instructions.

Brandel presented himself with as much alacrity as a fifteen-year-old boy could manage when asked to change into his best on no notice. He'd attended her to the palace often enough that Barbara found nothing to blush at in his bow or his manners. He dealt confidently with Elisebet's questions, but Barbara could imagine him thinking, *A test, Cousin?*

And then the Dowager Princess rose, thanked them and left with only the cryptic comment to Chautovil, "He will do."

Brandel clearly expected to be dismissed, but Barbara motioned him to a chair. "So, Maistir Chautovil, I believe I can guess what that was about, but perhaps you could explain it to my cousin."

Indeed, Chautovil seemed relieved to be able to speak at last. "In another two years, Mesner Atilliet will begin attending classes at the university. The Dowager Princess believes it would be advisable for him to have the experience of studying among other boys. But there have been…difficulties in identifying suitable companions."

Yes, Barbara thought. The difficulties a boy encounters when he's been tied to apron strings far too long. When he's been kept apart from others his age except under the most stilted of circumstances. "Do I understand that my cousin has been approved as a suitable companion?" She could see why the suggestion had been made. Elisebet trusted her, though for the wrong reasons. The Dowager Princess didn't deal in subtleties. One was either her ally or her enemy, and Barbara had carefully avoided becoming the latter. There was another reason for the choice: Brandel stood a step below Chustin, both in rank and in age. A companion, but never a rival.

"As you say, Mesnera," Chautovil said with a nod. "You asked if I could recommend a suitable tutor. I offer myself, if that is acceptable to you. He would need to come to the palace for lessons, and I fear the hours must hang on Aukustin's convenience."

Barbara turned to Brandel. "Well? I give you the choice. Do you accept Mesnera Atilliet's offer?"

He considered the question for a gratifyingly long time. Had he considered all the implications? Likely not. He had come to Rotenek on the promise of training to be an armin—a declining profession. But the last place it would linger would be among the nobility with which he would now rub elbows. Some day Aukustin would want a trusted man standing behind him. Had it occurred to Brandel to imagine himself in that place?

Whatever thoughts he had were left unsaid, for he answered simply, "Yes, Cousin Barbara."

* * *

For some, the month of December might be a time for quiet domesticity. A time to gather family in, to shut out the wind and cold, only venturing out for the slow rhythm of Advent services. It had been years since Tiporsel House had seen anything resembling that idyllic vision. In recent years, Barbara associated December with unexpected attacks and arrivals. This time Margerit's concerns took pride of place—peaceful, but no less disruptive. There were properties to examine, lectures to arrange. The printing of Frances Collfield's plates always seemed to require Margerit's personal attention. But December passed, as it always did, and Barbara looked forward to some breathing space in January once the flurry of the New Year's Court was past.

This year the court itself made no demands on either of them beyond the duty to be present, to witness and to appear one's best. Margerit wore a gown that evoked a scholar's robes in crisp golden taffeta, her soft brown curls peeking out from beneath a small velvet biretta. Barbara thought the color was not the most becoming she could have chosen, but it matched well with her own preferred outfit, a near-military outfit in peacock blue, the hussar-style jacket braided in gilt, softened only by the sweep of her full skirts. The fashion gave her the excuse to wear her sword.

Every nobleman in attendance who had the slightest pretension to ability in the fencing salle considered it an essential accessory on this night, even if his blade were packed away in a cabinet the remainder of the year. Most had the good sense never to draw it, but the evening of the New Year's Court was fabled for the settling of festering debts and old scores of honor out in torch-ringed duels on the Plaiz. The New Year's celebrations brought the elite of Rotenek together more closely and more intensely than any other event. Fueled both by wine and by the expectations and disappointments that swirled around the court at this season of gifts, it was said that more duels were fought this night than during the entire remainder of the year.

This year the court itself provided no surprises except for a thinness in the company from a wet cough that had spread through the upper city. The festivities settled at last into the noisy revelry of the ballroom, the quieter currents in the corridors and courtyards and, distantly, the more raucous activities out in the Plaiz, including the faint, bright clash of swords.

Movement in the hallways and side rooms was as much of a dance as those done to music in the Assembly Hall. No one wandered unpartnered. Barbara watched the sets form up: Peskil and Mainek, their heads bent closely in speech, with Peskil's son trailing behind, partnered by some less important hanger-on. The armins, as always, discreetly followed in train like a peacock's tail, though not so bright. And over there, Antuniet was trying not to look bored as Mesnera Chaluk droned on. In her position as Royal Alchemist, Antuniet had perforce learned more patience, but she hadn't yet learned to enjoy these affairs, nor had she learned the trick of shedding an unwanted conversation smoothly and easily. Jeanne would be in the ballroom, enjoying the gossip and drinking in the delight of the younger set, and most likely dancing herself.

Barbara nodded at old Chozzik in passing, wondering if she should pause for longer speech. He'd been a close friend of the old baron—to the extent that Marziel Lumbeirt had had friends—and that was worth acknowledging. But Margerit had pulled her on to greet the Pernelds. She had been cultivating their daughter Valeir for her talents as an auditor. The parents were skeptical that theological studies would be an asset to a girl about to pass from her dancing seasons to the marriage market.

Another nod in passing, this time to Baron Mazuk deep in conversation with someone whose back she couldn't recognize. She hoped they could slip by without Margerit being importuned for an investment, but he caught her eye eagerly and exclaimed, "You've missed your opportunity, Saveze. Antoz will be enjoying the rewards you could have had."

If it hadn't been for the slight jerk of recognition at her name, Barbara would have thought that the smirk on the stranger's face as he turned was only for his supposed good fortune. Certainly it could be nothing more personal. His face was unknown to her and the name tickled only vaguely at the back of her memory. But the smirk deepened as his eyes slid across her and to Margerit. Barbara had only just begun to bristle at the man's impudence when he let out a bark of laughter.

"You!"

His eyes had gone past them to someone beyond. Barbara turned. There was no one in his immediate field of view but the armins and Brandel, trailing at the prescribed distance behind their charges. She would have thought the stranger merely in his cups—which he almost certainly was—except that Tavit had gone bone-white. She saw his fingertips brush the hilt of his sword in a gesture she recalled well. Not a threat to draw, just reassurance of its presence.

Again the bark of laughter. "I should have known a freak like you would turn up in this sort of company!"

Tipsy or not, that went beyond anything that could be ignored. Antoz... she cast her mind back a year and more. That was where she'd heard the name before. Tavit's last employer. The one Perret, her swordmaster, had called a bad business all around. A bad business that had left Tavit with bruises he'd still carried when she first met him. She briefly wondered if Tavit stood ready to avenge that business now, but he seemed frozen in place.

She turned back toward the stranger. "Mesner Antoz—" She gauged the degree of provocation to give that would let him know how closely he stood to danger. "Mesner Antoz, perhaps you could explain what sort of company you believe him to have fallen into?"

He didn't seem a man familiar with the thrust and parry of words that served as prelude to more direct action in Rotenek. Perhaps things were done differently in his rural circles. And though Mazuk's man stood close at hand, there was no one whose posture proclaimed him to be Antoz's armin. That was no surprise for a country gentleman, but it meant he had no one to soften or make good his offense.

Mazuk recognized the dance they'd begun. In the past, he'd traded barbs with her that brushed the edge of challenge, but he'd always had the sense to step back. He plucked at his friend's sleeve and leaned closely for a whispered caution.

Antoz shook him off. "Oh, I know who this is well enough," he retorted loudly. "The Duchess of Lautencourt and her wife!"

Barbara felt Margerit's hand grip her elbow painfully. The affair had gone past the point of return. At the edge of her vision she could see Marken closing up to loom protectively over Margerit, but there were strict rules to the game. No matter how outrageous his behavior, Antoz was of noble rank and there were limits to Marken's license to answer a matter of honor. And Barbara knew the insult had been aimed at her.

This was Tavit's cue to take up the challenge. She could hear the tension in the sound of his breathing behind her but still he made no move. Not fear, she was certain of that. But concern for his own grudge against the man? Never duel in anger—that was one of Perret's hard rules. Like an old friend, she felt the presence of her own blade where it lay against her thigh and assessed the stranger. She could take him. Easily. And if it weren't for the slight to Tavit if she were forced to dirty her own hands, she might enjoy it.

But she wasn't the only one who had noted Tavit's inexplicable hesitation. On her other side, Brandel stepped forward and stumbled his way through the unfamiliar words of the formula.

"You have besmir— bestir—, you have sullied the name and honor of Barbara Lumbeirt, Baroness Saveze. Do you stand ready to uphold your words with your body?"

"And who are you, boy?" the challenger demanded. "Boy? Or are you a woman like the rest of them?"

Oh, he was well beyond forgiveness, but Barbara knew she'd answer for any harm that Brandel might take. Why had she allowed the boy to wear a sword tonight of all nights? She dropped Margerit's arm to take up the challenge for herself and found Tavit recovered at last. He stepped in front of Brandel to repeat the boy's challenge in a precise, clipped voice.

Antoz might not know the formulas of a Rotenek duel, but his answer left no question of his willingness—nay, eagerness—to cross swords with Tavit. A crowd had begun to form around them in the wide corridor and Barbara saw the signs of wagers being placed. Most of that crowd followed them out into the sharp chill of the palace foreyard and thence into the Plaiz. Several men had picked up blazing links to light the circle that formed.

Barbara made one useless effort to send Margerit home.

"No," she replied hotly. "This concerns me as well."

Mazuk was thrust unwilling into the role of arbiter, making the last, useless request for reconciliation, then giving the signal to begin.

Tavit moved slowly at first. If Barbara had feared his own anger would make him careless, that was answered. His face was still pale in the torches' flickering light, but now it seemed like carven ice. Antoz was more skilled than one might expect for a man so clearly unused to the formalities of dueling, but it was a skill with little depth. His feints were only what they seemed, his errors were not a duplicitous invitation to overreach.

Barbara recognized the moment when Tavit had finished taking the man's measure and began to work in earnest. Two minutes later there was a sigh from the crowd as a crimson stain spread across Antoz's bare shirtsleeve. That should have been the end: the insult answered, honor served. But Antoz stared at the wound in surprise, as if it were a fresh affront. Tavit had stepped back to give him time to recover and acknowledge his defeat. That extra step meant that Antoz's sudden lunge fell short and he stumbled as Tavit beat the blade away. There was a scramble as he turned and they engaged once more and then that long suspended moment as they came together when the watchers knew one man would fall but did not yet know which.

It was Antoz's blade that dropped to the cobbles with a clang as he sank slowly to his knees and then pitched forward.

Tavit stepped back, holding his empty hands out to his sides. Barbara caught his gaze and gave a small, sharp nod then turned to Baron Mazuk.

"Perhaps you would be so good as to notify the magistrate's men." On a night like this, someone would be standing conveniently to hand. Barbara looked around at the crowd that had begun to filter away and named two of the men who had followed them out from the palace corridor. "Stand witness, if you please." There were formalities to endure when a duel ended in death, even in as clear a case as this.

Now Margerit agreed to be sent home. Brandel was bullied into accompanying her. And after the authorities had come and gone, only Tavit remained, waiting silently, his still-bloodied blade now retrieved and his coat draped over one arm despite the chill.

Barbara expanded on her approving nod. "Good, quick work. A pity it came to that, but the law should be satisfied." She fished out a handkerchief and handed it to him. "Best clean that off. I thought we might walk back to Tiporsel. We could both use the fresh air." There were questions still to be answered.

The road was dark with no moon to light the way and only faint pools of illumination from lanterns set into the gateways along the Vezenaf. A carriage rattled past and then turned in front of them onto the approach to the Pont Ruip.

Tavit finally broke the silence with, "You'll be looking for a replacement, of course. Brandel…he's a promising boy but he needs years yet of training. I'll stay until you find someone."

"What in heaven's name are you talking about?" Barbara said. "You hesitated—anyone might at their first serious challenge—but not when it mattered. You'd worked for him, hadn't you? Not surprising if you might balk at that."

"Not that." Tavit's voice was bleak. "They all know now. You heard him. How can I protect the name of Saveze when my own is questioned?"

Know what? Barbara sifted back through the accusations Antoz had made but could recall none directed at Tavit in particular save that first one. *A freak like you.* It had meant nothing at the time except as insult. She knew little of Tavit's past—that wasn't uncommon for an armin. She knew the things that mattered: that Perret had vouched for him and that he'd given good service.

"Whatever passed between you and Antoz, I find it unlikely that it would outweigh what I've seen in the last year."

"What you've seen—" Tavit's laugh held no humor. "Mesner Antoz saw more than you did. I thought I was safe—that only my skills and my service would matter here. I thought the rest could be…could be left behind. I thought…I never knew how Antoz guessed—how I gave myself away—but when he knew, he would have forced me to be a woman for him."

"To be…" Several possibilities spun out in Barbara's imagination. The first was that Antoz had been the sort to press his attentions on serving men. But that made no sense with the rest of what had been said. *A freak like you.*

Then it came to her. Not what she had seen, but what she hadn't seen. All the small clues that she had failed to make sense of: the beardless cheek, the slight, almost delicate build, the excess of modesty when they traveled together that she thought had been for her sake. *He saw more than you did.* There had been a time when such a failure of perception would have meant disaster for her duties. She was growing soft and lazy.

"Tavit," she said gently, "you should have known that I, of all people, would have no objections to a woman as armin. You should have told me."

"I'm not—" Tavit's voice choked off. And then more roughly, "I'm not… like you. I'm not…oh Christ, I don't know what I am. I only know what I'm not. They all tried. They tried to make me be a woman, but I'm not."

The silence spun out between them. Barbara still struggled to understand what Tavit was telling her. It was important—of that she was certain. And moment by moment something was slipping away. Something they might never regain, if lost.

"Who do you want to be?" she asked at last.

Tavit's expression couldn't be seen but there was a long ragged sigh. "I want to be armin to Baroness Saveze."

"And who has any say over that but me?"

"The scandal—" Tavit began.

"What scandal? Do you think Antoz went boasting to all the world of his mistake? And now he's dead."

Yes, Barbara thought, that was the most convenient part. If she hadn't seen the duel herself, she might have thought it too convenient.

"I doubt there will be gossip. But if there is, I'd rather not give the world reason to believe that anything that was revealed tonight was a surprise to me. That would damage my reputation far more than my choice of armin."

Once more the silence hung between them in the dark but this time it was easier, more thoughtful. And then, as one, they turned and continued up the Vezenaf.

CHAPTER NINE

Luzie

Early January, 1824

Luzie closed her eyes and leaned toward the keys, trying to imagine the notes spilling from the fortepiano out into the parlor, filling the space like drifts of mist off the river, the way Serafina had described. Only a week remained to finish the commission for Maisetra Honistin, and with every day that passed she despaired. Something magical, she'd asked. Like what you wrote for Baroness Saveze. As if magic were something one could produce on command. The Pertulif settings had been easier. His poetry could inspire anyone to flights of passion. And she hadn't known she was supposed to be writing magic. There was so little to work with here. A sonata for my daughter's betrothal party. She'd met the young woman briefly—too briefly to have a sense of what hopes and dreams might be woven into the strains of the music.

Luzie opened her eyes again and scratched a few more notes onto the staff. The parlor looked the same as it always did: a cozy, comfortable space as far removed from magic as one could imagine. It was impossible to tell whether the phrases were worth keeping or whether she should begin again with a blank page. Perhaps she should beg Maistir Fizeir for his opinion. He wouldn't hesitate to be honest with her. But every commission made her ground firmer. She'd been able to send the entire fee for the last one to Iuten. You see, Papa, my music is in demand now. She couldn't afford to disappoint her patrons.

"That was lovely," Issibet commented from the sofa, where she bent over her sewing in a pool of lamplight. The work wasn't opera costumes this evening, but the long overdue mending of bed linens. Issibet couldn't bear to have idle hands and it might be months before Alteburk would find the time.

Luzie nodded and thanked her absently. Issibet thought whatever she played was lovely. Quiet company was appreciated, and Issibet's uncritical enjoyment was comforting, but not much to the point. In the pause before she began the strain again, Luzie heard the front door open and close. She felt, rather than saw, Serafina pause in the doorway as her fingers moved over the keys, trying to recapture the image she was reaching for. Without breaking the sequence, Luzie threw a quick smile over her shoulder and tilted her head to invite her in.

It was a deliberate habit now to make that invitation. In the first months of her residence, Serafina had seemed to slip crosswise through the movements of the household. After that disastrous affair dressing for the palace dinner at the end of October, Luzie realized it wasn't only shyness, but a deliberate reticence, hidden under the uncertain schedule of her studies and masked by her outward moods.

Elinur had opined that Maisetra Talarico thought herself above sharing a table with working women. But that night of the Royal Guild dinner had broken an opening through the hedge of diffidence. When your shoulder had soaked up someone's tears, it seemed unnatural not to move on to exchanging Christian names. Once you had done that, you noticed the hesitations and excuses. Now Luzie made certain to draw the scholar more closely into the rhythms of the house.

Serafina settled onto the bench beside her bringing a wash of sharply acrid scent. Luzie's nose crinkled. "Have you found a new pomade? I prefer the one you found at the market. It was almost as nice as the broken one."

After a moment's confusion, Serafina laughed. "I've been sitting all day for Olimpia. No wonder I reek of turpentine and linseed oil! I'm sorry, I'll go change."

"No, no, stay," Luzie urged. "I want your opinion on something." Yes, now she could recognize the aroma of the painter's studio. "I thought her piece for the palace was finished."

Serafina looked away. "This was just…she finds my face interesting, she says. She's been doing sketches…studies she calls them."

Interesting enough for regular visits to the studio over the last two months! It was easy to see what Olimpia Hankez might find fascinating in the luminous tones of Serafina's skin and the bright glance of her eyes. Serafina seemed embarrassed to speak of it. Did she realize how sought after Hankez was?

"Will we have a portrait to hang on the wall?" They had grown easy enough that some teasing was permitted.

"No, it's only for her private notebooks." Serafina's cheeks darkened in what must have been a blush. "What did you want to ask?"

Luzie spilled out her concerns with the sonata. Her hands moved restlessly over the keyboard, punctuating her doubts. "I never thought about it before, this thing you say my music does. But now they expect…they expect miracles.

I feel like the girl in Rumpelstiltskin. Everyone expects me to spin straw into gold because they've seen me do it before, and I don't know how!"

From the sofa, Issibet chided, "You're making too much of this. You're already a good composer. Don't tie yourself up in knots just because you have a few commissions."

Serafina laid a hand on hers where it still rested on the keys. "There isn't a single work of yours I've heard that hasn't sung with power. I don't think it's possible for you to fail." Her fingers tightened before releasing. "Play it from the beginning."

Luzie shuffled the pages and found her place. The first chords rang out, dissolving into runs in the treble while the bass settled into a restless rhythm.

"Wait," Serafina interrupted.

Luzie paused with her hands over the keys as Serafina glanced around the room, tracing invisible patterns.

"For a betrothal, you said? I think it begins too…too deeply, too many colors. The power is there but it's…" Serafina waved her hands, clearly finding it as frustrating to explain as it was to try to understand. "Give me just the upper part."

Luzie picked out the treble line one-handed as Serafina nodded in time. And then, because she couldn't bear to leave it so naked, her left hand added just a note, here and there. The barest skeleton of the original part.

"Yes, like that. Now it's green and soft, and spreads out without pushing. A young girl in a garden at the beginning of spring, when only the first shoots are rising through the earth."

With that image in mind, Luzie moved on to the second theme. Serafina's descriptions were entirely different from what she had envisioned for the music, but she could see how they matched up, side by side. Not the essence of the music, but a cipher, in the same way the black notes on the page were not the sound but only instructions for the sound.

Measure by measure they began to build a vocabulary, a language. In the manuscript for the third movement she found herself scribbling notes couched in colors and textures, with little diagrams of sharp-edged shards and smooth spirals. It was still her music—that hadn't changed—but she could see new patterns in how the pieces fit together. Distinctions that she might once have felt her way toward by ear, but that were entirely apart from the rules of harmony.

Luzie sat back and gave a deep sigh, feeling drained. There was a waiting stillness from Serafina beside her. "Is it like that for you?" she asked. "All the time?"

Serafina shrugged. "Not like that. Not so strongly. But yes." She searched for words. "The great miracles…they're like storms. They move you—change you—whether you will or no. Most people, if they can sense anything at all, only know the storms. Or they know a storm has passed because the limbs have been torn from the trees, or the ships were heeling over almost foundering. But I…I feel every breath. The air is never still, whether it's the sharp cold before a snow, or the cool breeze coming off the river in high summer, or even just the rush of air behind someone walking past. And sometimes, even if I can't feel the wind, I see the leaves moving high in the trees, or the way a kite hangs suspended above the hill." Her eyes had gone unfocused, seeing all those things before her within the parlor walls.

Luzie shivered. It was frightening to think herself a part of that vast invisible force. And yet…to think that one might call the wind and send leaves skittering down the cobbles, or drive the ripples on the river into caps of foam. She stared down at her hands. What was it good for? To warm the spirits of a hesitant student? To send chills down the spines of a salle full of listeners, curious to experience the frisson of something more than music?

Serafina was watching her again with that wary caution. Impulsively, Luzie threw an arm around her and drew their heads together briefly. "Thank you. Thank you for giving me that."

* * *

Rain beat against the glass of the parlor windows when Luzie began packing the latest batch of Fizeir's copywork into her music case. She pulled the curtains aside and peered out, trying to guess how long it would last. January should have snow, not rain. It wasn't a good day to travel across town, but she'd promised delivery. And she needed distraction. On today of all days, she needed that.

It was growing harder to fit in the time for Fizeir's work, and the pay was little enough compared to the new students, but she hated to lose her contact with the man. She could never really call him a mentor—certainly not a patron—but he was the only composer who had condescended to comment on her work. How she wished her father were closer! Fizeir had promised to look at the commission for the Honistins. It wasn't that she didn't trust Serafina's opinion, but she wasn't a musician. Together they'd coaxed and teased the work into something Serafina called bright and marvelous, but how many listeners would be able to see it as she did? The piece needed to work purely through the ears as well.

The wind slackened briefly and Luzie held the case close under her arm for a quick dash across the little bridge and over to the edge of the Nikuleplaiz where it would be easy to find a fiacre. At least she needn't count teneirs in that fashion anymore. The rain had turned the little chanulez into a brief torrent, washing out the stench of the mud, but she held her breath by habit while crossing over. If the spring flood were low again, they'd need to dredge, and wouldn't that stink!

By the time she arrived across town, the storm had settled into a sullen drizzle. Fizeir's mood, in contrast, was as cheery as the bright coals cracking on the grate.

"Finished already? Good, good." But he set the bundle of scores aside, next to a folio inscribed across the cover with the title, *La Regina di Saba*.

"Your new work?" Luzie asked.

Fizeir quickly laid his hand across the title, then changed his mind and pushed it toward her, with a finger across his lips and a broad wink. He was notoriously close-mouthed about new compositions. Sometimes everything but the title was kept a secret from all but the cast until opening night. Once, he'd canceled an opera entirely when the singers had performed excerpts at a private party before the opening.

Luzie appreciated the confidence as she opened the cover to scan the beginning of the overture. Not another tragedy, but a Biblical spectacle. In some ways she admired Fizeir's disdain for the modern fashion for operatic farce. Surely the grandeur of the stage was meant for more than adulterous comedies. "And who is singing your Queen of Sheba?" she asked.

"Benedetta Cavalli," he said shortly.

The temperamental Italian soprano would do justice to his work, Luzie thought, but it was hard not to imagine Serafina's face instead in the role of the ancient Ethiopian queen. Perhaps they could go to the opening…no, even her careful budgeting wouldn't yet extend to good seats, and Serafina was so shy. She wouldn't subject her to the common crowd. Issibet could be relied on to arrange something once the chaos of the opening was past.

Fizeir closed the cover of the folio and slid it away from her reach as he handed her the note with his payment. "You had a new composition you wished me to judge?"

Grateful that he'd remembered, Luzie found the sonata at the back of her case. She waited anxiously as he played it through, first deliberately and then at speed with broad showy movements of his hands. She scanned his face, looking for some sign of the surprise and delight that Serafina always betrayed. But perhaps he wasn't sensitive to—what did they call it? *Fluctus*? And that was why she had asked his opinion. She needed that distance.

Fizeir gave her a small, tight smile as he returned the manuscript to her. "It will do for the purpose. I'm sure the Honistins' guests will enjoy it. You seem to have found your calling."

He meant it for praise, Luzie knew, but she'd hoped for more. "I'm enjoying the opportunity for longer works," she said as she packed the papers away once more. "I'm working on another motet like the one I showed you last spring. Perhaps some day I, too, will try my hand at an opera." She had meant it as a jest, but even as the words escaped her mouth she knew it had been a mistake.

"You? An opera?" He was too startled for polite lies. "You have no idea what that would require. And who would perform it?"

"My father's work was performed at the Royal Opera House," she said quietly.

"Your father was a great composer and Alpennia is the less for his retirement. Perhaps some day your brother will take up his banner and continue the name."

Luzie bit her lip and nodded as she turned away. There he was wrong. Gauterd was a superb performer, but he would never make a name as a composer. Perhaps one of his sons. It would be good to see a return of the Ovimen family to Rotenek's concert salles.

* * *

Luzie hadn't expected to return to solitude, but Issibet was still at the opera house sewing room, with the opening coming so soon. Elinur had taken to her bed with a wet cough—she would need to make sure that Silli made up some broth for her. The cough often ran through the city at midwinter but rarely this badly. The apothecary's physic was having some effect but perhaps she should send Charluz for a thaumaturgist. No, Charluz was out for the whole day. And there was never any telling when Serafina would come or go. A cough could turn bad so easily. It could... A dull ache began to grow beneath her heart.

The house was still except for the faint pattering of the rain on the windows again and the distant footfalls and clinks of Mefro Alteburk and the maids at their work. Luzie brushed her fingers across the keys of the fortepiano, but she'd lost all chance of denying the date. The tenth of January. Ten years to the day since Henirik's death on yet another cold, dreary winter day.

Luzie crossed to the secretary desk and fumbled in the back of a drawer until her fingers closed on a small round object. She took it out and sat in a corner of the sofa by the front window, opening the chased cover of the pocket watch and gently touching the dark curl of hair tucked into the case. The timepiece itself had stopped ten years past and she had never rewound it. Some day she would pass it on to Iohen.

She shut the cover again and closed her fingers around it. No portrait to gaze on. They'd always meant to have their likenesses taken, but time had slipped away. She could still see his hands—the way they drew the watch from his waistcoat pocket and clicked it open, all in a single movement—but his face had faded.

A tear slid down her cheek, then another. She no longer mourned the loss of the man she'd thought to share her life with. Now she mourned the loss of the memory of him. Life had always been as it was now. Alone. Even her sons had been given up to the dreams Henirik had traced for them. Every summer they were more and more strangers. It had seemed so important to hold on to Henirik's home here—equally important to send the boys to the school he'd chosen. Perhaps it would have been better to remove to Iuten with her parents where she could be near them all. It would have meant giving up teaching music, but she wouldn't have needed as much income.

Luzie wasn't sure how many hours had passed in reverie when she heard the front door open. Gerta had come in to poke up the fire but had carefully left without speaking. Luzie recognized the soft tap of Serafina's boots, met by the quicker staccato of Gerta's steps as she hurried to take her wet coat and parasol. A few indistinct words passed in the entry hall, then Serafina's face appeared in the doorway. Luzie expected her to withdraw silently. She was grateful when Serafina instead crossed the parlor to sit beside her and take her hand without a word.

"Usually it's at Christmastide that it hurts," Luzie began. "You haven't been here long enough to know. That's when we always come together in Rotenek. For the important folk, it's for the New Year's Court, but for people like us it's simply family coming home. My parents moved to Iuten a year or two after I married, and then it was Henirik and I who invited them all. My parents, my brother Gauterd and his family, if he wasn't traveling, and Henirik's sister Anniz before she married. The house would be full of music and baking. And somehow the night was always clear and fine to walk down to Saint Nikule's for midnight Mass. We'd walk arm in arm singing noelle all the way—even Henirik who couldn't keep a tune to save his life!" Her voice caught.

"And now it's only me. My mother's too frail to make the journey in winter. And the boys go to stay with them for their winter holiday. Their school's only a half-day's journey from Iuten, and in any event they've grown too old to be tucked in here with me when the rooms are all let. Anniz is off in Suniz now. Gauterd was here two years past for some concerts, but it wasn't the same."

Though it all must have seemed like babbling nonsense, Serafina's hand squeezed hers tightly.

Luzie forced a smile. "Did you have a favorite holiday as a child?"

She felt Serafina stiffen. Had she touched on a tender spot?

"The feast of Christmas was a special time for us too," Serafina said quietly. "But my parents celebrated it as they did in their homeland. I don't know what other families in Rome did."

"Tell me," Luzie urged, when Serafina fell silent again. Anything was better than falling back into her own memories.

Bit by bit she coaxed enough of a description from Serafina to build a picture, eked out with memories of paintings she'd seen where dark-skinned figures lounged on carpets and cushions. She imagined a tray shared between them with curious flat leaves of bread—a type of crêpe, she supposed—used to dip up bits of spicy stew with paprika and ginger and onions.

"And then mother would sing," Serafina said, her eyes staring unfocused into the past. "There should have been a drum, she said, but she would clap along in time. I never knew what the songs meant because they were all in Tigrinya. I never learned it. That is, I must have lost it before I can remember. Papa thought we should speak Romanesco." She began crooning a wordless melody. It had the feel of calling and response, like the work songs of the bargemen on the docks.

Luzie stored the tune away in memory to copy down later. "And does she still sing the songs when you visit?" she asked.

Serafina's expression hardened. "My mother died, and my sister-in-law keeps a proper Roman household for them now."

"I'm sorry, I had forgotten." How could she have been so thoughtless? "But when you go home—"

"It isn't home," Serafina said. "It hasn't been home for a long time."

Luzie laid her arm around her shoulders and squeezed gently. "Then we have come to the same place."

"Once—" Serafina began. She turned and her eyes were shining. "Once in Palermo I was home again."

"With your husband?" Luzie ventured.

She shook her head. "It was a mystery—not quite a proper church mystery but more like what your guilds celebrate. It was in the piazza by the harbor. I don't even know what it was meant to do. I was a stranger there and I didn't like to ask questions. All I know is that the music surrounded me and embraced me and took me home." Now it was Serafina's cheeks that were wet with tears. "I was there again. Mama was singing, and I could taste the air of my childhood, and for one moment everything was right…and then it was gone. I have to build my own mysteries. It's the only way I can ever get it back." She shook her head again, but this time to shake something off.

Luzie knew how that story had ended: the long lonely journey here to Alpennia to study with Maisetra Sovitre, only to find that she hadn't the talent after all. Her arm squeezed Serafina's shoulders gently again. It was easier to comfort than to be comforted. "And now you are missing your husband too, no doubt. How can you bear to be parted from him all this time? You must be lonely."

Now there was a silence so long that Luzie was certain she'd stepped beyond the boundaries of their new-grown friendship.

Serafina's lips were pressed tightly together, but at last she said, "I was lonely before we parted."

Luzie felt a pang of guilt, recalling that not all marriages grew as close as hers had promised to. Serafina was here—alone—that said most of what needed to be said. "Did he have other women?"

A shrug.

Men could be such fools. "And you never took a lover in turn?" Such things were common in Italy, she knew.

Another pause. It seemed they had crossed over into a land of confidences. Serafina answered slowly, carefully, like plucking her words from within a nest of thorns. "It would break my marriage vow to lie with a man who was not my husband."

Something left unsaid hung heavy in the air between them, a door begging to be opened. "But…?"

In answer, Serafina leaned toward her, the sweet-spicy scent of her hair making a curtain around their faces. She pressed their lips softly together.

Luzie gasped in surprise and jerked back.

In an instant, Serafina was on her feet, crying, "I'm sorry! I thought— I never know how to behave properly. I thought you wanted…" She backed away with a hand covering her mouth.

Luzie stood too. Her thoughts tumbled over themselves, trying to sort out what had happened. But before she could collect them there came the sound of the door and Charluz's cheerful voice in greeting.

CHAPTER TEN

Margerit

Mid-January, 1824

January had been alternating between wet sticky snow that turned the streets into an ugly mess, and gray days of constant drizzle that dampened the spirits of travelers and stay-at-homes alike. Frances Collfield paced the front parlor, grumbling that no one would venture out to the exhibition of her prints, until Bertrut was driven to snap at her. Brandel, at least, was as careless as a duck of the weather. Between his new studies at the palace and practice at Perret's fencing salle, he was rarely underfoot.

Even Margerit found herself looking up constantly from her books to stare out through the panes of the French doors of the library across the dull expanse of the Rotein where it flowed at the foot of the gardens. Every time the weather changed, anxiety clutched at her as she wondered if some new threat had slipped through the protective walls. It was only a storm. There were ordinary storms, after all. Not everything had hidden meaning. Not too long ago, she had been so confident that she understood the protections that the mysteries cast over Alpennia. Now there were so many questions, and not only her own. She glanced down at the brief note she had been folding and unfolding. *You have my every confidence. AA* The fact that Her Grace had felt the need to send it spoke volumes. It was only rumor, but it was said that the guildmaster of Saint Benezet's had challenged her appointment.

She looked out across the water once more. Curiosity replaced worry when she saw Barbara striding up the path from the private wharf at the river's edge, a heavy driving coat swirling around her ankles. Had she been out on the river? The landing was rarely used in wintertime except for deliveries. It was scarcely a day for pleasure boating.

A few minutes later the library door opened and Barbara entered, divested of coat but still wearing boots and traveling clothes.

"I have a riverman waiting down at the wharf. Could you manage a little excursion?" she asked, bending over Margerit's chair for a brief but unhurried kiss.

"In that?" Margerit swept her hand toward the windows where a soft patter of drops had obscured the view once more.

"In anything at all. I received a message this morning from Eskamer."

Margerit's heart leapt. There was good news for a change! Some of her most treasured books had come from the pawnshop owner. Given that, she was willing to overlook his less savory reputation when it came to more conventional valuables. "What has he found this time? Or won't he tell you?"

Eskamer played his little games; he had a living to make, after all. But she'd pay any fair price so long as the goods were sound.

"This time it was a bit of early news as a gift. It seems Mesner Chasteld has died at last. It seems the cough took him, though he'd been poorly for a long while." Barbara waited while that information sank in.

"The poor man, God rest him," Margerit exclaimed as she crossed herself and promised a prayer for his soul. "But now we may never see what else that library of his could offer up." She felt a moment's guilt that the man's death itself meant little to her. She'd never met him that she could recall. But she was intimately familiar with the contents of his bookshelves. The early draft of Gaudericus with Tanfrit's notes had only been the most valuable of the works that Eskamer had brokered for the elderly recluse. Who knew how long it might take his heirs to sort things out? She said as much to Barbara.

"That's why Eskamer suggested we might want to make a little inventory of our own," Barbara said. "He's well known to the staff there. He thinks he can get us in to look things over before word spreads too far."

Even bundled up warmly, Margerit was glad of the canvas shelter arched over the back of the riverman's boat. The armins made do with an oilcloth in the bow. The riverman himself plied his oars with little heed of the water rolling off his heavy woolen coat and cap.

Margerit leaned into Barbara's side, stealing some of her warmth. "I still don't understand why we couldn't have taken the carriage."

"If rumors get out that we're interested in Chasteld's library, I know a dozen other collectors who might descend on it. As it is, we'll have to forsake decency. The corpse is in the church but not yet in the ground, I understand. But if we drive up in a carriage with the crest of Saveze on the door, we might as well post our interest in broadsides in the marketplace. Chasteld's place has its own wharf. This way we won't attract notice until we've staked our claim."

The old Chasteld place—it seemed to have no other common name—lay a short distance beyond the sprawling edges of Rotenek just by the village of Urmai. Back when the city had kept within the ambit of the old walls, Urmai was considered sufficiently distant to serve as a floodtide destination or a summer residence. Some Chasteld ancestor had built a sprawling villa there. Now Urmai was thought too near the bustle of the city to be truly fashionable, but in the sweltering heat of summer, its public gardens were an easy distance for a day's outing.

In midwinter the place was less inviting. A strong-backed riverman could make the trip downstream in less than an hour—better than a carriage ride if the streets were crowded, and more discreet, as Barbara had noted. The broad stone steps of the private landing were thick with sticky mud, less from the low level of the water than long neglect in cleaning. Marken sacrificed the dryness of his boots to help secure the boat, and Tavit scrambled out after him to offer a hand to the passengers as the riverman sculled gently to steady his craft.

Margerit noticed the briefest of hesitations as Barbara reached out to take the offered hand. A check, and then a second check as she grasped it and stepped across to drier ground. Margerit knew what lay behind that reflex. They kept no secrets between them—certainly not ones that might touch on safety or reputation. Barbara had related the aftermath of the duel at the New Year: Tavit's revelation and her confused acceptance of it. Now Margerit could see the corresponding flinch in Tavit's expression at that silent reevaluation of trust. Not trust in his loyalty or abilities, but in what services it was right to expect. Barbara herself would have raged at such doubts when she had held the post of armin. And she knew it, and pushed past those doubts. But Margerit could tell the matter was still a wound between the two of them.

The riverman was dismissed to take his ease in Urmai proper, glad of the day's sinecure, and they followed the leaf-strewn path up to the twin stairs arching to embrace the grand entrance doors. It took three times pounding with the iron ring to summon faint footsteps within. A crack opened in the smaller wicket door.

The woman who confronted them had a suspicious and careworn face. She looked too young to be housekeeper for such a large estate, but she wore a ring of keys at her waist and peered at them with a proprietary air. "Yes?"

Barbara stepped forward. "We regret to intrude on your recent loss, but Eskamer the bookseller suggested that—"

"If you're friends of that thief Eskamer, then you may go to hell!" she spat out and would have closed the door in their face except that Marken laid an immovable hand on it.

Margerit hurried to take a softer approach. "Forgive us for overlooking the introductions. I am Margerit Sovitre, thaumaturgist to Her Grace Princess Anna. In the past, your late master has sold me several ancient books that have been valuable to my work. We were hoping to assist in sorting out Mesner Chasteld's library to advise his heir in how to dispose of it. And this," she added belatedly, "is my friend Baroness Saveze. If it is convenient for you, would it be possible…?"

The housekeeper's brief temper had retreated into wariness and she hastily curtseyed to the both of them. "I suppose you may come in if you must," she conceded.

They followed her through the wicket door into the gloom of the echoing entryway. The housekeeper picked up a lamp from beside the door and led the way between another pair of arching stairs and into what must once have been the ballroom beyond.

Light filtered in through filthy windows set high in the walls above the gallery. Lumps of covered furniture huddled around the edges of the room, thick with dust. The housekeeper turned when she heard their echoing footsteps pause. "Mesner Chasteld had been an invalid for a very long time," she said by way of explanation. But that scarcely explained the neglect.

"Where is everyone?" Barbara asked. The house had a stillness that spoke of a deeper absence than only the late owner. The air was chill and dank.

"Gone," the housekeeper said shortly. "Been leaving one by one for years now. And taking most of what's valuable with them." She fixed Barbara with a critical eye. "Your friend Eskamer doesn't ask many questions."

Margerit winced silently. They knew what sort of man Eskamer was. She wondered now whether her books had indeed been purchased from Chasteld or obtained only by way of some greedy footman who'd pocketed the money himself. And who was Chasteld's heir? No one close enough to have kept an eye out for him. Or had Chasteld been one of those sharp-tongued, bitter old men who drove away anyone who might have taken care for his interests? He seemed to have kept at least one loyal servant, as attested by the presence of Mefro Montekler, as she introduced herself.

They stopped to gather two more lamps before unlocking the dark oak door to the library. The chaos was more orderly here: close-packed shelves, volumes stacked two and three deep on small tables. Mefro Montekler cleared spaces for the lamps saying, "There's no point to opening the curtains. The ivy's grown so thick it wouldn't matter."

Even so, Barbara crossed to the window and pulled aside a heavy drape to let in the green-filtered light. A different light caught Margerit's eye.

"What—?" She followed Barbara to examine the stiff fabric of the drapery. Pale ghosts of figures showed on the side that had faced the glass. Not brocaded arabesques, but a face, an arm, the folds of an ancient gown. It was an old tapestry, repurposed for its thickness and weight to keep sunlight from the books. But what she had seen was not the designs themselves but the faintest overlay of *fluctus*, following the fabric as it moved. "How curious," she said, explaining to Barbara what she'd noticed. "That's the second time this year I've seen a fragment of mystery bound into an ancient object. There isn't enough to tell what it was meant to do. Not enough for me, at least. I wonder what Serafina might make of it." But the books were calling more strongly, and calling was what she hoped they'd do in truth.

Barbara was looking over the contents of the room in something like dismay. "We could be weeks in here and still miss the best of the lot." And to the housekeeper, "I don't suppose you could find us an empty ledger book and pens to start a catalog?"

Margerit stopped Barbara with a hand on her arm and then pulled open her reticule. "We may be able to work more quickly. Mefro Montekler, could you find me a couple of wax candles? The lamps will do for light, but not for this."

The housekeeper frowned at them suspiciously, as if she expected to return to find the room entirely emptied. And it didn't help that Marken and Tavit had taken on that alert, wary stance of an armin in uncertain territory. They must seem quite the invading army! But at last Montekler shrugged and disappeared to return with a few stubs that had clearly been dug out of neglected sconces.

"I hope these will do."

Margerit nodded and set them beside the materials she had laid out: several small packets of parchment, marked with words and symbols.

Barbara grinned at her. "Antuniet's book-finding charm?"

"I thought it might be useful today," Margerit answered. "That was why I was so slow getting ready."

It was the little mystery that Antuniet had once used in Prague to find her book of alchemical secrets—an adaptation of an old nurse's charm to play sweetheart games at floodtide. But now when the contents of the packet were burned, rather than pointing to your true love, the smoke would pick out the object you would find most useful.

When Margerit lit the largest of the candle stubs and cracked the seal of the first of the packets, Mefro Montekler stepped back and crossed herself. Margerit felt a twinge of guilt. The housekeeper was right. It was too easy to treat small mysteries like this as mere sorcery and not a gift to be granted. She echoed Montekler's gesture with her hand and said, "In the name of the Father and the Son and the Holy Spirit, lend your grace to my work today. Hear the pleas of my intercessors to allow what I would accomplish." Only then did she continue on with the words of the ritual as she tipped the fine contents of the packet into the candle's flame.

The floodtide game was meant to be showy, with a cascade of bright sparks choosing the target. That wouldn't do at all in a room full of books, and Antuniet had altered the charm so it would produce only smoke. The dark thread hung in the air over the candle for a long moment, then curved gently toward a corner of the room. Margerit followed it, scarcely daring to breathe for fear of disturbing the air. It took one more working to trace the path to the particular tome it had picked out. She pulled the book from the shelf and brought it back to the lamps. A dark powder streaked the covers and left stains on her gloves.

"How long has it been since there was a fire in this room?" she asked.

Mefro Montekler shrugged. "Last winter, perhaps. We've had to save the coal for the inhabited rooms."

Her tone was not one of indifference, Margerit thought, but more of resignation. How long had she been struggling to manage like this? Margerit opened the covers of the book carefully. At least the pages weren't touched by rot. An early, minor work of Chizelek, but leafing through she could see annotations that might be of more value.

"Is it worth the trip?" Barbara asked, leaning over her shoulder.

"Perhaps. Let's try again." Margerit moved to a different part of the room and relit the candle stub.

There seemed promise enough in the collection. The finding charm identified three books of interest and sometimes seemed to hesitate as if confused by the bounty. What a shame it would be if any of it succumbed to the damp before it could be examined properly! Margerit turned to Mefro Montekler decisively.

"I need to have a fire in this room. Constantly for at least a week to dry things out and at least half of each day after that until other arrangements can be made." In the face of the housekeeper's protest, she said, "I will pay for the coal and for a girl to tend it. I'll send someone to make arrangements before the end of the day."

The housekeeper gaped at her, but before she could speak there came the tinkling of a distant bell.

"I thought there was no one else left," Barbara said.

Montekler looked pained. "My grandmother," she said, almost in a whisper. "She's an invalid. Mesnera, may I—"

Barbara gestured permission and, after the woman had left, said, "Well, that might explain why she didn't leave with the others. What a sad ruin! I never knew Chasteld well. He was a recluse even in the baron's time, though he'd put in an appearance at court a few times in the year. If I'd known…"

But what was there to know? A man had a right to keep his life private.

There were two more little envelopes prepared for the finding charm still laid out on the table. Margerit picked one up, saying, "No point in letting them go to waste." This time she began near the window and the trail of smoke first caressed the edges of the faded tapestry before flattening itself against the window, leaving a smudge of soot on the glass. She peered out, trying to see past the trailing ivy to the grounds beyond.

Barbara gestured to Tavit to undo the latch, noting apologetically, "A bit of air won't do any harm, even on a day like today."

This time the thread of smoke drifted out straight through the window frame and into the curtain of leaves, but whatever goal it sought was lost in the falling drizzle.

Barbara looked at the litter of emptied packets. "Perhaps on our next visit?" She motioned Tavit to fasten the window again.

"I wonder…" Margerit began. When Antuniet devised the charm, she had needed the smoke to point the way, given how uncertain her *visio* could be. But a visual sign was only an echo of the underlying *fluctus*.

Margerit picked up the unused pen that Mefro Montekler had found and examined her palm. "These gloves are already ruined," she said, dipping the pen into ink and tracing the same symbols and words that adorned the scraps of folded parchment. When the pattern was complete, she laid the pen aside and cupped her hands together, whispering the charm into the space between. As she opened her fingers, a bright thread of *fluctus* escaped and drifted off through the glass and into the yard beyond. She grinned at Barbara. "A treasure hunt! Shall we follow it?"

Without Mefro Montekler to guide them, the closed-up house was a maze. They came out at last into what had been the gardens. Unlike the great houses in the city that turned their faces to the street, this one faced the river, and its private spaces spread out on the landward side to fade into orchards and stables and the other outbuildings of a property that had once been as much a rural estate as a mansion. Three more times Margerit cupped her hands around the finding charm and followed the trace of power with the others trailing behind her blindly.

The *fluctus* knew only direction and took no heed of the ground underfoot. Once it led them into the stable yard, until a wall blocked their path. At last it flickered out and abandoned them beside an old stone and timber cottage. They'd gone well beyond direct sight of the mansion, but still within its grounds. At one time, the cottage must have been made for habitation, but in some distant past it had become a shed for livestock, with a low stone wall added to form a yard.

"What now?" Barbara asked as Margerit looked around uncertainly.

"I don't know. The mystery thinks there's something here that would be useful to me. I rather doubt it's a book this time! Not in a place like this. Antuniet's ritual doesn't specify books. I think there must be something of the user's intent involved. But in that case I don't know what we're looking for."

There was a gate hanging crazily off its hinges that let them into the little yard. The door to the cottage itself was long since gone and the opening let in barely enough light to see the noisome remains of straw bedding. Margerit ducked back out quickly and examined the yard from within. The wall had been built from odds and ends of stone: smooth boulders tumbled by the river, small worked squares that must have been repurposed from some other source, a tall broad slab that stood the full height of the barrier and might well have determined its course. On second examination, the shape of that stone became familiar and she went to crouch before it and touch the traces of carving that still showed through the moss.

A sharp stick uncovered the edges of lettering and the shape of an escutcheon above, though the device on it was only recognizable as bearing birds of some sort. Barbara joined her, scraping gently at the moss to reveal the beginning of the inscription. HIC IACET...

"No surprise," Margerit said. "I wonder what churchyard they pillaged for this?"

"The stone is set deeply. If I didn't know better, I'd think it marked the original grave. Let's see whose memory we're meant to call to mind."

They worked more carefully now, picking the dirt and vegetation out of the lettering. The end of the line held only a single name. Margerit's heart began hammering as it came clear: TANNFRIDA.

Barbara laid a hand on her shoulder. "She wasn't the only woman by that name. Don't assume—"

But Margerit had attacked the obscuring moss more frantically. Why else had the mystery led her here if not for this? The drizzle started again, but she took no notice of anything except what the stone revealed. The Latin was clumsy and ambiguous, abbreviated to fit the stone and not the standard formulas of a churchyard monument.

HIC IACET TANNFRIDA
DOCTORA UNIVERSIT'
ROTANACI CURAV'
SUSANNA SOROR
CARISS' EIUS

"Doctora Universitatis Rotanaci," Margerit breathed. "It must be. But…?" So many questions. Why here? Why did the dozzures at the university deny she had ever taught there? Tanfrit's scholarship was legendary, even in the few scraps that survived. Why was she buried here in obscurity, commemorated only by Susanna, her most beloved sister?

"Why here?" she asked aloud.

Barbara offered a hand to help her rise. "You know what the legends say, that she was a suicide. They couldn't have buried her in a churchyard."

It wasn't the question she'd meant to ask and the answer made no sense. "But those legends say she threw herself in the Rotein from a broken heart and was lost," Margerit countered. "This isn't lost."

"It could be a cenotaph," Barbara cautioned. "But no, not if it says *iacet*. And yet—"

They stared at each other in wonder, forgetting all the rest of the world around them. "This is it," Margerit said abruptly.

"What?"

Margerit gestured back toward the Chasteld mansion. "This is where I'll have my school. Don't you see? It was destined. Academia Tanfridae, Tanfrit's Academy."

She could see all the objections tumbling through Barbara's mind.

"It's a ruin. It could take a fortune just to make the place habitable."

"Then I should be able to get the property at a good price," Margerit countered. "Think. The location is perfect: close enough to the city for day students but enough space for boarders. Close enough to travel from the city for special lectures. Plenty of room to set up a printing press or any other project Akezze can think of. We can—"

"Are you certain this is what you want?" Barbara asked. "Are you sure this isn't just sentiment? There are other properties we've looked at that would do as well. Better, perhaps. You won't get as much casual attendance for your lectures here."

It was a question worth asking, Margerit knew, but the fire in her blood burned the same as it had the first time she created a mystery of her own. "What is the difference between sentiment and divine inspiration?" she asked with a smile. "Yes, I'm certain."

Barbara nodded sharply. "Then let's go see if Mefro Montekler knows anything about who Chasteld's heir might be. Though if she doesn't know, I'm sure LeFevre could have the answer for us by tomorrow."

* * *

There was a cousin, Montekler had said. Or perhaps a great-nephew, she wasn't sure. There had been letters from him in recent years, but no visits. Was he likely to be interested in selling? She'd shrugged and said he'd be a fool not to. She fell short of indicating that she thought anyone would be a fool to buy, especially not in front of someone who might be her next employer.

The riverman left them at the landing nearest to LeFevre's office, then continued on, taking Tavit to fetch back a carriage. There was no need for misdirection here.

LeFevre was as doubtful about the Chasteld estate as Barbara had been, and less willing to be convinced by signs and portents. "Maisetra, I cannot advise it—though I don't recall that my saying so has changed your mind in the past."

Margerit had been carefully marshaling her arguments on the ride up the river. "The place is in poor repair, it's true, but that should be to our advantage. And the location should be as well: too close to the city for a summer place, too far for a residence. Barbara says Chasteld's heir has a house near the Plaiz Nof. He'd have no good use for the estate."

"Unless he has shipping interests," LeFevre countered. "If the river continues to run low, a speculator might decide that property in Urmai would be a good investment."

Barbara had been holding her tongue but now she asked, "And what would my father have done?"

LeFevre studied her thoughtfully. "He would have bought it," he said at last, "as a speculation." But then a grin spread across his face. "And all the while he would have convinced Chasteld's heir that he meant to turn it into a charity school or an orphanage and gotten a better price thereby."

And then they both laughed, though Margerit couldn't entirely see where the joke lay.

"So," LeFevre continued, dismissing his qualms. "I will approach the new owner about taking this old ruin off his hands with the understanding that you will be thinly stretched to make it habitable for your students and that we are considering several other properties and must make a decision soon. If he has time to think, the price will be more than it's worth."

Margerit nodded, knowing how painful it would be if it slipped through her fingers.

"And then your work will begin. Who do you have in mind to see to the repairs? Who will oversee the property for you? How will you divide the expenses from your own?" he continued. "And who will see to your faculty? Or did you plan to do that all yourself?"

It was a real thing now, Margerit realized, not merely an idle conversation among friends. By the time the deed was in her hands, she would need to have begun on the answers to those questions. But it would prove a good distraction from useless worrying over the flawed mysteries. If she stopped to think too long, she might never regain the courage.

CHAPTER ELEVEN

Serafina

Late January, 1824

Serafina gazed out over the expanse of faces in the common seats and then up across the tiers of boxes. Maisetra Ponek had begged a favor from the manager to identify a box in the lowest tier that would be left empty on this, the final night of Fizeir's *La Regina di Saba*. The angle was awkward and the singers were close enough that their painted faces looked like garish masks. It didn't change the music, though.

Luzie was listening intently to memorize each note and phrase. Serafina thought back to the first time she'd seen an opera in Rome, slipped into Costanza's box discreetly after the overture had started. She'd been introduced only to those who visited with similar discretion. She'd never been certain whether Costanza was more reluctant to introduce her as a lover or a cousin. What had they seen? She no longer recalled. Last year Margerit had brought her once, but she'd declined further invitations. The boxes required as many roles and costumes as the stage. Margerit hadn't said anything about her performance, but neither had she insisted further.

Serafina didn't know what to think of the music. Luzie seemed to think it good, but Jeanne's opinions had been sharper when the subject came up in passing at Tiporsel House last week. Too old-fashioned, she said. Too safe. But how could one judge what was old-fashioned if one hadn't seen the new? All music seemed flat now without the mystical currents held by Luzie's every phrase. Surely there were other composers who could evoke them—others beyond the anonymous man who had written the mystery in Palermo. If she went to more concerts she might find them, but that would require...

Serafina's attention came back to the performance as the scene changed to the court of Sheba and a tall dark-haired woman commanded the stage in garments evoking both royal robes and ancient splendor. She could be none other than Queen Makeda—no, Fizeir gave her the name Nicaula. Except for a leopard skin draped across her ample bosom like a sash, there seemed little of Africa about her and nothing of what Serafina knew of her homeland. But Luzie had intended this as a treat and the music was pleasant enough for what it was.

Her eyes wandered back to find Margerit's box in one of the upper tiers on the far side. Margerit wasn't there, but among the small cluster of faces she recognized Jeanne by the tilt of her head and the distinctive movements of her fan. Luzie noticed her gaze and followed it.

"Someone you recognize?" she whispered.

"The Vicomtesse de Cherdillac," Serafina returned, and then added impulsively, "We could go visit during the interval if you like. Didn't she invite you to one of her salons?" If she must challenge herself, why not now, for Luzie's sake? They'd both dressed in their best for the evening so they wouldn't be too far out of place. She could try to hold her tongue and not say any of the things that Jeanne's friends found so unexpectedly amusing.

Jeanne was entertaining in something less than full state. It looked to be little more than a private party among friends and she welcomed them as such. "Maisetra Valorin! It's been entirely too long! Surely you know Maisetra Noalt. No? Then you should, for the Noalts have built a beautiful new salle and will want to fill it with music as well as dancing. Maisetra Noalt, you simply must commission a piece from Maisetra Valorin."

Serafina watched her friend dragged off to discuss business, or what passed for business in the opera house. That made it worth having ventured to the upper levels. She moved to one side of the box hoping to escape notice but Jeanne was relentless, pulling her over to join several of the other guests.

"Serafina, I should have guessed you'd want to see *La Regina*, you should have told me before. You've met my friend Count Chanturi haven't you?"

She hadn't, but she nodded as the man made an exaggerated bow over her hand and murmured, "Enchanted."

"Are you enjoying the opera?" she asked him. It was a safe enough topic.

Chanturi waved his hand in a gesture that could not be interpreted. "Fizeir has delivered what we always expect from him. But I would be interested to know what you think of his ancient Abyssinia."

What was she meant to say? It was impossible to guess. She was saved by the return of Luzie and her new patron who exclaimed, "And you must be my Africa!"

Serafina could manage nothing more eloquent than, "I beg your pardon?"

Luzie rescued her by explaining anxiously, "Your friend Olimpia is designing a mural for the ceiling of the Noalts' ballroom."

"The continents and the seven seas," Maisetra Noalt proclaimed. "And you must be my Africa. Your friend Maisetra Valorin tells me that Olimpia Hankez has been painting you."

"Not painting, no," Serafina said, still floundering for a response. "Only drawings."

"Then there will be no need even to trouble you to sit for her. It's settled then."

She wanted to protest, but would it lose Luzie a commission? She nodded mutely.

The venture achieved its second purpose when Jeanne invited them to stay, as the musicians began signaling the second act. "I scarcely see you at all these days! Has Margerit dragged you off to view her ancient ruin? And what do you think of Fizeir's Sheba? You never did give Rikerd an answer."

"I think that Maistir Fizeir knows different stories than the ones my mother did," Serafina said carefully.

But Jeanne only laughed. "No doubt! He tells the story we expect to be told. You should have seen his Iulius Caesar! But I think dear Benedetta has done well in the role. Now hush, they're starting!"

It was during the love duet toward the end of the second act that Serafina first noticed it: a thread of magic weaving in and out of the queen's theme, just barely at the edge of perception. So he has the talent as well, she thought. Perhaps Fizeir's popularity was not so mysterious then. She thought he must be blind to it like Luzie was, for the *fluctus* came and went randomly, like the chance reflection of light from a ripple on water. Serafina leaned against the rail, straining to see better. There was something familiar about the flavor... or was that only the way of mysteries in music?

At her side, she felt Luzie shift restlessly. Had she seen it too? Was it only her own magic she was blind to? Serafina leaned closely to whisper, "What do you—" She hesitated. The dim light betrayed something akin to embarrassment on Luzie's face.

"I didn't know he would..." Luzie began.

Of course. No wonder the flavor was familiar. "You wrote that."

"No. Not..." Luzie was shaking her head. "It was one of my little études. I sold it to him last summer. Shh."

Was that how these things worked, Serafina wondered, settling back in her chair. Was music sold in the marketplace like sausages? She could see more clearly now which of the threads carried the power. The play of the two voices wove together. Only one carried that extra burden but she could see what might have been if the effect were more deliberate.

When the curtains closed again before the last act, Serafina returned to that thought. "You should write an opera of your own."

She could see Luzie's confusion as the others turned in interest.

"Oh goodness, no!" Luzie began. "That's far beyond..."

Count Chanturi rose to pour wine for them all and offered a glass to Luzie saying, "What would you venture? A comedy? A history? Though I don't know that I can think of anything in Alpennia's history that would be worthy of an opera." It was clear from the humor in his voice that he considered the idea no more than idle conversation.

"What about the story of Tanfrit?" Serafina asked. "Margerit has been telling me all the scraps she's discovered."

Chanturi raised an eyebrow. "Tanfrit?"

Jeanne tapped him chidingly on the arm with her fan. "One of Margerit's ancient philosophers. Don't you remember me telling you? They seem to have found her grave on that property Margerit bought for her college. You'd think she'd found a piece of the True Cross. It has all the makings of a great tragedy: raised to the heights of fame and honor, a tragically unrequited love and then at the end she throws herself into the Rotein in flood!"

Luzie was listening in fascination. "Serafina, you never told me that part. The vicomtesse is right, the story would be perfect for opera. But I could never…"

"Perfect, even if it's not true?" Serafina protested. "Margerit thinks most of the story is nonsense."

Chanturi chuckled dryly. "True history makes poor theater, as a rule. Invention is better. If you pass it by, perhaps I should suggest that one to Fizeir. God knows he could do with fresh ideas! If you will forgive me, I think the evening has already been long enough for me." With a bow, he left.

The image kept hold of Serafina's imagination all through the final act. Was there enough remaining of Tanfrit's story to bring to life in such a place?

* * *

The thin winter sun struggled through the narrow window in Olimpia's bedroom, such that late afternoon seemed more like dusk. The sunny rooms were reserved for painting. Serafina rolled over and squinted trying to gauge the time.

"Must you go?" Olimpia said. She twined their legs together and buried her face in the loose cloud of hair.

"Not yet, but soon." Serafina reached across to adjust the wick on the lamp, bringing a warm glow back to the room, then relaxed across Olimpia's body, drawing in her heat against the chill of the room. Their stolen afternoons were a warm refuge against so many things. There was nothing of her failures here, no struggle to find her place. But the mood had been broken and she sat up in the middle of the bed. The covers slipped off her bare shoulders as she fumbled for a ribbon to tame her hair until she could braid it.

"Just like that; don't move." Olimpia rolled off the side of the bed and snatched up the sketchpad that was never far from her reach.

The instruction was familiar by now. Serafina paused with her hands reaching behind her head as Olimpia's hand moved quickly across the surface of the paper. "Do all your lovers have my patience?" she asked. Talking was permitted; moving was not.

"Mihail only visits for one thing and then he's gone," Olimpia said, pausing with her head tilted to consider the work. "And Renoz won't ever stay still. If I can't capture her in three lines, she's done. Done."

The last was meant for her. Serafina slid to the edge of the bed and held out her hand to see. It was only a rough sketch, the sort of study that littered the walls of the studio. Olimpia had captured her in midmovement: her elbows akimbo as she gathered up her hair into the ribbon, a single sinuous line following the arch of her back down around the curve of her hip to where her feet peeked out from the jumbled covers. The merest impression of dark eyes and a tilting smile. "You make me beautiful," she said.

Olimpia took the sketch back from her. "You are beautiful. I make you see it."

Serafina looked again. It was only charcoal on paper without the underlayer of Olimpia's talent bringing it to greater life, yet it captured something more than a mirror did. "And what would I see if you drew mysteries for me?"

A shake of the head. Olimpia didn't care to have her work described in mystic terms. "I'd rather learn you the slow way. It's only fair." She gave a little half smile.

"But when they come to you for portraits—" Serafina waved her hand out at the studio where several unfinished works stood under their discreet covers. "—you give them your visions?"

Olimpia shrugged. "Sometimes they get a true portrait; sometimes they only get paint. I tell them it depends on whether the muse is kind, but in truth it's for my own reputation. Not everyone would be flattered by having their soul laid bare on canvas. Once I look, I can't choose not to see, but I can choose not to paint it."

Whatever inspired her—whether muse or fancy—when the spirit moved through Olimpia's hands, it could open a window even for those with no special vision. They might not know what drew them to the portraits, or why one inspired love and another doubt. Serafina wondered idly whether Luzie would see something in the paintings that she couldn't see in her own music. And Margerit…she had one of Olimpia's sought-after portraits, but she'd never admitted its hidden power. There was more magic in the world than could be encompassed in Margerit's theology. Some day she would see that. The cold air stirred across her bare skin and Serafina found her discarded chemise and pulled it on.

"Would you like to see my new project before you go?" Olimpia asked as she buttoned up her work dress and covered it with a paint-stained smock. There was a mischievous gleam in her eye as she led the way out into the studio.

She unrolled a series of pen sketches on the floor, weighting them with this and that. A bearded man astride a dolphin, a woman in Greek robes with her arm draped across the neck of a bull, a dark-skinned man dressed in a skirt of feathers and holding up a colorful parrot. Serafina recognized the pose in the next sketch and a sense of dread settled in her stomach. She had become more familiar with her body as seen through Olimpia's hands than through her own eyes. Her limbs were sprawled across a carpet as they had been across the bed a short time past, but now with a leopard skin draped carelessly for modesty—she thought suddenly of the Queen of Sheba parading on the opera stage, but she, at least, had been given regal dignity. Serafina's eyes traced over her rounded belly, her breasts bare and dark-nippled, her arms crooked around a pair of spears, her hair floating loosely and transfixed by a pair of ostrich feathers, her face…

She looked up at Olimpia, feeling the painter's excitement and pride like a blow. "That's not…that's not me," she said.

"Of course not," Olimpia said. "It's Africa. I thought I'd arrange them…" She stopped. "Serafina, what's wrong? Maisetra Noalt said you agreed."

"But not…not…" Serafina struggled to find words for her dismay. She fell back on something Olimpia might understand. "This was private. This was just for you." She hugged her arms across the thin cotton of her chemise feeling the weight of other eyes.

Olimpia's voice was suddenly quiet. "Serafina, I'm an artist. Nothing that comes into my hands is just for me. I thought you knew that." She reached out to brush away an errant lock of hair and Serafina drew back. "You liked it when I put you in the banquet scene."

The painting of the guild banquet had been different. That had been her, Serafina Talarico, the foreign thaumaturgist. "This isn't me. It's not Africa. It's not anything but stage scenery." Serafina heard her voice shaking. "It's a painted whore for everyone in Rotenek to stare at. Do you think they don't stare at me already? And now this is what they'll see. When I agreed, I thought it would be…I don't know. I thought it would be different."

She realized that the betrayal was not in the exposure of her body, but that Olimpia could have looked at her so many times and seen this—seen a jumble of stage scenery and opera props. A dark-skinned canvas on which to paint someone else's fictions. Even without true vision she had expected more. She hadn't realized she was crying until her hand came up to brush the tears away.

"I'm sorry," Olimpia said. "It's not a portrait. It isn't you. It was never meant to be. I re-use faces all the time."

"This is the only face I have." Serafina turned and headed for the bedroom to gather up the rest of her clothes.

"Wait," Olimpia pleaded. "Don't leave, not like this. Let me try again."

Was she begging for the picture or for their time together? Those warm memories were slipping away already. They never lasted.

"Serafina…"

She turned and saw Olimpia standing, sketchbook in hand. That was how she would always picture her. In that moment, she knew she would never return to the studio.

"Serafina, I promise I won't use that one. Give me the Africa you know instead. The one you want people to see."

I don't have one, she wanted to cry. All I have is… The vision of her mother rose before her, what her mother had been before the shrinking and fading. She did have that.

She reached back and untied the ribbon from her hair. There was no one to braid it properly and no time, but she fumbled to twist long rows to catch it back from her face—a style she hadn't worn since a girl—and tied it in place again. The studio was littered with lengths of cloth and other oddments that might be useful when posing. She found a voluminous shawl of white merino, so thin and delicate it seemed to float in her hands. How had her mother wrapped it? Like so: over the shoulders and drawn up over the head. And what of Papa? He, too, was an anchor to her elusive past. She saw his hands always caressing one of his beloved old books with the strange writing she had never learned. She chose a volume from a table and tucked it into the crook of her arm then settled into the cross-framed chair placed where the light was strongest. It was a chair meant for sprawling and sultry looks but she sat erect, staring into a land she'd never seen except through stories.

This time there were no instructions, no brief touches to move an arm here, a fold of cloth there. Olimpia circled around to find the light she wanted then worked in deft strokes across the paper. Serafina could see the trailing wisps of *fluctus* echoing the movement of Olimpia's hand. She'd always wondered how it would look. So this was to be a true image at last—Olimpia's own way of saying farewell.

The movements slowed. A final stroke, a frown, a brief gesture with the charcoal that never touched the paper, a long out-drawn breath. "Would you like to see it?"

Serafina shook her head. "No, not until it's finished." She didn't want to know what Olimpia had seen within her. Better to have her heart broken no more than once in a day. She set the book aside and unwrapped the shawl, then slipped her gown over her head and let Olimpia do up the buttons.

There was no further apology at their parting, only one last kiss, and then Olimpia murmured, "I hope you find it," as she opened the door to the twilight chill.

* * *

Serafina had meant to be home for supper but the hour had passed along with her appetite. There was no hope of slipping unseen up the stairs with both Charluz and Elinur settled in the front parlor with handwork while Luzie practiced at the fortepiano. She almost wished for the days when there had been a stiff distance between them.

Her voice betrayed her, and then there was all their bitter sympathy to bear when she dared give them only a piece of her sorrow.

"Well I don't know what you expected," Elinur said as she offered up a crisp white handkerchief for the tears and a waspish opinion on the morals of artists. "Letting her draw you naked like that. No wonder if she thought you a bit loose."

Charluz followed up with a cup of tea and her own opinion. "For all the time you've spent posing for her, I'd think she might at least have done a portrait for you. Now there would be a coup! I hear that Countess Peskil has been waiting two years to commission one from her."

But Luzie shooed them away after a bit and, when they were alone, sat down beside her on the sofa. "It wasn't just the painting, was it?"

Serafina shook her head mutely in confirmation and felt the other woman's arm encircle her shoulder. It was a motherly gesture. She leaned closer not trusting herself to speak yet. At the far side of the room the clock ticked off the moments, sifting a stillness over the room. She drew a long shuddering sigh.

"Were you…" Luzie's voice trailed off. "I have guessed that…that you are very lonely here."

The close press of Luzie's body became both uncomfortable and tantalizing. What was safe to confess? It was tempting to pour her heart out, but she had betrayed herself too far once before. Luzie wasn't Jeanne, to sympathize with where that loneliness might lead. Serafina straightened up and moved a little apart, dabbing at her face with the sodden handkerchief.

"You must think I'm foolish, being put all out of countenance by a silly painting."

"And will you…sit for her again?" Luzie's hesitation betrayed her understanding but no word of condemnation followed.

"No," Serafina said. "That's done with. She's going to use a different pose. There's no need for me to return. Will you play for me?"

"Of course," Luzie said and rose. "I have a new tune for…no, that one isn't ready yet. I'll save it for a special occasion. But I've been playing with some ideas you mentioned. About Tanfrit. Not a whole opera! But maybe a song or two. What do you think of this motif?"

Her fingers brought forth a spill of notes like the rush of water, echoed by threads of blue and green that wound throughout the room.

* * *

Tanfrit and the college were becoming rivals met on every street corner. In the space of weeks, Margerit had nearly disappeared from view, like a woman in the flush of a new affair. The urgency that had driven their studies in the wake of the *castellum* was set aside. Twice now the walk up the river to Tiporsel House had found the library empty and all plans swept away by the need to consult carpenters and masons. Serafina had found a note of apology suggesting passages and questions to review, but a knot of discomfort grew as she sat alone reading. Every face in the doorway felt like a challenge. Would she like tea? Did the fire need poking up? The servants were easier to ignore than Maisetra Pertinek's polite inquiry if she expected Margerit back soon. She could hear the question they didn't ask. Why are you here?

Why was she here? What was the use? She was no closer to any understanding of her own failures. What was the use of knowing why the Lyon rites worked for some saints but the Penekiz tradition was best for others? How did it help to know when to use Latin or Alpennian to set out a markein when the mystery she cared most about had no scope beyond her own heart? Why should she care if Alpennia were under siege from unseen forces? Perhaps she should return to Rome. She had learned enough to pursue her own studies now. There had been a letter from Paolo, passed through many hands, the last time she spoke to the bankers. There were difficulties in Paris. He had hoped to return by summer but that was not possible. She should not expect him before the fall at the earliest.

That was more notice than she usually had. There would be plenty of time to make plans. She needn't chance the storm-cursed land route via Turin or Milan in winter, or the roundabout passage on one of the river barges all the way down to Marseille to brave a sea voyage. She could wait until late summer to set out and he need never know she'd been gone. Not that he would care, so long as she were waiting for him.

The maid came in to close the curtains on the darkened river view and trim the lamps once more. "Will you be staying to dine, Maisetra?" she asked.

Serafina tried to think back to the last chime of the clock in the hall. "Oh, no, I should be going." It was growing late. She'd promised Luzie to be company for dinner tonight, with Issibet off visiting her sister and the others on a holiday trip to Akolbin. The house had been echoingly empty for days except for Luzie's students.

The streets of Rotenek had never seemed a dangerous place—not the ones Serafina kept to—so she was more startled than frightened when a shadow emerged into the faint pool of light cast by the lamps to either side of Tiporsel House's entry gate.

The man nodded to her. "Maisetra Talarico."

In the pale glow his face was indistinct and she scrambled for a name. He wouldn't have spoken unless they'd met. "Forgive me..."

He bowed more sharply this time. "Franz Kreiser. We met a few months ago at the Ambassadors Ball."

Yes, of course she remembered now. She remembered the uncomfortable moment when Antuniet had given him the cut, and then the awkwardly persistent questions that she hadn't known how to escape. She fumbled for something to say. "If you've come to visit Maisetra Sovitre or Baroness Saveze, I'm afraid they aren't at home."

"Ah, my loss." Oddly, he seemed neither surprised nor disappointed. "In that case, perhaps I might escort you a little way on your path?"

He offered an arm to her and she could think of no reason to refuse. Or was there? She had so few dealings with men outside of the company of her friends that she hadn't learned the rules very well. She wished Jeanne were here to ask.

"I've been hearing interesting things about your studies. Maisetra Sovitre appears to be quite impressed with you."

Had Margerit been discussing her with this stranger? Whatever for? The thought was deeply unsettling.

"There are…" His pause seemed calculated somehow, like a storyteller teasing his listeners. "…some curious questions I have been studying. I was hoping that Maisetra Sovitre might be able to assist me, but—"

In the dark she felt rather than saw him shrug.

"She is a very busy woman," he continued. "And your name came to mind instead."

Margerit should have asked her first, but it was warming to think she'd been considered a worthy substitute. "What questions were you investigating?"

He tucked her hand more closely into the crook of his elbow as they strolled down the Vezenaf. "I understand you have a talent for locating and observing the effects of a mystery at a distance. Have you ever tried scrying with a map? Some odd events have drawn my interest—mystical events—and I'm trying to trace their origins."

Serafina remembered the long frustrating sessions with Paolo with his maps and books. But perhaps she had learned some skills here in Rotenek. What he asked seemed akin to what they'd done with the *castellum*, overlaying their visions on the map of the countryside. "I've worked a little with maps. Margerit will have told you: I can see things, but I can't work mysteries."

Mesner Kreiser made a dismissive noise. "The mysteries I want to trace have already been performed. It's only a matter of determining where."

Kreiser left her before they reached the Nikuleplaiz, with plans to meet in the church in a few days time. His puzzle was replaced by hunger as she opened Luzie's door. The aromas that met her suggested that Mefro Chisillic had been coaxed into producing something more daring than her usual. Luzie's cook favored old-fashioned Alpennian country dishes, intended to fill stomachs rather than tempt palates. Today was different. Serafina sniffed again as Gerta took her coat and Luzie called a greeting from the dining parlor. A hint of ginger and cinnamon, more garlic than Chisillic usually cared to add. Chicken? No, duck. Luzie's favorite, though she didn't care for the stronger flavor.

"Just in time," Luzie said. "I've told Silli to begin making the crepes—though of course you wouldn't call them crepes but I don't remember what you called them. I only remembered the description."

"What I…?" Serafina thought back. When had they talked about food? Yes, a month past. That day she'd found Luzie crying and they'd talked about holidays. And then…oh, that had ended badly! She'd hoped Luzie had forgotten it entirely. She breathed in the hints of dinner again. A suspicion crept over her. "What are we having?"

"A special surprise! Come. I know you've been feeling low. I thought you might be homesick. So I described everything you told me to Mefro Chisillic and asked her to see what she could do."

Serafina let herself be led to the table with a sense of unease. It began to make sense. There was something like a stew—that must be the duck. Ginger and cinnamon and garlic and…yes, even cardamom. But studded with black peppercorns, not the hot red peppers that should have been laced through it. Something that might have been inspired by a dish of spinach, except that cabbage was the only green thing to be had at this time of year. And Chisillic was bringing in a stack of golden crepes before nodding to her mistress and returning to the kitchen. That must be meant to stand in for injera. All her cherished memories fed through an Alpennian kitchen and made as unrecognizable as Olimpia's Africa had been.

From Luzie's expression, Serafina knew she hadn't kept the dismay from her face.

"It's…it's not right, is it. I tried to remember all the details, but…"

No, it wasn't right. Nothing was right except for the impulse that had created it. Serafina swallowed the memory of hurt and answered that impulse. "It's almost perfect! But the meal needs the right setting. We never ate a holiday banquet at a table like this. We need to—" She glanced in the direction of the front parlor. Would Luzie find the idea too ridiculous? Would she laugh, or be too embarrassed? "We need to recline, like the ancient Romans did. And there must be cushions and…I'll show you."

She took Luzie by the hand and pulled her into the next room. The low tea table would do. "Pull all the cushions and pillows off the sofa and pile them beside it. Gerta, go get some bed pillows too."

Gerta gaped in open-mouthed confusion until Luzie laughingly repeated the command.

"Now bring in the dishes and lay them out here. Never mind the silver, we won't need it." Serafina grinned to see her own dismay now reflected in Luzie's expression. "You'll see!"

When the room was arranged to her satisfaction, Serafina kicked off her shoes and sank down onto the cushions, patting the place beside her in invitation. When Luzie had settled awkwardly beside her, Serafina said, "Now this is how a holiday banquet is done in my home!"

She sang something that no one else would know were not the prayers her mother had said before a meal, then tore off a corner from a crepe on top of the stack and daintily scooped up a morsel of duck. "And this is how we honor guests at our table." She popped the bite into Luzie's mouth almost before Luzie realized her intent.

It might have been a disaster. Serafina could still remember her sister-in-law's voice railing at her mother. Savages. Uncivilized barbarians. How can you live like this? But soon they were giggling as Luzie fed her in turn, holding up a napkin to contain the initial spills. And nothing was said of the choice of spices or the too-sweet taste of the bread.

"It wasn't just dinner, you know," Luzie said when they were sated at last. She struggled to extricate herself from the nest of pillows and wiped her fingers carefully on a napkin, saying, "Wait here," as she crossed to the fortepiano. "I noted the tune down as soon as I could, but I'm sure I've made as much a mess of it as I did of dinner. I hope you won't mind."

The theme was brief and repetitive, transformed into variations like a student étude, but Luzie had captured the mode perfectly from memory. There were no words, of course, but the cloud of sound and colors that rose around them took on the shape of that never forgotten voice and reached back through time. The walls dissolved. The music touched her, caressed her. Fingers playing with her hair. The scent of spice. The whisper of fabric. Laughter. How could she remember laughter? When had there been laughter? Memories of her mother's love had always before been wrapped in longing and regret. Had she forgotten so much? A warm cheek brushing against her own in greeting. A voice raised in song to the rhythm of the day's chores. Her father's strong hands lifting her up to his shoulder to watch a procession go by. Her brother's quick energy running ahead into the crowd. Her mother's face…her face…

The music ended and the parlor echoed with a different sound. Sobbing. Whose?

"Serafina! I'm so sorry! I didn't mean to—"

Serafina shook herself free of the spell. Her own sobbing. It was still there—the lost world of her childhood, that place she had been transported to that time in Palermo. The place that no longer existed in this world. It was still there and the door could be opened again.

The cushions shifted as Luzie crouched down beside her. "I'm sorry," she repeated.

"No, you don't understand. It was beautiful. So beautiful." Serafina grasped for the words to explain. "You gave it back to me. You gave her back. That's what I came to Rotenek to find: how to get back there again."

She knew that Luzie didn't understand. Couldn't understand. She was making no sense at all. Luzie's arms were holding her and it took all her strength not to turn in them and try to return some measure of gratitude in the only way she knew how.

She thought briefly of Paolo's letter and dismissed it. These were reasons to stay: Luzie's magic, Margerit's confidence in her work, even Kreiser's intriguing project.

CHAPTER TWELVE

Jeanne

Late February, 1824

Jeanne set her book aside on the cushion beside her and reviewed the letters on the silver tray that Tomric held for her examination. She selected the two that lay on top. The intended recipient of the third was clear by the signs of foreign origin, even without the name penned neatly across its face. The butler crossed to where Antuniet sat at the ornate secretary desk to complete his delivery.

"And, Tomric, will you let Cook know that we'll be four for dinner rather than three?" Jeanne reviewed the planned menu in her mind and added, "Tell her to add stewed pigeons if she thinks the mutton won't be enough."

"Yes, Mesnera."

Antuniet looked up from turning the letter over in her hands and asked, "Who will be joining us?"

"Tio's husband will be in town after all."

"Ah." Antuniet's response included a hint of relief at the prospect of something to leaven Tio's court gossip. With a brisk movement she cracked the seal on her letter and turned to spread it across the blotter.

Jeanne skimmed over the contents of her own messages with a broadening smile but she waited until Antuniet sat back and looked up before sharing them.

"This is curious, Toneke. My dressmaker begs the favor of a word with me. You remember Mefro Dominique? I wonder what that could be about? It certainly isn't a dunning letter! And Maisetra Tizun is quite anxious to know when she will be invited to my salon again, although she carefully avoids mentioning the topic at all."

Antuniet turned. "And will she? Be invited?"

Jeanne folded the note and set it aside. "That will be up to Anna. Selecting the guests is the most important skill. I think she's ready to take charge of that part. A few mistakes will only improve the lesson."

There was something much like a snort from Antuniet's direction, but she had turned back to the desk. "And do your guests know that their fate is in the hands of a chit of a girl who isn't even out in society and wouldn't be received in their own parlors?" The amused affection in her voice gave the lie to her dismissive words.

"Of course she would be received. Maisetra Manzil is." Manzil's salon was famed among the more politically radical set. Jeanne had kept her success in mind when making plans for Anna.

"Estir Manzil is a married woman. Her hosts have no need to worry that their sons will show unsuitable attentions to her. Though," Antuniet added with the touch of regret that always intruded, "I suppose they needn't worry about Anna attracting those."

Jeanne hastened to break the mood. "Have you discussed your plans with Princess Annek? Does she approve?"

Antuniet's head turned sharply. She looked more than startled, almost guilty.

"The trip to Prague." Jeanne gestured toward the letter that still lay spread under Antuniet's hand. "Is she worried? I do wish you'd let me travel with you. There's trouble on the borders. The Osekils have put off their visit to Baden." The question had always been deflected, never rejected outright.

"Princess Annek is concerned that I finish the current commission before I leave. Beyond that…" She shrugged. "I don't plan to take any foolish chances. Jeanne—" Antuniet looked down at the letter again. She seemed to come to some decision and crossed over to perch at the other end of the settee. "Jeanne, I didn't want to speak of this until there was a decision to be made."

"Mmm?" Jeanne hid her trepidation behind a mask of curiosity. This wasn't Antuniet's usual style. Bold, direct and tactless. That was her way.

Antuniet spoke quietly but steadily, staring down at the folded letter in her hands. "You know what it meant to me to restore the honor and legacy of the Chazillens. But there's no use in a legacy if it can't be passed on. I have Princess Annek's word on it—her charter—that my name and rank will pass to my children. But for that, there must be children."

A worm of doubt twisted in Jeanne's heart. What was she saying?

"I know it would mean a change to our lives. An intrusion. And it may be too much to ask of you. But I am asking." Still her eyes remained fixed on the letter.

Jeanne sat stunned, as if the house had collapsed about her, leaving her soul bare in a raging storm. How could she not have seen this coming? In any other person, she would have suspected—would have seen a change, a coolness. But no, it was all of a piece. She should have known that if Antuniet chose to marry it would come from the head and not the heart. She would know if Antuniet's heart had changed, but the paths her mind took could be hard to follow. To ask this of her…

"Toneke, I…" She felt tears start and fumbled for a handkerchief. "I don't know what to say. I know it's selfish of me."

Jeanne could see Antuniet stiffen. Of course she knew this would tear them apart. Such a short space of time they'd been happy here together! And how had it come to this? For years her heart had always skipped lightly past infidelity and betrayal, never letting any of her lovers plant deep roots in her life. Not until Antuniet.

"Toneke…" she began again. "I remember when you said…when you offered to…to allow me to have other lovers." It had seemed quaintly charming at the time, despite Antuniet's distress. The offer had been easy enough to refuse. "Is it wrong that I can't find it in me to be so generous? No, Toneke, it isn't fair of me, it isn't right. But not here. I couldn't bear to share you with a husband here in my own home. And you have no right to ask that of me."

Now Antuniet looked up in startlement. "With a…?" She cast the letter aside and reached to grasp Jeanne's hand, capturing it in its fitful motions. And then, unexpectedly, she laughed. "Oh, Jeanne, no! I have no intention of acquiring a husband! Only a child."

Jeanne gaped at her as she sorted through the implications. "Only…but Toneke, the scandal!" And how like Antuniet to propose such a thing so calmly. "Here I thought I was the daring one. You'll lose your position at court, you know. Princess Annek can choose to overlook our…our friendship, but she can't overlook that! What on earth will you tell people?"

"I've thought it through carefully." Antuniet composed her face into earnestness. "There are three Great Works in alchemy: the philosopher's stone, the transmutation of metals and the creation of a homunculus. If I were to create a child by my art, it would be mine as much as any other, and there would be no reason for anyone to call me wanton or unchaste."

"And can you do that?" Jeanne turned the wonder over in her mind. "I've never seen anything in DeBoodt's text about—"

Antuniet released her hand and made a dismissive gesture. "He doesn't touch on those techniques, but my old teacher Vitali has been studying them." A faint smile crossed her face. "You didn't think I was traveling all the way to Prague only to return his zodiacal watch did you?"

"A child." Jeanne let the thought sink further in. "And would you…would you carry it in your own womb?"

There was a hesitation. "There are other ways, but that is the simplest."

Something in her words—in the careful phrasing—slipped into place. "Toneke, tell me the truth."

The stillness that came over Antuniet confirmed Jeanne's suspicions. "Toneke!"

"Jeanne," she began more hesitantly. "Do you really want the truth? It might be better if you could tell people you know of no reason to doubt the child's alchemical origin."

"Rubbish, Toneke. I'm a much better liar than you are. Now who is that letter from?" Jeanne held out her hand. The letter had precipitated this conversation. It must hold the key.

With a sigh, Antuniet handed her the creased sheets. Jeanne scanned through the lines of elegant writing.

I will not pretend to understand your reason for asking this of me, and I confess it is not entirely a flattering offer. Perhaps that is only fair. At this time in my life, there are no impediments to what you ask. So for the sake of the affection I have always sincerely felt for you, I extend my invitation for you to visit me in Heidelberg.

The signature was more florid than the body and she could only make out the initials G von L. At the bottom of the sheet, cramped and in a less formal hand, there was a postscript. *I could wish you had felt able to trust me before.*

"Heidelberg?" Jeanne asked. "You went there after you left Prague."

Antuniet nodded.

"You told me once about a man you met in Heidelberg."

Another nod.

"I hadn't thought it was a pleasant memory for you."

"No, not pleasant," Antuniet said. She seemed to be released from a great weight. "How could it have been? But he was—" She chose her words with the same precision she might have chosen materials in the workshop. "He was young and selfish, but no more than any other man would have been. You remember what I was like! I was terrified and I didn't trust anyone. I never gave him the choice to help me from generosity, rather than in trade for my body. Perhaps he would have. I won't blame him for that. And—" She spoke more briskly now. "—he's of good birth and far enough away to avoid gossip. And if I must do the thing, I would prefer not to add to the number of men in the world that I have lain with. Call it fastidiousness if you like. Heidelberg is on the road to Prague. No one will think it strange if I break my journey there. I can—"

Jeanne stayed the babbling with a finger across Antuniet's lips. "Shh, I understand. And I will go with you. Don't even think of leaving me behind! You still make plans as if you were alone in the world. A child!"

Her imagination began listing the things that would be needed. The old nursery in the top of the house had been used for storage since she was a girl. So long empty!

Antuniet broke in on the reverie. "Jeanne, you shouldn't answer me too quickly. I can make people believe my story—there are amulets that can help with that—but it will mean changes. Difficulties. Think carefully."

Jeanne reached out and brushed a fingertip across the irregular red stone that hung suspended at Antuniet's throat. "This is my answer, now and always, dear heart. Thinking can come later." She smiled wistfully. "Do you know, I sometimes regretted not having children. Pierre...he was an old man. It wasn't that sort of marriage. But Toneke, you know it isn't as easy as all this! Some women try for years. You can't simply—"

"I'm not some women. I'm the foremost alchemist in all of Alpennia. And even short of the Great Work, it will be no lie when I tell people that I got my child by means of my art. DeBoodt describes amulets to make even a barren woman fertile. I've been testing some of the formulas. They should more than suffice for my needs." Antuniet smiled as she always did at a new challenge in her work.

One couldn't help but believe.

* * *

Motherhood was still on Jeanne's mind when Tio and Iohen Perzin joined them at the dining table that evening. Tio had changed with motherhood, despite her intentions. Once, she had been all rough edges and sharp points, straining against what society expected of her, restless in her boredom. She had joined in conspiracy with Rotenek's eccentrics and rebels as they urged each other to new lengths of daring against convention. Now her edge was turned outward. When she lowered her voice to share the latest scandal, there was more of reproach than admiration.

"Iaklin is making her husband look like a fool." Tio glanced across the table at her husband, but Iohen was giving close attention to the meal. "She wants Silpirt to leave the foreign service. Take up some post that will keep him at home. And just now when Albori needs experienced men for the negotiations!"

Jeanne aimed for a noncommittal response. "I should think you would sympathize. You weren't happy about the time Iohen spent in Paris last year."

"Only because I couldn't go with him!" She reached over to lay a proprietary hand on her husband's where it lay on the table. "Iohen is Albori's right-hand man. He relies on him to advise Her Grace in his absence. But Iaklin has no such excuse. She needs to think of their future, not a few lonely months."

Tio hadn't been lonely. Not that she'd ever dipped into *that* kind of scandal. Jeanne smiled, recalling the harmless flirtation Tio had conducted with her to fill the time. Tio was desperately in love with her husband, but boredom had led her into scrapes that she wouldn't care to have him know about. Iaklin had lent a hand in covering a few of those. What had happened between them?

"Perhaps the two of you should find some charitable project together," Jeanne suggested. She saw Iohen begin to choke in laughter then cover it with a sip of wine.

It was the sort of bantering conversation that Antuniet found tedious and Jeanne had learned to let her be. But now she spoke.

"Mesner Perzin, I hadn't thought we would have the pleasure of your company this evening."

"Ah yes." Iohen seemed glad to turn to a new topic. "I'd meant to travel down to Nertul on business—problems with the mill there, a bit of unrest—but there's a debate coming up in sessions that my father wants me to track."

He paused. Jeanne guessed that he was deciding whether the subject was of interest to ladies.

"Ehing thinks something needs to be done about all these canals," he continued. "Thinks they're drawing down the water levels. Total nonsense of course, but as there's nothing can be done about the weather, there's a faction that wants to be seen to take action. Another faction thinks it should all be beneath the notice of the upper council."

And the Perzins fell awkwardly between the two, Jeanne knew. The mill in Nertul was an investment, not a trade, but they couldn't afford to be cavalier about the income.

"And what does he think could be done?" Antuniet asked. "I've heard they want to dredge the channel around the wharves in case the river's low again this summer."

He nodded. "That's what the commons are talking about. Falls within their purview, after all. But Ehing thinks the transport canals are holding water back from the Rotein. Wants a bill to keep all the locks open until the river's normal again. I expect your cousin Saveze will have something to say to that, Mesnera Chazillen. Hasn't she been dabbling in that field?"

Antuniet shrugged. "My cousin's business is her own. She—"

Tio interrupted, concluding that the conversation, like the river, was in danger of becoming dry. "Speaking of Baroness Saveze, Jeanne, have you read that novel?"

Jeanne winced. Were people still talking about that? She signaled to Tomric to have the next course brought in, hoping that Tio might lose interest. "Try the cauliflower. My cook has a new way of preparing it. Very delicate."

Tio would not be put off. "I have my own guess as to the author, of course. It's not in Lady Ruten's style but I hear her sister has been trying her hand at writing. I don't know what they have against your friends, but one must admit they've made quite a spectacle of themselves."

"That they have not!" Antuniet said sharply. She wasn't usually so quick to Barbara's defense, but she had little patience for Tio's sharp tongue.

Iohen shifted uncomfortably. "A duel is something of a spectacle, you must admit, even at the New Year."

"Oh come now," Jeanne said, trying for levity. "You can scarcely say someone wrote the novel because of the duel! That's putting the cart before the horse."

"No, no, that's true," Iohen admitted. "But Baron Mazuk still carries a grudge. He lost an investor that night. And he and Saveze have been butting heads in council…"

He seemed to sense that the conversation had gone beyond what was proper for the dinner table and Antuniet had retreated into silence. But Tio would require a firm hand to return to safe ground.

Jeanne cast about for a better topic. "I've discovered a brilliant new soprano. That is, Count Chanturi has discovered her, but he leaves it to me to see that she takes. Tio, what program do you think would be best: old favorites or a new piece?"

And though Tio's taste in music was not to be relied on, she was flattered enough to be asked that she took the bait.

* * *

Several days later, Jeanne's thoughts returned to the note from Mefro Dominique and she sent a reply. Several more days passed before she found the time to travel down to the neighborhood near the Nikuleplaiz where the dressmaker's shop stood. There had been just enough of a delicate hint to pique her curiosity. A favor, Dominique had said, and so not some new fabrics to be shown only to special patrons, or any of the other imaginable reasons Dominique might have to contact her.

At the chime of the bell on the door, Dominique herself came out from the back rooms to greet her and invite her into the side parlor that served both for fittings and as a workroom. Two girls scrambled to their feet at their entrance. She recognized the dressmaker's daughter, of course, but the other girl was new. She was nothing much to look at, with mousy brown hair pulled tightly back under a linen cap, a whey-faced complexion, a long thin nose and sturdy arms that spoke of hard work, but her eyes were bright and curious before she remembered to look down.

Dominique gave them brief instructions. "Celeste, go to the front and see to anyone who comes. You may leave your work here. Rozild, do you think you can see about fetching some tea for our guest?"

Jeanne saw a flash of panic in the girl's eyes before she nodded and slipped through the rear door to the private rooms. "A new apprentice?" she asked. Dominique certainly had the custom to support one, but usually the extra work was hired out.

"No, Mesnera, not an apprentice, though if I dared take her on, that would be a better choice."

Dared? Well, who knew what these arrangements required. Every trade had its rules. Jeanne made a shrewd guess. "Is it possible that the favor you want has something to do with the girl who is not your apprentice?"

Dominique nodded with a glance toward the back rooms, and so Jeanne held her tongue until—after a lengthy wait—the girl returned with a tea tray that would not have passed muster in any respectable household.

"Thank you, Rozild," the dressmaker said in dismissal. "Take your sewing upstairs until we're done here."

She waited until the footsteps had faded overhead before continuing. "Rozild was in service until recently. Not a parlor maid," she said with a rueful smile and a nod toward the tea tray. "Laundry and mending at one of the houses near the Plaiz Nof. She helped out with the sewing when the Maisetra and her daughters all needed new gowns at once. That's how I met her. She's a good girl, quiet and well-mannered. There's not an ounce of vice in her."

"And yet," Jeanne observed dryly, "she is no longer in service."

"No."

There were several possibilities. She wasn't particularly pretty and she looked scarcely more than fifteen, but men didn't always care about that, and no one would ask whether she'd been willing or not.

"Is she with child?" Jeanne felt an inward shiver. Such a fine line between respectability and shame. A girl like Rozild couldn't bluff her way through with tales of alchemy. But why had Dominique come to her? There were charities for fallen girls.

"No, it's nothing like that. Mesnera de Cherdillac, it's not my business to make judgments of my betters, so I hope you will forgive me if I speak of things that are not spoken of. Rozild was accused of a…a particular friendship with one of the other housemaids, if you understand my meaning. She has no hope of being given a character." Dominique's hesitation seemed born, not of reticence, but of uncertainty over the right words. Her gaze was direct and without accusation. "I hoped that you might know of an employer who would overlook that particular sin."

"Ah," Jeanne sighed.

It had been a risk for Dominique to bring the matter to her. If her own position in society were more fragile, she might have bristled at the thought of her amours being gossip among tradesmen. But she had survived for years by the secret smile and the discreet silence—long before Antuniet had come to complicate her life. Jeanne realized that she didn't even question whether she would help the girl. There was an invisible bond as strong as that of a mystery guild among women who loved their own. She could no more think of refusing than she would if Ailis or Ermilint or any of the rest of her circle came to her for help.

Dominique was still waiting for an answer.

"I will see what I can do," Jeanne said. "My own household is far too small—" Though it would need enlarging by the end of the year…but no, that was too long to wait. "How soon will the girl need to find a place?"

A shrug. "I have work enough to keep her busy, but I'm not allowed to take apprentices. Because I am foreign, you see. Not unless I have special permission from the guild. Eventually there will be questions."

"I'll give you an answer by the end of a week." Who did she know who kept a large enough staff that there would always be a place for one more? And who could not possibly object to the reason for the girl's fall? The answer was obvious.

A few minutes later, as the fiacre rumbled over the cobbles up the Vezenaf, Jeanne composed several possible appeals in the event that Margerit rejected the first. That presumed she was at home, which could not be relied on. But the footman at the door escorted her into the parlor with a promise that the Maisetra would be there presently.

"You're tired," Jeanne exclaimed on seeing her. "And here I am with one more demand on your time."

Margerit returned her embrace. "It doesn't matter. I hope nothing's wrong? Antuniet's well?"

"Yes, perfectly well." It was hard not to see suspicion in every innocent question. How would she ever last until summer! "I've come to ask a favor for a complete stranger."

After refreshments had been brought and sampled, she related the whole sad tale, concluding with, "So I thought of you. I didn't think to ask what the girl is good for beyond laundry and sewing, but no doubt she could be trained up."

Margerit frowned in a way that was less promising than she'd hoped. She stood abruptly, exclaiming, "Does everyone in Rotenek think my house is a refuge for…for…"

"For sapphic servants?" One might as well be shocking, Jeanne thought. "No, I'm the only one to think that."

"Jeanne, you don't understand. I need to be very careful. Things have been…difficult." The sweeping gesture of Margerit's arm was vague and all-encompassing.

"Yes, yes, I know," Jeanne guessed. "That ridiculous novel."

"It isn't only that. I'm still fighting with Archbishop Fereir over the Mauriz mystery, and now I have several important guildmasters challenging my appointment by Her Grace," Margerit said. "I can't afford to have any shadows cast over my school. I'm asking people to put their daughters into my hands. I can't have them think—"

Ah yes, the school. That could be her fatal weakness. "And which of your students, if she were accused, would you cast off to satisfy the gossips?" Jeanne asked quietly. "What standard will you hold them to that you couldn't meet yourself? Respectability is a fragile thread to hang your dreams on. Who will you give the power to break it? Where would you be now if you'd hesitated over what people would think?"

Margerit turned and Jeanne could see the shadows she feared, but there was an air of surrender in her voice. "Very well, I'll see what I can do for your laundry maid."

CHAPTER THIRTEEN

Luzie

March, 1824

Maisetra Orlin was late in bringing Mari for her lesson. It spoiled the morning entirely for other work and there were two commissions to complete before Luzie could steal time to contemplate Tanfrit's song. Songs—really, it was growing into a small cycle. The commissions were nothing of note: a new dance for the Peniluks' ball, a setting of a French poem for the Lozerik girls to perform. Small requests that showed she was still riding the horse of fashion. Tastes would move on soon enough. It was perilous to refuse anyone. The money was good—better than it had been at any time since Henirik's death—but there was no saying it would last.

She needed work that would establish her reputation more solidly. She might dream of an opera someday, but that would require patronage. And yet, a month after the idea had first taken hold, Tanfrit kept invading her thoughts: a march for the entrance of the dozzures of the university, a theme that might grow into Tanfrit's first aria. It was madness. She had no libretto, no book. The lyrics she'd penned for the song cycle were nothing of note, just something to wrap the music around. And for now there was only time to finish the second movement for the Peniluks' dance and snatch a bite to eat before going out to the afternoon lessons.

The dinner table that evening saw all five of them together. That was unusual enough that Luzie brought out a bottle of the better wine and lingered at the table. Work could wait another hour.

"Luzie, will you join us for carnival at last this year?" Elinur asked. "Surely you can take one day away."

She would have refused—carnival brought sad memories—but she saw a bright eagerness in Serafina's face. Elinur wouldn't think to invite her directly. "What about you, Serafina?" she said. "Were you here for last year's carnival? Did it compare to the famous one in Rome?" They fell to discussing revels of the past and somehow she found herself agreeing to the excursion.

The commissions should have come first when Luzie rose from the table, but she took up the pages with her Tanfrit sketches instead and continued tinkering. Issibet and Charluz lingered in the parlor with mending when the others had gone up to bed. There was always mending. Eventually Luzie found herself alone and set all the compositions aside to play whatever her fingers called up. A bit of waltz. A difficult piece by Fauvel that she had been trying to master. When she heard restless footsteps from Serafina's room overhead, she moved into the tune written for her. It should have a name, but nothing had offered itself yet. The footsteps stopped, then descended the stairs.

"I didn't mean to disturb you," Luzie said without looking up from the keyboard.

Serafina settled onto the bench beside her and Luzie paused for a moment to make room.

"You didn't disturb me, but I thought you might be calling me."

"Perhaps I was." Composing always seemed more joyous with Serafina there, even when she only listened. "I don't know about this Tanfrit work. It's all so—" She wasn't even sure where the difficulty lay. "I keep trying to write something small, but it wants to be big. And there's so little to work with. She was a famous philosopher and no one knows anything about her. She taught at the university or maybe she didn't. She died for love and lived to an old age. How do I find a story that will make sense in two or three songs? Where do I even begin? I need—"

"Two or three songs?" Serafina asked. "I thought it was to be an opera."

Luzie shook her head and stared down at her hands. "That's beyond me. Most operas begin with a play, or at least a novel. I have nothing but gossip."

"We have more than that," Serafina offered. "There are bits and scraps scattered throughout Maisetra Sovitre's books. Margerit says that every thaumaturgist of the age was in correspondence with her. 'We are the threads in the web God weaves, even a weak weft can make strong cloth.' Gaudericus wrote that she said that to him when he was in despair. And Lorenzo Valla mentioned in a letter that he met her in Rome just before she returned to Rotenek and that she encouraged him to visit. There's more like that in the lives she touched. Baroness Saveze says there's an old ballad about her and the flood when she died. That's where the story about her suicide came from. 'Let the waters rise up...' I don't remember how the rest of it goes."

Luzie remembered hearing it as a child, but she'd forgotten any connection to Tanfrit. *Let the waters rise up and wash away my sorrow.* The phrase caught at her imagination and she lifted her hands to the keys. A torrent of notes spilled from the words into her fingers. She heard Serafina's sharp intake of breath.

"Yes! Use that."

After a few more repetitions to set it in her mind, Luzie found her pen and set it down on paper for later. "So. Now I have three motifs. But still no story. And I can't well go digging through Maisetra Sovitre's library!"

"I could."

"What?"

"I spend half my time there. And Margerit is too busy planning her college to work with me most days. I could copy out all those bits and scraps for you. If you wanted me to."

"Would you?" Luzie asked eagerly. "Then I'll know if there's enough story to be found."

"Enough for a whole opera?"

Did she dare to dream that far? No need to voice it yet. "Enough for two or three songs, at least."

* * *

The carnivals of Luzie's youth had been filled with music and dancing—that was no surprise. The city's mystery guilds drove the festivities and Rotenek's musicians were well represented. The itinerant players who were little better than beggars claimed rights to play among the tents and booths out beyond the Port Ausiz under the patronage of Saint Iulin. At the other end of the city, the more staid revelry in the Grand Salle was overseen by the Guild of Saint Sesille, whose membership was by private invitation. Falling between the two, all manner of performers from the theaters and concert halls gathered under the name of Saint Chenis. It was primarily a social guild and Luzie still paid the fee to stay on the rolls. Her father's membership had given her that right.

When she'd married Henirik and come under the ambit of Saint Nikule, they had enjoyed the smaller celebration held in the Nikuleplaiz, rather than traveling out the east gate to the larger revels. Saint Nikule's festivities still had a wild and raucous air—the nearness of the wharf district on the opposite bank saw to that—but the crowds were smaller. It felt more like a village festival.

She had always felt safe under Henirik's eye, no matter how rude the joking and pranks became, but she hadn't gone out to the plaiz during carnival since his death. At first there had been the excuse of mourning and of the boys being so young. Later, she had shrunk from the idea of going out into the holiday crowds without an escort. In recent years, Elinur and Charluz would come home, dangling the strings of their masks, laughing at how they'd danced with this stranger and answered back the jests of that one. But the thought of encountering her students' parents…Carnival gave license but people still remembered afterward what license had been taken. Now, with Serafina's enthusiasm added to Elinur's invitation, somehow this year it felt right.

A late storm had left crusts of snow in the shadows and discouraged any festive dress more elaborate than a heavy cloak and a domino mask, though the players in the guild shows shivered through their lines in their usual costumes. The small party took turns explaining the crowd's laughter to a bewildered Serafina, who struggled to follow the clipped workmen's dialect on the stage. Then they bought hot crisp pastries from a man tending a fry-pot in the shadow of the statue of Saint Nikule and sat on the low surrounding wall to eat them. The statue sat lower than the main plaiz and its surrounds gave some protection from the chill wind.

The rivermen were doing a brisk traffic bringing carnival-goers to the landing. It was cold enough that the smell of the mud and weeds on the lower steps was barely noticeable. A small crowd of sturdy children were earning coins providing a steadying arm to those disembarking to climb up under Nikule's watchful eye.

"Why is he down here and not in the middle of the plaiz?" Serafina asked, looking at the bronze saint where he held up his hands in blessing.

"Because he's here for the boats, not the land," Charluz answered. "The barges always come by for his blessing on their way downriver."

Elinur added, "They say cargoes used to be unloaded directly into the Nikuleplaiz so the saint would keep an eye on thieves, but that must have been a long time ago. It's too shallow here for barges, even when the river isn't low." She laughed. "They'll have to throw the bucket at him again, come floodtide this year."

Serafina glanced at her curiously. "What do you mean?"

Luzie took her turn to explain, "The start of floodtide is marked when the river reaches the feet of the statue. If there's no flood, they draw a bucket from the river and pour it out." It sounded a little silly when told like that. "It was because of the fever originally," she said. "The flooding stirs up the putrid mud and brings the fever." Luzie shivered, and not from the cold. It hadn't been river fever that carried Henirik off, but it had taken her brother Ianilm when they were both still children. It had swept through the city that year striking rich and poor alike. "Ever since the city was founded, people leave at floodtide, if they can. The fever's rarely as bad now as it was in Domric's day, but floodtide became a holiday for its own sake. Shall we walk again? The stone's too cold for sitting."

The sound of fiddles and pipes drew them to the smooth-flagged yard beside the church where dancing had started. Not the quadrilles and waltzes favored in ballrooms, but jigs and round dances. Luzie watched Charluz and Elinur drawn off immediately by eager partners but she shook her head politely at the hand offered to her.

"Go on," Serafina urged.

"I don't like dancing with strangers," Luzie explained. "But you should dance."

"I don't know how."

At first Luzie thought it was only modesty until she saw Serafina's panicked look. "Not at all?"

A shake of the head. "My family, we weren't...we didn't..." She shrugged helplessly.

"Don't tell me your husband never took you to balls," Luzie teased. Immediately she was sorry.

Serafina gave a little half smile meant to turn away sympathy. "He told me he enjoyed having a wife who didn't expect to go to parties and wouldn't pester him."

Luzie added that to things Serafina had said in the past. "Was he ashamed of you?"

Another shrug. "No, not the way you mean. But he took no interest in society. He could have. His family has money. But he only cares about his books and manuscripts."

She'd gone this far, why not dare more? "Did he love you at all?"

Serafina turned on her with pointed questions. "Did you love your husband when you married him? What has love to do with it? We marry because that is what one does. Do you know? Paolo doesn't even realize I'm not in Rome. He's been off in Paris hunting down books for the Vatican for two years. He expects he can return anytime he likes and I'll be waiting with clean linens on the bed and all his correspondence organized and dinner on the table as always. This time I grew tired of waiting."

Luzie flinched in the face of Serafina's anger.

"No, I never minded that he didn't take me to concerts or dances or to meet his family. I wouldn't even mind if he went to other women. But I minded that he never taught me mysteries like he promised. I minded that I did all his work in the archives when he was gone and he never said a word of praise. I minded that he expects me to wait at home until it suits him to return."

It had been a mistake to ask the question; there was nothing that could be said to that. "I'm freezing again. If we aren't going to dance, there's less wind under the arches and we could have our fortunes told." And the drifting smoke from the food-sellers would be less noticeable there. Luzie took Serafina by the hand and led her to the covered walk that bordered the plaiz, where they were besieged by market-women with trinkets and charms.

"Ribbons, Maisetra? Fine silks and laces?"

"A candle with a blessing from the Holy Mother, guaranteed to cure the cough."

The woman who offered it turned away briefly to hawk and spit. It might have been only the smoky air, but Luzie made a note not to trust her cures.

"What would you buy? Combs for your hair, Maisetra?"

Luzie pushed past the more forward of the hawkers to the stretch where the charm-wives gathered. They were less inclined to besiege their customers, and instead waited for a need to be presented before they gathered around to argue the efficacy of their wares over those of their rivals.

Serafina gazed at each of them in fascination. What did she see? Luzie wondered. She leaned closely. "Can you tell which of them can work mysteries and which are frauds?"

"It's not…" Serafina looked down, realizing that she had been staring. "It's not quite like that. Some of the charms have power and some don't. At least from what I can see. But some may only show it when used. And some of the women, I can see that they…Margerit would say they have the ear of the saints. You can see the echo of holiness following them. But that doesn't mean that all their works have power. It's complicated. They don't always know what they're doing, you see."

Luzie didn't see at all. She laughed at the thought. No, she didn't see at all. "Who shall we ask to tell our fortunes?"

No sooner had the question left her lips than they were surrounded by offers. Luzie looked sidelong at Serafina, waiting for a sign.

"If you want the hope of truth, that one," Serafina said, nodding at an older woman wrapped in red shawls, sitting behind a barrel that served as a table, back against the building wall.

They were all older women, of course, and a few old men. Who would trust a young charm-wife? And who would try to scrape a living peddling cures and market-charms if they still had the strength for more certain work?

The woman turned sharp eyes on the both of them, looking from face to face, but she didn't rise.

"What do you care to ask, maisetras?" She unwrapped a set of cards and began shifting them around in her hands with quick, jerky movements.

Luzie looked at Serafina who nodded at her to go first.

"There is a…an endeavor that I have begun." Did she really want to know what her Tanfrit songs might become? Why had she chosen that question?

Before she could either offer more details or change her mind, the woman shuffled the cards one last time and laid out several on the barrelhead, keeping a fingertip of her left hand on each to keep the breeze from shifting them.

"Ah, they speak clearly," the fortune-teller began, tucking away the remaining cards and pointing to those displayed in turn. "It is a long path you've set your feet on. You see here? But a dark stranger will help you to your heart's desire."

Luzie glanced at Serafina again. They both grinned like schoolgirls. A dark stranger indeed. It didn't take any mystical visions to suggest that.

"Beware the man who will betray you. He has less power than you think. Not enough to destroy your work, but enough to destroy your dreams. That is all the cards say."

It was the sort of vague answer that anyone could give, but Luzie pulled a few coins out of her reticule and placed them in the woman's hand. "Thank you. Serafina, what will you ask?"

Serafina nodded to the woman, almost like a little bow. "I ask nothing now, but if I have a question that needs a true answer, I will return, Mefro. I—"

Whatever she had meant to say was lost in the noise of a sudden quarrel from farther down the arches. A thin man in a barge worker's coat was shouting, "I know you have it!" as he grasped the wrist of a dark-skinned girl who twisted to break free.

Serafina started forward but Luzie pulled at her sleeve saying, "It's nothing to do with us. Probably a pickpocket."

"I know that girl," Serafina answered, shaking loose in an echo of the other struggle. She pushed through the crowd and joined several of the old charm-wives who confronted the man with little more than scolding tongues as weapons.

Serafina drew herself up with a haughtiness that Luzie had never seen in her before.

"Let her go and be about your business. Celeste, shall I call the city guard?"

The girl shook her head violently but finally managed to twist free. "I told you before, I don't do that sort of thing."

The bargeman swore but seemed daunted by the closed ranks of women arrayed before him. His voice turned more wheedling. "You could if you wanted. You've done it before. For her." And then, directed to Serafina, "This isn't your affair. What's she to you?"

By now Luzie had edged her own way through and joined Serafina at the girl's other side. The man was deeply gone in drink and there was no telling—

"Fire!"

The shout came from down by the statue of Saint Nikule.

"Fire!"

More voices took it up, and in the confusion of running steps and sellers quickly scooping up their wares Serafina gathered the girl to her side and the bargeman disappeared. They made their way edgewise through the crowd out into the main plaiz where pointing hands and shouts drew attention to a plume of smoke on the far side of the river.

"The old warehouses on Escarfild Island!"

"Not the new wharves?"

There was a splash of oars as a wave of rivermen took off from the tie-ups at the stairs to see if rescue were needed.

"Will it spread?" Serafina asked anxiously.

"Not to this side," the girl, Celeste, said confidently. "Probably not off Escarfild with the air so still."

Luzie offered more reassurance. "Escarfild used to be an island with a channel between. It silted up years ago, but there's a break in the buildings. Everything's falling to ruin there. Probably some poor soul lit a fire to keep warm and it spread."

A pall of more than smoke lay over the carnival festivities. Some were running toward the nearest bridges to see what assistance might be needed. The players were shedding their costumes, certain that frivolity was no longer the order of the day. Charluz and Elinur were nowhere to be seen.

Luzie turned to Serafina who still kept an arm around the dark girl's shoulders.

"I thought I'd see Celeste home. In case that man returns."

Remembering his drunken anger, Luzie nodded. "I'll go with you."

"Thank you, Maisetra," the girl said, "but there isn't any need."

"It's not far out of our way," Serafina assured her. "It's no trouble." As they made their way through the thinning crowds at the edge of the Nikuleplaiz Serafina collected herself enough to do introductions. "Celeste is the daughter of Dominique, the dressmaker—the one who made that beautiful red gown for me. And she's quite talented at working little mysteries." She turned to the girl once more. "That man who was bothering you, will he come back, do you think?"

Celeste shrugged. "He always comes back and he always goes away. He thinks I should make charms for him anytime he asks, but I don't do the kind he wants. Not for why he wants them. He wouldn't hurt me, though. Too afraid of Maman." And almost as an afterthought she added, "He's my father. At least he says he is."

Luzie felt embarrassed, like she'd stumbled into a private quarrel. The dress shop lay down one of the narrow streets paralleling the river where the smoke was lighter than it had been in the open plaiz and the panic that the conflagration had sparked grew faint in the distance. Serafina and the girl Celeste chatted about relics and candles and different colors of inks and all manner of things that made no sense at all.

"Is she your student?" Luzie asked when they stopped at last in front of the shop front with its neat gold lettering.

Serafina shook her head and looked wistfully after Celeste as she unlocked the door. "No, there's nothing I can teach her."

Luzie thought she saw the girl stiffen but then she turned and curtseyed before closing the door behind her.

"She works with an entirely different sort of mystery than what I'm studying," Serafina continued as they began walking again. "Mine's all books and philosophy and studying the symbols and meaning. She's like a cook, taking the recipes she's learned and changing a bit of this and that until it tastes just right. She has the ear of the saints and just enough vision to improve on the mysteries she's been taught. In some ways, she knows more than I do. But it's nothing at all like what Margerit teaches."

Luzie considered the image: changing this and that in a recipe. That's what it felt like when Serafina worked with her on the music—if one could imagine a cook who had no taste at all.

* * *

In the weeks that followed, Serafina brought back scraps of Tanfrit's life scribbled on bits of loose paper: the quotations scattered throughout Chizelek and Pontis—Luzie was learning all their names. What could be gleaned from Tanfrit's commentaries on Gaudericus, beyond the obvious fact of their friendship. The accusations of later writers who wavered between charging her with laying the foundations for the mechanist heresy and dismissing her work as of no moment at all. The memorial stone from Urmai. A copy of an old broadside ballad that told of two lovers whose pact with the devil was punished by a flood that had changed the course of the river.

"But Baroness Saveze says that's nonsense," Serafina pointed out, "because there are maps of the city from well before Tanfrit's day that clearly show the river in its present course."

Two different women emerged from the fragments. There was Tanfrit the scholar who had traveled abroad to study, who had been in correspondence with the foremost men of her day, who had returned to Rotenek in triumph to take up a position at the university, who had laid the foundations for understanding the mechanics of mysteries and for what might have become a science of miracles. And then she disappeared entirely until she died in obscurity near Urmai and was remembered only by a beloved sister.

And there was Tanfrit the heretic who had tempted Gaudericus from an orthodox path with the promise of earthly power, and who had been ill-paid for her pains when he made—or refused—a pact with the devil to be given perfect knowledge in return for foreswearing all other loves, mortal and divine. Tanfrit the vengeful who called down (or was punished by) a storm that drove the Rotein out of its banks and through the streets of the city. Tanfrit who, in despair at her unrequited love (or driven by madness), threw herself from the Pont Vezzen into the furious waters and was swallowed up. The stories all contradicted each other. Sometimes it was Tanfrit herself who sold her soul for power and was rejected by the more saintly Gaudericus.

Serafina spread the scattered papers before her. "It's impossible. How can she be both a famous scholar and a villain? How can she be Gaudericus's inspiration yet not figure in his most famous work? Why would the university have appointed her to the faculty if she were a heretic? And if they did, why should they deny it happened to this day?"

But within all the contradictions, Luzie saw the connecting threads. And—seeing them—she finally admitted to herself that nothing short of a complete opera would do justice to Tanfrit's life, even if it would never be performed on stage. Perhaps she could include a few songs at a time in recitals. She began sorting through the notes and laying them into something of an order. "If I were writing a biography, I'd need to find answers," she said. "But for this I only need a story. Look here. What do we know? Her family were weavers—"

"How do you know that?" Serafina asked.

Luzie looked over the pages again. "It's here…no, I guess I assumed. But she's always using weaving as a symbol. The web God weaves. And here where she talks about a guild being the fibers spun together into a thread, and how the thread is strong because of the spinning, not because of the fibers. It made sense. But maybe it would be better to start with the end. The climax will need to be when Tanfrit calls up the waters and throws herself into the flood."

"Why?"

"Because it's the most dramatic part. And, of course, the end of her story," Luzie explained.

"No," Serafina said. "Why does she drown herself?"

"For love, of course. Don't look at me like that! It's a tragedy; it has to be for love." Even as she said it, Luzie knew it for the wrong answer. "Or perhaps that's only part of it. There's the bargain with the devil."

Serafina threw up her hands in exasperation. "That's no better. And I won't have you turning either of them into heretics. Not if you want my help. It's bad enough that Tanfrit's writings are all lost and that no one has dared to publish Gaudericus for nearly two centuries. Did you know that Margerit is planning to print an edition of his works? I don't want feelings stirred up against it."

They went through the different stories again. Perhaps not fallen, only tempted?

"We need a villain," Luzie suggested. "A rival scholar who wants…I know! He's in love with Tanfrit and jealous of Gaudericus. He offers Tanfrit the secrets of forbidden mysteries…or perhaps he offers Gaudericus the secrets but on the condition that he foreswear all other love than the love of learning." She looked over at Serafina to see if the idea were acceptable.

"I don't know…" Serafina said slowly. "It might fit. If the rival carried false tales between them that each had taken the devil's bargain?"

Luzie nodded slowly. "Gaudericus will be the heroic tenor of the work, so he can't be entirely unredeemable. But perhaps he doesn't repent of his path until after Tanfrit dies?" Her mind leapt to the next scene. "Yes, and then the final aria will be his repentance."

"And the university giving up entirely on women scholars," Serafina added sourly.

She'd meant it as a poor joke, but Luzie seized on the idea. "Yes, that gives the opportunity for a chorus to join at the close."

"A chorus," Serafina said. "Where will you get this chorus? I thought you were only planning a few voices."

Luzie laughed and set a finger to her forehead. "In here. The same place I can get the scenery and the costumes and a soprano who can do justice to the role. If I thought about that, I'd never dare to set pen to paper."

"So it will be an opera after all?"

"I…perhaps." It was as far as she was willing to go. "Now the first act, that will be when Tanfrit returns to Rotenek, having been invited to teach. She'll meet Gaudericus after a long separation. I think they must have been childhood friends. That would work. There should be another female role. A confidante, someone she can sing her secrets to."

"What about the sister? The one who had the gravestone made—Susanna."

"That might work," Luzie said thoughtfully. She took up her pen and between them the ideas followed one after the other.

* * *

Serafina's teasing question haunted her. *Where will you get a chorus?* When the audaciousness of the project overwhelmed her, Luzie set Tanfrit aside until the doubts had faded. Or, not faded, but they could be ignored once more. To attempt an opera without a book—no libretto, not even a script from the stage to adapt—she was mad. She was no poet, and borrowing the scraps of Tanfrit's own words wouldn't go far. But the inspiration always came back when she returned to the music. *Let the waters rise up and wash away my sorrow.* That brought a shiver every time she played it. Endings were easy, beginnings, more difficult.

The commissions were all finished for the moment. The impatience to be done with them was replaced by the worry that there would be no more. But it meant that evenings could be spent on Tanfrit.

Serafina had become an essential part of the project, sitting beside her at the fortepiano and turning through the pages of notes, then urging her on with demands and suggestions. It was a partnership like none she'd ever known. It wasn't only that Serafina was more familiar with the scholar's history—able to pull out the quotations from ancient books that might inspire a scrap of tune—she also kept the story more true to the woman Tanfrit might have been.

"Here in the first act, when Tanfrit returns to Rotenek, it should be triumphant," Serafina pointed out. "What you have sounds more melancholy. This is a woman whose name is on everyone's lips, at the peak of her fame. Perhaps a bit self-satisfied and overproud. That would fit with the later story."

Luzie tried to summon up the mood Serafina described. Perhaps her own experiences were the wrong model; she still found success hard to believe. "How do you see her?"

Serafina looked into the distance with an impish grin. "A bit like Margerit Sovitre, I think. Very...intense and sure of herself. Taking for granted that everyone will see the world the way she does."

The memory returned of the Royal Thaumaturgist sitting her in her parlor, calmly discussing the theological implications of a mystery in music. Yes, she might do something with that. "And then, when the offer comes to her—of the forbidden learning—it doesn't occur to her that Gaudericus might view the matter differently."

"Exactly!" Serafina nodded vigorously. "But here—" She returned to the notes for the second act. "I think the romance doesn't make sense the way you present it."

Serafina had argued against the romance from the beginning, but there was no help for it. What else could drive the tragedy to its proper end?

"I think," Luzie suggested slowly, "they must have been childhood sweethearts. Before Tanfrit left for her schooling. Then the duet in the first act can suggest the stirrings of love as well as Gaudericus welcoming her home as a colleague."

"Hmm," Serafina said doubtfully. "Is there truly such a thing as childhood sweethearts? Did you have one?"

"There were one or two boys I liked...my father's students. I don't think they ever knew. I was much too well-behaved for that! I didn't meet my husband until I was twenty." She thought back to that meeting. Henirik's face was indistinct and all she could recall was the awkwardness of speaking to a near stranger who asked if she would allow him to court her. They'd become easier together later, much later, not knowing how short the time would be. An unexpected wave of loneliness washed over her. A hungry memory of touch. She shook it off. "And you?"

Serafina turned her face away and Luzie couldn't tell if she were staring into the past or unwilling to share her thoughts beyond a shake of her head.

"Well, it doesn't matter," Luzie continued. "It's what the audience will expect. No one would believe they fell in love over philosophy!"

"Sometimes—" Serafina's voice was wistful. "Sometimes it might happen that two people might meet mind to mind, but that the only way they know how to speak of it is in the language of the heart—of the body. Philosophy does not teach one how to speak of love."

She looked back, and Luzie felt the weight of a question between them.

"Is that..." she began. "Is that what it was between you and Olimpia?" She'd never asked Serafina about the painter since that evening.

"No, Olimpia was loneliness, and needing someone to hold me."

Luzie felt her face grow warm from hearing her own thoughts echoed back to her.

Serafina bit her lip, steeling herself to continue. "But it's how it is with you. Sometimes...sometimes the heart wants something so deeply, so desperately, and yet the only thing you have to offer is your body."

Luzie's heart beat faster. The waiting silence between them drew out painfully. She reached out and took Serafina's hand. It was trembling even more than her own.

Serafina brought their linked hands to her lips and left a kiss where their fingers entwined, dark and light together like the keys of the fortepiano, then lifted her eyes, with a frightened look.

"Serafina, I..."

"Shh, don't worry. I won't—"

"No, wait. Serafina, I need to think about this. But...but thank you." Her stomach was fluttering like a baby bird. What did it mean? She wasn't...she didn't...

"Don't worry," Serafina repeated and rose from the bench, allowing their fingers to slip slowly apart. She gave a hesitant smile, then left the room.

Luzie twisted her hands together until the shaking stopped, then she picked out the beginnings of the theme she had begun to associate with Gaudericus and alternated it with Tanfrit's triumphant return. The latter shifted and slowed and the two phrases twined together.

CHAPTER FOURTEEN

Margerit

April, 1824

Margerit read through the letter to Sister Petrunel again, then reached for a pen to add her signature at the end. Though the Orisules had given permission to approach Petra, her former governess might well consider her current position at the Orisul school in Eskor a pleasant retirement compared to becoming headmistress of a fledgling college. But Petra could be a bridge to the Order as a whole. There were teaching positions still to be filled. And Margerit trusted her experience. It would be one fewer worry.

Would Petra agree? Margerit hadn't seen her governess since the day she'd left Uncle Fulpi's house in Chalanz to return to the convent school. So much had happened since then! And what had Petra heard about her? Not so much about…other things, but about the mysteries? Surely Petra had recognized her *visio* at some point during their years together. Why had it never been part of their lessons? Looking back, she saw that her governess had deliberately discouraged her from those paths of thought.

Margerit held up the letter to shake off the sand and check that the ink was dry then held it out to the thin, gray-haired woman who stood waiting.

"Thank you, Maisetra Ionkil. That's the last of them for now. I'll write the letter to my cousin myself and you can include it in the package to the Fulpis. When you come tomorrow, bring the college accounts to review."

"Not tomorrow," Maisetra Ionkil reminded her. "I need to secure the lumber for the new roof. It's contracted, but I won't rest easy until we have it on site. And I don't care to leave the builders unsupervised at the moment."

A flutter of panic was stilled by the woman's calm certainty. "Was there any trouble?" Three warehouse fires on the south side of the river. Only the last had damaged goods, but that damage had included half the cured lumber in the city.

"No trouble you need to concern yourself with."

Margerit set aside further inquiry. Necessity was forcing her to leave much in other hands. "Then we'll meet again the next day. I'll see to the letters to the Fulpis myself. That will be all for now."

It wasn't entirely true that the builders needed Ionkil's personal supervision. The architect LeFevre had recommended was a solid man for the job. He'd focused on returning the structures to good shape without adding too many decorative touches, though she'd had to promise him a chance to redesign the gardens later before he would accept the contract. He'd been the one who suggested Maisetra Ionkil's name when she'd mentioned her search for a business agent.

"Ionkil's widow is who you want," he'd said. "She should have inherited the trade but—" No need to finish the thought. No one would believe she'd been his equal partner. And if they believed it, they still wouldn't hire her.

There had been a tiny worm of distrust that he might be placing a confederate in charge of his own payroll. The first meeting with Marga Ionkil had lessened that concern with her sharp and perceptive questions. The woman's skill in securing the lumber they'd need before scarcity put the price out of reach set the seal on Margerit's approval. LeFevre's vote of confidence was scarcely necessary. Future plans hadn't been discussed, but for now Margerit saw no reason to look elsewhere when the repairs were finished and it was time to find a manager for the college itself. Assuming the widow was willing to trade her current rooms for an apartment in Urmai. An apartment at the academy. Margerit kept reminding herself to call it that. The Tanfrit Academy. An ambitious name for an ambitious project. If not for the gravesite, she might not have had the impudence to claim it.

Maisetra Ionkil had slipped just as easily into place as secretary for Margerit's ever-increasing correspondence. For a brief time it looked like Frances might fill that role. The botanist had been at loose ends and underfoot all winter, impatient with the delays in the printing of her book. But Frances was hopeless at everyday details. An unwritten letter had lost them the chance of a lecture from a scholar traveling through to Barcelona. She'd quietly stopped asking for that type of help.

Margerit sighed at the memory, comforting herself that Frances would soon be off collecting specimens for the summer and by the time the college opened, there was some hope that her treatise on lichens would be bound, and copies shipped off to satisfy her English subscribers.

And now there was no putting off the letter to Iuli.

My dearest cousin, I hope you and your parents are well. I greatly enjoyed the verses you sent with your last letter and I have taken the liberty of having them set to music by the talented Luzie Valorin, whom you might have heard of even in far-off Chalanz. I enclose the music with these letters and hope to hear you perform the song someday.

It pains me to tell you I will not have that opportunity this summer, even though you learn it in time for your coming-out ball. As you know, I have decided my college must be ready in time for the fall term, and I will have no chance for travel this summer, neither to Chalanz nor to Saveze. I would very much have loved to host your ball at Fonten House as I did your sister's, but our lives move on and Fonten House is no longer part of mine.

Margerit paused, chewing on the end of her pen and thinking what more to say. She couldn't tell Iuli the truth: that Uncle Fulpi had suggested in the strongest terms that her presence would be unnecessary. He hadn't gone so far as to say unwanted. While she had owned property in Chalanz, the prestige of hosting Sofi's ball in the mansion on Fonten Street had more than balanced the Fulpis' concerns for the family reputation. The abstract family pride in an absent relation who was an heiress and the Royal Thaumaturgist was always put in peril by her presence. Her presence brought with it an inconvenient baroness who had a habit of wearing men's clothing, not to mention an affection between the two of them that couldn't entirely be excused by the conventions of friendship.

With Fonten House sold, Uncle Fulpi was happy to accept her offer to underwrite the expenses of Iuli's coming-out, but had expressed his strong preference that only her purse and not her person attend. Iuli would be disappointed, but there was no help for it. Her cousin's parents had the power to forbid their continued correspondence entirely and Margerit knew how much it meant to Iuli to have at least one person in the world who encouraged her writing and wanted her to continue dreaming beyond the future that Chalanz offered.

Perhaps I will be able to visit next year at floodtide. I know it seems so long to wait! It would have been an eternity when I was your age and I will miss your entire dancing year. Write to me when you have time and make sure to save up all the memories from your ball to tell me.

Your loving cousin, Margerit Sovitre.

* * *

There had, of course, been no expectation that Sister Petrunel would come in person to discuss the offer. Eskor was nearly a week's travel if one hadn't the need or the funds for a traveling coach and staged horses. But her answer arrived in little more than the time required for the mail.

My dearest Margerit, if you will still allow me that familiarity,

As you may guess from the promptness of my response, your request has already been discussed by the superiors of my Order and they have granted me leave to accept. Indeed, they have encouraged me to do so in a manner scarcely falling short of instructions, though that removes none of my joy. The guidance of young women's minds in the paths of knowledge and wisdom has ever been the Orisules' calling and it would be a heavy responsibility for someone untried without the support and advice of experience.

There were several pages of that advice regarding preparations to be made and a request for thoughts on the curriculum and faculty. Margerit wondered if Sister Petrunel would be relieved or dismayed at how few decisions remained on that end. The contracts had not yet been offered, but the maiden term was planned with a light schedule, drawing from those who had participated in the lecture series. Time enough for more formal goals when those first steps were found to be steady.

There was an answer of a more personal nature at the end.

I have, indeed, followed the news of your career with interest and an unbecoming pride, though I cannot claim to have set you on that path. Perhaps I should have suggested to your uncle that you be sent to the convent school, where you might have received better guidance. I could have taught you theory, but that might have been worse than ignorance. A talent such as yours brings dangers as well as joys, as you have learned. But if you have wondered at my silence on that matter, consider the path you faced then. You would not have been allowed a contemplative life. An educated woman can be an ornament to her household and family, but would a mystic be content in that setting? I could not foresee that God would grant you the freedom to spend your days in service to Him. I lacked that faith, and so I thought only of your happiness. I hope that you will forgive,

Your friend Petrunel.

Margerit read through the paragraph again. It made a type of sense if Petra were so certain that delving into the mysteries required a contemplative life, if that were the only model she had for a woman studying thaumaturgy. She sighed and folded the letter in her lap.

Barbara had come into the library while she was reading and took the movement as a cue to come bend over her for a series of kisses, working slowly down from her forehead to her mouth.

"I've been missing you," Barbara said as she straightened again.

Margerit laid her hand over Barbara's where it rested on her shoulder. "No long lazy mornings."

"Not when the council sessions have everyone's blood up. Why did I ever let Lord Marzim talk me into caring about politics? Everything else gets squeezed into the edges of the day. I rarely see Brandel except at Perret's fencing salle in the morning and at the supper table. Do you know? He managed a touch on me today. I think it surprised him more than it did me. I'm afraid that will ruin my suggestion that he spend more time with the pistol than the sword." Barbara pulled away to sit in the matching overstuffed chair but stretched her long legs out to put their ankles in contact under the ruffled edge of Margerit's skirts.

Margerit set the letter aside on the table between them. "At least Maisetra Ionkil has been freeing me from quite so many trips to Urmai. I only go to see the progress for myself now, not because they need me for orders and decisions."

"I envy you your new factotum! But are you suggesting you've been waiting here for me to have time for you?" Barbara teased.

Margerit smiled, knowing no answer was needed. "I thought you had your agents in Turinz well established."

The answer was a sigh. "I have a man here in Rotenek who's taken over the accounts and correspondence from LeFevre, but he hasn't the skills to manage a working estate. There's Akermen in Turinz—he does well enough— but I need a second to back him up. I think Akermen is too deeply entangled in village affairs, for all that he has wider ambitions. And I worry...well, no need to go into it all unless you care deeply about rust in the wheat and apple moths." She laughed bitterly. "Akermen has been hinting around about curses and sorcery, but I can't tell whether he thinks magic is to blame or he wants me to pull strings with the Royal Thaumaturgist for mystical assistance."

"Do you plan to replace him?"

A wry smile quirked the corner of Barbara's mouth. "No. He's a bit of a revolutionary—a relic of his days at university—and eventually it will be good to unsettle things a bit in Turinz, but not until I've gotten the place back on its feet. You know I've set Brandel to studying accounting with LeFevre. I've thought—"

"I know what you've thought," Margerit interrupted, "but is that fair to Brandel? I can't see him content to spend his days over ledgers and letters."

Barbara shook her head in agreement. "Not all his days, but it's no bad thing to be able to oversee your own affairs, as you well know. And LeFevre... he needs to have people he'll trust."

The rest was left unspoken between them. It was still impossible to imagine anyone else in charge of their properties, but LeFevre had given up the pretense that his eyes would improve with rest. A detailed memory of the matters under his charge would serve for some time yet, but the day would come...

Margerit turned the subject away from that painful topic. "So what is the council up in arms about now?"

"Tolls on a dead horse."

Barbara's voice was so carefully even that Margerit suspected a joke. "Truly?"

"If a horse drops dead while entering a toll gate but has not completely passed through, does the full toll accrue, or half or none?" Barbara's slow, rolling declamation mimicked that of Lord Ehing. "When the horse was ridden by Peskil's son and the toll accrues to Lord Seuz, it becomes a matter for serious debate. In truth, the practical business of governing only seems to come from the common council these days. Once they have a bill worked out, someone will take it up for debate among the nobles. Marzim bullied me into attending the sessions this spring because of the water rights question, but if it weren't for this puzzle Kreiser set me I'd have quit in disgust."

"Are you still working with him on that?" Margerit couldn't help some uneasiness at that connection. Whatever concern the Austrian had in weather mysteries and other disasters, it was unlikely to be to Alpennia's benefit.

"He's still only teasing me with hints, but it isn't just the frozen passes and river levels. You know that as well as I."

One fire was bad luck. A bad winter season for the cough happened now and again. The histories spoke of tremors in the earth back in Domric's day. Crops were known to fail for no reason. But taken all together it felt that the luck was draining out of Alpennia. It was maddening to think that the flaws in Mauriz's protection might be to blame and no one had listened to her. More maddening still to know that some were blaming her own *castellum*.

"What hints has he let slip?"

"An unusual increase in letters between certain parties. A sudden interest in the esoteric among the clubs in Paris and London. Nothing that's provided any answers yet, except that there may be more than one party in conspiracy. We need more of the pattern. Kreiser is gathering information outside Alpennia. My task is to collect it here, and the issues raised in council sessions provide a great deal."

Barbara leaned forward and her eyes brightened as she gestured a map through the tangle. "Take just the water issues alone. You'd think the old guard would consider such matters beneath them, like Chalfin, pontificating that the Rotein will rise and fall as it always has and it makes no sense to try to pass laws on the river. But too many of the noble families rely on water, one way or another. As long as enough rain falls, those who rely on crops are happy, but what happens to the shipping families if the stretch down to Iser is full of shoals? Salun has asserted that all the new canals are holding up water that should flow to the Rotein, which is nonsense, of course. It all flows downstream eventually, but he's proposed destroying the locks on anything connecting to the Tupe, the Esikon or the Trintun."

That caught Margerit's attention. "The Trintun? But that's the one—"

"The one that Mazuk's invested in. And he's taken it as a personal attack. He can't afford to lose that access for his ironworks. He's not the only one, but he's been very pointed about implying that the causes aren't natural. And evidently I'm somehow to blame for that."

"Has there been trouble?"

"No worse than anything before." Barbara shifted uncomfortably in her chair, then leaned forward to squeeze Margerit's hand briefly. "There are people who resent my presence in council. They always have, but at first I was only a novelty. Someone they thought they could ignore. The young baroness. Saveze's bastard. If I'd kept my nose out of the debates and only shown up for the ceremonies, it wouldn't have mattered. They can't challenge my right to be there, so they try to find some other weakness. Like you. Like rumors of sorcery. Like that duel at the New Year's court. Don't fear that Princess Annek will let it come to anything. It's tiring, that's all."

* * *

In time for the last lecture of the season, Antuniet had finally agreed to present a talk on the basics of her alchemical art and the spectacle of the Great Works. They could claim the Salle Chapil, thanks to Lent putting the usual damper on balls and more frivolous uses. It had taken a year's worth of coaxing to convince Antuniet and, at the last, agreement had come too swiftly for Margerit to be comfortable with claiming it as a personal victory.

Returning from securing those arrangements, Margerit found Tavit sitting on the bare wooden waiting bench to one side of the entryway. He rose hurriedly at her entrance.

"I thought there were sessions today," Margerit said to him as she pulled off her gloves and laid them on the sideboard to look through the letters displayed there.

"No, Maisetra," he replied. "The baroness had an errand east of town. Her cousin attends on her. She thought both boys would enjoy the ride. "

Both boys? Ah yes, Aukustin. His name was regularly on Brandel's lips now that they shared a tutor. The Dowager Princess Elisebet had relaxed her worried grasp on her son enough to let him run more loose than ever before, though Barbara's company scarcely counted as loose.

But if Barbara had no need of Tavit, why was he waiting at the door? She glanced over at him where he waited expectantly and nodded permission to continue.

"Maisetra," he began and licked his lips nervously. "Maisetra, I was wondering if I might have a word with you. Privately."

The last was said so very precisely that her attention was seized.

"Yes, of course," she said, setting the letters down. There was nothing in them that couldn't wait.

She nodded down the hallway toward the office and led the way, closing the door behind them. She sensed the library would be too informal for this discussion. She pulled a chair out from the desk and sat but didn't waste the effort to invite Tavit to do the same.

The silence drew out uncomfortably until at last he began, "Maisetra, how much do you know of what passed after the duel at the New Year?"

"After the duel? I know…" She considered carefully what he might mean, but only one topic seemed a likely explanation for the hesitation: the question of his—even in her mind she stumbled over the word—his past. "I know that you have not always been what you are now," she said slowly.

It was an awkwardly delicate way of phrasing it and even as she spoke, it seemed false. The Tavit who stood before her was the one she had always known: tall, slender and wiry, with close-clipped, curly dark hair and the sort of intense expression that Barbara had cultivated in her own days as an armin.

The sort of look that warned off trouble before it could start, especially when one didn't have the intimidating bulk that someone like Marken could wield. She might have expected there to be a curious double vision: the Tavit she knew and the Tavit she knew of. But in the end there was only one.

"The baroness and I do not keep secrets from each other," she added as the silence stretched out, wondering if that would spur him to reveal whatever concern he had.

He nodded briefly, taking her full meaning, and said, "Then you know there has been trouble at the council sessions."

The leap to more recent affairs confused Margerit at first. "Yes, Barbara told me something of it."

"I'm not speaking of the substance of the nobles' debates," Tavit said, waving his hand in dismissal. "The details aren't important." His brows were drawn together in a frown. In a sudden explosion of intensity he said, "I can't do my job if she doesn't trust me!"

Margerit blinked in confusion. "Do your job?"

Tavit moved restlessly about the room. Whatever had driven him this far still struggled to find expression. Discretion was an armin's second most important skill, and to break it even this far…

"The baroness…there are those on the council who find her presence unwelcome. I'm sure you know that."

It was much the same as what Barbara had explained. For her youth and her sex, yes definitely. For her opinions and alliances, perhaps. Margerit nodded to encourage Tavit to continue.

"If it were only the subjects under debate, it would be no matter. But debates are duels like any other, always looking for a weakness, a stumble."

Now that Tavit had begun, the words came in a flood. And it was clear he'd been studying the dynamics of the council as if it did, indeed, involve blades. "There have been insinuations, remarks in passing. Her friendship with that Austrian spy has been thrown in her face. You…your name has not been mentioned in specific, but when people speak of 'meddling in the mysteries' there are knowing looks."

"None of that would matter," Tavit continued. "But Baron Mazuk has never forgiven her for the loss of his investor, and he was there at the New Year's duel. He heard everything. And Feizin has some old grudge that I've yet to untangle. Something dating from the old baron's time. And there are others."

He took a deep breath and closed his eyes briefly to gather courage. "It started when Feizin asked the baroness just what it was she was plotting with the Austrians. When she said they were looking into the unnatural weather patterns in the Alps, someone in the back rows said, 'You'd know unnatural; like calls to like.'"

Margerit couldn't prevent a little gasp. Gossip was one thing, but to voice such a thing in open session?

"I don't know who said it first, but it was Feizin who pressed the point when debate was closed for the day. I tried—" He shrugged helplessly.

That was how such things went, Margerit knew. A provocation, an insult or slight that couldn't be ignored. It was an armin's duty to see if it could be turned aside. To distract or prevent it before it happened, if possible. To give the offender opportunity to back down and, if that failed, to see the matter through. Nothing said in council itself was actionable, but afterward...

"If Feizin was determined to push it to a confrontation—" Margerit began.

"But he wasn't," Tavit said. "It was only a feint, anyone could see that. A test to see where her defenses were weak. It was the baroness who pushed it to the drawing of steel. And it was all I could do to keep her from bloodying her own sword."

"Another duel?" Margerit asked anxiously. The question gave the lie to her claim that Barbara kept no secrets between them. Or...no, there had been something in what she'd said the other day. "Did you—?"

Tavit shook his head. "To a touch only; his man took a scratch, that was all. Enough to put the matter to rest for now. But it should never have come to steel!" he insisted. "She won't let me do my job. She no longer trusts me, yet she refuses to release my contract."

Margerit shifted in her chair as a picture began to form. The discomfort came not from the confidences that Tavit was sharing, but from the need to share Barbara's own inner thoughts, as best she could guess them. It didn't feel quite proper. What were the rules for this sort of thing? Who would one even ask?

"I think," she said slowly. "I think it isn't that the baroness doesn't trust you, but that she doesn't trust herself."

Tavit frowned slightly and waited as she struggled to explain.

"You must remember," Margerit said, "that Barbara was an armin herself. Think how much depended on her ability to keep track of everyone and everything about her. It...it worries her that she's ceased to notice such details. That she's felt safe enough—secure enough—that no one's life depends on what she sees or fails to see. She didn't notice that Maistir LeFevre's eyesight was failing until he told her. That pained her, I know. And though she knew that you had secrets in your past—who doesn't have secrets? She hadn't guessed at the shape of them. That made her vulnerable."

"No," Tavit said harshly. "I make her vulnerable. I should be her shield and instead I've become a breach in her walls."

"She must not think so." Margerit struggled for an explanation he might accept. "The baroness has always been very fierce in protecting those she is responsible for."

"Protecting?" It was a view he hadn't considered. "I don't need her protection!" Now he sounded exasperated.

"Don't we all need it?" Margerit asked. Protection was a tightly woven web: Barbara's rank, her own money, the Pertineks' veil of respectability, the formal dance of the armins. "No, it's not what she's supposed to do, but it's a habit she has a hard time discarding. She doubts herself. And she blames herself for that man you killed at New Year's." Barbara had said as much in private in the days that followed.

The idea slowly settled into Tavit's understanding. He laughed bitterly. "I'd forgotten the first piece of advice that Marken gave me when I was hired."

"What was that?"

"He told me not to let the baroness do my job for me. But that she'd try."

Yes, Margerit thought. Marken would have seen that from the beginning. "Would you like me to speak to her?" she asked.

A violent shake of the head. "No. No, this is between the two of us."

Between him and Barbara, yes. She had already stepped beyond what was proper.

* * *

The Salle Chapil was nearly full for Antuniet's talk, but with a different mixture of people than usual. Were there truly so many interested in transmutations? Or were people merely unsettled and looking for distraction? The city felt uneasily on edge as it hadn't since the days, six years past, when Prince Aukustin's health had begun to fail. Tonight's audience wasn't only those who wanted a glimpse of the Royal Alchemist—one they rarely got in more social venues. Margerit recognized a few older faces from the university faculty. And there was Mesnera Farin, the mathematician, and several of her friends. Now there was a prize to have captured! Margerit's own following had largely been drawn from the younger set—the women who still thought of themselves as students. But the eccentrics of the older generation—the scholarly ones, that is—had largely kept away. This might be Jeanne's doing, though the vicomtesse herself hadn't come. Was that by Antuniet's request or Jeanne's own decision?

Those who hoped for the story of the famous alchemical gemstones were disappointed. Not that the lecture wasn't entertaining. Antuniet had a crisp, dry delivery that hovered at the edges of wit. The occasional nervous titter from the audience was rewarded with a brief pause that could have been either appreciation or impatience. She knew her subject well, and knew how to make the quest for physical and spiritual transformation sound as exciting as a heroic novel. A willing audience brought out Antuniet's hidden dramatic talents.

Tonight she spoke of the Great Works, the ones that could set the seal of triumph on an alchemist's career. The distillation of elixir, the stone of transmutation, the growing of a homunculus. Margerit was surprised to hear Antuniet discuss philosophy more than science. She always seemed concerned with results above reasons. But tonight she touched on the spiritual motivations of the scientist. On the aspirations and changes that the art worked on the practitioner. On the perfection of the soul that went with the purification of matter. The echo of divine creation. It was a better choice for this audience than a more technical lecture would have been, but so very different from Antuniet's usual style!

Antuniet was more gracious to those who stayed after the lecture than Margerit might have expected. She usually had no time for idle conversation. But perhaps, like Anna, she had been practicing at Jeanne's salons. Anna was certainly growing more confident and assured in company. But Antuniet had never lacked in confidence, only in patience.

Margerit glanced over the remaining attendees and left her post by the main doors. Those who might expect a personal farewell had left. Antuniet had only a few people around her now and Margerit extracted her tactfully with an offer of a carriage ride home.

"Are you tired?" Margerit asked her, as Antuniet seemed to wilt visibly once they had come out into the porch of the salle.

Antuniet answered with a small grunt, then added, "I've grown accustomed to having Jeanne as a shield. But we thought…well, never mind."

It still seemed strange to hear "we" dropping from Antuniet's lips so easily. Margerit had feared the partnership wouldn't last. The start had been rocky enough, but now it seemed stronger with every passing month. Soon they would be setting out on a new journey together.

"When do you leave for Prague?" Margerit asked. "I don't imagine there's any point in waiting for floodtide proper, and who knows when that will come."

"In two weeks," Antuniet replied. "And still so much to be done. I've been meaning to ask you. Would you look after Anna for the summer?"

"Of course," Margerit answered, trying to calculate how to fit another responsibility into her days.

As if the thought had been voiced aloud, Antuniet waved her hand to brush it away. "She won't be any trouble, I promise you. It's only that there's no work to be done at the palace in my absence and I think she might be glad of the occasional outing. Just give her the freedom of your library and she'll be happy."

The Plaiz was never entirely empty except in the hours halfway between midnight and dawn, but this late in the evening it was quieter than usual. Only a few carriages rattled across the cobbles on the far side by the palace. Café Chatuerd was dark, but a few lesser establishments still catered to late diners. The stars were crisp overhead and a thread of mist wound its way across the empty space.

A thread of mist? Margerit looked again. It was a low, pale wisp of *fluctus*, floating above the ground like the fog that rises off a stream in winter. Margerit's gaze followed the trace across the open square and down toward the river. Her breath caught.

"What's wrong?" Antuniet asked.

Her first thought was of another fire in the warehouse district. A small stretch of the Rotein—barely visible between the buildings where the road turned down to meet the Vezenaf—was ablaze with light. It wasn't the reflection of flames, but a more intense glow like the one threading through the Plaiz.

"Do you see it?" Margerit asked.

Antuniet blinked. "I don't…"

Margerit grabbed her arm and pulled her toward the waiting carriage. "Come on," she said.

Marken scrambled to a perch behind and the coachman asked, "To Mesnera de Cherdillac's?"

"No," Margerit ordered. "Down toward the river."

Margerit let down the window and leaned out for a better view as they rumbled over the stones.

Antuniet did the same on her side of the carriage. "What in heaven?" she exclaimed as they came closer to the river's edge.

Like the strand she'd seen in the Plaiz, the currents of divine power drifted slowly above the surface of the water in streams and eddies that mimicked the waters below, except that the flow—if it could be said to be that—seemed to be moving upstream.

"A new attack?" Antuniet asked.

Margerit's voice was tight and her heart beat sharply in her chest. "I don't know. I can't even tell where it's coming from."

The *fluctus* spread out as far as she could see in either direction, as far as the bends in the river. She turned to Antuniet. "I can't usually see the workings of a mystery at a distance, but Serafina might know. Line of sight doesn't seem to matter as much to her."

She rapped on the roof of the carriage and called up to the driver, giving Maisetra Valorin's direction.

The river was mostly hidden from view until they rumbled across the Nikuleplaiz. Now she could see that the water was clear further downriver. Then houses blocked their view again. A brighter trace followed one of the chanulezes that led off through Serafina's neighborhood. No, not just a trace. A bright glow pulsed and dimmed above the brick-walled channel, like the flow from a pump head that tumbled and roiled through a sluice. And the source of that spill was the dark ivy-covered house of Maisetra Valorin.

CHAPTER FIFTEEN

Serafina

Late April, 1824

Serafina leaned on the end of the fortepiano and watched Luzie's hands move over the keyboard. She never tired of watching those hands, of imagining what other tunes they might play. No, that was too soon. Too soon. Issibet was on the sofa with her sewing, constantly in Serafina's awareness. Even a touch that might once have seemed harmless now burnt like a coal. Guilt magnified everything.

Light filled the room in swirls and eddies. Serafina kept up a quick commentary on what she saw, using the code words they had slowly developed between them. When they spoke of music, they fell into Italian together, in a jumble of dialects that still failed to hold the words needed to describe what they were attempting. They fumbled and stretched to find a meeting point.

"The third time through is weaker," she said. "It needs...It needs to start from a different place but move toward the same finish. Not like the call and response of a *tutela* mystery. More like a *castellum* where the echoes are the same but different each time, and build up layer on layer. Or like a painting."

She thought of watching Olimpia at work: the sketches, the underlayers, the glazes, the highlights. Each utterly different and yet all shaping the figure on the canvas.

Luzie paused and then tried the strain again with the chords modulated to a wilder, more mournful sound.

"Yes," Serafina said slowly. "That might work. Now again from the beginning."

It was a slow, tedious process, this working out of Tanfrit's aria. And it was only the first of the major songs they'd tackled. The mystic undertones could only be seen in the structure as a whole. With each revision they went back to the beginning—the beginning of that song, at least. Heaven knows how long it would take if they needed to play the entire sequence to see the success of each change!

Luzie was endlessly patient. She might not be able to see the details of the *fluctus*, but she knew music. Serafina marveled at how Luzie turned her frustrated, incoherent suggestions into exactly the right structure of sound that filled the house with power and made the hairs along her arms stand on end.

The sharp crack of the door knocker cut through the room. Luzie looked up in startlement as the notes and their echoes drifted into corners of the room.

"Who can that be?" Issibet asked.

Charluz had gone up to bed already. Had Elinur lost her key? It was far too late for visitors. Serafina saw a start of fear in Luzie's eyes.

"Something's happened!" she said anxiously. "A message?"

They heard the maid's quick steps from the back passage to the door.

Margerit's voice was the last thing Serafina had expected to hear.

"Is Maisetra Valorin at home?" The question held a sharp edge.

Serafina hurried out into the entryway. "Margerit, what's wrong?"

Not only Margerit, but Mesnera Chazillen. They bustled into the front parlor and with no warning Margerit demanded, "What are you doing?"

Serafina exchanged confused glances with Luzie, who rose from the music bench asking, "What do you mean?"

Issibet quietly set her sewing aside and left the room without a word.

Margerit seemed to collect herself and repeated her question in a calmer tone. "Just now—before we knocked on the door—what were you doing?"

Luzie's confusion was not abated. "Composing," she said, gesturing toward the manuscript notebook on the instrument.

"We've been working on Maisetra Valorin's new project." Serafina searched Margerit's expression for some clue. "You remember—the one about Tanfrit that I've been borrowing all those books for."

Mesnera Chazillen cleared away some of the confusion, by noting dryly, "The entire Rotein has been awash with mystic light tonight, and you seem to be the source."

"The Rotein?" Luzie echoed, bringing her hand to cover her mouth in concern. "Let the waters rise up," she whispered. "Did anything happen?"

Mesnera Chazillen gave a short laugh. "No, not unless 'anything' includes the most startling magical working I've seen in years. But it was only the *fluctus* itself as far as I could see. No concrete miracles."

Even Margerit's concern seem to have ebbed. "Then it was only your…
your musical effect?" she asked.

She was still unwilling to give it the name of mystery or miracle.

"I hadn't thought—" Serafina began. "It was quite brilliant in the parlor
here. I hadn't noticed that it spilled outside. But you say there's no harm done?"

"Well, no," Margerit said. "No harm." She seemed more subdued now.
"How could there be harm? It's not as if…"

"No harm, perhaps," Mesnera Chazillen interrupted. "But anyone with
the slightest sensitivity who was within sight of the river tonight will wonder
what's afoot. Some of the more esoteric mystery guilds are paying close
attention to unusual workings."

Margerit was still frowning, but more in puzzlement. "I'll drop a word in a
few ears and let them know what happened. But you might want to see if you
could…No. No, there's no need for that," almost to herself. Whatever she had
intended to say was left unfinished. "We're so sorry to have disturbed your
evening. Maisetra Valorin. Serafina."

And with the pleasantries completed, they took their leave.

Luzie sat down and stared dazedly in the direction of the door. "I hadn't
realized it would disturb anyone," she said. And with a little laugh, "I only used
to worry about being too loud! Do you think I should—"

Serafina's mouth twitched. It was just like Margerit to think that anything
mystical in the entire city was hers to approve or disapprove. "What you
should do is work on that chord in the last section. I know you said there are
rules to the progression, but—" Her hands tried so shape her meaning. "It
finishes things too simply. Too predictably."

She sat down on the bench and, as Issibet hadn't returned, she dared to lift
Luzie's hand to kiss. "Tanfrit has just gone into the waters," she said. "Nothing
will ever be simple after that."

* * *

Every neighborhood of every city had its own rhythms of conversation
as the seasons passed. Serafina could have identified any month and
neighborhood in Rome by the talk on the streets. No doubt someone more
experienced could do the same in Rotenek from the interplay of the floodtide
holiday and the way it danced around the timing of Easter. Every district had
its own concerns as the days stretched out with still no sign that the mountains
had escaped the hold of winter and let the water flow.

Along the Vezenaf and in the wealthy neighborhoods north of the river,
there was an uneasy edge of impatience at this time of year. Serafina brushed
against it at Tiporsel House. The social season that dictated Jeanne and
Margerit's lives might end with Easter or with floodtide, whichever came
later. Or it might stretch beyond them if both came early. For now, the upper
town still concerned itself with balls and concerts, but the talk looked ahead
to the summer with the nervous fretfulness of a racehorse at the post. Who

would one visit for floodtide? Who would return to the city after that, and who would remove to their country estates? Who had invitations and who still waited for them? What meaning could be read into that lack?

One year past, Serafina had been living on the edges of the university district. There, the talk as the summer term began had all been guessing when the long delayed floodtide holiday would bring a break in studies. Some hoped for sooner, to have done with the uncertainty. Some wished for later, when the time could be put to better use over books. Akezze said every student guild had a mystery to try to influence the river's rising, but there was no telling whether their petitions canceled each other out or had no influence at all.

Here in the district around the Nikuleplaiz, concerns were more practical. Precious stores were moved to upper levels of buildings in anticipation of rising waters. Gutters and drains were cleared. It might not be necessary, but if it were, there would be no time for preparations.

Easter passed, and the joyous cries of, "Christ has risen!" changed quietly into, "Has the water risen?" In past centuries, some wag had nicknamed the steps leading from the river landing up to the statue of Saint Nikule after the apostles. Instead of saying, "The water has reached the ninth step," it would be "Iohen has his feet wet today!"

The apostles seemed in little danger of drowning this year. The first hint came as an almost imperceptible muddying of the central channel. Luzie's cook returned from the market with the news that Tomos and Mazzi were swimming now. But after another week passed, it was clear that the holiday would only be signaled with a bucket.

Elinur and Charluz made plans to travel to Iuten for the week's holiday. Issibet would join a friend in Urmai for at least the first few days. Luzie began talking eagerly about the return of her sons from school. Serafina hadn't realized her own plans were in question until supper one evening when Charluz asked, "Which of your rich friends will be hosting you for the summer?"

"None of them."

Luzie frowned and Issibet said, "Now what is the use of having friends with fine houses if they won't invite you for a proper holiday? What about that vicomtesse who visits now and then?"

"Mesnera de Cherdillac has left town already," Serafina explained. "Foreign travel for the summer." She didn't bother to add that Jeanne herself depended on the hospitality of others for her holidays. "And Maisetra Sovitre is staying in the city all summer, preparing her college."

"But Baroness Saveze—" Luzie began.

Serafina shook her head. She'd heard this one rehearsed the last time she'd been at Tiporsel House. "She's traveling between her estates, but not hosting guests. Too much back and forth, here and there, all summer. And there's no one else who would think to invite me." No one she'd be comfortable accepting an invitation from.

Luzie looked surprised and concerned. They hadn't discussed the summer, or any sort of future for that matter. The conversation they had begun that night in March had never been completed. "I had thought…It's the boys you see," Luzie said. "Last year, Iustin was off in Falinz all summer. And the year before Issibet was on tour with the company. There's usually someone leaving a room empty. I don't know…"

Serafina saw at once what would be expected. Of course Luzie's children would come first for her. "You needn't worry. I'm sure I can make other arrangements for the summer. Soon there should be rooms at the college in a fit state for guests."

Luzie looked stricken. "I didn't mean to put you out. We'll think of something. It's a pity the boys are too old to just pull out the truckle bed in my room!"

But if something could be arranged, Serafina didn't see what it would be unless there were a spare room in the attic where the maids and the housekeeper slept. Charluz and Elinur already shared a room. Issibet's restless nights were legendary and she was jealous of her space. No offers were forthcoming and Serafina passed around another helping of dessert to cover the silence.

* * *

Summer plans still stood undecided when the priest of Saint Nikule's carried a bucket of muddy river water up the steps to pour over the feet of the saint, setting the city astir like an anthill. Once the exodus had been accomplished, Luzie's house mirrored the upper parts of the city, empty and echoing.

The half-empty house and the lack of lessons gave an opportunity to clean from top to bottom. Extra hands were hired and Serafina took the strong hint and made herself scarce. The library at Tiporsel might have been a refuge, but Margerit and Barbara had taken a brief private holiday, as credit against the summer's separation. It would have felt odd to rattle around in their house with just the servants.

On the first day, she simply went walking, up past the Plaiz Nof and around the back side of the palace grounds, through the public part of the gardens, along the poplar-lined paths and past Antuniet's now-quiet workshop, then down to the front of the palace and the cathedral. Her thoughts turned to Mesner Kreiser and the sessions they had spent trying to trace mysteries. It had been too like Paolo's teaching at first: maps and verses and small rituals. She had flinched at every failure, expecting scorn. Then Kreiser had placed a small broken stone in her hand, closed her fingers around it and said, "Tell me its story."

Her vision loosened. She saw a valley…no, a hillside. Both at the same time. Permanence, tumbling, movement.

"What is it—" she began.

He shook his head. "You tell me."

The slow, cold thoughts of stone. Mist tracing through the mountain valleys. No, not mist. Power. A mindless, formless power—not like the bright crispness of *charis* in the mysteries. Movement, wakening, fracturing.

"The earthquake?" she asked.

Kreiser nodded. "Where did it come from? What caused it?"

But that was elusive. She could see the trace of *fluctus* but it was like no ritual she had ever observed. More like a natural, malevolent force, with no beginning and no end.

He took the stone from her hand and replaced it with a small whitened bone. "Tell me its story."

She could find no sense or pattern in the visions she reported, but Kreiser had seemed pleased and suggested another session. Was he still in town? She wasn't certain, but it didn't matter. She could think of no way to approach him that would fit into the rules Jeanne had drilled into her.

On the second day, she went to visit Akezze in her lodgings at the edge of the university district. They went to one of the student cafés, nearly empty for the week, to sit among the worn oak benches, with the shutters thrown open to catch the summer breezes, and drink cheap wine. They talked of everything that had nothing to do with mysteries: the exciting plans for Margerit's college, Akezze's own private students, from the ambitious clerks who longed for political office to Aukustin Atilliet himself.

Serafina listened to Akezze's wry and self-mocking stories of how she came and went at the palace now, and might have a hand in shaping the thoughts of the next prince. But there was another thread in Akezze's stories. The third time that young Mesner Atilliet's tutor was mentioned as Cherstuf rather than as Maistir Chautovil, Serafina interrupted, exclaiming, "Do you have a sweetheart?"

There was no chance of missing the blush that spread across Akezze's pale, freckled skin.

Serafina laughed. "I thought there must be some attraction at the palace other than teaching young men to work proofs! And does he feel the same?"

Akezze sighed. "We haven't really discussed it. He's in no position to support a wife, and I don't care to give up my hopes of starting a girls' school back in Falkoiz. I've saved up quite a bit of money thanks to Margerit's connections." Her mouth twisted in a smile. "I've been working with the orphans' school here in Rotenek to get experience. It isn't just a matter of teaching classes, you know!"

"I thought Margerit had plans for you to teach at her college," Serafina said.

"For the first few years, perhaps." She shrugged. "I'll see. It depends on what direction it goes. I know Margerit expects it to be an excited gaggle of book-mad girls like she was, but it could end up just another finishing school. I have no interest in spending the rest of my life teaching elocution and rhetoric to debutantes. She's put an Orisul in charge of the place and they have a reputation for safe and ornamental learning, at least for the secular students."

Safe and ornamental. That was a description that would never fit Akezze. It didn't fit Margerit either, but Margerit was wise enough to know her own style of careless study would not do for a formal institution. And what was her own place in all this? She was only a student herself. There was nothing she could contribute to Margerit's plans. There was still everything to learn. And to what end? It seemed increasingly unlikely that she would ever put it to use. Even Kreiser's scrying seemed to have no larger purpose.

With mysteries on her mind, on the third day Serafina went to sit quietly in the church of Saint Nikule to watch for scraps of everyday miracles as the parishioners came and went.

It was one of the first exercises Margerit had suggested that she tackle. One of the first Margerit had done herself. To sit quietly in a place of worship and watch the signs and effects of people as they performed ordinary prayers, desperate petitions, private desires. It was meant in part to remind one of humility: that God and the saints do not answer prayers for power, or for virtue, or for need, but for reasons of their own, unknowable by mortals.

The purpose wasn't to judge, but to see—truly see—the workings of divine grace. But was it divine grace? Margerit was so sure in her faith. Serafina had learned to be silent with her doubts.

If the traces of luminous color, the wisps of half-seen power truly were a sign of God's blessing, then the priest who tended to the altar at Saint Nikule's was a holy man. For a while, Serafina watched him at work with the light following his every action like an afterimage, lingering in the candles as he lit them, briefly brightening the pages of a prayer book, hovering in the air in the shape of the cross as he rose from his knees and returned to the sacristy.

Did he know? Did he have *visio* as well? What might it do to the spirit of a priest to *see* that echo of grace in his own work. Did those who ordained and appointed him know? Growing up in Rome it was too easy to think the choices of the Church were made for worldly reasons. And however such decisions were made, they were unknowable to those outside the hierarchy.

If *fluctus* reflected divine grace, then why should it respond so brightly to old Mefro Efriza, sitting on a bench before the Lady Altar, speaking bright words into the scraps of scribbled prayers and charms that she had brought, then folding and sealing them within to be sold in the marketplace for a teneir or two.

From the way that she worked, Serafina could guess that she had both talents: to do and to see. What was it Efriza sold? Scraps of luck, both good and ill. The ability to draw the eyes long enough to make a sale or attach a heart. Or the ability to turn the eyes away from things best not observed. A bit of strength to see one through hard times, or a curse to drain the strength of rivals. Efriza had few scruples—the poor couldn't afford them. And why should someone with such talents remain poor all her life? An accident of birth could have gained her training and status as a professional thaumaturgist like Maistir Escamund, who waited on the Dowager Princess. Where was the grace of God in all that?

But the priest and Efriza were only the extremes. In between were those whose abilities and motives were less certain. Those who might have been deserving of grace, however one might judge deserving.

What do I deserve? Serafina wondered. Does it matter whether I deserve it? Is my failure a lesson in humility or a judgment on my own sins? The sin of pride? The sin of lust for things I shouldn't desire? She had never truly repented of that.

A familiar figure moved through the shadows of the church, only her white linen cap showing brightly in the candlelight. Serafina watched as Celeste genuflected before the main altar before moving to the small shrine of Saint Mauriz to one side. The city's patron saint was honored to at least some small degree in every church that had more than a single altar. Serafina quietly moved to a different vantage point, the better to see what happened. She felt a stirring of guilt she hadn't felt when observing strangers.

At first, Celeste was lit only by the flickering glow of the waxen candles in the shrine, as she raised her face to the saint's image and moved her lips in prayer. But then she sat back and, like a number of other petitioners, drew out the paraphernalia for small mysteries. She was more self-conscious than the priest had been, less perfunctory than Efriza.

Like the old woman, she seemed to have brought the apparatus for future mysteries, drawing in the saint's power and fixing it for future use. It was a different tradition than the one Margerit followed, even apart from Margerit's focus on the large public mysteries. Serafina thought back to Celeste's erteskir, the small private shrine she had seen at Dominique's house, with its chest filled with bits and snippets of apparatus. The candle from the cathedral, jars of herbs and powders, scraps of paper written with names and symbols, strips of red flannel.

Serafina imagined generations of charm-women passing down recipes by faith, and now and again those recipes falling into the hands of one whose petitions would be heard, as Celeste's were.

And she *was* heard. As she held each object and spoke over it, a glow coalesced around her hands and, through them, entered into the objects. Sometimes it faltered and then she would hesitate, try again and perhaps discard the item. She was sensitive enough to guide her own work in the details. To pick and choose from what she'd been taught. And how did she understand the workings of mysteries? What did she know of what she was doing?

When Celeste finally gathered up her things and dropped a single coin in the offering box by the shrine, Serafina followed her out into the porch of the church.

The girl turned at her approach with a sharp intake of breath, and then relaxed into a wary greeting.

"Good day, Maisetra."

"I shouldn't have surprised you," Serafina said. "May I apologize by sharing a bite to eat, or are there chores calling you home?"

Celeste hesitated, perhaps weighing the excuse to decline. "There's no need for apology, Maisetra," she said stiffly.

"If you wish," Serafina said with a nod. "But I would enjoy a word with you, the same." Would it frighten the girl off to show too much interest? "I hoped you might tell me something about your training."

"If you wish," Celeste echoed, and fell in beside her, walking across the open space of the Nikuleplaiz.

It wasn't a market day, but there was a woman in the corner of the square selling fritters and they found a place to sit along the embankment that looked out over the river. Serafina thought of the last time the two of them had met there. The charred ruins of burnt warehouses were still visible on the other bank. Before she could think better, she asked, "Has your father given you any more trouble?" No, how could she have said such a thing? That wasn't something one asked!

Celeste only shrugged. "He's off downriver again. I won't have to worry for another couple of months. And he doesn't really bother me—not unless he's drunk, or when he wants something from Maman."

A silence, and then Serafina tried again. "How did you learn to work mysteries?"

"I don't do mysteries," Celeste said hurriedly. She sounded almost frightened. "Just charms and such! Nana Charl taught me."

"Your grandmother?"

Again the diffident shake of the head. "Don't have any grandmothers. Nana was—" Now she seemed to turn shy. "When I was a girl, Maman got sick. Baby sick, you know? Nana took care of it. I decided I wanted to be able to do that, to keep people alive when they were sick. Maman wasn't too sharp for it. You can get in a lot of trouble doing charms, especially if you're—" A quick apologetic glance. "—if you're foreign, you know? But Nana said I had the knack and she'd teach me. She wouldn't take just anyone to teach." It might have been pride or boasting, but she said it as simple fact.

"She taught me all her charms—the ones she could remember. Maman taught me a few things too. Stuff she learned…back there." Celeste gestured to indicate some far-off time and place. "Some I got from watching other folks. And the rest I figured out for myself. There's always something to learn." She looked sideways with a little challenge. "Who did you learn from?"

"From books, mostly," Serafina answered. "And some from Maisetra Sovitre and her friends. But I can't work mysteries, nor even charms."

Celeste leaned toward her to whisper, "Most of them can't either," she said, nodding in the direction of the arches where the charmwives congregated, though there was no one there to overhear at the moment. "But don't tell anyone I said that. If you start pointing fingers and telling tales, things might happen to you."

The laws of the street, Serafina thought. Part of those dangers that Mefro Dominique worried over, no doubt.

"There was one woman," Serafina began. "The one with the cards. She told my friend's future. She knows what she's doing."

Another sly, sidelong glance from Celeste. "I thought you said you couldn't do charms."

"I can't do them but I can see them," Serafina said.

"Ah," Celeste answered.

Somehow there was a world of acceptance in that one word.

"Why did you have to learn from books?" Celeste asked. "Didn't your own Maman teach you?"

"She didn't know any. Not any in a language I knew." But Serafina thought back to all the little songs and exclamations that had made up her mother's daily rituals. The ones that had first stirred her visions. What you said over the bread to help it ferment. What you sang to keep spiders out of the house. She had explained what they were for in her careful, halting Romanesco, but Serafina had never learned the charms.

"Maybe that's why the saints don't listen to me," Serafina suggested. "Because I should be talking to them in Tigrinya." It was a thought that had come to her now and then, when her father told stories of the marver ceremonies back in his home.

But Celeste made a rude noise. "I can't understand the priest's Latin, but the charms still work for me. Some can and some can't, that's all. No use fretting."

No use fretting. Serafina wondered if that were a phrase Celeste heard often from her mother. On impulse she asked, "Have you ever thought of studying from books? Maiestra Sovitre is beginning a school. Some of the classes will be about mysteries. She—" Even as said it, Serafina was certain the question would come out badly. "She has space for students who can't pay the fees if they have talent. Like you do."

For the briefest of moments Celeste's face brightened before closing down again. "And what would Maman do if I were off at classes all day? Who would help her take the measurements and do the sewing and run errands to the market? I have to go," She stood and brushed the crumbs from her skirt. "I need to finish my work before supper."

Serafina rose too. She had no response to offer. "Thank you for your company. Do you...have you used up the Mauriz candle I gave you?"

Celeste's eyes narrowed. What did she think the offer meant? "There's still some left," she said. "I don't need anything."

And then with a brief curtsey she was off.

The talk with Celeste had lightened Serafina's mood more than she had expected. No use fretting. Could life be that simple? To do what you can and let go of what you can't? But how could one know what was possible and what should be set aside?

One decision had fallen into place without conscious thought. In the parlor after supper, when the day turned to music as it usually did now, Serafina ventured, "Wherever I end up staying for the summer, I'd like to come back to keep working on the opera with you, if I may."

Luzie looked startled. "Of course! I thought…I mean, I assumed, I hoped…" Her answer fell into confusion.

"I can stay at Urmai, at the Academy. It's easy enough to come and go by the river."

"Would you prefer that?" Luzie began slowly. "I was thinking—"

Whatever the thoughts were, she struggled to voice them. Serafina could see Luzie's hands shaking a little over the keyboard.

"I have room," she said quietly. "My room, that is. I was thinking…"

Serafina's heart thudded heavily. What offer was she making? How mortifying it would be to guess wrong!

Luzie struggled to continue. "I don't know if…" She took a deep breath and began again. "What I want to say is, I wouldn't mind trying." She moved her hand the short distance to cover Serafina's where it lay in her lap and looked up to meet her eyes.

This is different, Serafina thought. She's no Olimpia, certainly no Marianniz. This could go so badly wrong.

And yet it could be so right. She remembered the evening with the near-disastrous dinner and then the music that had swept her back to that sweet, safe, comfortable place inside. Perhaps this place could be home.

"Shall I move my things tonight?" she answered. "There isn't much to gather up."

CHAPTER SIXTEEN

Barbara

June, 1824

Summer was already out of balance and it had barely begun. When floodtide came late and by fiat, half the families simply left for their summer estates. There was no reprise of the social season after the holiday, nor any sense of a deliberate close.

The council debates had accomplished nothing of value, not by Holy Week, or even by the floodtide exodus. Princess Annek released them with a summons in hand to return at midsummer. In the usual way of things, it would have been a hardship to come all the way back from Saveze simply to sit in the Assembly Hall and listen to speeches in the heat of a Rotenek summer. But with Margerit staying in town, it would be a pleasure to return.

Barbara first turned her journey south to Turinz, as she had the year before. Confidence had slowly replaced uncertainty, but affairs in Turinz were not yet so predictable as to require only a light hand. She glanced back at the traveling coach. Maistir Tuting had done well enough in keeping the books so far but he had no experience with managing a working estate. Shipping and warehouses were more in his line. Young Akermen in Turinz was punctilious in his reports, but they felt less than candid. Odd gaps and omissions led to probing questions; details were forthcoming only when pursued. The two men had yet to pull evenly in harness.

A sharp whistle from Brandel where he rode ahead signaled the approach of another vehicle. The broad road allowed for two vehicles to pass—no need even to slow to a walk. She heard the quick hoofbeats of Tavit closing up from behind. He'd done his duty this morning and advised her to travel in the coach. The dignity of Saveze and all that, and it was safer than the open road. She had, as usual, listened to the suggestion and declined. She felt too fidgety to be closed in a box all day. Tavit had become almost tiresome in his insistence on the protocols. His insistence on reminding her, at least. Hence, his choice to bring up the rear where he could keep an eye on the entire party and bear the brunt of anyone overtaking them from behind. It was a concern meant for wilder roads than this. Turinz had no reputation for highwaymen.

A battered wagon packed tightly with barrels passed at the leisurely pace dictated by oxen.

So, Barbara thought. Nothing's traveling by water yet. Or perhaps Mazuk had forgotten the agreements made last year. Or was he waiting to see if the council regulated canal traffic after all? He'd never been that cautious before. When they rounded the bend near Sain-Mihail it was no surprise to see the canal standing idle.

Barbara cantered over to the edge with Tavit following closely behind. The ditch had been completed, at least that much was forward. The narrow, stone-faced channel skirted gracefully around the scatter of tumbled boulders that had forced its path across the boundary into Turinz. Now the two sections that had stood separate last year were joined. The water was low and stagnant—only the several feet that rainwater had filled.

Whatever the delays, they must be of Mazuk's own making. He blamed her; that much was clear from the way he needled her every time they met. It wasn't her fault he'd had to look so long and hard for investors. Nor her fault that he'd settled for one whose irascible temper had led to his doom. It *was* by her word that certain other of his projects in Turinz had turned sour, but those were ventures he'd had no right to begin. She turned her horse's head back toward the road.

Barbara had managed one brief visit to Turinz during the winter, feeling helpless to address the plague of crop disasters. The tenants in her title-lands were still wary, but glad of assistance. Even without the new problems, it would have been some time yet before Turinz had its feet under it again. And with only the bare skeleton of the title-lands, the position of Count Turinz would never again be prosperous. It was well she had no need for it to be so.

Akermen met them at the manor. Barbara had hesitated over opening it up for the few weeks she would be staying, and with such small company. But there were certain standards to maintain, hospitality to offer. Not a lavish show—that would give the wrong message in these times—but a solid generosity. And she wanted to test Akermen's abilities and judgment.

The man had taken her at her word that only a few principal rooms need be prepared and a minimum of temporary staff. He looked harder now, more worn. Less the promising new man freshly returned from the university. He'd spent his years in Rotenek studying the usual program: history and rhetoric and law, with a smattering of radical ideas for leavening. It occurred to Barbara they might have spent time in the same lecture halls. He was of an age for it. She must see that those ambitions weren't squandered.

Clerks learned in law were easy to find. More valuable was a man like Akermen who had grown up hearing the talk of farmers and discussions of how to bring land to its best use. One who wasn't too proud or too disdainful of those roots to return and take up the challenge of such practical problems. He wouldn't be content here for all his life, but for now their goals might serve each other.

Akermen met them wearing a town-made suit of sober cloth, agreed to share a glass of wine at the welcome, but declined the invitation to dine, excusing himself on the grounds that she would be tired from the journey. He exchanged glances with Maistir Tuting—looking for all the world like two strange dogs taking each other's measure—and promised to return in the morning with all his accounts and surveys drawn up.

The paper accounts and surveys were only the first look at the status of the estate. The ritual of riding the markein once around served a more practical purpose here than it did at Saveze. Rituals had their own worth and power, but here the first purpose would be viewing the state of the land and meeting with her tenants on their own ground.

Tuting stayed behind, being of no use on a horse. Akermen hadn't the seat of a gentleman, but he'd grown up riding across these fields.

Barbara suggested that Tavit, too, might take a holiday. "Brandel can attend me for the circuit," she offered. Brandel should learn the habits and customs of holding property. It was never too soon to make his face familiar, should matters alter. One never knew.

But Tavit asked stiffly, "Mesnera, do you forbid me from accompanying you?"

"Not at all," Barbara exclaimed in surprise. "I only thought…There's little enough to defend me from out here."

"Forgive me, Mesnera," Tavit said, the tension in his voice easing slightly. "But this is still uncertain ground for you." He threw a glance over where Akermen waited out of hearing. "I would ask that you allow me my own judgment in how you should be attended."

Lately Tavit had become…no, not prickly. Nor was stubborn the precise word. But insistent. Yes, perhaps insistent was the right term. What would she have done with their positions reversed? But back in the days when she had been an armin, her status had been peculiar. Irregular, if you will. Her duty had been measured in wild swings between rigid protocol and silent obedience. And then there had been the time of freedom as a new baroness, looking to her own safety and honor and trusting only her own judgment. And Marken's, of course. That went without saying. Marken had a lifetime's experience and judgment to draw on.

But Tavit was right. He was doing nothing more than what an armin was bound to do. She nodded. "As you think best."

But, oh, how it grated to have her own judgment called into question.

Summer found the Turinz lands better than she'd feared but worse than she'd hoped. She was no farmer, but there was a life, a vibrancy to the patchwork of green and gold fields, a firm solidity to the vineyards climbing the sides of the steeper hills, a sweet promise in the ranks of apple trees that edged every lane.

She ventured the opinion, "The harvest should be enough to see everyone through, if luck holds."

Akermen's glance was unreadable. "Must we trust to luck, Mesnera? I thought we might have higher assistance than that."

Did he mean it for a joke? "God willing, if it needs to be said!" she answered. "But a personal miracle is beyond me."

"You are a friend of the Royal Thaumaturgist…"

"And she is trying her best for all Alpennia. We aren't the only ones in need." How to explain that Margerit's efforts were made on a longer scale, at a higher level? But perhaps… "There is a parish guild, is there not? What mysteries do they have for the crops? Perhaps they might be examined and made stronger."

It was a vain thought. Margerit wouldn't have time for such a task this summer. Not with the school to be built. But the promise returned some of Akermen's enthusiasm.

Her manager's enthusiasms came between them again in the last days of her visit. They had been speaking of what measures might be decided on in the extended summer council sessions, when he unexpectedly said, "There are likely to be new elections for the common council next winter. Do you favor anyone in particular? It's unlikely that Perkumen could be dislodged from his seat, but the other one is less fixed."

"I have my opinions, like anyone else," Barbara replied with amusement. "But as I have no vote in the matter, I don't see that they're of any importance."

He looked nonplussed. "I had thought—" A glance at Brandel.

Good heavens, did he think she meant to set her cousin up in politics? Now that the thought occurred to her, it was a reasonable suspicion, if she had been inclined that way. No doubt other lords whose bloodlines crossed over into the burfroites might find it convenient to install a relative in the lower council.

"My preference," she said evenly, "is for someone of experience and clear thinking, who will bend to neither fear nor favor. My preference," she emphasized, "is for laws to be made from sound judgment rather than loyalty. And yes—" She waved her hand to stop any protest. "I know well how these things truly work. But I have no mind to meddle unless there's need."

Akermen looked disappointed before his face smoothed into blandness again. Clearly he had his own interest in the seat, but she was loathe to encourage him at this time. It would be impossible for her own estate manager to take up a place in council without giving the appearance that he would be her creature. And Turinz couldn't be overseen by someone who spent months at a time in Rotenek for the sessions.

* * *

The journey to Saveze was longer than it would have been, except for her choice to avoid traveling across Mazuk's lands. An excess of caution, perhaps, making the detour to Rapenfil more awkward. There Brandel left their party for a month's visit with his family. But soon enough the white walls of the Orisules' convent came into view on the mountainside, followed by the verdigrised roofs of the manor at Saveze.

Saveze, in truth, needed little of her oversight. Cheruk had its affairs well in hand. And without the distraction of other guests—and most especially of Margerit, so far away in Rotenek—the days dragged as she waited for word from her expected visitor.

Two summers past, Kreiser had sent a message to her secretly at Saveze, when he was persona non grata after the business with Antuniet. The wind had blown in several different directions since then and she had more of his measure. She still didn't entirely trust him, but their every interaction carried the thrill of sparring, of matching wits with someone who enjoyed the game as much as she did.

This time, a letter awaited her when she arrived, the superscription indicating that he'd written it at Geneva. She knew he'd planned to hunt down more evidence of mystic disasters. The Swiss were close-mouthed and wary—not given to interest in thaumaturgy at the best of times. But when something beyond the vagaries of fortune struck, they suspected their neighbors and made free with accusations. In Lombardy and Piedmont they had strong opinions of whom to blame for the forces that locked the mountains in winter, though with no better evidence than anyone else had. They, at least, had been trying to peck away at the southern edges of the disruption with rituals both great and small.

She knew Kreiser was mapping the ambit of the effects as best he could, with information gleaned in the spring through some sort of scrying, though he'd declined to elaborate. The letter held little more than a hint of his current travels lest it fall into another's hands. He named the date when she might expect him. Two weeks after her own arrival.

When Kreiser did not appear as appointed, she gave it little weight. Travel in the mountains was chancy at best, even without the state of the passes. The innkeeper at Atefels had been instructed to expect him and returned her a sorrowful tale of how the trade in travelers was sadly diminished, even from the previous slow year. Those who came through told of harrowing treks between piled snowbanks higher than their horses and no passage for coaches at all.

Barbara began to fidget. Not from concern for the man himself, but from the unease that disrupted plans always stirred in her.

Then a messenger rode down from Atefels, followed in two days by Kreiser himself. He was traveling lightly, accompanied only by a man who combined the functions of aide-de-camp and valet. Though there was space in plenty at the manor Barbara directed him to the village inn. One of the irritations raised against her in the council of nobles was her seeming friendship with the Austrian. She preferred being able to deny that Kreiser had been a guest in her home.

A dinner invitation carried no such risk. The manor's dining room with its long oak table was too large and echoing for use in the absence of a full set of summer guests, but it supplied space for the series of maps Kreiser unrolled from a long cylindrical case. Tavit satisfied his sense of duty by playing the butler, standing by to pour drinks and attend to any immediate needs. Barbara had no doubts of the discretion of the manor staff, but this service kept their discussions more private. Too, it avoided any awkward implication that she felt the need for protection in her own home.

Kreiser had never stated plainly just what level of mystical sensitivity he possessed. His interest in Antuniet's alchemy that had first brought him to Rotenek gave few clues, for alchemy could be pursued without any special talents. But as Kreiser began listing some of his observations in the mountains, Barbara compared them to the ways that Margerit and Antuniet discussed their visions. She guessed he fell more toward the lower end of the middle. Far less sensitivity than Margerit possessed, but more than Antuniet, though he shared with her cousin an air of frustration every time the subject came up.

"I've succeeded, I believe, in mapping out the current spread of this zauberwerk, though the eastern parts I know only by rumor. The original scope is harder to estimate." He traced his finger across the map. "We still believe it was intended to disrupt certain key travel routes. But the spread and the secondary effects confused the matter. I doubt the net was meant to be cast so wide."

We, he said. Barbara took that for the Austrian government. Or perhaps only certain agencies within it. She saw her own investigations embedded in his analysis: the collected travelers' reports on weather and road conditions up to Geneva, over to Turin. The earthquake, the crop failures, the outbreaks of fever, even the warehouse fires in Rotenek. Anything that one might have expected the saints' protections to have eased. She reviewed the essentials. "Nothing at this end of the mountains in the early part of twenty-two. Certainly nothing affecting the weather, for floodtide came as expected that year. That only started a year past, but by then the mystery had taken firm hold. Snow blocking the passes well into the summer and no floodtide to speak of."

Kreiser grimaced and continued. "If the authors had put a bit more effort into specifics it might have saved a great deal of harm. Your Rotein is only a small part of it. The Po would be affected worse if not for the difference in rain patterns. The southern Swiss cantons have lost half their summer pasture this year. And travel from Bohemia…well—"

He bit off what he might have said. Their newfound partnership still had limits when it touched on Austrian concerns. "If we can find a way to break the central zauberwerk, the roads should return to normal in a year or so, even with two years worth of snowpack tied up. But that's just the lancing of the boil. The spell has spread and fragmented. Even if these other effects are tied to the original purpose, breaking that spell may not touch them."

Barbara could still be startled by Kreiser's use of the language of sorcery to describe the weather mystery. Margerit avoided those terms entirely, dividing the mystical world into religious ritual and the common charms of the untutored.

She turned her thoughts to the timing. "It was only this past autumn when Margerit commented on the fraying of the Great Mysteries at the eastern edges of Alpennia. She thought perhaps she hadn't been looking closely enough—it was Maisetra Talarico who saw it first. But perhaps there hadn't been anything to see."

"Yes," Kreiser said. "The beginnings were a year before. And farther east. I asked you once what you knew of events in Spain?"

Barbara felt a sudden sympathy for Brandel being quizzed on his studies. She had followed the ins and outs of Alpennian politics closely under the old baron. And when he had been Prince Aukust's emissary to the discussions at Vienna she had attempted to follow their concerns at a distance. But Alpennia had little influence outside its borders and there had been much to distract her at home since then.

"The restoration of King Ferdinand in Spain," she offered. "But Alb—people say that's long past." No need to name names. Kreiser might guess that she had Albori's authorization, but it wasn't part of the game to say so.

"It had been suggested back at the Congress of Verona," Kreiser continued, ignoring her stumble, "that a larger, more balanced force should intervene in Spain. Moving across the mountains here and then by ship. But…"

"But they couldn't get through," Barbara finished for him. "They would have been stopped before the pass. But wasn't the mystery already in place by then?"

Kreiser waved aside the objection. "By the time anyone gets to talking, the moves and counter-moves have already been made. Someone wanted to prevent that army from traveling to Spain. And even leaving behind artillery," he continued, "by the time they could march through under those conditions, the battle would have been decided. The debates were a meaningless show. The army never moved and France had a free hand in Spanish affairs."

"So you think it's France?"

Kreiser's sidelong glance was both amused and suspicious. "Do you?" He leaned back in his chair and seemed to be enjoying himself greatly. "If it were only that simple! I suspect everyone. There were some who signed to the accords who were quite happy to have had the matter taken out of their hands. Within my own government there are forces who have moved in the past to preempt the ministers' decisions. And there are companies of thaumaturgists on every side. Not all have the power to work something of this sort, but the ones who do are rarely those who boast that they could."

For a brief moment, all masks seemed to drop away and Kreiser looked more tired than Barbara had ever seen before.

"There's a good reason why my activities in Alpennia have not fallen under the most official channels," he said. "And why my public mission has been cloaked in playing at marital intrigues."

If it were a ploy for sympathy, it fell short. Kreiser's "playing" had left bodies in its wake the year before, and it was only good fortune that none of them had been people she cared for. But she could believe it had been nothing more than misdirection, for it had come to nothing in the end.

Barbara was no longer certain how much of Kreiser's tale was belated honesty and how much was still part of that game. If he could pretend to bluntness, so could she. "Why Alpennia? Why me? Why haven't you brought this directly to Princess Anna's ministers or to your own ambassador? Why quiz me like a catechism rather than stating what you need outright?"

Kreiser exhaled, halfway between a sigh and a grunt. "Alpennia is at the heart of it, I'm certain. Not in the way my superiors think, but they wouldn't take my word for that, and—" He leaned forward in a move that might still be playacting. "—I don't trust them any more than I trust you or the Russians or the French, though perhaps more than I trust the English. I have been tasked with determining whether we're dealing with external enemies or with hidden forces within the Empire itself. If this is the work of foreign thaumaturgists, I am to cripple them as best I can. And that is where I hope to have your support." His gesture took in the entirety of Alpennia. "No one in Vienna has the power to work at this distance, and we don't have anyone with the right talent in place in Paris. The Russians don't do this type of work. The English won't even admit to having thaumaturgists. The last thing I want is to get tangled up with the disaster that is Rome. You have the mystical traditions and people with the skills to help carry it off, as well as the will to do so. I can't be seen to be working directly with your government, but no one will notice my dealings with you."

Yes, Barbara thought. She had played at cat-and-mouse with him over most of his false distractions. No one would find anything suspicious in their continued entanglements.

"And if it turns out to be agents within Austria itself?" she asked.

Kreiser's face settled into grimmer lines. "Then it's possible I will be a dead man as soon as I make my report."

* * *

A summer season in Saveze should have been a time of productive idleness. The days should have been spent riding up the steep valleys, renewing ties with her tenants, enjoying a sky unconstrained by the press of buildings. It was the first summer she had spent away from Margerit's side for more than a few weeks at a time. The experience might have harked back to her girlhood—those years of preparation and practice, always waiting for the old baron's appearance and the chance that he might drop a word of praise or a promise of adventure. That had been a different world. Back then her life had spun around her patron—her father—like the moon in orbit. Now she circled an equal body, like two dancers in the waltz. When every necessary task at Saveze was complete and she gave the word to ready the traveling coach, her nerves tingled like a girl in her dancing season looking ahead to a ball.

Rotenek should have been quiet and dull at midsummer. The court should have been away, traveling between several carefully selected hosts and royal properties, mingling leisure and the never-ending press of state. The great houses along the Vezenaf should stand half-empty, with skeletal staffs attacking those chores that could not be attempted with the family in residence. The newer mansions along the city's northern edge supported a summer season in imitation of those in rural gathering places such as Chalanz, Akolbin or Suniz, but the grand salles in the city center fell quiet and the cafés around the Plaiz saw more businessmen than barons.

It was far from unprecedented for the councils to be called to return at midsummer. During the tense and troubled times of the French Wars, it had been as common as not, though the bills decided in those sessions had been for show. If not for the other attractions of Rotenek, Barbara might have begrudged the summons enough to ignore it. Little enough of moment would be agreed on in the council of nobles, even if they could choose among the concerns for focus. In truth, there was little enough that could be done. Fires in the wharf district were outside their concern. Disease might be addressed by sanitation and the funding of hospitals. The topic of canals had caught everyone's imagination, but there was no chance of agreement on action.

Lord Chormuin set the cat among the pigeons in the second week with a bill that would transfer all governance of water transport and its appurtenances to control of the common council. "For," he argued in his opening remarks, "matters of ordinary trade and industry fall within their ambit, so long as they don't touch on tariffs or foreign exchange. It should be beneath the dignity of this body to squabble over whether canal locks are open or closed."

One might suspect Princess Annek's hand behind the unexpected move. Most of Chormuin's acts aligned in some way with her preferred goals. But Annek had kept carefully silent on any of the more practical debates concerning the river, confining her influence to a suggestion for dredging the chanulezes. And despite his reputation for legal reforms, Chormuin had old-fashioned views when it came to the nobility dabbling in trade. This move might be nothing more than what it seemed: a distaste for having the nobles' council devolve into bickering over transport rights and investments.

Barbara sat quietly on the bench and kept her thoughts to herself as tempers drove the speeches to the edge of insult and beyond. Given the source of the old baron's fortune, she was scarcely in a position to be disdainful, however little of that fortune had fallen into her own hands.

And yet, mere snobbishness aside, Chormuin's point was sound. The maintenance of the wharves, the dredging of channels, repairs to the river walls and the chanulezes, all of these fell under the lower council unless specific private properties were involved. Was the construction of a canal like the building of a new warehouse—no concern to anyone save the owner? Or did it fall together with ancient regulations such as the discharge of tanneries—a matter of common concern and common welfare?

The questions stirred Barbara's fascination with the structures of the law, and she idly made notes of every point where a search of the Statuta might bear fruit. Law and precedent might be complex, but at least they were fixed, not like the question of what the consequences of canal closures might be. As voices rose around her, she confined herself to providing citations.

That reticence failed to save her from demands for support. Only absenting herself entirely from the Assembly Hall would have done that and she'd grown to enjoy the interplay even when the goal seemed vain. It felt like the excitement when she had watched the old baron at work as voices and opinions flew like shuttlecocks. Back then she had watched from the armins' benches at the side, with more focus on the currents of emotion than the details of law.

Tavit had that task now. No sooner had the staff been struck three times on the floor to signal each day's close than he was at her side, close as a shadow. He blamed himself that she'd lost her temper at Feizin back in the spring. It shouldn't have gone that far, she could admit that now. But it terrified her that someone like Feizin might feint at Margerit to strike at her. Her own place was secure. Was Feizin behind the guildmasters' attack on the Royal Thaumaturgist appointment? Margerit's position—her plans, her dreams—might still crumble if such filth were thrown and allowed to stick.

But the rituals of honor held. You kept the reputation you allowed others to give you. And as long as her arm was sure, no one would be allowed to cast that sort of dirt on Margerit. The honor of Saveze might be in Tavit's keeping, but Margerit's was in hers.

With her thoughts turned in that direction, Barbara started like a spooky horse when Tavit coughed discreetly at her back as they made their way through the press toward the doors into the Plaiz. But it was only one of Annek's pages, holding out a folded and sealed note.

She took it with a nod and broke it open. Yes, she had expected this since her return from Saveze. With a small gesture, she indicated the change in plans and direction to Tavit and turned to work back through the crowd toward the palace proper. There was a report to be made, and perhaps new instructions that would never see their way into a minister's dispatches.

CHAPTER SEVENTEEN

Luzie

July, 1824

Every summer morning brought Luzie the same slow-dawning awareness. An unaccustomed warmth under the covers. The scent of sandalwood and clove. One stopped noticing scents after a time. She no longer noticed the faint trace of lavender in the sheets or the otto of roses she had always preferred in pomade. But it was hard to imagine becoming oblivious to that sign of Serafina's presence.

She could hear footsteps and clattering from downstairs where Silli and the maids were up and about. And then a shout from one of the boys at their endless squabbles. There were only a few more moments to enjoy this rest, even on a Sunday, and no time remaining at all to pretend the world could be ignored. With every moment spent lying here, the comfort curled into anxiety. Oh, Gerta wouldn't come up until she rang, but there was no reason at all to lie abed. Someone would question it.

Luzie opened her eyes to the dark curve of Serafina's shoulder above the white linen of her nightdress and pressed her cheek against the warmth of her skin. She'd missed this and scarcely dared to admit it. Missed—no, not this precisely. Her marriage had been a different matter. But missed having a friend, a confidante, a companion...she flinched away from the word lover. A widow who took a lover was a figure of contempt. One who remained alone was an object of pity. But a widow could have a close friend. A special friend.

"It's getting late," Luzie whispered, and Serafina rolled toward her, smiling in a lazy stretch. At night, when the doors were closed and the lamps snuffed, and the darkness hid Serafina's amusement and her own embarrassment, they sated their hungry skins with touch and reached out to take what each other offered. Perhaps sometime she would be daring enough in daylight to study every unknown inch of the body that lay beside her. To explore the unfamiliar planes of Serafina's bones, the way her breasts melted into small puddles when she lay back as she did now, the way her skin shaded now darker, now lighter in unexpected places. But mornings were shy, as she returned to being uncertain just what it was that they had become to each other.

"We're going down to Urmai today after services," Luzie reminded them both, as she threw back the covers and moved to pull the cord that summoned Gerta with a pitcher of hot water.

It was fashionable to complain that the heat was oppressive in Rotenek in the summer. If you were rich and had the misfortune to be stranded in town, there were barges that would take you drifting lazily down the river where the breezes were cooler. Once you were out in the current, the stink of the mud along the banks was barely noticeable. If you hadn't the wherewithal for a barge with chilled wine and soft music, you could still hire a riverman to row downstream to the gardens at Urmai.

It wasn't only the gardens, of course. There were acrobats and clowns, shows with performing monkeys, and dogs that would dance on their hind legs, games of strength and chance. The entertainments changed from week to week. Whatever might lure the city-dwellers out for a day's pleasure.

This year Hennik was grown old enough to pretend indifference to the shows and games, though he laughed and shouted easily enough when Rikke was the excuse to stop and watch. Hennik had come home from school all lanky and awkward and putting on grown-up airs. When had he grown so tall? Mother had written at midwinter that he'd topped her by an inch or so, but it hadn't prepared Luzie for the change.

His stories were still full of Efrans Perkumai and the Feizin brothers, though this year there were no awkward invitations that must be declined. But more than that had changed. Hennik spent half-days over his books, sending his brother off to play alone while he conned his Latin and frowned through a book on geometry in hopes of advancing early. In explanation, he'd only muttered something about examinations, but those were still two years in the future.

Someone must have been putting it into his head how much his future depended on doing well and gaining a scholarship at the university. He certainly hadn't picked that up from his schoolfellows. Luzie suspected her brother. Surely it was too early for Hennik to turn from a carefree boy into such a sober young man!

After the services at Saint Nikule's, she announced the outing to the boys. They could still be surprised into unguarded excitement. As they descended the steps from the plaiz to where the rivermen waited, Hennik demanded rudely, "Why is she coming?"

Luzie glanced at Serafina, the target of the question. "Iohen Valorin! Where are your manners? Maisetra Talarico is coming to show us around the grounds at the new Tanfrit Academy. She'll be teaching at the school there and if not for her we wouldn't have a chance to visit."

"I don't want to go to a school!" Rikke protested.

Serafina had composed her expression and took a teasing tone with Rikke. "It's a school for girls, so you wouldn't be allowed to study there anyway."

Rikke made a face. "Then why are we going at all?"

"Because it's a beautiful house," Luzie said briskly. "And Maisetra Talarico wants to show it to me. And then we'll go to see the fair."

And to settle the matter, she stretched her hand out to help Serafina into the boat, giving a gentle squeeze to say, what can you do with them?

For the most part, the boys took as little note of Serafina as they did any of the lodgers. Which was to say, as little note as they did of the furniture. But as the novelty of the boat ride began to pale, Rikke observed, "You talk funny." A sharp glance pushed him to add, "Maisetra Talarek."

It might have been just his tongue stumbling over the foreign name and giving it an Alpennian flavor. Luzie took a breath to demand manners again but Serafina took it for a question.

"Yes, I do. I began learning your language last year. So you must help me if I don't know the right words."

That seemed to satisfy Rikke's curiosity, but his older brother demanded, "Why do you talk to my mother in Italian? Black people come from Africa. I have a book that says so."

Serafina answered more stiffly this time. "But I come from Rome. And in Rome we speak Romanesco. That's a type of Italian."

Luzie felt torn between Hennik's clumsy curiosity and Serafina's discomfort.

"My parents were born in Ethiopia," Serafina added. "That is in Africa, as your book says."

Luzie loved to hear Serafina tell her parents' stories, but she took her cue from the tone of weariness and pointed ahead to the right bank. "Look, there's the landing for the academy. We're almost there."

The outing was not as complete a disaster as Luzie had begun to fear it would be. The boys fidgeted through a tour of the principal rooms but brightened when Serafina took them to the former stable where the printing press had been set up. They took to racing about on the overgrown garden paths while Luzie and Serafina wandered down to visit the small building now called Tanfrit's cottage. Then there was the walk down to the fair outside Urmai proper and all the entertainments to enjoy.

By the time they returned up river in the fading twilight, it was worth the extra teneir to ask the riverman to take them up the chanulez to a closer landing than the Nikuleplaiz so the sleepy boys would have only a short walk.

In an ordinary summer he could have left them no more than a block away but though the channel looked passable he grumbled and declined to go further than the first bridge.

Sunday might be a day of rest, but once the boys were safely in bed, Luzie descended to the parlor where Charluz and Elinur were reading and Serafina waited by the fortepiano.

She looked up with an eager smile. "I want to hear you play the university theme again. I had an idea for how to change it in the second act."

Luzie settled onto the bench beside her, took a long, slow breath to settle her mind, and let the music flow.

When she worked with Serafina on the score for *Tanfrit*, Luzie felt that she had a masterpiece in her hands. By whatever invisible sense Serafina possessed, her descriptions urged the composition into places Luzie would never have dared explore on her own. But in the light of day? Alone with the notes on the page? Doubts sprang up around her like a sudden ring of toadstools in the garden.

Serafina was no musician—she would be the first to admit that. And this work was ambitious. Settings for poetry and small concertos were no practice for the scope of an opera. She was so immersed in it herself, it was hard to judge the music properly. Certainly not by the strict rules of harmony and counterpoint that had been drilled into her by her father. This composition played around those rules. Teased at them. Expression was more important than order. The doubts crept in, and she wondered if she'd grown too intoxicated by the joy of the collaboration. Had the flaws in her work become like the scent of lavender in the sheets, too omnipresent to notice?

And so, one day when no lessons were scheduled, she took up her courage along with the notebook where she had laid out the structure and motifs and she went to call on Maistir Fizeir.

It was good fortune that he was in the city. At the beginning of summer, he'd been traveling with one of his patrons, but the family had returned a few weeks past and he hadn't found another invitation for the remainder of the season.

His greeting seemed stiff but he welcomed her into his parlor and Maisetra Fizeir joined them briefly for tea and cakes, then took her leave with a smile and a comment that surely they wanted to discuss business. It was kind of her to treat it as a social visit. Not all wives were complaisant about their husbands' female colleagues.

Fizeir composed his expression into a kindly invitation and asked, "So what may I do for you today, Maisetra Valorin? Your success has meant that I've seen little of you this spring."

"I hadn't meant to stay away," Luzie said by way of apology. "It's only that I'm busy enough that I don't need the copywork. And I felt awkward asking for your time only to look at my compositions." It wasn't entirely the truth. The new commissions had carried their own judgment of her success. But this was a different matter.

He sniffed and said, "I would have thought you'd gone beyond anything I might offer."

Luzie winced. "It was only that I didn't want to make demands on your time. But now…"

He smiled. "But now you wish my advice?"

"That's it," she agreed, nodding. "I've been working on…that is, I've been contemplating a new project. A rather large one."

Why did she feel the need to soften her intent? Here in Fizeir's parlor they were surrounded by the signs of his accomplishment: the bound volumes of his earlier compositions, the ornate mantel clock engraved with the names of his proud patrons. It seemed brash to admit her plans before a man whose work had graced the largest salles in Rotenek for a generation.

"I've been working on a cycle of songs. A rather extensive one."

He looked startled and doubtful.

She drew out the notebook and fidgeted with it in her lap. "There's an old story—a legend—about Tanfrit the philosopher. My lodger, Maisetra Talarico, is studying thaumaturgy, you know. With Maisetra Sovitre. And she was telling me about the legend, and—" Luzie shrugged. "It caught my interest. Perhaps you're familiar with the story?"

He nodded.

"I thought it would make a good subject. Something rooted in Alpennian history, rather than the old classical tales." Was that an ill-advised comment? Fizeir's specialty was the old-fashioned *opera seria*, however much they were fading from fashion.

"Perhaps," Fizeir said slowly. "Whose verses are you working from?"

"I'm not," Luzie confessed. "There aren't any. I'm writing the whole thing myself. And I thought perhaps you might have some ideas. I have several of the songs worked out, and ideas for the rest."

He reached peremptorily for the notebook and she let him take it to leaf through the pages. It was a bare skeleton of the acts—outlines of a structure with snippets of music in the margins and the beginnings of a libretto. Half of the starts were lined out. There were places where she still hadn't decided between several possible scenes. Luzie suddenly wished she'd thought to make a clean copy to show him.

"This is an opera!" he said, with an accusatory tone. "Whatever were you thinking?" He stood and moved toward the instrument in the corner without asking leave.

She hadn't brought the scores for the fully worked sections. That would have seemed too much of an imposition on his time. But he played around with the motifs, elaborating on them and extending them. Luzie relaxed and sat back, enjoying how his skillful hands turned the familiar phrases into something that one could imagine filling the opera house.

"And is this your libretto?" he asked, turning the page to the lines of verse.

"It's a start on it. I'm not a poet, and for the most part I've begun with the music." She had stopped denying the nature of the project.

"Well you've set yourself quite a challenge," Fizeir said, closing the notebook and returning it to her. "The story is quite inspiring, I agree. Perhaps in other hands…" It seemed he might continue in that vein, but instead he said, "I think you would do well to play to your strengths. And what in heaven's name do you imagine you could do with it if you did finish?"

"I…" There was nothing she could say to that. He was right, of course. What had she expected, that he would offer to find her a patron? Yes, she admitted, that had entered her fantasies.

"Your work is very well suited to the chamber," Fizeir said kindly, echoing her thoughts. "I rather liked those settings of Pertulif that you did."

Had he? Luzie thought. That wasn't the impression he'd given at the time. Then, he'd suggested that those works were too ambitious and that she should return her hand to composing student études. It was as if…

It was, she realized suddenly. It was as if even his praise was a weight tied to her hands to discourage her from aspiring too high. It was impossible that he was jealous of her work! The man was the most famous living composer in Alpennia. And yet every time she'd brought her work to him for advice, the advice had been to set her sights lower, to stay close to the schoolroom and parlor. To close her talent into a box and set it on a shelf rather than letting it out to fly.

"I thank you for your advice, Maistir Fizeir," she said, gathering her things to go. "I will consider it."

CHAPTER EIGHTEEN

Margerit

Late July, 1824

Margerit balanced on the stepstool and poked between the volumes to see if anything had fallen to the back of the shelf. She looked down at Anna's waiting face.

"That's it, I'm afraid, for alchemy. I thought I had a copy of the *Trinosophia*, but I might have lent it to Antuniet. Have you spoken with your father yet about attending classes?"

"Not directly," Anna said hesitantly. "I've talked about the academy, of course, but…"

"Would you prefer me to talk to him?" Margerit asked. She'd been spending half her days this summer meeting with parents of the girls she had marked out as most persistent at her lecture series. The girls themselves might be eager, but their parents took some coaxing toward the idea of allowing a more extended education. Something beyond a few years of finishing school or safely tucking them away at a convent during the hazardous years before they were ready to come out.

"Would you?" Anna asked. "I'm afraid he might think that I—"

"That you were presuming? Not at all," Margerit said briskly. "You are exactly the sort of student I had in mind!" She turned back to the shelves and ran her finger over a few spines. "Now what else might you be interested in? Some of the newer philosophers perhaps? Hegel or Mazzies?"

Anna shook her head. "Jeanne…that is, Mesnera de Cherdillac thinks I focus too closely on philosophy anyway. I don't suppose you have a copy of de Gouges' *The Rights of Women?*"

"The what? No, I doubt it."

"And Papa thinks I should read more Jewish writers. Mendelssohn?" she asked. "Or Rodrigues?"

"Good heavens, I have no idea. Do you have titles?" Perhaps *she* was too closely focused on philosophy.

Her next question was interrupted by the maid at the door, announcing, "Sister Petrunel has arrived for you, Maisetra."

Ah, the morning had slipped away faster than she thought. Ordinarily she would have received her here in the library, but she didn't want to dislodge Anna. And Brandel should be at his studies here soon as well.

"Show her to the parlor," Margerit said. "I'll be there as soon as I've gathered my notes."

"Or I can help you with that," Petrunel said cheerfully, on the maid's heels.

Margerit pushed a curl out of her eyes and descended the steps carefully. "It's no trouble Petra," she said with a grin. The sight of her former governess always brought a wave of nostalgia and that sense of being under firm and confident direction. Not that she would return to those days…

Her manners returned to her. "Sister Petrunel, I don't know that you've met Anna Monterrez. She's Antuniet Chazillen's apprentice in alchemy. I'm keeping an eye on her for the summer while Antuniet is away. Anna, this is Sister Petrunel from the Orisules who's to be headmistress of my college."

Petra nodded and Anna had already risen to dip a brief curtsey.

"Monterrez? The jeweler's daughter?"

"One of them," Anna replied, and then to Margerit, "I can find something on my own. Don't let me keep you."

When they were settled in the parlor, Margerit took up their previous day's conversation. "Now about astronomy—"

They had been working their way through the planned curriculum, piece by piece. Petra was so thorough that Margerit sometimes despaired of her leaving the instructors themselves any choice in the matter. But only a few of them had experience in regular teaching. As Petra pointed out, classes were a different matter than presenting an evening's lecture in a public salle. It was important to show that the students would be given a strong and solid program.

"That girl seems an unusual choice for an apprentice," Petra commented.

Margerit laughed. "When has Maisetra Chazillen done anything in the usual way? But Anna is perfect for her. And she's the sort of student I want. Serious and studious, but one with no opportunity to pursue a higher education in the usual way."

"Do you mean she's to be one of your students?"

"If her father agrees," Margerit said. "That seems to be the case with so many of them! I think I have enough parents convinced for a respectably sized class. It makes sense to start with a small group, focusing on the girls with the most interest. With more, half might drift away and that would dishearten them."

"But a Jewish girl…do you think she will be comfortable?" Sister Petrunel seemed to be taken aback and was searching for some tactful objection.

Margerit frowned. She hadn't thought that Anna might feel alone in that way. "Perhaps I should ask Maistir Monterrez if he knows any other girls who might be interested."

"That wasn't quite what I meant," Petra said tartly. "Would she be permitted to study at a Christian school?"

"I'd scarcely call it that," Margerit protested. "It's true I plan to cover thaumaturgy in the curriculum, and that means a certain interest in theology, but nothing formal." The university dozzures might consider that to be too great a trespass into their own gardens. "I hope there's no reason why Jewish students wouldn't feel welcome."

Petra said slowly, "I suppose I had assumed…"

Oh. That possibility hadn't occurred to Margerit: that hiring Sister Petrunel and filling some of the teaching positions from the ranks of the Orisules might give the impression that her college was meant to be an extension of the convent schools.

"I never meant it as a religious school, as such," Margerit ventured, watching Petrunel's face for reaction.

"But you mean to teach thaumaturgy."

"As a philosophy, yes. And as a study of practices. I'd like—" She'd mentioned this only to a very few people. "I'd like to see if we can encourage the development of talents in that direction. You yourself said that it's difficult for girls to get good instruction in thaumaturgy outside the convent. Even the ancient authors talk about the difficulty of passing on traditions when each mystery guild keeps its own secrets so closely. Everyone says Alpennia has a strong tradition of mysteries based on the work of people like Fortunatus and Gaudericus. But that's centuries past. Where is the new work? Where are their ideas being taught and expanded? I know groups like the Benezets are said to teach their own members, but the guilds guard their traditions too closely. The university doesn't encourage practice. Not in any practical sense. If thaumaturgy is to revive in importance to the state—"

She hesitated, wondering how common that knowledge was. Princess Annek had privately encouraged her plans for the school but perhaps she hadn't meant that support to be public. "Not just the Great Mysteries and the protections of the *tutelas*, but things that are useful. Like the healing mysteries you do at the convent. Think how much more could be done with more trained thaumaturgists. Or combining ritual with new agricultural practices. We've all heard about the failed ceremonies during the French Wars. What if Prince Aukust could have called on a practiced corps that could direct the guilds…?"

She let the thought trail off, realizing how self-important it sounded that she might change the face of Europe on the basis of a group of schoolgirls.

Sister Petrunel seemed to have something of the same thought, for she asked gently, "And what makes you think that you should be the one to accomplish this?"

"Because I've been blessed with the skill to know who has talent. True talent. The sort that can be developed. Maisetra Talarico is even more sensitive. She can see traces of ancient mysteries that we've lost any ability to recreate. And I'm blessed to be surrounded by colleagues who understand that mysteries can be tuned like a harp or built like architecture. Not just rituals to be acted out the same way we always have. It's important that we don't waste those talents just because they happen to have been given to young women who are only allowed to dream of being wives and mothers."

"I see," Sister Petrunel said slowly. "Quite an ambition. I hadn't realized you were planning a school for sorcerers."

Margerit winced at the word even though it was said in jest. "That's not what I mean. The thaumaturgy would only be one part of the curriculum—for those with the interest and skill. The rest of the girls should have a chance to expand their minds as well, no matter what subject they turn to. We shouldn't be wasting mathematicians or legal scholars or historians either."

"Of course. Then perhaps we should continue discussing those parts of the curriculum," Sister Petrunel said.

* * *

Barbara returned late from the council hall, but it made little disruption in the rhythms of the household. Aunt Bertrut and Uncle Charul were traveling for the summer—visiting in Chalanz for a while, and by now most likely ensconced at Marzim with the crowd of Pertineks. With no regular round of dinners or balls over the summer, Tiporsel House had fallen into the habit of dining *en famille* in the lower parlor overlooking the back gardens where the windows could be opened to catch the faintest of breezes.

As the clatter of dishes quieted, Margerit listened to Barbara quizzing her cousin on the day's lessons. Brandel had returned from his visit in Rapenfil full of family news and was enjoying the novelty of being treated as an adult among adults at the dinner table, expected to join in the conversations rather than keeping silent. Barbara was taking the opportunity of her irregular spaces of free time to drill Brandel on some of the more practical skills of an armin's duties. He was practicing regularly with pistols now, as well as the sword, riding out past the Port Ausiz to shoot at targets when the parade grounds were empty.

Academic studies were suspended for the summer as Chautovil was Aukustin's tutor before all else and the Dowager Princess Elisebet's household had removed to Fallorek. Perhaps Brandel would be invited to join them next year. Elisebet had not yet chosen to take further notice of her son's school-fellow, but Barbara had admitted to having thoughts in that direction and it colored the form of Brandel's less martial lessons. Not only courtly skills like dancing, but the subtler dance of how an armin followed his charge through a crowd, always at hand but never intrusive. How to move soundlessly in ways that whispered or shouted to those around. How to listen for the details of speech and address that gave clues to thought and intent, and might signal some more overt challenge.

Margerit had come to appreciate the results of those skills, first from Barbara and then under Marken's watch. But she'd never before heard them laid out as a lesson plan so baldly. She asked Barbara about it that evening, when they had retired to their room and she had dismissed Maitelen to finish brushing out Barbara's long tawny hair on her own. It was still too warm and sticky for bed and the long, even strokes of the brush were a more comfortable intimacy.

"Who taught you?" she asked as the golden wave fell loose and she lifted the brush again. "Those things you're teaching Brandel, who taught them to you?"

Her movements raised a scent of lavender and well-dressed leather and even a hint horses still lingering. She loved how Barbara's presence evoked memories of adventure. It took her back to the first time they'd spoken, years ago in the park in Chalanz.

"The baron taught me, though not in the same way." Barbara tipped her head back to lean into the slow movements. "And, of course, he had other armins before me. They were willing to give advice once they saw I was to be more than a curiosity. The baron—" Now Barbara's face twisted in not entirely pleasant memories. "He taught more by disapproval. He would say, 'Attend me' and then my only guidance would be frowns and sidelong looks."

Barbara could speak of it more calmly now than she once had, when the wound of his betrayal was more raw. Margerit had enjoyed far less of the baron's irascible personality, but she could easily imagine how it must have been. She turned the conversation away from that sore point. "Is there any progress in the council?" She set the brush aside and began twisting the hair into a loose braid.

A wry humor infused Barbara's answer. "We seem to be on the verge of agreeing that administration of water transport has always been within the ambit of the common council. A commission has been funded to oversee dredging, though the execution will take longer to plan. That may be the best we can hope for."

Margerit tied the ribbon off and then leaned down to place a kiss where an old scar made the part in her hair jog sideways. "And will that be an end of it?"

"No." Barbara leaned back against her but their eyes met in the dressing table mirror. "The commons are being more sensible than we are these days. They can decide whether closing off the canals will make the slightest difference in how high the Rotein runs, and we can return to squabbling over toll roads or whatever the latest outrage might be. No more council until the season begins again, though. Too late for most to remove entirely for what's left of the summer, but I expect the plaiz should be a little more empty for the next month. And what of you? Is the college taking all your time?"

"Not all," Margerit answered. "I have a new mystery to work on for the court. And there's always time for you." Summer heat or no, the bed was calling.

* * *

When Margerit stepped down from the carriage in front of Maisetra Valorin's house, she could hear the faint sound of the fortepiano from the front walk. It was only student lessons, with none of the unsettling pull of Maisetra Valorin's own music. Serafina must have been watching from the parlor window, for she opened the door before there was a need to knock and closed it again quietly behind her.

"Will we have everything we need to start working today?" Serafina asked as they settled themselves on the cushions and the carriage jerked into motion.

"I think so," Margerit answered. "Princess Annek finally found the time to draw up the remaining requirements for the ceremony."

It was only a minor mystery: some changes to the routines of the palace guards. They were accustomed enough to the ceremonial nature of their work that the additions would be no burden. Whether those changes would evoke any additional protection would depend, in part, on the participants. As with any mystery, the repetitions by enough different individuals were sure to catch the ear of the saints at some point. This was a subtle armor. Therein lay both its strength and its flaw. How many such rituals had been established in the past, only to be discarded by those who could see no immediate value?

Indeed, most wouldn't have thought developing them worth the trouble, except for the convenience of having a thaumaturgist attached to the court. When she had first been appointed, Margerit might have considered it a waste of her talents. And it was frustrating to hear the constant reports of failures and disasters across the land and face Annek's refusal to set her to work on them. But in the past three years, she'd grown more appreciative of how Annek chose to use her skills. It was not enough to have power, it must be seen to be used and that use must be seen to be effective and successful. The palace rituals were—not exactly practice, but a foundation. Annek had hinted that others were at work on the Great Mysteries. Enough. Margerit was tired of battering at those doors. On these small things, she could apply her talents fully, and there was a chance to teach Serafina the more practical aspects of the art.

Margerit realized how lost in thought she had been when Serafina asked, "It's going well? The preparations?"

"I'm sorry! Yes," she replied hastily. "It's only that there's so much to do still. I don't know how I'd manage without Sister Petrunel. You've met her, yes?"

A nod.

"You'll like the new workroom, I think," Margerit continued. "Perhaps I shouldn't have had them finish it before the classrooms were done. But I couldn't bear the thought of one more project on the library table at home."

"I remember," Serafina said with a smile.

Yes, that had been the first time they'd worked together. Serafina was newly arrived in Rotenek, and Princess Annek had required a truth-seeking mystery to counter the accusations of sorcery that had been made against her son, Efriturik. The research and sketches had overflowed the library and taken over the parlor, to Aunt Bertrut's dismay. That was when the thought had first fastened itself in her mind: to have a larger place, a dedicated space for this sort of work. The academy had been an afterthought back then—a place that could include a lecture hall so that she needn't compete with balls and concerts for space during the season. Now the school had taken first place in her heart and plans. But the workroom—that was a delicious luxury.

The long oak tables invited the placement of notes and diagrams. Standing lecterns had wheels so that the reference books could easily be moved with the work. At one end of the room, an open space was tiled in a decorative grid, the better to practice movements and note the placement of the larger apparatus. At the other end, she had brought in from a storeroom an ancient standing cabinet, crowded with drawers and tiny compartments, in which some Chasteld ancestor had assembled a collection of wonders and curiosities. By the time of Chasteld's death, the valuable items had long since disappeared and it contained fragments of broken seashells, the tusks of some unknown beast, a jumble of minerals of a common sort and, behind one glass-fronted door, a pile of feathers that must once have been a stuffed and mounted bird. Margerit had claimed it to store and organize the various bits of common apparatus that experimental mysteries might call for. Candles of various sorts, oils, bits of parchment, small vials of water, both holy and distilled, inks in all colors and substances and, in one locked compartment, her small, precious collection of secondary relics, bits of wood and cloth.

But for now, they would be working with ideas alone—with the structures of symbol and logic that would invoke and bind together the divine grace symbolized in those objects. Margerit looked over to where Serafina waited with patient resignation. In the beginning, there had been hope. That was before failure had become a habit. It was time to move beyond that past.

"This time I want you to design the mystery and direct me in performing it."

The resignation fell away, replaced with curiosity. "Me? How can I design it if—"

Margerit spread out the outline of the current palace ceremonial and handed Serafina the description and specifications that Annek had drawn up. "Begin with the markein as we always do. What will be the limits of the physical ambit?"

Serafina frowned down at the paper. "We'll need something to represent the palace grounds." She turned to the open tiled floor and asked, "Do you have a stick of chalk?"

CHAPTER NINETEEN

Serafina

August, 1824

Serafina carefully avoided noticing the two pairs of eyes that turned to meet her when she entered the dining room. It had been a late night and a late morning. The boys were there, not to linger over breakfast, but for an early luncheon. Usually someone else would be present and the silence would not be so pointed.

Iohen Valorin didn't like her. Serafina had yet to untangle precisely what it was he disliked beyond a vague jealousy of anyone who took his mother's attention. He found excuses to come into their conversations, to come between them when walking, to have inconvenient need of his mother's time. Luzie was patient, mingling excuses for his demands with guilt over the long separation they endured during the school year. Serafina was patient because there was nothing else to be.

"Good morning Maistir Iohen, Maistir Orrik." She took a chair at the far end of the dining table. They were not on such terms that she could use Luzie's pet names for them.

"Good morning Maisetra Talarek," Rikke replied.

Serafina hadn't decided whether there was malice behind his continued mangling of her name. It might be nothing more than a childish tongue turning it into something more Alpennian. Roman tongues had turned her father's name into Talarico. Another change scarcely mattered and she didn't care to betray how much it needled her. Rikke's guileless questions often fell barely short of rudeness. Iohen's rudeness was more subtle and more studied. He returned to his meal without a word.

Gerta came in and placed a small basket of rolls and a pot of butter on the table before her, asking, "Will that be enough, Maisetra? Or would you rather have luncheon? Cook says she has more of the cold pie but you usually only want bread in the morning."

"That will do," Serafina answered.

"There's a letter for you," Gerta added. "Not a regular letter, but a note that a boy brought round. Would you like it now?"

Serafina nodded, thinking it would save her from having to make conversation. Her heart had squeezed tightly at the word "letter," but it couldn't be from Paolo. All his correspondence came through the bankers.

The outside bore nothing except her name and a plain drop of red wax to hold it closed with no design on the seal. She could see a trace of *fluctus* threaded through the wax. Not Margerit, then. She wouldn't bother with anything that elaborate and she certainly had no need for urgency. They saw each other often enough for ordinary questions. Before breaking the seal she examined the patterns of power it carried. Not the ordinary sort that traced whose hands opened the message, but one bound to the ink in some fashion. If the wrong person broke the seal, would the message disappear entirely? It seemed it might be so, but she couldn't be certain. And who would be sending her such messages?

The answer was found in the small looping "K" at the bottom of the page. So the Austrian was back in town. But was there any need for this secrecy or was it merely a habit with him? The message itself was simple, if indirect.

I would like to make further use of your insight. I hear that you are fond of the gardens at Urmai. There is a statue of Prince Domric that shows to advantage in the afternoon light.

The afternoon? With no other indication, he must mean today, unless he expected her to travel down to Urmai every day until he appeared. He presumed a great deal to think she could drop any other plans she might have made. But there were no such plans and the location would cause no comment. She traveled down to the academy often enough, and one might run into anyone by chance at the pleasure gardens. Secrecy raised more questions than openness.

When Kreiser had first contacted her, she'd acceded as a favor to Margerit, not realizing that he'd never claimed that authority except by implication. His questions had seemed harmless. Had a certain object been touched by mysteries? To what purpose? Who had performed the rite? Where? Half the time she could see no trace of power. Only rarely could she follow the traces beyond the immediate event. As his questions moved from Alpennian matters to a wider search, she'd become uneasy about how far her cooperation should go. She knew too little about what interests the Empire might have in the Papal States—only that they did have interests. And she'd thought too little about how deep her own loyalties might be. She'd never had any reason to question her place in the forces that moved through the European courts and capitals. She had no allegience to Alpennia beyond personal bonds. Neither did she have the bone-deep attachment to Rome that Paolo and Costanza and even her brother's wife Giuletta had. But the thought that she might find herself spying for Austria against the city of her birth…

The scrying he'd asked for was uneasily similar to what Paolo had wanted. But this time—with Kreiser's help—she had succeeded. Success was intoxicating. Somehow, step by step, she'd become enmeshed, and now she was uncertain how to refuse. How important was Kreiser here in Alpennia? More important than she was, that was certain. *Could* she refuse?

She folded up the paper and slipped it into a pocket in her skirts.

When Gerta next came through clearing away the boys' plates, she said, "If Maisetra Valorin asks, I'm going to Urmai for the afternoon."

The maid nodded. She was accustomed to serving as a calendar for the lodgers. "Will you be late for supper? Cook will want to know."

Serafina calculated. "She shouldn't wait on me."

Meals were more predictable in the summer and Chisillic had higher expectations for promptness than in the eat-and-run of the winter season.

At the other end of the table, Serafina saw Iohen lean down to whisper something in his brother's ear and then nudge him sharply.

The younger boy looked over at her with what might be a genuinely innocent expression. "Why do you sleep in my mama's room?" he asked.

There was no guile in his voice, only curiosity, but Iohen was watching her under suspicious brows. Did he guess anything near the truth? Or was he only fishing for some tender spot? Who knew what the imagination of schoolboys might turn up.

"I sleep in your mother's room," she said carefully, "because I gave up my own room for the two of you." She couldn't tell whether Iohen was satisfied or not, but Orrik simply nodded and reached for another sweetbun.

* * *

She still hadn't become accustomed to the rules of Alpennian society with regard to men and women, though she could always go to Jeanne for plain answers. She had presented herself as a married woman, and therefore the company of unfamiliar men was not forbidden to her. If she had been accompanied by a lady's maid—or lived in those high circles where one might employ an armin—then she might dare to meet a man such as Mesner Kreiser in a private parlor at a café. It was only Luzie's own strictures against male visitors that prevented him from coming to her at home. So many rules! She had been shielded from the need to know them in Rome by a girlhood spent outside ordinary society. Her father's colleagues had scarcely considered her female, and when they did, his presence served as chaperone. After her marriage, Paolo's position gave her the same protection. Costanza had been the one to open her eyes to how those rules could be used to a woman's advantage, as well as how they could bring about her ruin.

The boat ride down to the school was more than familiar, though she usually tried to beg carriage space for the return to save the sharper upstream fare. The riverman who answered her hail knew her from previous trips and asked, "The Chasteld landing?"

She thought about telling him to continue down to the gardens, but something in Kreiser's caution infected her and she only nodded. There was time to walk from there and then there would be no reason for anyone at all to remember.

She knew the monument Kreiser had specified. The gardens were not as full as the time she visited with Luzie and the boys. The children that played along the hedge-bordered paths today lived here, as did the shop girls out on a midday break. The visitors were a different mix as well: courting couples of respectable families, attended at a safe distance by maids or governesses, clumps of students from the university who hadn't escaped the city for their more abbreviated summer season, walking with heads together in argument.

Serafina settled herself on a bench and looked around to see if Kreiser were in view. Her heart skipped. An achingly familiar figure was winding through the paths with an awkward case in hand.

Olimpia Hankez noticed her, hesitated, then shifted her path. "It's a lovely day," she offered.

It was what one said in Urmai. One praised the cool breezes that had first made the spot popular so many years ago. One admired the gardens and made note of whether the crowds were thick or thin. One didn't exclaim in surprise at the sight of a former lover.

"You've come for work?" Serafina asked, nodding at the art case under her arm.

"I thought I'd set myself up and sketch. I need new faces," Olimpia said, with a rueful twist of her mouth. "And you?"

"I'm meeting someone," Serafina returned, trying to keep the answer as uninviting as possible. She could still be moved by Olimpia's energetic grace. The betrayal hadn't changed that. Luzie hadn't changed that. Luzie filled a different place in her life, in her heart. A quieter place. Other spaces were still empty. Olimpia had filled one of them for a time. There had never been any word of forever between them. How could there have been? Olimpia dealt in bodies—explored them, appreciated them, immortalized them and then moved on. And for her? She barely knew what she was searching for.

From the corner of her eye she caught a glimpse of Kreiser's ruddy face. Olimpia saw the movement and followed it. Her eyes widened slightly. Had she recognized the Austrian? Or did she think it an assignation? Or both perhaps?

She said only, "It was good to see you again," and moved on.

If Kreiser had noticed Olimpia he said nothing when he settled himself on the bench and placed a well-worn atlas in her lap. Even before she opened the covers she could feel the tingle of some mystic residue within the pages. There were no preliminaries this time.

"I thought this might help. Open to the marked page," he instructed.

She found the ribbon and spread the book across her lap. It was only a section of land, taken out of context, with little markings for roads and rivers, tiny buildings indicating towns, and a faint glow perceptible only to the sensitive where Kreiser had marked a pattern of symbols across one part.

Next he opened a small case that shone brightly with *fluctus* and unwrapped layers of cloth to lay a frozen lump in her outstretched hand. It became slick with melt and made her fingers ache with the cold.

"Don't worry about where the ice itself came from," he said. "Follow the cold. Trace it back to its origin. Use the map."

Serafina clenched her fingers around the ice, holding it away from the atlas and hoping that she could find the thread before it had melted away.

The last time they had worked together she had become lost in the visions, like one wandering in a fog. There had been no landmarks, no sense of distances or scale. This time the search was more focused and the atlas provided an anchor. She stared down at the page, trying to shift her mind into that floating state where even the faintest trace of *fluctus* would be apparent.

It had been easier to achieve within the walls of a church, where every habit and instinct called to those inner eyes. Here it took more conscious effort to remove distractions one by one: the laughing children, the small flock of songbirds in the tree behind her, the still unsettling memory of Olimpia's appearance. She stared fixedly at the pages of the atlas so long that her eyes swam and the ink moved on the page. No, that wasn't the ink. The mystic sigils had lifted up and were no longer tied to the paper.

She closed her eyes and followed those guides to their home. Not the page, but the land itself. She was a bird soaring high, a cloud drifting across the land. She could feel the cold of the snow-capped peaks sinking into her bones, spreading from her shivering fingers, even here in the sunlit gardens.

Yes, there was the shape at the heart of it. It felt like a rounded mass with waves lapping outward. Or like the opening petals of a rose. This was the pattern it had been impossible to find before, when the ripples and cross-ripples of those waves echoed back and forth across the landscape, confusing her senses. In her mind, she plucked away the petals from the edges of the mystery one by one. The later echoes, the spreading influence, the currents that the curse had traced across field and mountain. There was the core, the bud, the central mystery as it had been set.

She felt giddy at her success. This was different from observing the formal ceremonies in the cathedral. This was wild and uncertain, a puzzle to solve.

A sudden laugh behind her brought her back to Urmai. One hand was damp and empty and the other hovered over a page, pointing to one of the small black marks set on the page.

"Yes." Kreiser let it out like a sigh. "Now for the harder part. That may be where the mystery was first invoked, but it's unlikely that the celebrants worked it in that spot. I want you to cast your mind through and past. Find the source or sources."

It took some time to compose herself again, returning to the landscape with its snow and peaks and full-blown rose of light nestled in one mountain pass. The giddy joy was gone and she set to work plucking the petals away again, one by one, to reach that core. It was easier this time, now that she had that image to follow. Now what? A stem, a branch, roots in the soil pointing to what had sprouted and nourished the mystery. She could feel them, like encountering a cobweb in the dark. Insubstantial but resistant. Invisible yet present. Her finger brushed a strand and it twitched and jumped, as if plucked at the other end. But there *was* another end. She could feel it stretching out, anchored somewhere...

And then there was only the park, and the atlas, and Kreiser sitting patiently beside her. Was it the image of the cobweb that betrayed her? She moved her fingers over the page again but could no longer pick up the strands. They melted away like the lump of ice had. The touch of her mind wasn't delicate enough to trace the threads from across the gulf of miles. They were there, they led somewhere, but...

With a sigh, she rested her hands on the pages, tired from holding them raised above the book, and opened her eyes. "I'm sorry," she said. "I haven't the skill."

Kreiser was staring at her curiously. "If that was a failure of skill, may I aspire to fail so badly."

"What does it mean?" Serafina asked. She brushed her fingertips across the skirts of her dress, still feeling those clinging strands.

He shook his head and said slowly, "Shall we try a different question?"

He placed a bright gold coin in her hand this time. For a moment she thought it was payment, but he opened the atlas to a page somewhere near the back.

"No mysteries or disasters this time. Can you trace what path that coin has taken?"

Serafina recognized the outlines of the coast where Ravenna stretched up toward Venice. This had nothing at all to do with the weather mystery. "No," she said. "Do you think me a child? I won't do your spying for you."

There was a hint of amused respect as he took the atlas back, saying, "No harm in asking. I will let you know when I have further questions."

Serafina stayed on the bench after Kreiser left, in deference to his impulses to discretion, though he could hardly have concerns for his reputation as she did. If his intent in arranging the meeting for Urmai had been that no one should take note of their meeting, it had failed, but only from chance. Across the other side of the small square, Olimpia was sitting with her sketchpad on her lap. Well, there was nothing to be either ashamed or afraid of in speaking with Kreiser in a public place, but best to make that clear by her actions. She rose and went to lean over the back of Olimpia's bench where she could see the drawing in progress.

The page was covered with charcoal studies of faces and heads, crowding each other like sweets on a platter. A laughing child, no doubt in quick motion for it was indicated by only a few hasty lines. An old woman and a young one, their heads together in conversation, drawn more carefully this time. They might have been mother and daughter—must have been, for Olimpia's talent had shown the young woman's soul shining from under the other's lined face. Or perhaps they had been sisters? And it was the wrinkles that were the illusion, showing the woman one would some day become? There were endless stories hidden on that page.

Serafina breathed a sigh of relief that her own figure did not appear.

"Were you looking for this, perhaps?" Olimpia said, bringing out a separate paper from the case beside her on the bench.

Serafina had previously seen only the ordinary drawings Olimpia had done of her. She'd refused to look at that last allegory. Was this what Olimpia saw through her true vision? It was only black and white: lines and shading and smudges. Between those marks, wisps of mystic color traced, weaving in and out around the two figures on the bench. It was an illusion that the drawing moved on the page, just as the color itself was an illusion. Kreiser was indistinct: a shoulder, a turned head. Serafina saw herself framed, her hands hovering lightly over the atlas, her face raised and her eyes closed, the better to see the visions that came through it. Although the figure was small and lightly sketched, the face held an expression suspended between concentration and awe.

"But it isn't right," she protested, gesturing to the surrounding currents of *fluctus* in the drawing. "None of that was there. I know. I can't—"

"I don't draw what's there, I draw what I see," Olimpia said quietly.

"May I have it?" Serafina said without thinking. She couldn't afford Olimpia's work! The woman took commissions from the wealthiest people in the land.

"If you do me a favor." Olimpia laid a plain sheet of tissue on top of the drawing to prevent smudging and rolled it carefully into a small tube.

Serafina made a questioning sound, not committing herself.

"I've been asked to do a portrait of Maisetra Sovitre with her college as the setting."

Serafina didn't ask who the patron was, but the answer came anyway.

"Evidently Princess Anna liked my painting of the guild dinner. Now she wants portraits of some members of the court. I'd love to have a chance to paint the alchemist! I have plenty of studies of Maisetra Sovitre herself from the painting I did last year, but I need someone to show me around the college grounds. I'd like to show it in progress, half-finished, coming into being from wrack and ruin."

Yes. Serafina could see the symbolism in that. It was one of Margerit's passions: to bring things back from obscurity and disuse into life again.

"I know you have something to do with the academy," Olimpia continued. "Could you take me there? Show me around? Help me find a good setting while the repairs are still half-finished?"

"It might be too late for that," Serafina pointed out. "The work is on schedule to open with the Mauriz term. The main buildings are all complete, but I think there's still scaffolding on some of the outbuildings." She tried to visualize various vistas in her mind. "You could put the mansion itself in the background—"

"There's still hours and hours of light," Olimpia said. "Could we go now?"

This was the first time Serafina had looked at the renovations with an outsider's eye. When Luzie had visited, they had spoken mostly of what the school would become, but Olimpia wanted to see that becoming. The remaining work in the main buildings was all inside—the finishing of the classrooms and the residential areas. The printing house, too, was finished and now busy with activity as the Poor Scholar printers worked to finish Mesnera Collfield's book before she returned and classes began. It was mostly the farther outbuildings that remained incomplete.

They wandered along the paths, now well-trodden by workmen. Olimpia made maps of where the structures stood with little notes about their condition and how they would show against the mansion itself. Serafina took her to visit Tanfrit's cottage with an air of sharing great secrets. It had been cleared and cleaned, and the smell of fresh carpentry and new plaster had replaced that of the barnyard.

Olimpia paused for a brief sketch while hearing the history and significance of the building. "And what does Maisetra Sovitre plan for it?" she asked.

"I don't think she's decided. In her mind it's something of a shrine. Not like in a chapel. There's a chapel on the grounds already that the students will use. It isn't sacred in that sense." Not in that sense perhaps, but there was a stillness, a depth to the place.

Olimpia must have had something of the same impression. As she looked around, she said slowly, "No, there's nothing of that sort here. But lives can make a place as sacred as relics can." And then more briskly, "We're making this too complicated. I think that for the background I shall simply need to move things around." She frowned at her notes. "I'd like to use the front facade of the main building. The view from the river approach. I think I'll just add some scaffolding back on." She gave Serafina a sidelong smile. "It's the advantage of painting what I see rather than what's there."

Somewhere along the path out to the cottage, the awkwardness had fallen away. The memory of that last sitting remained, but without the sting. Might they still be together if Olimpia had used her vision before? But no. Magic was no solution to the human heart.

"I'll introduce you to Mefro Montekler, the housekeeper," Serafina said, nodding in the direction they had come. "And Maistera Ionkil as well. They'll see you settled with anything you need for your work."

As they returned to the mansion proper, Serafina ventured, "The portrait of Maisetra Sovitre, will it be a…a true portrait?" She was never quite certain how to speak of that special quality in Olimpia's work.

"I think it must. That's what Princess Anna is paying me for. She's too sharp to be put off with excuses about muses and inspiration. I only hope she's careful about which courtiers she asks me to paint!"

The printing project had spilled out of its own buildings into what would become the dining hall. Stacks of finished folios crowded against bundles of color plates carefully layered in tissue. The air was thick with the tang of printer's ink. Someone had been assembling signatures in a corner of the room, but there was no one at work just now. Serafina hesitated at the entrance to the room. The disarray seemed to have become a point of contention for the three women gathered there.

"Sister Petrunel," the housekeeper was saying firmly, "I told them they might use the space, so there's no point to scolding the printers over it. They aren't in anyone's way at the moment and they hope to be finished before the term starts. If they aren't, we'll find some other space."

Akezze was standing beside her with arms crossed, making a united front against the headmistress.

To cover the awkward interruption, Olimpia paused to examine one of the plates, a careful drawing of a tree-like structure, with some details enlarged to one side. Serafina saw Akezze's head turn to take note of them, but the argument continued unabated.

"It wasn't your place to give them permission," Sister Petrunel said. "The school is under my administration."

"Begging your pardon," Montekler replied. "The buildings themselves are under my authority. It's the teaching and the students that are your concern. And as the teaching hasn't started yet—"

"But the printers themselves—" Petrunel began.

"Are not yours to direct either," Akezze pointed out. "And I would ask in the future if you have concerns about them, that you bring them to me."

Petrunel bristled visibly. "I see I was mistaken. I had thought that the publications were under the name of the academy."

"Not entirely," Akezze explained. "Maisetra Sovitre plans to have certain works published under the academy's name, but the printers have been given a lease for the space. That's a separate arrangement from the school. But even it they were, that would fall under Maisetra Ionkil's concern, not yours."

"If this—" Petrunel held up one of the printed pages. "—has nothing to do with the academy then it has no business here."

The argument seemed to have circled around to its beginnings again and Serafina thought an interruption might be welcome.

"Mefro Montekler?" she said, pulling Olimpia along after her. "I wanted you to meet Olimpia Hankez, the painter. She'll be in and about working on a painting of Maisetra Sovitre."

The others nodded to them and Montekler took Olimpia aside to speak in low voices about her needs.

Akezze returned to the matter of jurisdiction. "I believe Mesnera Collfield will be teaching botany here, so her book is not entirely unrelated."

"Teaching?" Petrunel asked sharply. "Her name hadn't been mentioned to me."

Now Akezze hesitated. "I might have misunderstood."

It sounded to Serafina that the misunderstanding was on the other side, but perhaps that wouldn't be polite for Akezze to suggest.

"If she limits herself to the physical sciences, I suppose…" Petrunel began. Then she turned to Serafina. "And I suppose you'll be teaching as well, though goodness knows what!"

Serafina shook her head and her tongue faltered. "No…I…I'm only a student like the others."

"A student?" Sister Petrunel looked her up and down. "You're old to be a student. In what?"

"Maisetra Sovitre has been teaching me thaumaturgy. How to create mysteries."

"Ah, you must be the Talarico woman. Yes, Margerit spoke of you. She had given me the impression that you had studied elsewhere. But surely she hasn't been teaching you herself!"

It was clear from the woman's tone that this was news to her. Serafina knew that Margerit softened the importance of her own instruction when speaking to others. And she could see how Sister Petrunel's opinions might lead one to skip over topics that she might object to. But Margerit had always spoken glowingly of her former governess. How was it they hadn't yet butted heads over this subject?

Serafina glanced over to Akezze and saw the same worry in her eyes.

CHAPTER TWENTY

Jeanne

Early September, 1824

The sky cracked open with a blaze of lightning as they crossed the border into the low, forested hills of Helviz. The coachman called down that he'd try to make Pont-Sain-Pol before dark. Jeanne relaxed into the cushions. The fury of the storm was nothing to the tense suspicions of the soldiers in the past week on the road. Travel papers that should have seen them safely through the morass of jurisdictions between Bayreuth and Strasbourg had been questioned at every turn and they had only once made the mistake of mentioning the nature of their visit to Prague. The closer they came to Alpennia the sharper the looks. What would Antuniet have done without her to coax and cajole? But Antuniet had done this before, and very much alone. Jeanne glanced over and saw her staring pensively out the window where rain lashed the glass into impenetrability.

"Are you thinking of the last time?" Jeanne asked.

Antuniet's head turned from the window. "The last time?"

"That you traveled this way," Jeanne said. "The last time you returned home."

"No," Antuniet said. And then, "Yes, I suppose. It's different this time, but there's still that uncertainty. Will my project succeed? What will the reception be?" She looked back toward the window. "That's no natural storm. No wonder the people back in Les Bains were frightened. What have we come back to?"

Jeanne took her hand. That much, and no more. Toneke hated to be fussed over, and yet she longed to fuss. Throughout the whole journey she'd wanted to offer comfort when it might not be wanted, or even needed. And, of course, Marien was perched on the forward seat, studiously not seeing anything she wasn't meant to see.

Not all of Antuniet's outward calm was for show. When it came to the central purpose of this journey, she had made her calculations, weighed her choices, and set out with eyes open. Perhaps it was enough to be here, beside her, accepting those choices.

They'd sent word ahead from Basel of their expected arrival. Not the precise day or time, of course, yet Tomric had the door open in welcome before the hired groom had even let down the steps. And while the men dealt with trunks and boxes, and Marien took their coats and bonnets, Ainis bustled out to promise tea as soon as the water could be heated.

"Never mind the tea, but heat enough for a bath," Jeanne said. "Toneke, you'll want to lie down for a bit until its ready."

Antuniet gave an exasperated sigh. "Jeanne, I don't need to be cosseted like that!" She leaned closer and lowered her voice. "There are foundations to lay before we let the world guess that I'm in a delicate condition. I need to have Margerit set me up with another lecture so I can share the fruits of this summer's research. All in the most theoretical terms, of course. Just enough to let them all draw their own conclusions."

"Then if you won't lie down, at least sit," Jeanne urged. "It makes me tired to look at you. And I'll spend the time sending out a few notes to let people know we've returned. I suppose you'll want to go see to your workshop tomorrow. Shall I let Anna know to meet you there?"

Antuniet nodded and Jeanne settled down to work.

* * *

By midmorning the next day, Jeanne found herself still staring at the remaining stack of correspondence yet to be opened and wondering if there were anything that couldn't wait for a few more days. Despite her protests against being cosseted, Antuniet was barely stirring upstairs and Cook was already asking when luncheon should be served. At least it was a week or two before anything resembling regular visiting would start again.

To belie that thought, she heard the faint chime of the doorbell ringing in the back, and the quick steps of Ainis hurrying to answer. Before Jeanne could decide whether to be annoyed, Anna was there in the doorway to the parlor saying, "I hope you don't mind. I know your note said the palace workshop this afternoon, but then I wouldn't have a chance to welcome you back as well."

When had she grown so tall? They'd only been gone four months. But no, it was only fresh eyes from the absence. This new Anna had been emerging all the last year, leaving behind the shy, studious girl for a poised young woman.

Where once she might have dashed across the room into Jeanne's welcoming embrace, now she moved gracefully, taking Jeanne's hands to kiss then letting herself be enfolded in her arms.

"And just as well," Jeanne said, "For Toneke is still barely stirring. How was your summer?" She held Anna at arm's length and examined her again. "It's good to see you again. Ainis, go up and let Mesnera Chazillen know that Anna is here."

The workshop was forgotten and the three of them spent the afternoon sharing stories of their adventures—the ones that could be shared—while Anna recounted her summer studies and the changes in her family.

"Both my older sisters have new sons! That's three boys now. Papa says they're making up for all of us being daughters."

When the talk turned to Prague and the wonders of Vitali's work, Antuniet glanced over briefly in warning then took Anna's hands in hers and fixed her gaze intently.

"There was a special purpose to my visit there, you know. A Great Work that I needed assistance on. You remember that secret project from the spring? The amulets that I said not to ask questions about? I didn't want to speak of it until I had some confidence of success, and you mustn't go telling anyone else quite yet. But I have succeeded in creating a homunculus—a living being— through the power of my art."

Anna's mouth opened into a little O and her eyes widened. Jeanne couldn't tell whether it was awe or disbelief. This would be the first test. Would Anna find it harder or easier than most to believe the story that would preserve Antuniet's good name?

"But how? Where?" Anna began, looking around as if she expected the child to be tucked into a corner of the room.

"As to how, I'll be sharing some of that in a lecture soon, I think. Is Margerit planning to move all the public talks down to Urmai, do you know? I think it would be of interest to a wider audience."

And, Jeanne thought, more important for our friends to be convinced, than for a group of schoolgirls.

"I don't know."

Antuniet waved a hand in dismissal. "Never mind. As to where, I couldn't very well wait in Prague for the project to be completed. I have too many responsibilities here." Antuniet nodded at Anna with a smile. "But I couldn't very well be dragging a sealed cucurbit halfway across Europe, so I decided to complete the cibation in a more traditional way." She briefly touched her belly in a gesture that was becoming more natural each time.

Anna's mouth opened wider as understanding dawned. "Truly?"

Jeanne noted surprise, but neither shock nor doubt. So Anna accepted the alchemical story as true. If enough people did, the others would hold their tongues.

"Now tell me," Jeanne interrupted, sensing that it would be best to let the idea take root on its own, "how is Margerit's school progressing? Is it all settled for you to be a student?" They had worried that Maistir Monterrez might balk at that step.

"I think so," Anna replied. "Maisetra Sovitre said she would speak to Papa. Oh! And he asked me to give you this." She opened her reticule and drew out a folded note. "Perhaps that's what it's about."

Antuniet took the letter from her and looked to them for permission, but when she had read it she only folded it again and set it aside saying, "Tell your father I'll come speak to him tomorrow."

Only when Anna had gone did she hand over the note for Jeanne's perusal, saying, "Maistir Monterrez is calling in a debt."

"Is there some trouble?" Jeanne frowned over the lines.

"The task itself will be easy enough to perform. When Monterrez made the setting for this—" Antuniet raised her hand to the irregular crimson stone that lay always against her throat. "—he gave it as a gift. No, not a gift, an exchange, with the price to be claimed in Anna's name at a later date. He wants me to make a special amulet for her that will overcome the disadvantage of her face."

It took Jeanne a moment to realize what he meant. There were long stretches when she forgot entirely the corded mark that traced down the side of Anna's cheek. Only now and again, caught in a reflection or an odd angle that stripped away familiarity, did it still catch at her vision.

"What does he want?" Jeanne asked.

Antuniet shrugged. "He leaves that to me." She gestured at the letter. "I suspect he has in mind some sort of illusion. I'm more concerned with why he's chosen to make the request at this time. She's a young woman now."

Jeanne nodded. If Anna had been born into the upper town, she would be looking forward to the beginning of her dancing season. There was one obvious reason for Maistir Monterrez to turn his mind to how others saw her.

A thoughtful look crossed Antuniet's face. "Do you recall that formula in DeBoodt's book that you once suggested that we try? 'To ensure that the true worth and beauty of the bearer is seen.' I think that one might answer Monterrez's request."

* * *

With the season not yet started, the rules for visiting were more haphazard than they would be later. Given Margerit's schedule, Jeanne thought the best time to visit Tiporsel House might be earlier than would ordinarily be polite. Even so she almost missed the opportunity. As she stepped down from the fiacre outside Tiporsel's gates, she could see Margerit's town carriage standing waiting at the door.

From the midst of the small party that bustled out the front door, Margerit stopped in surprise crying, "Jeanne, I hadn't heard you were back!"

As they embraced, Jeanne said, "I see I've caught you at a poor time."

"Yes," Margerit said. "And Barbara's out for the morning, I'm afraid. Frances and I were just leaving for Urmai. The first copies of her book have been bound! But…would you like to go with us? Or have you other visits to make? I can't wait for you to see what the place looks like now! We need to pick up Serafina as well. She and I are working on some new mysteries. But I could find someone to show you around the grounds. I'm counting on you to help make my Tanfrit Academy popular!"

Jeanne quickly weighed the options. There was no particular guarantee that any of her other calls would be more successful. She hadn't yet sorted out who had stayed in town for the summer or who might have returned early. "I'd be delighted."

The summer's travel had often meant long stretches of companionable silence. The ride to Urmai was quite a change—as full of chatter as a ballroom in high season! For all that, there was a brittle, almost frantic tension within the carriage. Nothing like the usual excitement of the start of the season. One might expect Margerit to be on edge with the debut of her academy, but it went beyond anticipation. Mesnera Collfield recounted in detail her disappointing attempts to collect samples in Piedmont. The lingering snow had baffled all her efforts. Serafina was uncharacteristically quiet until Margerit continued an earlier conversation with, "…and I hope you'll take notes during the Feast of Saint Mauriz this year. There's nothing more I can say about it, and Archbishop Fereir is unlikely to change his mind about my analysis. But at the least we can record the continuing fractures."

And then the conversation slipped off into the mechanics of mysteries again. Jeanne pulled the curtains aside to look out the carriage window as they approached their goal. The college grounds had truly undergone a transformation. Jeanne had visited the old Chasteld place when Margerit first bought it, of course. A dreary edifice of patched roofs and ivy-encrusted walls, the gardens overgrown with neglect and the air of ruin about it. Nothing at all like it had been when she was young before Chasteld became a recluse. The difference was as night to day. Now the stone gleamed, the windows glittered like polished crystal, and what had once been the ballroom was transformed into a temple of learning with new furnishings and warm draperies.

When they went through to the dining hall, Mesnera Collfield gave a sudden cry of delight at the sight of two bound volumes carefully laid out beside the bundles of folded pages. The rest of them watched in amusement as she brushed fingers over the embossed cover. The black leather had been tooled to look like stone, with the botanist's beloved lichens growing in the crevices.

Akezze Mainus came in from the back of the house, saying, "I thought I saw you arrive. What do you think?"

"I didn't realize they'd be beautiful!" Mesnera Collfield breathed. She opened the cover reverently and began leafing through the pages.

"I know we'd planned to do plain covers," Akezze said. "But the women decided to make a few in special bindings. By way of advertisement, you might say, to show off their skill."

The crowd increased by the addition of an older woman in a religious habit. Jeanne searched her memory. This must be the Sister Petrunel that Margerit had spoken of, the headmistress.

The newcomer said briskly, "I hope this means that we can clear this mess out of the college buildings."

"There's plenty of time yet," Margerit answered. "Though we'll need to find some other solution before we start on the next project."

"And what will that be?" Jeanne asked. Her curiosity was idle but the tension in the room begged to be broken.

"What I want to do," Margerit replied slowly, "is an edition of Gaudericus. It's a crime that in this modern age one can't find a printed edition of such an important work. But I don't think we're quite ready for that. Someone will need to compare all the copies we can get access to so we can draw up a corrected text."

"Gaudericus!" Sister Petrunel said. "Wouldn't it be better to begin with something a trifle more orthodox?"

Jeanne looked from her to Margerit, who seemed to have missed the edge of criticism.

"All the more orthodox books have had recent editions," Margerit pointed out. "I can easily get enough copies of Fortunatus and the important parts of Chizelek for the students to study. And of course all the standard classical works like Bartholomeus and Aukustin and Atelpirt. But it would be awkward indeed to try to teach from Gaudericus with only the single copy."

"Teach?" This time the dismay was impossible to miss. "You weren't planning to teach the Mechanists were you?"

"Oh Petra," Margerit said. "I know Gaudericus is difficult, but he's the best foundation for theoretical thaumaturgy that we have. Everyone agrees on that. If we're going to take a modern approach to mysteries, there's really no substitute."

Without knowing anything of what might have passed during the summer, Jeanne could tell the precise moment when disaster was inevitable. The only other person in the room who seemed to sense it was Serafina, whose face turned to a guarded mask.

"Maisetra Sovitre," the nun said, bringing Margerit's explanation to a halt. "This will not do. This will not do at all. You appointed me to oversee your curriculum, and at every turn you have dismissed or ignored my advice with regard to this subject. The order of the Orisules cannot—*cannot* be involved in a project so cavalier about the mystery traditions. You of all people should see the dangers of amateurs meddling in the mysteries. You may view writers like Gaudericus as ordinary grist for your mill. That only shows the flaws of self-education. I blame myself. I can see now I made a grave mistake in choosing not to teach you better as a child. But this will not do. It simply will not do."

Now Margerit realized the depth of the disagreement between them. "But, Petra, you knew I meant to teach thaumaturgy."

"I knew that thaumaturgy would be taught," the nun said, "but you had given me the misapprehension that the curriculum would be in my hands to guide. If you wish to turn this institution into a salon of dilettantes, radicals and heretics, that is your choice. I'm sorry, but I cannot give my countenance to it any longer."

"What are you saying?" Margerit asked in dismay.

"I'm saying that you need to find a new headmistress. I will pack my things and be gone as soon as transportation can be arranged."

"But I…" Margerit didn't complete the thought.

It was clear that the decision was final. Jeanne could tell it had been some time in coming, but Margerit, it seemed, had been blind. She had always expected those around her to share in her enthusiasms. Jeanne wondered that Barbara hadn't seen the looming conflict and warned her.

"I'm sorry," Sister Petrunel repeated with finality. And then she left the room to a stunned silence.

Margerit sat heavily on a nearby chair, her mouth still hanging open in shock.

"What will I do?" she asked in a small, lost voice. "Classes begin in a little over two weeks. What will I do?"

Jeanne pulled a chair over and sat beside Margerit, taking her hand and asking softly, "She hasn't left yet. Would it help to apologize? To ask her to reconsider? It does sound like you've been contradicting her decisions."

"Contradicting?" Margerit said. "But that's not…I was only explaining what I wanted. I hired her to run *my* college, not her own. Not to run an Orisul school."

Margerit had started out bewildered and doubtful, but her resolve strengthened as she continued, "She didn't want us to teach thaumaturgy. She thought she should have control over the printing house as well, or at least to have authority over them. For heaven's sake, she wanted to approve every servant that Ionkil and Montekler hired! She wanted to say who might and might not teach." This last was said with a quick glance at Frances Collfield.

"It would be reasonable," Jeanne suggested, "for a headmistress to have authority over the choice of teachers."

Margerit turned to her. "She thought we shouldn't accept Jewish students."

Taken each by each, they were small matters. Someone else might have backed away, step by step, deferring to what seemed a reasonable expectation, until the field had been abandoned in defeat. But not Margerit. Margerit always had that naive confidence in her own vision. That certainty that the things she wanted were right and reasonable to want.

"Well," Akezze said briskly. "I don't see that there's any help for it. We'll just have to go forward on our own. The curriculum is mostly settled. I assume we may lose the Orisul teachers as well. We'll need to make plans against that.

Draw up some lists and identify the crucial positions. We can muddle through the first term and that will give you time to find another headmistress."

"Why not you?" Serafina had been standing quietly to one side, clearly trying to be invisible among the currents of tension.

"Me?" Akezze asked.

"You said you wanted to start your own school. You told me you'd been helping at that orphanage to gain experience."

Akezze glanced over at Margerit who had a desperate hope suffusing her face.

"Would you be willing to take on the duties?" Margerit asked. "It's a lot to ask. Just for the first term or so, until I can find someone else. You've been here since the beginning. You know everything we've been planning."

Akezze was silent for a few minutes as if working through a calculation. Then she said, "It's an offer that might be better made after the heat of the moment."

Margerit shook her head. "I have every confidence in you. There's no time to waste. Will you do it?"

Akezze nodded. "Since you ask. Just for the first year, as you say. Eventually you'll need someone that your upper-town parents will respect as an equal. But for now, I can take up the reins."

While the two of them settled to discussing details and sent for Maisetra Ionkil to inform her of the change, Jeanne found herself led away by Serafina to tour the grounds. The rest of the property had been as transformed as the main building and Serafina's voice fell into what seemed a rote speech at each building.

As they entered what was clearly Margerit's mystery workshop, with its long tables and scattered papers, Jeanne observed, "You've served in this function before."

Serafina smiled. "I don't know how it is, but I end up leading all the tours. I suppose it's because I'm so useless at anything else."

"Who's telling you you're useless?" Jeanne chided. She looked around at the makings of the mystery that Serafina had just been explaining. "A few years and you could be quite as proficient as Margerit in devising all this."

Serafina shrugged. "But not in performing them. That's a weakness. I always need someone else to test the structures for me. Theory is one thing, but without the skill to invoke the saints, there's no way to work on my own. It's like Luzie's music, Maisetra Valorin's that is. I can tell her where it calls up power and which parts falter, but I can't even play the pieces myself much less compose them. And what I can play is only sound."

"And how is that nothing at all?" Jeanne asked. "That's more than most could do. How is that different from a composer who writes the music for others to play?" She tucked her hand under the crook of Serafina's elbow in a companionable way and urged her out into the main hall again. "And how is your friend, Maisetra Valorin? What is she composing?"

There was the faintest hint of embarrassment in Serafina's reaction. Jeanne's curiosity stirred. Was there an intrigue to pursue? Maisetra Valorin hadn't seemed the type, but one never knew. Her curiosity would lie unsatisfied unless Serafina gave encouragement. There were rules of delicacy. She had played by them herself all her life: things one might know, but could never ask. The precise nature of Serafina's relationship with her landlady fell into that category unless she were given an invitation.

"She's been working on a…on some songs about Tanfrit," Serafina explained, and hurriedly added, "They aren't ready for performance yet. I never knew that music was so complicated to create. It's like…" She reached for a comparison. "It's like that point when the dressmaker has taken all your measurements and cut the cloth, but the gown hasn't been assembled and trimmed yet."

Jeanne laughed. "Then I will wait patiently and not peek into the fitting room!"

By the time they had hunted down the others again, Margerit had left behind her initial dismay. They were gathered in the offices where Margerit, Akezze and Maisetra Ionkil were huddled over the account books and records. Sister Petrunel was nowhere to be seen but everything was in tidy enough shape that her participation in the transition wouldn't be needed.

"Margerit dear," Jeanne said. "Serafina says she must abandon me for her mystery work, and it's clear you'll be sorting things out for the rest of the day. Do you suppose I might borrow your carriage and driver to return home? He'll be back long before you're finished here."

Margerit looked up briefly, just long enough to take in the request. "Oh, yes, of course." And then her attention was lost again.

* * *

When Antuniet disappeared into the palace workshop for the next few days, Jeanne was glad she had stored up the summer's long stretches of close company. Now they barely saw each other between breakfast and bed. In addition to Maistir Monterrez's commission, Princess Annek had delivered a long market list of small projects that had accumulated over the summer. Small, but of troubling import. Efriturik had returned from his service in Paris with several of his amulets chipped or cracked. It might have been only the rough life of a cavalry officer, but Antuniet was troubled and spent late hours poring over DeBoodt's annotations in preparation for examining them. Replacing those stones would be a priority, not only in obedience to the princess his mother, but for the friendship that had grown in the year his services had been lent to Antuniet's work.

The new demands would take careful thought. Annek's first set of commissions had challenged Antuniet's skills to the limit. She had been provided no more than a list of names—cabinet officers and members of the court—and the traits to be strengthened or countered. The challenge went beyond simple alchemy. Antuniet had finally bent her pride and called on Barbara's knowledge of the court to chart a path. It had been a collaboration they both came to enjoy—a place where the skills of the two cousins could complement each other. Now they took up that partnership again and it was one more demand on Antuniet's time that took her away from home. Jeanne schooled herself to patience and turned to her own neglected tasks.

Then over breakfast one morning, Antuniet asked, "Would you like to do some alchemy again? I'm starting to work on Anna's jewel. I thought you might…"

In the early days, alchemy had been the excuse to spend time in Toneke's company. And that first commission from Princess Annek had required as many hands as could be scraped together for the ceremonial roles. Jeanne had no nostalgia for the tedium of grinding *materiae* or picking the fired stones out of the matrix, but the ceremonial processes themselves—those had an attraction for her dramatic soul. And as it was for Anna's sake…

"When would you need me? How long will it take?" It was another week or so before the true start of the season, but it wouldn't matter if the project spilled over a little.

It was like stepping back into a familiar parlor. The great moveable furnace stood on its groaning wheel, framed by the brass inlay of zodiacal symbols in the tiled floor. She could visualize where the orrery clock would go when it finally arrived, keeping time to the movements of the stars and planets. Antuniet had been in correspondence with a clockmaker in Geneva but God only knew when the passes would be clear enough to transport the mechanism safely. For now, there was the familiar sight of Toneke pulling out Vitali's zodiacal watch on its chain from her pocket. Returning it to her mentor in Prague had been one minor excuse for the journey, but in the end he had closed Antuniet's hand around it again, making it a gift.

"For luck," he'd said, "since it's served you so well."

And now Antuniet nodded. The alignments were correct for the beginning. Anna sifted a measure of powder into an iron vessel, describing aloud how the serpent would begin the calcination, and turned the vessel to align correctly with the stars. She signaled to one of the apprentice boys to begin slowly working the bellows on the fire beneath. Now Jeanne stepped forward with her own addition, calling on the lion to devour the serpent.

Jeanne had only the faintest idea of what the physical changes within the vessel might be, but she kept fixed in her mind the images from the alchemical manual. When used correctly, the symbols and gestures would work the change in matter. She'd seen the results often enough to trust.

This was only the first step, of course—the processing and purification of the ores and materials. Next would come the solution, the separation, the conjunction, each cycle applied to the *materiae* individually then combined as a whole. And then there would be the tedious cycles through the twinned cibations, marrying spirit to matter within the furnace, enhancing the natural properties of the gem and growing it in size and strength.

They would need another woman to assist with the twinned cycles. A woman, but not necessarily a maiden. One to mirror her in the role of queen, just as Antuniet and Anna would mirror the salamander. But for now she stepped back, waiting in turn as Anna and the youngest apprentice mixed the flux in preparation for the dissolution.

Antuniet checked the watch again. "Two hours before the next process. Princess Annek is sending someone over with the damaged stones I need to examine, so take some time to clean up now." This to the two boys.

Efriturik himself was Annek's messenger, somewhat shamefacedly bringing the damaged amulets in the hilt of his ceremonial sword and ring. He, too, had changed in the past year. Any man of his age would look dashing in the bright uniform of a cavalry officer, and Jeanne felt no qualms at all about staring in admiration. But his year attending on the Alpennian embassy in Paris had brought a new depth and seriousness.

"I swear I didn't abuse them," he said as Antuniet took up a jeweler's loupe and examined the spiderweb of fractures through one of the stones. "And it's odd," he continued, "that it would be that one, and not the one at the end of the pommel."

There was a touch of genuine anxiety in his voice. He'd had a hard time throwing off the reputation of wild and careless youth, and only half that reputation was undeserved. But he'd always taken the alchemy seriously and Jeanne knew he wouldn't have damaged the gifts negligently.

"If it had been only the one," Antuniet said thoughtfully, "I might have thought I'd overlooked flaws between the layers of the stone. But three? And look." She held up the ring. "This one is not merely cracked but discolored. That wouldn't happen from knocking it about."

She frowned and stared more closely, cupping her hand around the ring to enclose it in darkness.

"What is it?" Efriturik asked anxiously.

"The damaged stones are the ones meant to protect against sorcery and curses, not the ones for physical protection. It may need a simple adjustment of the formula, but I'd like to have Margerit look at them first."

With business done for the moment, Jeanne asked, "Can you stay for tea? How long have you been back? Anna," she called into the next room where the girl was being unaccountably shy. "Anna, can you scare up a pot of tea for our guest?"

"I'm afraid I haven't time today," Efriturik began. Then he stopped, staring at the doorway to the back room. "Ann—Maisetra Monterrez." A pause. "How good to see you again."

He stepped forward and started to bow over her hand, but Anna hid it away under her apron saying, "Oh don't, I'm filthy!" so he only completed the bow with a flourish as if that had been what he intended all along.

"You're...taller than you were," Efriturik said. Then he looked sheepish, realizing how silly that sounded.

But his own embarrassment seemed to erase Anna's and now she put on the air of a practiced hostess, learned through last year's salons.

"It was so kind of you to come visit us, even for so short a spell. I hope we'll have the pleasure of more of your company sometime soon. I know Mesnera de Cherdillac longs to hear anything you can tell her about the Paris fashions. Though I'm sure you paid more mind to Parisian politics! I would love to hear your thoughts on what will come if the French king's health is, indeed, failing."

"Why yes, yes of course," he answered after a moment's hesitation.

Jeanne saw Anna's eyes glance toward her quickly for permission. "Mesnera de Cherdillac has been holding some little salons at her house. Perhaps you could join us for one? There is always delightful company and the conversation is pleasant and lively. But you must excuse me, I need to help prepare for the next process."

With a little curtsey, she went to join the apprentices at their work.

It was all Jeanne could do not to smile too broadly as she watched Efriturik's eyes follow her. Yes, the last year had been well spent indeed. Anna would soon be able to match the elegance and poise of any society hostess. Maistir Monterrez's jewel scarcely seemed necessary.

* * *

If the work on Anna Monterrez's amulet went smoothly, the same could not be said for the damaged stones brought back from Paris. Jeanne would have heard only those parts that Antuniet shared at the dinner table if not for her own presence in the workshop. Now, in the idle hours waiting for the best alignments, she listened as Antuniet talked over the puzzle with her apprentices.

There had been a time when Jeanne would not have believed Antuniet could be such a patient teacher. Even so, it wasn't teaching as much as tracing out her thoughts before them and periodically loosing sharp questions regarding some of the more simple problems.

Perhaps I should be an alchemy apprentice myself, Jeanne thought, *if I can discern so easily which of the questions are simple!*

"What can cause a layered stone to crack?" This question Antuniet directed at the older of the two boys.

He frowned in effort, then closed his eyes as he recited, "Impurities during separation, the wrong flux chosen for putrefaction, too low a heat during cibation, or performing it under the wrong stars, too high a heat during sublimation…no, too short a time?"

Antuniet's glance shifted to the younger boy. "You should know the last one."

He looked down uncomfortably and whispered, "Quenching the matrix when it hasn't cooled enough."

"What else? Even more important than those. Anna?"

This one Jeanne thought she could have answered, having watched through many of those initial failures.

"Trying to marry types of stones that will not suit," Anna said promptly. "Adding a new layer that will destroy or reject the last."

But most of those could be ruled out, Jeanne knew. The amulets that Princess Anna had requested for her son hadn't been among those early experiments. And even that first set of alchemical gems had seen no failures of this particular sort, only one or two small chips and scratches that could be blamed on rough handling of the softer layers.

Antuniet returned the flawed gems to their case with a sigh. "I need to question Mesner Atilliet further on anything unusual that might have happened. Anna, check the inventories and see if we have any twins to the discolored ones that were held back a year past. Margerit wanted to compare them."

The puzzle was set aside as the minutes ticked closer to the alignment for the next step.

* * *

When the day finally came, the final fixation and enhancement for Anna's jewel was a gentler process than the creation of the stone itself. It would abide no physical heat at this stage, now that it had been shaped and polished and engraved and set into a simple gold band. As with all the ring amulets, the setting had been shaped to allow the underside of the stone to be in contact with the wearer's finger. Jeanne felt disappointed at how plain it looked: a rounded square of dark green, flecked with red. The engraving was not a design of birds or flowers but a few letters in the Hebrew script. That had been Maistir Monterrez's addition, after consultation with Antuniet—that and the shape of the ring. The power would come from the stone itself but the inscription carried its own meaning. Monterrez had joined them for this last part, watching the proceedings with interest and pride as Anna performed her part.

When the enhancement was complete, Jeanne cleaned off the last remnants of the bath with a soft cloth. "After all those steps, I'd expected something more eye-catching."

Antuniet took it from her and held it to the light to examine closely. "Complex and brilliant are not the same thing. The complexity is inside the stone—all the separate crystals with their individual properties joined together. That's what makes it possible to adjust the effects so finely, to enhance the revelation of inner truth without focusing on mere physical deception, to open the eyes and the heart in tandem. It's a far different process than for a simple bloodstone used against wounds and bleeding."

She turned the ring over once more and nodded in satisfaction then passed it to Maistir Monterrez. "This is your gift," she said.

It had all the air of a formal ceremony as Anna hesitantly raised her hand. He slipped the ring on her finger with a few quiet words that had the air of a blessing.

Jeanne had never seen visions. Not the sort that Margerit described, nor even the brief glimpses of *something* that Antuniet used to guide her personal mysteries. But she had sometimes felt that thrill—something like a convulsive shiver—that came during the *missio* of the Great Mysteries in the cathedral. This was nothing like that, yet between one moment and the next, something changed. A veil was drawn, or perhaps removed. It became a struggle to remember that Anna's face had been marred. If she concentrated, she could still trace the thread of the scar, but it wasn't important. The eyes slid away. For the rest...how could the amulet have made any improvement? Anna was Anna: eager, curious, poised, thoughtful. *To ensure that the true worth and beauty of the bearer is seen.* Anyone who couldn't see that without assistance was blind indeed.

Maistir Monterrez appeared satisfied. He squeezed his daughter's hands and kissed her lightly on the cheek. "I've done what I can to ensure your future. Now I'll leave you to your work."

Jeanne lingered after he had left, until it was clear that Antuniet would be kept busy for another hour or two directing preparations for the next day's work. The only sign of the previous event was the way Anna sometimes paused to stretch her hand or glance down at the ring. Could she feel the amulet at work? Or was it only the unfamiliarity of its presence on her finger? Would she see a change in herself when she looked in a glass?

A brief knock on the workshop door interrupted Jeanne from gathering her things. When the younger apprentice opened it, Efriturik's familiar voice was heard.

"Mesnera Chazillen, I know I'd promised an afternoon to you in two days' time, but I have an errand in Fallorek. Would you have time today?"

Antuniet visibly suppressed the impatience she always felt when plans were disrupted. She glanced around and signaled the apprentices to leave off their work, saying briskly, "Today is better than later. You two may go," to the apprentices. "Anna, I'd like you to take notes, could you go find the account book we started? And Jeanne, I promise I'll be home in time for dinner."

Jeanne touched Antuniet's hand, in lieu of a kiss, and allowed Efriturik to help her on with her coat. She couldn't resist asking, "And do you see anything different about our Maisetra Monterrez today?" She was sorry immediately when she saw Anna freeze in the doorway as she returned with the ledger book in hand. She hadn't meant Anna to hear.

Efriturik tilted his head quizzically and said, "I don't think she's grown any taller since a week past. And if she's dressed her hair in a new fashion, I can't see it under that cap." He shrugged. "You must forgive me."

"Never mind," Jeanne said hurriedly. "I hope you find some clue to your damaged stones. Toneke, until dinnertime then."

She turned over that last exchange in her mind, as she stood waiting for one of the palace pages to summon a fiacre for her. And, with a stroke of revelation, her heart dropped. Efriturik...and Anna. No wonder he needed no assistance to see only her inner worth! And Anna—oh, the poor girl! Had this been in her mind all along when she wished for more social polish? And did they each know that the other...? Oh, but it was impossible. Completely impossible. The only saving grace was that they were both sensible enough to know it.

CHAPTER TWENTY-ONE

Margerit

Mid-September, 1824

Two days, Margerit thought. Could there not be more than two days of classes before the next disaster? They'd barely recovered from Petra's departure.

Two days with twenty students—fewer than she'd hoped but more than she'd expected. There were some she already thought might drop away. Who might find it too difficult to balance the glitter of the season with lectures, or who had thought the studies would be a lighter burden. There was a solid core of ten or so that she had harvested from the lectures and knew to be dedicated. Several more who wavered and might yet join them. Their reasons were mixed: studious burfro girls with academic ambitions like she'd had, girls of good family looking to delay entering society for varied reasons, a few with some degree of thaumaturgical talent whose parents had embraced the chance for training. She had been startled and delighted to find the auditor Valeir Perneld among those, even though she'd been out for two years and there were even rumors of a betrothal in the offing.

No charity students yet, to her disappointment. One couldn't count the two Poor Scholars who had joined the thaumaturgy students as charity. The foundation paid fees to the Academia Tanfridae just as they did to the university. Just as they had until now, that was. But there were girls unsuited to the Poor Scholars whom she'd hoped to attract as well. That would be an important sign of the academy's goals.

Two days—just barely time to see the beginnings of a routine. And now…

Margerit glanced across the cold marble floor of the antechamber to the chancellor's office at the hard bench where Akezze sat, head bent in discussion with Maisetra Nantin, the directress of the Poor Scholars. She couldn't shake off a sense of guilt, though there was no way she could have predicted or prevented the decision of the university dozzures.

The chancellor had kept them waiting for hours, hoping they would be discouraged enough to leave. Margerit envied the calm patience that Barbara could summon in situations like this. Waiting is a weapon, she had said once. But whose hands held it here? Margerit couldn't help growing more and more discouraged with every minute that passed.

They were ushered into the wood-paneled office and offered chairs only marginally more comfortable than the benches they'd left. Margerit took the one farthest to the side. This wasn't her grievance, however much she might have precipitated it.

In their previous brief encounters, Margerit had identified Maisetra Nantin as a formidable woman. Every inch of her appearance was held to the same strict standards as the young women in her charge. Crisp, regimented waves of steel-gray hair edged the opening of her bonnet in lieu of lace, and the sober black of her coat escaped giving the impression of a religious habit only in the modish style of its cut.

Without waiting for the chancellor's invitation she launched into her petition with the air of a family matriarch chastising an errant nephew.

"The Foundation for Poor Scholars has had a satisfactory arrangement with Rotenek University for nearly two hundred years. You have benefitted from that arrangement for the price of a very small burden. Our students have never brought the university into disrepute or caused even the slightest disruption. I would ask—" said with the tone she might use to her own charges, "—that you explain why this arrangement is no longer satisfactory."

Margerit imagined that most men, facing the directress's disapproval, might scramble for the easiest means to satisfy her, so as to cut short the time suffering under that regard. But Chancellor Epertun spent his days handling unruly students from the most power families in the city. If he were the sort to wilt before autocratic demands he would not have survived.

"Maisetra Nantin," he said, countering her role of matriarch with the air of a wise and kindly uncle, "the university has long had a tradition of accommodating charitable endeavors so long as it does not interfere with our mission of educating the sons of Rotenek. But it cannot be denied that the presence of women in the lecture halls is a distraction."

The claim was disinguous. It might be true of the frivolous girl scholars—the ones who attended lectures for idle amusement. Indeed, some of them were attracted by the opportunity for safe and meaningless flirtation under the guise of study and the watchful eye of a chaperone. But the same could never be said of the women of the Poor Scholars. They lived lives as strict in propriety as any convent.

"When there was no other alternative," he continued, "we were happy to make certain accommodations." Accommodations that did not extend to allowing the women to participate in debates or discussions, and certainly not to the granting of degrees.

"But as we know," the chancellor said, "it is no longer the case that there is no alternative."

Margerit flinched as he gestured toward her. "Chancellor Epertun, my academy has barely opened. It would be difficult to take on another thirty or forty students on no notice, and the scope of our curriculum...we don't offer all the subjects that the university makes available."

The chancellor grimaced in what might have been amusement or triumph. "Then you will appreciate the difficulties we have suffered in allowing unsuitable students into our halls."

Was he deliberately goading her? She had been one of those "unsuitable students."

"Our decision is made," the chancellor concluded. "Rotenek University is now closed to women. I see no use in continuing this conversation. Maisetra Nantin, the fees that you paid for access have been returned to you. I advise you to see what arrangements you can make with Maisetra Sovitre."

The directress appeared ready to persist, but Akezze—who had kept silent during the exchange—touched her lightly on the sleeve and rose, saying, "We thank you for your time."

When they were free of the university's corridors, Margerit broke the silence. "I never intended this. I never expected..."

"We could do it, I think," Akezze interrupted her. "If you are willing. It isn't as many as forty students. Perhaps only twenty taking advanced studies. The rest are taught within the Poor Scholars house itself." She looked to Maisetra Nantin for confirmation. "We'd need to scramble to cover the medical studies, but for the rest..."

Margerit reviewed the difficulties in her own mind. The numbers...no, that could be managed. It would be within what she'd hoped to achieve in time. But could the rigid discipline of the Poor Scholars' House be accommodated? Maisetra Nantin would be as formidable as Sister Petrunel had been in a conflict, and might be just as unwilling to view her as an equal in authority. But with Akezze as go-between... "Perhaps we should find a private place to discuss this further," she suggested.

As she stood aside to allow Maisetra Nantin to enter the carriage first, Margerit spared a thought for the frivolous girl scholars who would have no similar alternative—girls like Amiz Waldimen and Verunik Felix and the others who had been her companions when she first came to Rotenek.

* * *

On returning home to Tiporsel House, there was barely a moment for Margerit to sense something was amiss. It was in the way the footman at the door glanced sideways with an ostentatious air of not telling her something important. But there, just beyond him, was Barbara, pacing the floor with a scowl and clearly waiting for her arrival.

Barbara jerked her head in the direction of the corridor to the back of the house and led the way, saying, "I've already sent a messenger to your aunt and uncle."

Margerit's stomach clenched. "To Aunt Bertrut?"

"To Chalanz, to the Fulpis. Best to reassure them with no delay. I took the liberty of suggesting that if the matter hasn't gone beyond all hope of repair, it might make sense to put it about that the visit was planned." Barbara paused at the closed door to the office. "I've left the scolding for you."

The confusion resolved itself. Margerit slipped through the door and shut it behind her.

The figure that stood nervously before the small hearth might have been taken for a boy except that the cap that had hidden her tumbling riot of chestnut curls was now clutched and twisted in her hands. Margerit could guess the rest of the story from the ill-fitting brown wool coat and trousers—respectable enough not to provoke questions about a young man traveling alone on a public coach—and the small valise at her feet, barely large enough for the most basic necessities. Knowing her cousin, the first of those necessities were her journals. The stricken look on the girl's face suggested either that Barbara had not been honest about the scolding or that her cousin had grown mindful of the enormity of her situation.

"Iulien Fulpi, what are you doing here?" Margerit demanded, seizing her cousin by the shoulders and shaking her violently. She wanted desperately to embrace her instead, relieved at safe passage through hazards only imagined now that they were past. "You're too old to be running wild! What were you thinking?"

Iuli's mouth quivered. "You promised."

"What?"

"You promised you'd be at my coming-out ball. You promised I could visit you. You never sent for me. You promised I could spend part of my dancing season here in Rotenek, and when I try to ask my mother and father they won't talk about it." Iuli's mouth was quivering more strongly and Margerit couldn't guess whether it was genuine emotion or the result of long practice.

That was entirely like Iuli: saving up every daydream and wish and turning them into promises.

"I never promised any of that. It was always up to your father to decide. And now you'll be lucky if he lets you walk to the park and back without a vizeino to chaperone you once I send you back."

"Margerit, I can't go back, not yet. Not until…I want…I couldn't bear it. It's like I can't breathe. Like I'm running through hallways looking for something."

There was enough of growing desperation in her voice to give pause.

"What is it you want?" Margerit asked more quietly.

"I don't know!" It was close to a wail. "I only know I can't find it at home. I don't want to have all the doors closed on me before I've had a chance to find out. Sofi didn't care. She's happy with her betrothal and her own household and staying in Chalanz forever."

So Sofi had landed a fiancé. It was news that her uncle hadn't seen fit to share yet. But Iuli was close to hysterics and that wasn't like her at all. Margerit took her by the hand and settled the both of them on the window seat that looked out over the alley between Tiporsel and the neighboring house. It was the only place in the room that two could sit side by side.

"Iulien, I'm listening. What do you want? I can't promise you anything—I never could. But I can't do anything if I don't know." She pulled out a clean handkerchief and passed it to her cousin.

Iuli dabbed at her eyes and her voice drew back from its frantic edge. "Margerit, you always had your books. You knew what you wanted, even when you couldn't get it. You had Petra and your godfather to give you hope. All I ever had was you. And then you never came back."

Margerit was struck to the heart. She knew Iuli had idolized her, and she suspected that there had been no one else her cousin had dared to share her poems and stories with, but she hadn't thought it was more than a girl's hero worship.

"Iuli, I'm sorry I didn't come," she said. "I was so busy with my school this summer." It was the excuse she was permitted to give. If the Fulpis had allowed, she would gladly have made the journey even if only for the one day of the ball itself. "But, do you have any idea what danger you put yourself in to travel alone? Even like this?" She gestured to take in the disguise. "If you had been discovered you'd be ruined for life. Even if nothing…nothing worse had happened." She shuddered. At Iuli's age, she herself wouldn't have known how bad that something worse could be. And even now, if word of the adventure trickled back to Chalanz… "Your parents must be frantic."

"I left them a letter," Iuli began in a thin voice, as if she knew how little that meant.

The letter must not have included any hint of her destination or the Fulpis would have overtaken her on the road.

"And how did you get these clothes? And arrange for the coach fare?" The trip from Chalanz to the capitol was not an outrageous fee, but more than the sort of pin money Iuli would have been allowed.

"I asked a friend to buy them for me," Iuli explained, beginning to sound more like herself. "And you can pay for the fare on the coach itself, you know."

"But where did you get the money?"

There was a pause and then a small quiet voice. "From my book."

"Your…book." Margerit tried to puzzle out a meaning from that word.

"From what the publisher sent me for my novel. Lissa…my friend keeps the money for me. She'll send me the rest when I need it. I thought it was better not to carry too much in case of thieves."

So she wasn't entirely such an innocent. But… "Your novel?" Margerit repeated, still feeling stunned.

"Yes. I won't be a burden on you if Papa is so angry he refuses to send me an allowance. Lissa did the correspondence for me because I couldn't use my real name, of course. And she said the publisher might cheat me if he knew I was so young. She thought it was just a lark at first, but since the book sold she's been very strict about showing me the accounting. I—"

"Your novel." A sick feeling grew in Margerit's stomach. She rose and crossed the room to the secretary desk and opened a lower drawer. This was one book she refused to display on the library shelves.

Delighted recognition lit Iuli's face. "Did you like it?"

Margerit held up the copy of *The Lost Heir of Lautencourt* like a cudgel. "You wrote this?"

Something in her dismay penetrated Iuli's enthusiasm.

"You know I did. I showed it to you. Margerit, what's wrong?"

"Don't lie to me! I never saw this until all of Rotenek started whispering and laughing over it." Margerit found her hands trembling and she set the book down on the side table.

"I did! I gave you a copy two years ago, when you were in Chalanz for Sofi's ball at the end of the summer. I changed it a little after that, but not so very much. You never said anything about it, so I thought you didn't mind." Iuli's voice faltered.

Margerit cast her mind back. Two years? But she would have… A faint memory came: Iuli slipping away on the day they were leaving Chalanz, handing her a thick notebook. She'd set it aside unread because of the jouncing of the carriage. What had become of it? Had it simply been lost during the journey? Or slipped down behind the cushions, forgotten all this time? Could she have prevented all this trouble if she'd only paid closer attention? And Iuli wouldn't have asked, thinking that her scribblings were simply being ignored as usual, after all the trouble of copying it out for her.

"Oh, Iulien," she said and sat back beside her cousin in the window seat. She felt sick.

"I know it's not very good," Iuli began.

"That's not it," Margerit said. "It is good." And it was, she had to admit that. "It's good enough that people thought perhaps Lady Ruten had written it."

Iuli brightened briefly, but when the silence stretched out she ventured, "What's wrong."

Where to begin?

"Iuli, anyone reading that novel knows it was about me. Me and Barbara. You couldn't have made it plainer if you'd used our names. You've made us the subject of a great deal of gossip."

"Oh." Iulien digested that for a moment. "I tried to change things around as much as I could. Is it so very bad?"

"You have me fall in love with my armin and marry him. A man who turns out to be my benefactor's long-lost son."

"I made up the part about falling in love, but there had to be a love story," Iuli protested. "It can't be a proper novel without a love story."

Margerit sighed. It was too late for anything except truth.

"Iuli, you wondered why your parents wouldn't let you join me for a season in Rotenek. Have you wondered why they told me not to come to your ball? This is why: because I fell in love with my armin and we live together as if we were husband and wife. And the only thing that keeps us safe from scandal is that the world chooses to believe we are nothing more than very close friends. Do you understand what you've done?"

Iuli was staring at her with her mouth in an O. Perhaps the depth of her carelessness was sinking in. But then her expression turned into a smile of delight as her eyes brightened. "Oh Margerit, that's so romantic! That's even better than my story!"

Did she truly understand the seriousness? Or was her head still full of fancies and adventures?

"Iuli, a man has died because of your story. He insulted me over it, and Barbara challenged him, and Barbara's armin killed him. Now do you understand?"

Now it was Iulien's turn to echo helplessly, "Died?"

Margerit sat quietly letting Iulien's imagination work through the rest of the consequences.

When the stillness seemed to stretch out into eternity, there was a small, quiet voice, "I'm sorry."

Margerit felt her heart melting as it always did in the face of Iuli's sincerity but she hardened herself…and then stifled a laugh, realizing she was fretting over Iuli's behavior the way others had fretted over her own. Well, what was done was done. Time to worry about the future.

"Barbara sent a messenger to let your parents know where you are and that you're safe. If I know her, she found someone willing to ride all night. And if I know your father, I expect he'll be banging on my door in two days' time, ready to drag you home and lock you in your bedroom for the rest of the season."

"Yes, he would do something positively gothic like that," Iuli said. Her voice was still subdued and it was agreement rather than protest.

"It is also possible—" Margerit repeated the word to suppress any hopes, "—*possible* that he will take Barbara's suggestion to save your reputation and his own by claiming that this visit was planned. A precipitous decision. We would need to find a reason that would be accepted. No one would believe that I invited you here just to enjoy a Rotenek season—not just now. Everyone knows I have no time for anything but the academy."

Iulien looked up hopefully. "Your academy."

"Yes," Margerit replied, catching her meaning. "Now that might be believed, if your father judges it best to smooth things over. And that means if all of Chalanz hasn't already heard. We could say that you wanted to spend a term or two as a student and that your father changed his mind to allow it at the very last minute. And that's why there was no time to tell your friends and neighbors back in Chalanz about it."

Already she was composing a letter to follow Barbara's hasty message to the Fulpis.

"No promises," Margerit said quickly. "It still depends entirely on your father, and you know how little he approves of me. I won't have you thinking this is some sort of reward. If the excuse is that you wanted to study this badly, then you must become a student—the most dedicated one I have. No balls or outings of any sort for the first term."

She saw Iuli's mouth begin to open in protest and then quickly close again. That threat held more weight than her cousin than it would have for her. Whatever the cause of her current sorrows, Iuli had been excited about the delights of a dancing season. Impulse might have led her to run off in a grubby coat and trousers but she would soon regret the ballgowns left behind.

"As soon as I can arrange where your room will be, you are confined to it until we get you some presentable clothes. And if you take one step out of line, then back to Chalanz with you. If your father agrees to let you stay, he'll hold me responsible for your behavior. And now, before anything else, you have some apologies to make."

She watched Iulien putting on her most earnest face.

"I'm truly sorry for the trouble I've caused you, Cousin Margerit, but—"

"Apologies," Margerit said sharply, "do not include the word 'but.' And you don't owe them only to me. You owe an apology to Baroness Saveze and to Saveze's armin for the trouble and danger you put them in."

"The danger?"

Iuli still didn't understand. That innocence would need to change. "Duels don't happen the way they do in your stories. People who have the truth on their side don't always win. They're dangerous and messy and unpredictable. It could just as easily have been Tavit who died. And for what? For a lie. Because we didn't have truth on our side. That duel was fought to prove that Barbara and I are nothing more than friends. And that is a lie. And we won. Think about that."

"But I didn't know!" Iuli protested.

"No 'buts.' You knew in your heart well enough to put it in your story. Truth is a weapon and if you're going to use it you should know where all the edges are."

Margerit crossed to the door where Barbara was still waiting out in the corridor. At least some of their conversation would have been audible through the door.

"Iulien has something to say to you and to Tavit, if you could send to ask him to come up."

* * *

Dealing with classes and the new students filled the week before a return letter arrived from Chalanz. Enough time for the Fulpis to have received her proposal and considered it. Margerit had scarcely found time to speak two words to Iulien during that time except at meals. Aunt Bertrut had managed to assemble the beginnings of an acceptable wardrobe that permitted her to join the family at the table, and she and Uncle Charul had quickly been won over. Even Barbara seemed ready to offer grudging welcome. Brandel wavered between being intrigued and jealous at the addition to the household. Iuli's contrition was genuine enough to have begun to capture the hearts of the staff. But until that letter arrived, all plans were held in suspension.

Margerit scanned it over quickly, looking for Uncle Fulpi's judgment.

I am satisfied by the rapidity of Baroness Saveze's response that you had no part in enticing my daughter in this madness.

Her eyes traced further down. She didn't need to know whether she was forgiven or not. Ah, there it was.

As little fit as I consider you to oversee my daughter's conduct, I believe Baroness Saveze has the right of it. We can retrieve the matter by a visit of sufficient length to suggest intention. I hope I need not mention that is this is considered my daughter's dancing season. You are not to allow any particular attentions to or from men, nor to discuss her expectations. Furthermore, you are not to consider yourself a suitable vizeino. If my daughter is to be chaperoned in society, I expect my sister-in-law to be responsible for her conduct and reputation.

Well, Aunt Bertrut wouldn't consider that a burden. But she meant to hold to her first impulse. Iulien would need to earn that privilege. After a brief council of war with Barbara and the Pertineks, Margerit summoned Iuli to set out the conditions of her continued presence.

"You'll attend a full program of classes at the Tanfrit Academy. That is the only sensible reason we can give for your sudden presence. I'll help you choose the program and on days when you have classes you can ride down to Urmai with me in the morning. In a month's time we may allow you to go visiting on days when you are free. If you are allowed to go out in society, it will be under Maisetra Pertinek's supervision and she will decide what invitations you may accept."

Iuli nodded gravely.

"You are never to leave the house alone. This isn't Chalanz where you can run wild. If you have good reason to go out, you must either be accompanied by your maid or by Maistir Chamering, and then only to the Plaiz."

Here Iuli protested. "But you said I'd only have Rozild half time, just to dress me mornings and evenings! That means I can't go shopping or walking or anything!"

"Or by Maistir Chamering," Margerit repeated.

"Brandel isn't any older than I am," Iuli said, clearly feeling the injustice of it.

"It isn't a matter of age. Brandel's a man." It was stretching the point, but Margerit was willing to do so. "And he's in training as an armin, so his reputation rests on not allowing you to get into trouble. That's what protects you. Or," she added firmly, "you can simply stay home when you aren't in classes."

Margerit watched Iulien's face closely for signs of rebellion, but the girl had taken herself in hand once more. Good.

"If you follow my rules, you can start going out in the evenings after the Mauriz term is finished. And if you behave yourself for the whole season, then I might be persuaded to hold a ball for you in the spring. You'd be the envy of all your friends back in Chalanz. And if you don't follow the rules, I'll send you back to your father. Do you promise?"

"I promise." She looked subdued and chastened for now.

It wouldn't last, Margerit knew, but it was a start.

CHAPTER TWENTY-TWO

Serafina

Late September, 1824

The cathedral echoed with the soft voices and restless movements of hundreds of expectant worshippers. How could it be two years? She'd never expected to stay this long. Not quite two years. She hadn't arrived early enough that fall to see this ritual, the Great Mystery of the city's patron. That had come a year past at Margerit's side, sitting on the bench belonging to Tiporsel House. But Margerit had washed her hands of this *tutela*. She had mapped every flaw she could see and petitioned every ear she thought might listen. This time, Margerit would participate in the rite as an ordinary celebrant.

Serafina watched the preparations from an uncrowded space by one of the side chapels. She had nothing of Margerit's driving ambition and so nothing of Margerit's impatience at Archbishop Fereir's seeming unconcern. She wanted only to understand. The dais with the lay presiders was hidden from her view behind a row of pillars though the altar could be seen. It didn't matter. She would be turning her vision elsewhere, as she had that day in the park in Urmai for Mesner Kreiser. It was enough to be in the midst of the mystery and feel it all around her. That would anchor her vision when she cast it out to see where Mauriz's blessing traveled.

A quiet voice at her side asked, "Maisetra, are we truly permitted to be here?"

She touched Celeste's shoulder in reassurance. "Yes."

She guessed that the girl had been shooed out of the cathedral on some previous visit. Technically, the Mystery of Saint Mauriz belonged to the immediate parish—to the upper part of town where the palace and all the grand houses stood. And as the mystery marked the start of the season, everyone who had returned to town had taken their places, filling the benches to capacity. That was why she had positioned herself to the side. Luzie's house fell in the ambit of Saint Nikule's and therefore so did she. If she'd asked Margerit, she would have been welcome on Tiporsel's bench, but they were here for worship. Today she was here to work.

"What do you want me to do?" Celeste whispered.

"Just what I explained before," Serafina responded. "My *visio* may take me out of my senses for a while. Just watch over me in case something happens. But watch the mystery as well."

The two ideas had come together in her plans. It was unlikely that she'd faint or cry out—her visions rarely took her that way. But she meant to look more deeply than she ever had before. She wanted someone else at her side whose eyes were on this world. And she recalled the little shrine to Saint Mauriz—the erteskir that Celeste had shown her so proudly—and the fierce possessive way the girl spoke of the city's patron. She recalled the hints Celeste had given that a girl from the wharf district hadn't found a welcome at this ceremony. And so she'd begged Mefro Dominique for her daughter's company for the day. The cathedral staff knew her as Maisetra Sovitre's friend and would let them be.

Now the sounds of the choristers rose as the presiders entered the nave. The echoes gave the processional a haunting quality, but it was only music, not part of the mystery. Not like the way Luzie's compositions called up the *fluctus*.

Luzie. A sweet longing stirred in her. The summer was past, the boys returned to school, and there was no longer an excuse to share Luzie's bed. It would be different now. No longer the easy, lazy closeness of the summer nights and the faint scent of roses, waking at her side. No more of the way the darkness washed away Luzie's shyness. Now when their hands touched over the keyboard, it wasn't a promise for later, but scant bread to feed their hungry skin. More hungry now than before those months of being fed with furtive meals. In time, would the hunger dull? Or would it drive them beyond caution in a house where they no longer had an excuse to be alone?

It felt like Costanza once more—the brief teasing touches in public. Except that Luzie didn't mean to tease. Not the way Costanza had. And there was no private palazzo where they could retire for wanton pleasure under the guard of a smirking maidservant. The close homely circle of Luzie's servants and lodgers felt like a cage, confining them in separate prisons where they could only touch briefly through the bars.

Serafina smiled wistfully and shook off the image. What had she expected? Both their lives belonged to other people. There was no future, only scattered nows.

The choristers had quieted and a strong voice began chanting the *markein* from the space before the altar. Serafina leaned against the pillar and closed her eyes, watching the stirrings of power rise and filter through the echoes of the cathedral's stones in her mind. The altar, the cathedral, the parish around it, Rotenek, Alpennia itself. The mystery took shape in slowly spreading waves of light.

The flaws were familiar this time: the way the archbishop's words tugged and pulled at the structure of the *fluctus*. Serafina had a vision of a cracked fountain, where the water that filled it up and should have flowed out from tier to tier instead drained through cracks, leaving whirlpools and eddies within the basin. She set the image aside. There was a danger that imagination could shape perception, like the way Luzie's arias formed themselves into the figures from the opera's story. The image of Tanfrit floated before her and once more she set it aside.

The work with maps she had done with Kreiser helped. This time she watched as Mauriz's blessing and protection lapped out further and further across the land, like waves reaching up the shore and falling short to drain into the sand. It was hard to know what form the *tutela* had been meant to take. The mysteries in Rome were shaped differently. The Great Tutela of Saint Peter rose in three tiers like the papal crown, blessing the basilica itself, the city of Rome and all of Christendom as echoes of each other. This had a similarity of intent, but the outcome was different. Was that by design or was it part of the flaw? The image of the overlapping waves returned.

She had felt that sense of waves before. Last year, the dark chaotic surge of the weather mystery appeared to lap at the foundations of Alpennia's defenses. That mass of power over the mountains was still present. It felt ragged and corroded but even more powerful, in the way a madman could summon immense strength. Focused as she was on the *tutela* as it spread outward, she saw only fragments of the other, no longer as a pulsing force, but lashing out randomly like lightning or like tongues of flame, slipping down the valleys to meet with Mauriz's protection. The invading mystery had no aim or intent; whatever will had directed it had turned elsewhere. But neither were the defenses directed against it. The *tutela* kept slipping back down the shore, to its core, to the cathedral.

The shape of her visions shifted. The waves of the *tutela* left behind, not the flat sand of a beach, but a broad expanse of mud, cracking and shrinking in the sun until it looked like a crazed mosaic. And the chaotic mass that lurked at the borders of Alpennia flowed into the cracks, following the flaws like rain filling a streambed, like floodtide running through empty chanulezes, like ice water seeping into the fractures of a rock face, freezing and swelling until the stone sloughed off in layers onto the travelers below…

The human voices had faded from her consciousness. Her inner vision saw only what those voices called forth, invoked, invited. But what had they invited? More powers than the saints were listening. At last the awkward slosh and swirl of the *fluctus* called her attention to the mystery's conclusion, the way the *charis* brightened momentarily and then drew into itself, like the opening of a drain, pulling Saint Mauriz's attention back, turning inward and collapsing deep into the foundations of the cathedral where his relics rested. The murmur of ordinary voices rose around her and Serafina opened her eyes once more.

At her side, Celeste was staring at her with an intent and worried expression.

Serafina frowned. "I'm back."

She looked over the crowd to the Tiporsel House bench. Should she seek out Margerit now to tell her of this new vision? Was the change in the effects of the ritual itself or had her imagination given it new shapes? No matter; that could wait.

Whatever Celeste had seen for herself of Mauriz's grace, it seemed a private thing and untouched by the shadows that haunted her own visions. There was a hidden glow within Celeste as they walked back from the Plaiz. Serafina was content to leave the two of them to their secrets.

* * *

"Is she serious?" Luzie asked, when Serafina passed on the inquiry brought back from Urmai.

The dinner table seemed unnaturally quiet these days without the presence of the boys. Serafina had saved the note and its contents to provide them with conversation.

"Of course she's serious," Charluz said and helped herself to a second serving of buttered carrots. "The question is which of you would benefit more."

"It isn't—" Luzie hesitated. "Serafina, it isn't just because we're friends, is it? You didn't ask her…"

Serafina shook her head as she waved away the dish Charluz offered. "The college needs more classes that will attract students from the upper town. Margerit's worried that the presence of all the Poor Scholars will make people think it's meant to be primarily a charity school. You'd be quite a prize to add to the faculty."

Luzie blushed. "Only one day a week? I could manage it if I can convince a few of my students to change days. But I don't know about the rest of it. Lecturing in music theory? I've never done anything like that." She skimmed through the letter Serafina had given her. "And other items as agreed. What does she mean by that?"

"I think," Serafina said carefully, not wanting to frighten her off, "that Margerit has concluded there's enough in your music similar to the mysteries to be useful for her thaumaturgy students."

Luzie made a startled noise and set down her fork. "Truly?"

"She said something about having them practice observation and description. I think she only wants you to play for them. She said it would be safer than performing true mysteries all the time for practice."

Elinur asked doubtfully, "Are you certain you want to get caught up in that sort of thing?" With a brief glance toward Serafina, "It's all very well for scholars and philosophers, but not for the likes of you and me."

"I don't suppose there'll be any harm," Luzie said slowly. She toyed idly with the last remnants of stewed beef on her plate. "And she would pay me? Just to play music for them?"

Issibet took a more practical turn. "It sounds like it would be a fixed fee for the whole day. Be careful about how much you get asked to do. It's no bargain if you aren't home until midnight." She clearly had experience with that sort of contract.

Luzie still looked bemused. "I'll write up a note this evening that you can take with you in the morning, Serafina. I don't think I could start before November, though." She folded her napkin onto the table. "Now if we've all finished, I have a surprise."

She led the way into the parlor with self-conscious ceremony and settled herself before the keyboard.

For all that they often gathered in the parlor in the evenings with sewing or correspondence or other tasks and listened to Luzie practice, she never concertized or demanded their attention. This, it seemed, was different. Serafina felt a growing excitement as she guessed what it meant.

The strains of the overture confirmed her expectation, filling the room with such a rich texture of sound and vision that you scarcely guessed it was no more than the fortepiano. This was the first time she had heard the work played straight through. The first time complete with lyrics as well as music. As Luzie fumbled to turn the first page, Serafina rose and went to her side, turning the pages at each commanding nod.

Luzie chanted the songs, more than singing them, with only the instrument to fill in the melodies. And on the duets and trios, she held to Tanfrit's line and only sketched the others in fragments into the pauses. But it was done: from the initial proud, triumphant entrance, to the climactic crashing tragedy, to Gaudericus's soft final lament. It was complete and whole and Serafina could see the bones underneath that held it all together.

When the last notes had died away it seemed too formal to applaud, but Serafina sank down onto the bench to embrace Luzie as she turned to face them.

"It's wonderful!" she exclaimed. Her mind was still filled with the music, both heard and seen.

"It's just a rough draft," Luzie said dismissively. Then she grinned. "But it's done!"

"Next we should find you a patron," Charluz said. She, too, embraced Luzie in congratulations. "You can't take the next steps until you know whether it will be a chamber performance or the opera house."

"Don't tease!" Elinur chided. "But Charluz is right. You should start looking."

Luzie blushed. "Not yet! It needs to be more polished before I talk to anyone."

"I could ask some friends to inquire for you," Issibet said. "Or…Serafina, you're friends with de Cherdillac. She could be very useful. She's always matching people up with patrons."

"Please don't," Luzie begged. She was growing increasingly flustered. "I couldn't bear for anyone important to hear it until it's perfect."

Serafina had doubts that Luzie would ever consider it perfect, but there was no use in pushing if she found it so upsetting. "Never mind, then. When you're ready I'd be happy to ask the vicomtesse."

* * *

Serafina carefully laid out the series of sketches and paintings along the center of the table in the thaumaturgy workroom as the small crowd of girls gathered to study them. The students had taken to calling the room the Chamber of Mysteries as something of a joke and Serafina found herself almost using the name herself, though Margerit was scandalized at the thought.

She held an odd position: a student, yet not a student. She'd never felt strange that way working alone with Margerit, or with the small circle that gathered at Tiporsel House. But here at Urmai, she was reminded at every turn of how young the true students were. Sixteen, seventeen, eighteen. Girls not yet out, or in the slow start of their dancing season, or the Poor Scholars at an age when they would have just begun earning a living were it not for the chance given them by the House. A few were older: dedicated young women who had been following Margerit's lectures and had begged their parents for more. The sort who might have lingered a few years as girl scholars at the university until marriage claimed them one by one.

She was older than many of the instructors—women like Akezze at the beginning of their careers, still full of fire from their taste of academic life. But there were older ones as well. Mesnera Farin had dabbled all her life in mathematics and never before had the opportunity to pass that love on. Now she'd been coaxed into covering astronomy as well. They rattled around in the old mansion, even with the addition of the Poor Scholars, who arrived in clumps every morning in the back of a market wagon and made their way home at the end of the day by similar means.

Having watched the buildings change from damp ruin to vibrant life, Serafina still found the transformation striking. Sometimes she thought she could see the ghostly promise of what the halls and classrooms would look like in years to come when completely filled.

"Mais— Serafina, I don't understand." The question came hesitantly from Valeir Perneld.

The hesitation in her voice was not from what they studied, for Valeir was one of Margerit's most promising thaumaturgical finds: an auditor who heard the *fluctus* as choirs of angels. No, they all still stumbled over how to address each other. Margerit had declared that there would be no distinction of rank among the students. No constant reminder from mesnera to mefro of the distance between them outside these walls. And there, too, she held an awkward place. Not a teacher to be given the respect of a surname, and yet one who stood on familiar grounds with most of those who were. If the other students stumbled over addressing her as Serafina, she too stumbled to remember to address Akezze as Maisetra Mainus in their hearing.

"Yes, Valeir?" she said. "What is it?"

"How will it work to try to…to describe *fluctus* in pictures when I don't see it?"

Serafina paused in laying out the drawings to answer. "*Visio* is the most common way of perceiving *phasmata*, if the word 'common' can be used at all. But even for visions it isn't a simple question."

From the corner of her eye, Serafina saw two figures slip quietly into the room. Not tardy students, but Margerit herself and a stranger in the dark clothing of a priest. It wasn't at all uncommon for guests to observe the classes: parents who wanted to see what their daughters would be studying or simply the curious. And not surprising, perhaps, that a priest might be sent to examine what was being taught in the way of thaumaturgy. Margerit made a silent gesture to continue, so Serafina turned back to her topic.

"The *depictio* isn't a true image. None of these are, any more than letters written on a page are the sound of a word." She caught the eye of a plump, dark-haired girl at the far side of the table. "Helen, write your name on the board." She nodded encouragingly to indicate that this was not intended as punishment.

The girl traced the letters crisply and precisely.

"Now in Greek," she instructed.

With only the slightest hesitation, Helen wrote Ἑλένη.

"Now in Latin."

Back to the more familiar letters: Helena.

"Now," Serafina asked, "are those the same name?"

The students looked confused and uncertain.

"They're not the same…" Valeir began.

Serafina returned to the dark-haired girl. "Who is your name-saint?"

"Sain-Helen," she replied promptly.

"And if you read her life and miracles in Bartholomeus, what do you read on the page?"

Her eyes brightened in understanding and she said, "Sancta Helena."

"Is that two saints or one?" Serafina asked. This time she directed the question to the whole cluster of girls.

"One," they chorused.

Serafina nodded to indicate they'd done well. "So here you have a *depictio* that Maisetra Sovitre made during the Mystery of Saint Mauriz." She returned to the images they'd been studying. "If I had represented that same moment of the ceremony—" She cast her mind back, though it hardly mattered in detail. "—I would have called the currents here more of a reddish-pink where she has green. I would have said it pulsed slightly, which she hasn't indicated. And these lines here at the side are meant to indicate the aural part, but I rarely hear things during mysteries. Someone else who is a tactile sensitive might describe the same thing as a breath of warm air followed by a prickling as if an insect were walking on their skin."

Two of the girls shuddered at that description.

"And yet the mystery is the same. The grace of God through Saint Mauriz is the same." Serafina chose those words for the unknown priestly observer. Margerit was usually the one who insisted on the language of *charis* and miracles.

She returned to Valeir's question. "So when we practice recording how we perceive the working of power, you will need to decide for yourself how to describe what you experience, for it will be different from anyone else."

Abruptly she gathered up the pages they'd been studying and chose a different set. "Now let's look at this little healing mystery and work through the *depictio* that Maisetra Sovitre has provided."

It wasn't the lesson they'd been meant to do. But in the presence of the visiting priest she thought it best to set the Mauriz text aside. The church could be remarkably jealous of ceremonies they considered their own and it would be hard to discuss that one without touching on its flaws.

* * *

"Your friend Maisetra Sovitre will be here in a little while," Luzie said over breakfast. "She asked me to make sure you didn't miss her."

Serafina set her cup down with a clatter. "What?" Had she confused the day? And why would she pass messages through Luzie?

"She's bringing her cousin to see about lessons. I suppose she didn't want to wait until I have my schedule arranged, and I couldn't very well put her off. I hope the girl can manage with once a week. Have you met her?"

Serafina nodded. "I see her down at the academy, though not often as she isn't studying thaumaturgy." She thought of sharing the gossip around the girl's sudden appearance, but not with Charluz and Elinur present. "Margerit is very strict with her, so I doubt you'll have any trouble."

When Iulien had been settled at the fortepiano in the parlor and been quizzed on the beginning of a concerto to Luzie's satisfaction, Margerit admonished her, "I'll try to return before the end of your lesson, but if I don't you're to stay here and wait for me."

Serafina stood waiting with coat and bonnet. "Where are we going? There isn't time to go all the way to Urmai and back."

"I'll tell you on the way."

The carriage rattled along the narrow streets, heading back toward Tiporsel House, but as they turned away from the river and up the steep rise to the Plaiz, Margerit explained, "I'm hoping you can do me a favor. I simply haven't the time or patience at the moment—especially not the patience—and Father Tomos thought you would be acceptable. Though you mustn't repeat what I said about patience! He was with me when we visited your class the other day."

Yes, the priest. "Acceptable to whom?"

Margerit sighed. "I hardly know. The archbishop, but I don't know who else is involved."

A startled squeak escaped Serafina's throat.

"They want someone with *visio*, someone who can make careful observations. But they still have no interest in my analysis, so I offered your services instead. I hope you don't mind."

The carriage brought them not to the cathedral itself but to the offices that stood along the east side of the Plaiz beside it. They were led to an upper room that had the look of a small dining chamber taken over for other purposes. Serafina thought she recognized Father Tomos, though she'd paid little enough attention to him at the time, but the older man was unfamiliar until she saw past the plainness of his cassock.

He nodded to them both. "Maisetra Sovitre, I'm sorry to hear that your duties won't allow you to lend your assistance. Maisetra...ah...Talarico?" He stared at her curiously. "We have not yet had the pleasure, I believe."

Serafina's tongue froze in her mouth. How did one address an archbishop? She'd never thought to need to know. She dipped a curtsey and stammered something.

Margerit filled in the awkward silence. "I do regret that my duties to my college—after those to Her Grace, of course—leave me no time. Two years past, of course, I had fewer responsibilities."

If the archbishop noticed the edge in Margerit's voice, Serafina couldn't see any reaction to it.

"Indeed," he said. "Two years past the city guildmasters had not yet brought their concerns to me. Maisetra Talarico, has our request been explained to you?"

"Not...not in detail. I was told you wanted my visions..."

"We would like your powers of observation," he corrected. "The guildmasters and I will be restoring and improving the original version of the Great Mystery of Saint Mauriz. We need someone with the sensitivity to assess the results as we work."

So, Serafina thought. Margerit had won. Or...if not won, then at least the old men had belatedly come to the same conclusion she had. And though it was true that the college filled every moment of Margerit's time, it was also true that her pride had been hurt by the archbishop's refusal to accept her analysis. That analysis had been a masterpiece. Serafina had recognized it when she first saw it in Rome, knowing nothing of its origins. And they had treated it as a schoolgirl's exercise. Even now, they hadn't asked for Margerit's analysis or her talents in design, only for her *visio*. But if *visio* were all they needed, she could be an acceptable substitute. Serafina took a slow breath.

"Your Excellency, I haven't the skill that Maisetra Sovitre has in devising mysteries, but I have eyes to see, and I can know whether a mystery has achieved its purpose. If my poor talents can serve in her stead, you are welcome to them."

CHAPTER TWENTY-THREE

Barbara

October, 1824

When pressed to it, Barbara had to admit that she enjoyed the grand balls of the season. That is, she had begun enjoying them after the first few years, once the suitors had given up hope of her granting them anything more than a dance and a penetrating conversation about politics. Back when she had attended on the old baron, she had stood watchfully in the arcades and galleries, focused entirely on him and those around him. In those days, she'd wondered why he bothered with dancing masters and lessons in comportment if she were only to be a spectator. She'd denied it at the time, but she'd envied the bright and elegant figures in the center of the salles, knowing she had no entrance to that world except in Baron Saveze's service.

Then the world had turned upside down and she became Saveze.

Barbara had arrived late and danced a set with Rikerd Ovinze, and then another with Perrez Chalfin, before seeking out her hosts to exchange pleasantries. With several daughters of an age for dancing, the Alboris had become part of the backbone of the season—these grand events designed to introduce a parade of accomplished young women to a similar parade of promising young men. The family's connection to Lord Albori, the foreign minister, meant they could attract the cream of Rotenek society, despite not falling within the upper ranks themselves. She watched Renoz Albori move through the figures in a gown of apricot silk, overlaid with silver tissue. Her sister must have accepted an offer, or she wouldn't have been allowed to outshine her.

"Another triumph I see, Verneke," Barbara commented, nodding in Renoz's direction. "Mihail, I'm guesing the rumors are true that your eldest has settled her choice at last. Is your cousin here tonight? I haven't seen him yet."

Mihael Albori harrumphed in acknowledgment. "Yes, though I beg you'll allow him one evening without a word of affairs in France!"

Barbara smiled, knowing that Lord Albori himself had no such aversion. It was another hour before she found herself in company with the minister and, as she had guessed, he was deep in conversation over matters unrelated to the ball.

Estapez was asking, "Are you likely to be sent back so soon? I thought Perzin was to take charge of our interests in Paris."

"He's a good enough boy. Very sharp. But I expect Her Grace will want someone more experienced until matters settle down again."

Barbara guessed correctly at which matters they were discussing when Estapez returned, "But he'd been ill for quite some time. Surely the French ministers have everything in hand?"

"You're speaking of the death of King Louis?" Barbara asked. The question briefly drew their attention, and then the circle reformed and she was accepted into the conversation.

"Nothing is ever settled until there's a funeral and a coronation," Albori said. "There's no judging a king until he's worn the crown a while. We have no idea what sort of neighbor Charles will be."

It was the sort of idle banter that Barbara knew was common in the clubs, but she had access to it only at events such as this, or around the council hall. That made balls even more of an attraction than the dancing did. Nothing of any importance would be decided in such a setting, yet she enjoyed being accepted into the debate.

She both wished Margerit were at her side and was glad to spare her what she would find tedious. Politics amused her even less than dancing. Barbara scanned the room and her eyes settled on a tall figure at the far side. Now there was another person who appeared only grudgingly in the Grand Salle.

Antuniet stood regally at the edge of the knot of admirers surrounding Jeanne. They had come to a compromise, where Antuniet would accompany Jeanne into society on occasion, then drift away to quiet corners when the press and noise became too much. They had their little rituals to maintain the truce.

Barbara watched one of those rituals now as Jeanne reached out briefly to touch the crimson pendant that always hung at Antuniet's throat before returning to her audience. Antuniet turned to retreat to the far end of the salle where a glassed-in conservatory opened off toward the gardens and one might find some solitude even during the bustle of a high season ball.

Something in the way that Antuniet moved nagged at Barbara's attention. When you had trained with the sword for more than half your life, you never stopped seeing such things: a change in balance, a shift in how one carried oneself. They had met to consult on the current set of alchemical gems several times in the last weeks. Had she stood too closely to notice? Her gaze followed Antuniet's path across the salle. At first the impossibility of the suspicion baffled her. Yet the signs were unmistakable now that she looked for them. Barbara's lips thinned into a grim line as she counted back. Without seeming to follow, she too drifted toward the far end of the salle.

How dare she? With everything…Barbara's anger rose quickly to such a pitch that by the time she entered the conservatory on Antuniet's heels she had distilled her demands down into two words.

"Who? When?" They were uttered with a quiet intensity not meant to carry to the other ears in the room.

To Barbara's annoyance, Antuniet relaxed, as if a weight had been removed. She looked around the dim room at those other ears. "Is this truly a conversation you wish to have here and now?"

Antuniet inescapably had the right of it. Barbara said stiffly, "How early would it be convenient for me to wait on you in the morning?"

Good heavens, even to herself she sounded like she was arranging a duel.

"If you like, I think I could manage eight o'clock," Antuniet said coolly. "In my workshop, not at home. That will give us an hour or so before the others arrive."

* * *

Tiporsel House no longer kept to anything resembling society hours. Margerit had already risen and dragged her young cousin out of bed to go down to the academy for the day, so there was no need to dodge awkward questions about her own errand. They had promised each other—a promise often repeated but just as often bent—never to keep secrets, no matter what the excuse. But it was hard sometimes to find the line between secrets and mere suspicions.

Neither had Barbara meant to exclude Tavit from the nature of the errand, but it had been a late evening and Brandel was going to the palace for lessons, so it was natural to excuse her armin for the brief ride over. She dismissed the question of attendance for her return. Tavit worried too much.

The decision let her deflect her mind from the coming confrontation with questions to Brandel about his new duties.

"Have you come to an understanding with Maisetra Fulpi yet?" she asked. The two had squabbled a few times until Iulien had been made to understand that though she might be under Brandel's watch, she could only ask and not command his attendance.

"Oh, Iuli's a good sort, I suppose," Brandel offered, reining his horse closer so they needn't shout as they rode along the Vezenaf toward the Plaiz. "At least she hasn't asked me to stand around while she takes tea like Marken does for Maisetra Sovitre."

Barbara found the image almost enough to lighten her mood as far as a smile. "Being an armin is ninety-nine days of watching your charge dance and drink tea for one day of adventure."

"I know," Brandel said with an exaggerated sigh.

"Let me tell you of an armin's duty," Barbara said, launching into a story from the old baron's time and then concluding with the admonishment, "Maisetra Fulpi will give you a good deal of practice, I think, in heading off trouble before it begins without provoking outright rebellion."

And then they were at the gates of the palace and handed the reins to waiting grooms to go their own ways.

Barbara found Antuniet engaged in a desultory inventory of her chemical stores. The great rotating furnace had been poked to just enough life to heat the room but there were no signs of a firing in the offing. Antuniet's choice of the ground to face her was for more than privacy. This was her territory. Barbara breathed in the sharp scents of acid and sulfur that had become Antuniet's signature.

The anger that had simmered on the ride over now flared up in the face of her cousin's calm composure. Instead of the two questions from the night before, Barbara launched into, "Why? What in heaven's name do you think you're doing? Or was it simply an accident? I never would have thought you would be the one of the pair of you to go catting about on the side."

It was an ugly question, but Barbara felt the desire to shake that bland composure.

"The Chazillen legacy," Antuniet said simply. "That was my whole purpose from the beginning, you recall. I have a warrant from Princess Annek for my children to inherit my name and rank."

"And what sort of legacy will it be?" Barbara demanded. "How many lives do you plan to destroy for the sake of that name? Your own for a start. I doubt Princess Annek has use for open proof of fornication in her court! Jeanne's life as well, to be sure, though you'll certainly distract from the rest of the gossip about the two of you. But you might have given a thought to my reputation. It's been hard enough this year with that damned novel and the troubles in council and everything. And Princess Annek's reputation as well, if she doesn't do the sensible thing and simply cast you off."

A rare smile quirked the corner of Antuniet's mouth. "I rather think Princess Annek's reputation will be enhanced by patronizing an alchemist who can achieve the most difficult of the Great Works. No other crowned head in Europe in the last hundred years can boast of an alchemist who achieved a homunculus."

"A...homunculus." Barbara remembered listening to Antuniet's lectures on the topic but she'd thought it an idle game of philosophy. An amusement, using the sort of spiritual symbolism that alchemists delighted in. "A homunculus," she repeated.

"Why yes," Antuniet said briskly. "The principles are quite similar to that of transmuting metal. A more traditional path than my gemstone work. Different materials, of course, and the processes use entirely different symbolism than that for the Philosopher's Stone. But—"

"You can't be serious," Barbara interrupted.

"I'm quite serious. The proof is in the result, isn't it?"

For a moment—only a moment—Barbara believed it might be possible. She had seen wondrous things come out of this workshop. And it was clear that alchemists of the past had known the secret. But…

Her gaze returned to Antuniet's face. It held a challenge that was just a hair to the side of smug certainty. If anyone could convince the elite of Rotenek that she'd gotten a child without resorting to a man, her cousin could do it. All it would take would be enough sincere believers and the silent acceptance of the rest. Princess Annek might well see the advantage to such a proof of skill. And yet…

Barbara's eyes narrowed. "Perhaps I will accept that, in time, you could accomplish this. But I saw how long it took to develop the formulas for your talismans. What I don't accept is that you could master the skills in a single summer. There are far easier ways to get with child in that span of time. So let us return to my first question. Whose is it?"

"Mine," Antuniet said simply. "And I fail to see what business it is of yours."

Barbara gaped at her. "I think I might be forgiven for having some interest in what sort of man fathered the next Baron Saveze!"

A wave of confusion passed over Antuniet's face. "What are you talking about?" Her expression seemed genuinely bewildered. "The next…" Abruptly, her mouth fell open. She drew up a chair and sat heavily. "I…dear God, Barbara. I swear, I don't care to be thought slow-witted, but it had never occurred to me…"

Her shock was almost believable.

"But…Barbara," Antuniet continued. "It isn't possible. The Chazillen line was cut off from the title when Estefen…when we were disenrolled."

When Estefen was executed for treason. They had never spoken of that—not in so many words. And now was not the time.

"The direct family claim, yes. But you're still my cousin and my closest kin by the Lumbeirt line. From the moment your rank was restored you've been my heir-default."

"I thought…" she began. "I assumed that Brandel…"

Barbara shook her head. In the face of Antuniet's confusion, her anger was draining away and leaving only exasperation. "I won't deny that I have ambitions for him, but not Saveze. He has no claim there. And there's no one else." She laughed grimly. "And unlike you—or my father for that matter—I have qualms about getting myself an heir without benefit of marriage. So let me ask again, who was he?"

The silence stretched out between them. Antuniet broke it at last. "He's of good birth. And he lives very far away. He won't cause trouble and you needn't be concerned about his bloodlines."

She mentioned a name, but it meant nothing to Barbara.

"And Jeanne knows?"

"Jeanne was there."

Something in the tenor of Antuniet's answer made Barbara tilt her head quizzically. Antuniet nodded, her gaze steady, confirming what hadn't been asked aloud. Barbara felt an unaccustomed warmth creep over her face.

"I see it's still possible for me to shock you," Antuniet said. "I am sorry—"

Barbara waved the protest away. "And what is my role in this meant to be?"

Antuniet sighed. "I hadn't intended you to have any role at all. You may disown me if you think it necessary."

The idea was tempting, but if she rejected her cousin's story, that would be a sign for others to do the same. "I doubt that would serve any purpose," Barbara said. "Best to see it through. I shall be seen to be proud of your alchemical triumph."

Antuniet rose slowly from her chair. She looked more tired than the early hour might explain. "I was hoping that perhaps you might consent to stand as godmother."

Barbara found the request strangely pleasing. "I'll consider it." And then, just before turning to leave, she asked, "Tell me: could you produce a child by alchemy?"

"I think so," Antuniet said. "At least, I think it would be possible. But I don't know that I'd have the heart to work through the failures to success."

Barbara remembered batch after batch of flawed gemstones, lying cracked and shattered on the workbench before being returned to the fire. No. Antuniet had made some cold-blooded choices in her time, but surely that would be beyond her.

* * *

At the ball, Albori had passed on several observations on the French situation, prefaced by the comment, "Her Grace thought you might be interested." It was permission, not a command, and the encounter with Antuniet had swept them from Barbara's mind for a few days.

Albori covered the official channels of diplomatic communication. But if Princess Annek thought the death of the French king might relate in some way to the matters she was investigating with Kreiser, those channels would be inadequate. Not for the first time, Barbara wondered just how much of the Austrian's mission was reported to his own embassy, and whether the answers received through those different channels bore any resemblance to each other. Barbara's blood quickened at the thought of matching wits once more.

Having prepared the way with a request to meet Kreiser at his club, Barbara dressed once more in that mix of male and female garments she had chosen previously for passage into the halls of Sainkall's. As the weather looked unusually promising for the season, she sent word down to Tavit that they would be walking.

Tavit met her in the foyer, but Brandel was close at his heels asking, "Cousin Barbara? I have no lessons at the palace today. Might I attend you?"

He glanced briefly over at Tavit for permission. Tavit's expression gave nothing away. He was grudgingly generous about sharing duties with Brandel when there was no chance of trouble. Council sessions did not fall within that category. But this? Barbara recalled that Baron Mazuk was another habitué of Sainkall's and shook her head. And not for that reason alone.

"Brandel, as I recall, Maisetra Fulpi is also free of lessons today. Have you asked her whether she might want your attendance?"

"Oh, Iuli," he said dismissively.

Barbara's mouth hardened. "Did you think I was investing in all this training so you could follow around at my heels for your own pride? You have far to go to convince me you have the skills and experience to attend on a person of rank and title. And you could make up a great deal of that distance by showing me you can watch over a 'nothing of a country girl with few expectations and a modest dowry.'"

Brandel stiffened. He hadn't meant her to overhear that comment.

When Barbara was certain she had his attention, she added more patiently, "It was never my plan or my intention for you to replace Tavit. Put that out of your mind. Having Maisetra Fulpi in your charge is training, just as much as your time at Perret's fencing salle. Prove yourself and then we can discuss taking on more responsibility."

* * *

The porter at Sainkall's had ceased to be startled at her visits, but held to the strict rule that she be met and escorted by one of the members. Kreiser had taken the liberty of ordering wine for them—a sweet dark vintage that encouraged lingering sips.

Barbara opened the match with, "Interesting news from France."

"I suppose the death of a king is always interesting," Kreiser replied, "or were you thinking of fresher news than that?"

"Tell me something fresher and I'll tell you whether I had it in mind," Barbara countered.

He waggled a finger at her. "That's not how the game is played."

Barbara laughed. "I haven't come for games today. Yes, the death of King Louis. Do you think—?"

"Why has your Archbishop Fereir changed his mind about the structure of the cathedral mysteries?" Kreiser interrupted. "What does he know?"

"I doubt he knows more than anyone else," Barbara said. "He's simply decided to listen at last." Though not, apparently, to listen to Margerit.

"Indeed," Kreiser replied. "One of the people he's listening to is that Talarico woman."

Barbara hid her surprise. Margerit hadn't mentioned anything of the sort, but Margerit was quite distracted these days. "I hadn't realized you were familiar with Maisetra Talarico."

Kreiser gave one of his taunting half smiles. "I try to be acquainted with everyone who has useful talents."

"And what do you think of her observations?" Barbara asked. A probe, as she had no idea what those observations had been.

Kreiser either missed her bluff or was willing to divulge the information freely. "She thinks our weather mystery has gone entirely mad. That whoever devised it has lost all control and that accounts for the disasters plaguing Alpennia and her neighbors."

"We suspected that," Barbara offered.

"No, we knew it had gone beyond the original intent. I don't think even the people who created it could pull it back or dismantle it now."

"Isn't the termination usually built into the mystery itself?" Barbara asked. The ceremonies of the formal mystery guilds were rarely meant to come to an end. They added layer on layer to previous workings, like fresh plaster on a wall. It was only lesser mysteries—private ceremonies and the ones dismissively called market charms—that had a closely defined scope. "Had they meant this to stand in place for all eternity?"

Kreiser leaned forward and dropped his voice as if even the servants passing in the corridor might be spies. "A zauberwerk of this scale, of this power—it takes a great deal from those who devise it. Maisetra Sovitre will tell you that's why great mysteries are celebrated only by guilds. It takes a great deal of skill and…and essence to create a working of this size. You can't build it on the talents of one or two thaumaturgists alone, no matter how dedicated."

Barbara considered him skeptically. "So you don't hold that mysteries work through the grace of God?"

He gave a soft snort. "I won't deny the grace of God and I wouldn't say even this much in certain places. I won't claim that skill alone can explain the outcome of a mystery. But the world is more complex than that. I once saw a man burned to a shriveled husk because he called on powers greater than he knew. Was that God's grace? And this…this thing we face," he said, waving vaguely toward the east. "I think the more it grew beyond their intent, the less they could control it and the more it ate at them. Something has changed within the last two months. Two months ago it was like a vicious dog that could no longer be called to heel. Now it's gone frothing mad and I think we may conclude that it's savaged its former masters. And what else has happened within that span of time?"

Barbara's heart quickened. Had his mind turned the same place that Princess Annek's had? "I can think of several things," she said cautiously.

"Leave off the games, Saveze," he said. "We know approximately when this…thing was created. And we know when King Louis's health took a sudden turn for the worse. And now he has died and the mystery has fractured entirely. That's proof enough for me."

"You think the French king would sacrifice his life for this?"

"You Alpennians!" Kreiser said with unaccustomed impatience. "For all your famed scholastic tradition, you think miracles come in tidy little boxes. Let us be plain. This is sorcery. And sorcery is ugly. It's ugly for those who work it and for those they work against. And you—you've worked so hard to unlock the secrets of power and then tied them up again in formal rituals and mysticism. Your Gaudericus might have been a genius but he squandered it all for fear of angering the church. Guilds provide a safe source of power but they make innovation nearly impossible. So every sorcerer tries to adapt the rules of thaumaturgy to a smaller scale in secret, and when they fail, they fail like this. If men like Gaudericus had had half as much ambition as talent—"

"Then we might not have the results of his work at all," Barbara finished. Kreiser's complaint put a different light on the treatment of Gaudericus's work over the centuries. Perhaps fear of heresy was not the only reason to suppress his publications.

Kreiser sighed. "I think there's a circle—a mystery guild, if you will—in France that found a way to tie the royal person into the structure of their mystery to enforce France's interests in Spain. Such symbols have power. But they lost control. And the ambit of the mystery grew until at last it killed him. Whether you call it the grace of God or something else, no one directs the forces currently at play to lock the Alps in winter. And no one can predict what further damage it may do."

Barbara stared at him in horror as the consequences expanded in her mind. "You can prove this?"

"I can prove nothing yet, but I'd stake my life on it. Indeed, I have done so." Kreiser sat back, his expression now as mild as if they'd been discussing the merits of a pair of coach horses. "And I must say, it's a great relief to me."

Yes, it would be. It meant he needn't watch his back against his own masters. "So Fereir has been convinced to restore and strengthen the old Mauriz mystery. We put the All Saints' Castellum in the hands of a guild chosen for something other than the length of their pedigrees, and—"

"Alpennians!" Kreiser muttered once more. "You can't just build a wall around your pretty little country and keep the wider world out. You've tried doing that for centuries and this is what comes of it!"

In a way, it was an echo of what Princess Annek had once said. An echo of what Margerit had complained of with regard to the Mauriz mystery. The time was past for looking inward. Alliances might shore up the present, but as Antuniet was wont to say, no way out but forward.

Kreiser turned the conversation sharply around a corner once more. "Will your Princess be sending her son back to Paris do you think?"

Barbara answered carefully, "Mesner Albori didn't say."

"Mesner Atilliet has spent a startling amount of time in France in the last year, but perhaps there are…attractions there."

"It's a good place to learn statesmanship," Barbara offered.

"But a poor place to seek alliances, at least of that sort. French royal blood has grown thin."

Barbara declined to take that bait. The little she knew of Annek's thoughts on her son's eventual marriage were not ones she felt at liberty to share. "I haven't heard that there is any thought of a French marriage."

Kreiser looked at her narrowly and returned to a previous topic. "It's time for me to make plans for my own visit to Paris, though I'd like to know more of what I face. I wonder if you might introduce me to someone who has been with the Alpennian delegation there? Perhaps Mesner Atilliet himself?"

"I doubt I could manage that," Barbara replied. "We meet socially, but it would be awkward for me to extend him a private invitation. And Albori himself would be too obvious for your purpose, I think." Though, she thought, he would definitely need to be apprised of Kreiser's plans. "I might arrange a dinner that included the Perzins. Iohen Perzin is in line to take over the delegation to Paris and his wife is close to an old friend." Now that was a very delicate way to describe Tionez's relationship to Jeanne and Jeanne's to her. "Now that I think of it…"

Barbara's mind spun off in possibilities. Jeanne's salons. Jeanne had the standing to invite Efriturik as well as the Perzins. But no, it would be impossible to suggest that Kreiser be welcome in her house. Not simply because of Antuniet's continued enmity for the man. Kreiser had given the orders behind the attack on Anna Monterrez, and Anna was at the heart of Jeanne's salons. No, that wouldn't do at all. But perhaps…The complexities stirred her blood.

"I'll see what I can do," she concluded. "Expect an invitation."

CHAPTER TWENTY-FOUR

Luzie

Mid-December, 1824

The students drifted in, one by one, and set out their pens and paints on the table. It was an odd sort of music lesson; only one of the girls played an instrument at all. That is, only one of the thaumaturgy students. Maisetra Sovitre's cousin Iulien would be joining them today. Luzie moved restlessly around the room tidying up as they waited for that most important straggler.

The music room at the Tanfrit Academy had once been a small side parlor. With its red-flocked wallpaper and marble fireplace it might have been a room in the house of any of her students' parents, except that few of those would have boasted both a fortepiano and a double-manual harpsichord. There was talk of adding more instruments in future years. Luzie rattled around in the space as the sole instructor, brought in—as Maisetra Sovitre had noted—as a lure to parents concerned that their daughters be accomplished and not simply learned.

Mornings were individual lessons. After lunch the room filled with girls eager to learn music theory—not the principles of composition yet, but the basics of the science of sound. Luzie had felt out of her depth at first. She'd taught brief snippets of such things around keyboard lessons, but never anything so formal. As that first month passed—as November turned to December—she and the students came to an agreement of exploration rather than instruction. When the lesson was over, instead of musical notation the chalkboard might hint of mathematics or physics or some other subject brought in slantwise.

Once, in the first weeks, she'd gone to apologize to Maisetra Mainus for the chaos and lack of direction, but the headmistress had nodded gravely and said, "If there's love of learning, the rest will come. We're all feeling our way down this path. Do you have what you need? Are there any books or supplies lacking?"

Luzie needed do no more than mention that composition books might be of use and the printers were set to work producing sheets of staff paper.

But this class was the one that left her most unsettled and yet most joyful. Late in the day, the small group of girls identified as having thaumaturgical talent clustered around the fortepiano with notepads in hand and she would play. It might have been awkward, except that Serafina was there as their teacher, though she disclaimed the title.

"Begin with your nightingale song," Serafina had suggested in the very first session.

And so she had played that simple tune over and over again for an hour, learning to ignore the delighted exclamations and puzzled comments of the students as they learned to record on paper whatever it was they saw or felt.

She played more than her own compositions. By trial and error, she and Serafina had identified some works of the great composers who had imbued their music with power. And at least one of the sessions had dissolved into an argument of whether all music that had the power to move a heart partook of mystic forces, or whether one could distinguish those that disturbed what Serafina called the *fluctus* as standing apart from those that only touched the emotions.

It had taken most of November for her to sort out the thaumaturgy students. There was Mari Orlin, who had studied with her for years and shyly confessed that she had never understood that not everyone felt music as a singing in the blood, as a spiritual joy like she felt during prayer. And only now did she have words for the thrill she felt when playing Luzie's exercises.

There was Valeir Perneld who had joined the small group of students with private lessons, not to learn the keyboard, but for practice in distinguishing the notes of the instrument from those she heard only in her own mind. There were times, she said, when the two jangled in conflict, and other times when they sang in a harmony that left her breathless. Luzie had no idea what it all meant, but they had set out a plan for Valeir to learn composition in the spring so that she could record her "angel voices."

The girls from the Poor Scholars were not among her performance students, of course. They hadn't enjoyed the advantages of the others, though one said she'd played the fiddle on street corners as a child. But three of them had been found to have visions of some degree—perhaps only a soft glow, perhaps more. Doruzi perceived the music in pictures, describing the little nightingale piece as a tree growing into arches and rafters like the stones of the church.

Today Iulien Fulpi had been added to the class when Serafina had suggested trying a song, and Luzie had demurred at using the Tanfrit pieces. Back last spring, Maisetra Sovitre had given her several short poems and commissioned settings for them. Luzie had envisioned the author as a somewhat older woman, sharing verses among her friends and perhaps aspiring to a slim volume some day. Though the works could not be said to be mature, there was an energetic freshness about them, a startling imagery and a playful way with rhyme. If she'd known they'd been penned by a girl not yet out, she might have balked. It would be too easy for her composition time to be bought by amateur poets whose talents would do little to enhance her reputation.

But the verses had called to her, and as the resulting songs had been sent back to the provinces, she hadn't given it further thought. There had ben no connection in her mind between Maisetra Sovitre's poetic cousin and the girl she'd been begged to work into her schedule. Not until Iulien Fulpi had shyly opened her music case one day during a lesson and asked if they might work on a piece with the title "Souvenir" penned across the top.

"Where did you get this?" Luzie had asked.

"Cousin Margerit sent it to me. Maisetra Sovitre, that is. I was so thrilled!" The enthusiasm in her voice had been embarrassing. "She told us all about your mystical music. And of course I couldn't tell whether you'd done that with my songs, because I haven't any sensitivity at all, Margerit says. But just the thought that the great Luzie Valorin…"

Luzie remembered her sharp retort, "You needn't try to flatter me."

"I wasn't—" Iulien had looked down with a smile.

The girl was both utterly charming and completely impossible. Luzie did not envy Maisetra Sovitre having the charge of her in a place as tempting as Rotenek. If Iulien were properly out in society, instead of substituting a study year for her dancing season, she would be causing havoc and devastation. Assuming that…It occurred to Luzie that she didn't know what Iulien's prospects were.

Like all of Rotenek, she knew of Maisetra Sovitre's fabled inheritance, but she knew nothing of her family. What were their circumstances? And would Iulien cause more disruption as an heiress than if that charming personality were paired with only respectable expectations?

Those speculations returned as she listened to Iulien's nimble fingers accompany her only passable voice, while the thaumaturgy students sketched and took notes and laid splashes of color across their pages. If Margerit Sovitre were older, then Rotenek society might expect her to name her cousin as her heir. But surely Margerit still expected to marry and have children of her own. She wasn't yet at the point of being considered on the shelf, and her fortune made up for any deficiencies in traditional accomplishments. She might—

It was the sight of Serafina, moving among the students as they worked, that diverted that path of thought. Perhaps Margerit Sovitre had no plans to marry at all. She'd heard the gossip of course, but there were always speculations and rumors about eccentrics. It was one of the entertainments they offered,

as long as no actual rules were broken. But for as great an heiress as Margerit
Sovitre to decline to marry…did that constitute the breaking of a rule? Before
this summer it might not have occurred to her that a woman could have more
reasons to remain unmarried than a lack of opportunity. Or that two close
friends might be enough to each other to set at naught all the attractions of a
conventional life. If she had thought of it at all, she had accepted the story that
the odd way in which Maisetra Sovitre's and Baroness Saveze's lives had been
braided together was reason enough for their closeness. Now she wondered.
And wondered if Serafina would know.

She set the thought aside. It was mere curiosity and none of her affair.
Even the question of Iulien Fulpi's prospects was nothing to do with her. If
she wasn't careful, she'd become as nosy as the old women in the marketplace.

Iulien finished the song and sat quietly while the other students hurriedly
moved to finish their notes and sketches. Serafina was strict about the need
for swift work. This isn't art, she'd said. You can't ask a guild to pause in the
middle of a ceremony so you can catch up.

While they waited, Luzie commented quietly, "You've changed the lyrics."

"Only a few words here and there. It felt…I don't know, ill-fitting? Like
when I used to try on my mother's gloves and they were both too large and
too small." Iulien held up her hands, staring at the unfashionably broad, blunt
fingers. Not the hands of a great performer, but sufficient for the parlor.

"You have a way with words," Luzie said, thinking both of the song and
what she'd said about gloves.

Iulien ducked her head in what seemed to be a habit, but this time it
looked like genuine embarrassment and not coy pretense.

Serafina came over as the students returned their pens and brushes to the
cabinets. "That worked very well. It was a different flavor than your usual
work, and it's interesting to see how a different performer changes the effect.
A good exercise."

But there was an edge in her voice, as if the difference had surprised and
unsettled her. Not for the first time, Luzie wished she had the talent to see
her own work the way Serafina did. At times they spoke entirely different
languages.

* * *

With the break between school terms at the turning of the year, Luzie
dedicated her free days to composition. Christmas passed, with its familiar
rituals, then the New Year, celebrated more in the upper town with balls and
concerts revolving around the glittering court. As she worked to turn the
keyboard sketches for *Tanfrit* into a score that could be shown to potential
patrons, Luzie became ever more grateful for the copywork she'd done for
Fizeir. Splitting the parts for an orchestra—even a small chamber group—that
would stretch her even more. She'd learned the basic principles under her
father, but Fizeir's work had given her practice.

There had been another benefit to working with Fizeir: glimpses of his compositions before their debuts. He was notoriously close-mouthed about new work. Some of her own reticence in discussing her project outside a small circle had come from his example. *I don't care to puff it about and have interest satisfied before the curtain rises*, he'd said. Keeping such matters quiet was difficult among the close-knit community of performers and theater staff. But few challenged Fizeir's desires after the affair of his *Arturo en Avalon*, when the leading soprano had been dismissed the night before opening for having performed selections for friends in a café. People had learned to keep his secrets if they wanted to ride on his success. Luzie had made certain that he never had reason to doubt her own discretion.

But Luzie hadn't had time or need to do any copying for the composer since last winter, and Issibet had delegated the wardrobe for his new work *Il Filosofo Dannato—The Damned Philosopher*—to her assistant. So it was that the first inkling of disaster came on the morning after Fizeir's new opera debuted, when she was startled by an unexpected visit from the Vicomtesse de Cherdillac.

At hearing the reverence in Alteburk's welcome, Luzie hurried out from the parlor where she'd been preparing for the next lesson, saying, "Mesnera de Cherdillac, I'm afraid Serafina has left for Urmai already. I'm so sorry, but she doesn't seem to have left a message for you."

"I'm not here for Serafina," the vicomtesse said.

Something in the overkind tone of her voice suggested sorrow and sympathy. Luzie's heart clenched.

"Is something wrong? Serafina—"

"No, no, nothing like that! But perhaps we should sit. Do you have the time?"

Luzie glanced at the clock at the end of the hall and nodded. Dread was replaced by puzzlement as the vicomtesse allowed the housekeeper to take her cloak.

"No, no tea," de Cherdillac said, interrupting the beginnings of a request. "This isn't a social visit."

The vicomtesse took her hand and drew her down to sit beside her on the sofa and continued holding it like one breaking tragic news.

"Serafina has been talking about a composition you've been working on. About Tanfrit the philosopher."

"Yes?" Luzie acknowledged. Had Serafina gone against her wishes and asked de Cherdillac for her support?

"I thought so. And Margerit said something about her library being plundered for the research!" De Cherdillac smiled to indicate it was a little joke, but the expression didn't reach her eyes. "Is it very far along? Have you talked to many people about it?"

"Only a few friends," Luzie said slowly. "It's complete, but I'm still polishing it. It isn't quite ready to show to anyone else yet."

More gently, "Then there's no reason why the composer Fizeir would know of your plans."

"I…yes, I mentioned it to him in the spring. I used to do some work for him. I wanted his opinion on the initial sketches. He wasn't very encouraging, I'm afraid."

"Well he seems to have changed his mind," de Cherdillac said. "Last night he debuted his new work, *Il Filosofo Dannato*."

She nodded vaguely. "A new version of Faust, I thought."

"The story of Gaudericus and Tanfrit."

Luzie could only stare, open-mouthed. "But…he…there must be some mistake."

"No mistake," the vicomtesse said. "And I find it an odd coincidence. It would be a different matter if you had both been inspired by the same source. Were you?"

Luzie shook her head. "I don't believe it," she said helplessly.

But in her mind she could see how it had happened. What had he said? *Perhaps in other hands…* Of course he'd never thought she would finish a work of this size. He wouldn't have thought of it as trespassing. If he'd known, he surely wouldn't…

She stood and went over to where the overstuffed music case sat on the desk beside the fortepiano and brought it back to place it in de Cherdillac's lap.

"This is my work. Tell me. He must have done something entirely different."

De Cherdillac left the case closed, saying, "I'm not enough of a musician to compare the two. But you should see for yourself. Come with me tonight. I'll manage an invitation from someone. Bring Serafina if you like. I'll come to pick you up."

And then there was a knock at the door, and her student arrived, and there was no time to do more than agree.

* * *

Afterward, Luzie couldn't remember the names of their hosts, or who else had been present in the box. Only the stifling closeness of the velvet draperies and the growing unease as Fizeir's work rolled out through the familiar scenes and acts. It wasn't a copy. Far from it. Her libretto had still been incomplete when she showed it to him. And Fizeir's was in Italian, like all his operas. Only occasionally could she glimpse traces of her musical themes—the ones he'd seen that day in July. But the shape—the story that she and Serafina had devised between them—the pace and tempo of the work…He hadn't stolen it exactly, but he'd built an edifice in the middle of the ground she'd prepared for planting.

She sat rigid and silent in her gilded chair in the corner of the box while the others chattered through the interval. She'd meant to see it out to the end. But when the climax began…Fizeir had rewritten Tanfrit's aria to a mournful dirge. Let the waters cover me as a grave. She could take no more. She stood and hurried out with no farewell to her hostesses. Indeed, she had to bite her lip to keep her emotions silent.

She heard quick footsteps behind her in the nearly empty corridor then felt the warmth as Serafina draped her cloak around her shoulders.

The walk home was like a dream in a fever. She set out blindly, the cobblestones cold through her thin slippers, barely hearing Serafina protest that they could hire a fiacre. That it was too late at night to walk alone.

But walk she did—across the empty Plaiz and into the maze of narrow streets that lay between the palace grounds and the river. The quickest route home, though not one she would normally take. Voices came out of the dark. Questions, rough offers. She heard Serafina answer one back in gutter-Italian.

The cold couldn't touch her. The walk seemed hours and no time at all. The street turned familiar, the walkway, the steps to the door, the hall, the parlor. As she felt Serafina take the cloak from her shoulders, her eyes lighted on the music case where it sat on her desk. With a quick movement, she opened it and seized a handful of papers, crumpling them in her fist and throwing them at the hearth.

Serafina pushed past her with a cry and snatched them back, patting out the burning edges with her gloved hands.

A rising wail forced itself out of Luzie's throat and she threw the rest of the papers into the air, scattering about the room like dead leaves. She felt Serafina's arms around her as she sank to the carpet, wailing and sobbing.

Then the room was filled with people: Gerta, Alteburk, Elinur, Chisillic and the others. Serafina's voice explaining what had happened. Hands, touching, patting, holding her. The soft rustle as someone began gathering up the sheets of music. The gradual fading of her own sobs. The dusty smell of burnt paper, masked by the scorch of leather from Serafina's ruined gloves. The comforting kitcheny aroma that clung to Silli's clothing, as the cook's strong arms lifted her to the sofa by the front window. The sweet spicy scent of Serafina, who held her tightly and rocked her softly and whispered that everything would be all right.

"He stole it from me!" she managed at last. "It was mine and he took it!"

"It wasn't really very like," Serafina protested. "Not in the music."

"But don't you see?" Luzie protested. "Mine will never be performed now. Everyone will think I was just copying him. 'A poor imitation,' they'll say. No one will even touch it."

"Yours is better," Serafina said fiercely.

Luzie knew it was loyalty, not truth. What did Serafina know of opera?

"Yours is better," Serafina repeated. "And when it's performed, everyone will know whose is the poor imitation."

It was useless, Luzie knew, but she let Serafina tell her comforting lies. And then Charluz pressed a glass of brandy into her hand and she gulped it down, punishing herself with the fierce burn down her throat. They helped her up to her room and off with the crumpled gown. And Serafina's voice was saying, "I'll stay with her, in case she wakes in the night."

Then, much later, oblivion.

* * *

Comfort and familiarity. Serafina's warmth beside her in the bed. Serafina's arm resting easily over her hip, warm under the covers.

But summer was past, they'd had to...

Why was Serafina here? Memory. The opera. That blind flight through the dark streets. Her music...the fire. No, Serafina had stopped her.

The body beside her stirred restlessly and turned.

"It *is* better," Luzie said aloud.

"What?" came a sleepy voice.

"My opera. It *is* better than his, and I won't let him take that from me."

Serafina rolled over so they faced each other, warm breaths mingling in the cold morning air. "Of course it's better. His doesn't have any magic."

Luzie made a rude snort. "Magic doesn't matter. Most people can't see the magic. But my music is better. Fizeir's grown lazy," she complained bitterly. "No one dares to say anything because he's the great Alpennian composer. My music is better and he knows it. That's why he bought my tunes. It's why he tried to discourage me from taking commissions. Or maybe he truly believes women shouldn't concertize. But in his heart, he knows."

She sat up in the bed, drawing the coverlet around her for warmth. It would be some time yet before Gerta came in to poke up the fire.

"I will see my *Tanfrit* performed. Even if I need to do it in the middle of the Nikuleplaiz!" Plans began to form and she said decisively, "I may have lost the chance at a patron, but it could be just a concert. I'm going to write to my father and my brother to ask their help in finding musicians. And Issibet knows everyone. She might be able to sweet-talk some singers. I don't know where the money is going to come from..."

"Don't give up. Ask Jeanne," Serafina said sleepily.

"What?"

"The Vicomtesse de Cherdillac. Ask her for help. If anyone can find you a patron, she can. It's what she does. She likes your music. She likes you. Why do you think she came to tell you about what Fizeir had done? You don't need to try to do this all by yourself. Invite her to come and listen to your opera and tell her about your dreams."

Yes, Luzie thought. Fizeir had the acclaim of all of Rotenek, but she had Jeanne de Cherdillac and Margerit Sovitre and—most importantly—she had Serafina.

CHAPTER TWENTY-FIVE

Jeanne

January, 1825

Through the open door, Jeanne heard Ainis's steps heading for the stairs. She rose from the morning's correspondence and intercepted the breakfast tray.

"I'll take that up myself. Is she awake?"

Ainis shook her head. "I don't know, Mesnera, but she told me to bring it up by the clock."

It was the change in habits more than the physical changes that made the coming child real to her. Antuniet had never been a layabed. Now, instead of rising barely later than the servants to leave for the palace workshop to fire up the furnace, she often slept late into the morning, and that despite enjoying a respite from late society hours.

Instead of trying to manage the tray and doorknob with the efficiency of a housemaid, Jeanne went the long way through her own bedroom and the connecting dressing room. She placed the tray on the little side table and settled herself on the edge of the bed. Breaking open a steaming roll, she waved it under Antuniet's nose until her eyes blinked and opened.

"How are you my little pruzelin?"

Antuniet smiled at the joke. "So I've climbed the ladder from mere bread to pastry?"

Jeanne rested a hand on the bulge of Antuniet's belly under the covers and leaned over her, murmuring, "You are my bread, and my cake, and my pruzelin, and my soul," punctuating each with a kiss. She felt the baby move, even through the blankets.

Antuniet smiled, but then she groaned and rolled away. "I love you, but at the moment I love my chamber pot more! If you will pardon me—"

Soon she was once again settled comfortably, propped under the covers, and Jeanne fed her pastries and poured tiny cups of hot chocolate for them to share in turns.

"I miss you in bed," she said.

"You don't miss me being constantly up and down in the night and the way my belly would push you off the side! But I miss you too. Only a little while more."

They sipped and nibbled in silence, then Jeanne asked, "Are you working today?"

"Today, every day, for as long as I can. Is it selfish of me to begrudge Anna the time she spends down at Urmai? The new apprentices can't match her."

"I'm interviewing some nursery maids this afternoon," Jeanne said. "I was wondering if you might be there."

Antuniet's mouth twisted in a grimace. "You're much better at that than I am. Do you really need me?"

"I need you to have trust in the woman who will be caring for our child."

Antuniet smiled and echoed, "Our child." The words were a caress. "I have trust in you, Jeanne. You'll make a good choice. Is it so very difficult?"

Jeanne sighed. "I'm very particular."

"All the more reason why I trust you."

"I had dinner with the Peniluks last night," Jeanne said by way of turning the conversation. "They asked after your health and were all curiosity about the 'alchemical child.'"

Antuniet handed the cup back to be refilled. "Have I succeeded? Do you think they believe it?"

Jeanne knew she meant more than the Peniluks. "I think that the very idea of an alchemical child is such a six-months' wonder that no one wants to be the first to doubt it. Except for Barbara, of course. She doesn't believe a word of it."

"Barbara and I have an understanding," Antuniet said simply.

"And Margerit would love to believe that it's possible, but—"

"But she and Barbara keep no secrets from each other."

"Marianniz loudly proclaims that she thinks it's all a hoax and that you're fooling us with pillows and will produce some orphan brat at the end of it to claim as your own."

Antuniet groaned in exasperation. "Pillows wouldn't kick as hard!"

"But she's always like that and no one pays her any mind," Jeanne concluded. "Tio has been very convincing and has been telling lurid stories of her experiences in your workshop and puffing herself off as your close friend and confidante."

"Who would have thought Tio could be so useful?" Antuniet exclaimed in pretend surprise.

"Quite useful," Jeanne agreed. "For she has Princess Elisebet's ear and you know how eager the Dowager Princess is to believe in every mystery that comes along. If people put little weight on Elisebet's credence, neither do they want to contradict her. Has Annek spoken with you again more recently?"

Antuniet's mouth twisted in silent denial. Jeanne knew she'd spent long hours closeted with the princess months ago when the news of her pregnancy had first gone round the city. The disclosure of her unexpected condition had strained Annek's trust, and that trust had been guarded from the first. The princess gave no clue to what she herself believed, but she had given no public sign of doubt. Antuniet still held her place as Royal Alchemist—an alchemist who had mastered the second of the Great Works. What might have been scandal had been turned to fame. But there were bridges to repair in the palace.

* * *

Jeanne sometimes wondered if she'd wasted most of her life in arranging balls and floodtide parties. The challenge that Luzie Valorin presented to her stirred her blood as few things had before. It was the same quickening she'd felt when Rikerd had asked her to launch that violinist he'd taken on as protégée. At the thought, she jotted down Iustin Mazzies' name on her list. No, Iustin Ion-Pazit now that she'd married her composer.

Musicians…but what sort of venue would they be playing in? That made a difference. Maisetra Valorin had been thinking of a small chamber opera. Something they could stage in one of the public salles. But that wouldn't serve the purpose of showing off the work. A small stage, with no announcements in advance? No, it wouldn't do at all. Maisetra Valorin was correct in one concern. If people knew her opera's topic in advance, no one would believe she hadn't copied Fizeir. That presented difficulties. Difficulties required boldness.

She heard Tomric answering the door and rose to greet her guest.

"Luzie! May I call you Luzie? It seems long past when we should have exchanged Christian names. Now come sit and we'll discuss everything that must be considered."

She brought out her notes and lists for consideration. Musicians, singers, chorus, venue, a question mark beside the word "sets," and there—deeply underscored—the word "date." And in a smaller scrawl at the bottom, like something of no consequence at all, the word "funds."

"Now as we discussed before, the first decision to be made is the scale and the venue, for everything else hangs on those. From what you've told me, it's completely impossible to think of a performance before Lent. Even if all your work on the music were complete, there'd be no time to make arrangements. And though a private performance during Eastertide might be excused, I have a better idea. We need to catch the attention of the entire city, not just a few invited guests. Some place public. A place where everyone will already be gathered. I had a thought."

Jeanne held up her hand to forestall any objections. "There's a corner of the Plaiz where traveling players sometimes set up in the summer. You know the place, by the old tapisserie guildhall. They use it because the arcades catch the sound and provide a natural stage. It's within view of everything: the palace gates, the cathedral, the shops and cafés. We hold the performance on Easter Sunday, just after services are finished. The Plaiz will be full of people leaving the services. Barring some miracle—" Jeanne paused to cross herself on the chance that God was listening. "—the city will be on edge waiting for a sign of floodtide. They'll want distraction and something else to talk about. And even if we have that miracle, no one would be thinking of leaving the city that very afternoon!"

Luzie stared at her in disbelief. "That's daring."

"Daring is what we need," Jeanne said.

Luzie thought about it silently for long moments. Resolve stiffened her expression and she nodded. "Vicomtesse, I place myself in your hands."

"Good, then shall we move on?"

They drew up suggestions for the instruments. The outdoor venue needed an arrangement that would carry the sound clearly. Luzie would need to start thinking about the orchestration.

"I wrote to my father for advice," Luzie said hesitantly. "I hope you don't mind. It was before you offered to help."

Oh dear, Jeanne thought, but she asked, "Does he have any ideas?"

"There are a number of favors he could call in. Musicians who owed him their first chance. At the least, his name might carry some weight."

"His name?" Jeanne asked.

"Iannik Ovimen. I performed with him and my brothers before I married."

Iannik Ovimen, now there was a name she hadn't heard in some time. "I hadn't realized the connection," Jeanne said. "Yes, that may be very helpful. Perhaps—" She rolled an idea around in her mind. "Perhaps we could use the Ovimen name as a mask when making arrangements."

"I still don't understand how we can do that," Luzie said. "It's one thing for Maistir Fizeir to keep his debuts a surprise. I don't have that much influence."

"Leave it to me. Didn't you say you'd put yourself in my hands?" Jeanne moved on to the next part of the list. "Now, the principal singers need to be secured soon. I have plans for the role of Tanfrit. Have you ever heard Benedetta Cavalli perform? She's contracted with that company from Florence that will arrive on tour next month and I might be able convince her to stay on when they leave."

"Madame Cavalli?" Luzie's eyes widened. "She's well beyond my touch!"

"Ah, ah," Jeanne stopped her. "Didn't you say you'd leave it to me? And I assure you, Benedetta is not beyond my touch." A few delicious memories of that touch intruded. "She's a dear old friend of mine. And beyond that, I think I can convince her that creating the role of your Tanfrit is an opportunity not to be missed. Once I've secured her, she'll have ideas for Gaudericus. She's rather particular about who she sings with, given the chance, and that will be a sweetener as well."

Other details were briefly skimmed until Luzie placed her finger hesitantly on the last item on the page. Funds.

"Vicomtesse—"

"Please, it's Jeanne."

"Jeanne, where will we get the money? Favors and debts can cover a few of the roles, but even without the rental of a venue and elaborate sets…And don't tell me simply to leave it in your hands. I know too many people in the theater. I know how it works. Investors want a say in the performance, in the choice of performers. And if there's no hope of return…"

"You're right to be concerned," Jeanne agreed. "It's a very delicate matter. The man I have in mind…let me simply say that there's a debt he might owe in connection with your work." She could see that Luzie was bewildered but that discussion would be between her and Count Chanturi.

* * *

Chanturi was the first name on her list of contacts, even before writing to Benedetta. She hadn't cared to mention his name yet in Luzie's presence for he was one of Fizeir's foremost patrons.

She tracked him down two days later. Like most men, he didn't organize his life around visiting hours at home, but he was more than willing to invite her into the parlor with a brief kiss on the cheek in acknowledgment of their long friendship.

"You have that look about you," he said. "Like a general on campaign. What am I to do for you today?"

Jeanne's hand twitched. It was the sort of banter that called for the language of the fan—a language in which they both were fluent. Instead, she accepted the role of general and led a charge. "You financed Fizeir's latest opera."

Rikerd winced and poured out two small glasses of sherry. "Yes, a fresh idea, though not as fresh in the execution. Still, people were happy to see an Alpennian story for once, even one sung in Italian. I do wish he'd learn to write farce, though. It would bring me a better return. But what can one do? We must have new operas and who else will write them?"

"And what if there were someone else?" Jeanne asked.

"Do you mean Domric Sain-Pol? I've seen some of his work. Yes, he might be worth bringing along."

"No, I mean someone entirely different. I want you to finance another opera taken from the story of Tanfrit."

Rikerd choked on his sherry and set it aside. "A second *Tanfrit*? Are you mad?"

"Not a second," Jeanne said, "but the original. The one Fizeir took his inspiration from. The one that by rights should have been performed instead."

She waved her hand at the beginnings of Rikerd's protest. "Oh, I don't go so far as to suggest you financed a plagiarist, but Fizeir was familiar with the work and chose not to credit it. And you are complicit in that. I don't expect you to remember, but you were present at the conception of this one."

"Is this blackmail, then?" Rikerd's question wasn't in the least serious.

"Think of it more as a debt," Jeanne countered.

"A debt. So you're saying there wouldn't be any return on my investment." Now Jeanne truly wished for a fan in her hands. Words were such awkward tools! "Surely my friendship is a better return than mere money."

He smiled. "And how do you know that Fizeir was familiar with this original work that no one else has seen?"

"Because the composer showed it to him and asked his opinion. And then—voila!—Fizeir writes his own opera and it includes details of Tanfrit's life that are pure invention, and yet curiously the same as that original. Did you know that Fizeir has been purchasing compositions from this composer for years and passing them off as his own work?"

Rikerd waved the objection off. "It's done all the time. There's nothing in that."

"But consider," Jeanne continued. "If Fizeir considers this composer's work worth passing off as his own, it says a great deal for the music in question."

"You needn't work so hard to interest me," Rikerd said, taking another sip of his sherry. "I've never known you to send me off on a false trail. But who is this unknown prodigy?"

"Not so unknown," Jeanne said. "Now you must promise me to keep this all under the rose, even if you refuse. It's Luzie Valorin."

"Valorin?" he said in surprise. "The one who does that little mesmerism trick with her art songs?" His eyes widened. "Now I do remember. She joined our party for the closing of *La Regina di Saba*. And someone did mention Tanfrit."

"It's no trick," Jeanne scolded. "But never mind that. Yes, Luzie Valorin, who has written an opera that will set all of Rotenek on its head, if only she's allowed to perform it. The problem is that everyone will think she's the one who copied Fizeir's work, and not the other way around, until they hear it."

"You're that certain?" Rikerd asked.

Jeanne nodded.

Rikerd steepled his fingers in thought. "Fizeir won't be happy and I rather like the role of his patron. I meet a great many interesting people that way."

"Fizeir needn't know," Jeanne said. "I'm quite happy to keep your part a secret."

"But if my part is secret," Rikerd protested, "then how can I have the glory of having discovered this Valorin woman?" He was teasing again.

"I leave that entirely to you," Jeanne said. "I only ask that you keep it secret until after the performance." She rose and offered her hand. "Have we an agreement? The expenses should be modest, mostly salaries. But I'm afraid you won't see a penny in return unless there's enough interest for more performances in the fall."

Rikerd took her hand and raised it to his lips. "Then we shall need to make sure that it takes."

* * *

"Would you have time to come to the workshop tomorrow?" Antuniet asked over dinner.

"Always," Jeanne answered warmly. "Do I need to wear a smock?" She tried to think what the current commissions were that might require additional roles for the ceremonial preparations.

"Yes, but not for the work itself. Do you recall that portrait that Princess Annek commissioned?"

Antuniet had been complaining about the sittings for the last week, though Jeanne expected that they were a pleasant break from the more active work.

"Is it finished?" she asked. "You wouldn't ask me to come in working clothes just to view a painting!"

Antuniet grimaced. "I don't know whether the idea came from Olimpia Hankez or Princess Annek herself. But now there's to be something more monumental. A depiction of my first royal commission. I think it's meant to be a companion piece to the one of the All Saints' Castellum she did last fall. There's also to be one commemorating the battle of Tarnzais, but I think that commission went to Iosip. There won't be a bare wall left in the palace if this continues."

Jeanne smiled at that impossibility. But it was true that Princess Annek was ambitiously filling the palace with new works. Her father hadn't turned his attention in that direction, and the Dowager Princess had been a follower, rather than a leader in the arts.

"So will we all be included? Margerit and Efriturik and that friend of his, Charlin Osekil?"

"And Anna," Antuniet added, "and even Barbara if she'll agree, though I don't know that she cares to be considered part of that crew. You needn't worry about spending long hours posing. Hankez brought in models to do the rough layout. But now that she has the poses decided, she needs to do studies for the faces. It's easier to bring everyone to the workshop. She says there's something about the light that's hard to duplicate."

It wasn't entirely a reunion from those intense days when Antuniet's dream of redemption had burned as fiercely as the alchemical furnace. Charlin had already completed his sitting. And there was no hope of Margerit making the time, but Hankez had a full series of studies remaining from her own portrait. That one had been unveiled at the New Year, showing Margerit standing triumphantly before the college buildings, her arms uplifted in a gesture that might either be prayer or a command for the restoration to begin. You could see in her eyes the dream of what she hoped to build. But as the portrait was meant to show her in her role as Royal Thaumaturgist, the painter had traced hints and illusions of mystical visions throughout the background. Hankez might have been working from the sketches Margerit was always making of how she saw *fluctus*, but somehow she'd made the images come alive. Staring at the painting, one had the sense of actually seeing the mysteries as Margerit did. It was that elusive quality, Jeanne knew, that made Hankez so sought-after as a portraitist, though only a few of her works evoked it.

While Antuniet and the apprentices attempted to carry on their work, Jeanne took her turn posing. She was to stand before the furnace holding out her hands as if carrying a sealed crucible to be placed in the blaze. At first she'd been afraid she'd be asked to hold one of the heavy vessels while Hankez sketched and frowned and scribbled color studies in pastel. But before her arms even had time to become tired, she was told, "Enough. I have the hands. And you may sit now for the head study."

It was hard not to smile at the peremptory commands. It wasn't simply that Olimpia Hankez was famed enough that people put up with it. It was that you understood you were in the presence of a master who wouldn't waste your time and expected you not to waste hers.

Jeanne passed the time by trying to recapture her thoughts and feelings from the days the painting was meant to portray. Scarcely two years past and it seemed like another age entirely, one when she and Antuniet were still fumbling their way toward a place where both their hearts could live. Their hearts…her eyes went, as always, to the irregular crimson stone that lay on Antuniet's breast. *I don't know if it will come through the fire, but it's yours, if you will have it.* She had been speaking of the stone and her heart both. She watched Antuniet straighten momentarily and stretch to ease her back. They were still going through fires, but now they entered them together.

"Perfect." Maisetra Hankez set down her tools and signaled an end to the sitting. "You captured the spirit of transformation I was looking for."

Jeanne stood and stretched in echo of Antuniet's gesture. "May I see?"

The painter examined her critically. "If you wish. Not everyone cares to."

What sort of warning was that? Jeanne waited until Maisetra Hankez had cleared her things away then stood before the easel where several sheets of paper were clipped with sketches in various levels of detail. The last one, still commanding the center of the space, was in many ways the simplest. Only a few spare lines in pencil, without any of the color that was roughed in on the more complete ones. But Jeanne could see what Hankez had meant. The expression that had been captured showed none of her private thoughts, but said plainly, *we will come through the fire and we will be transformed.*

Jeanne let out an admiring sigh. It would be almost insulting to praise Maisetra Hankez's skill. This went beyond mere talent. She peered more closely at some of the other drawings. It was like a child's puzzle blocks with little bits of a larger picture scattered here and there. An alembic, a mortar, a pair of hands grinding, the play of light from the furnace on a faceless figure who was working the gears for the alignment.

There were a few head studies as well, but not ones intended for the larger arrangement. These seemed to be quick sketches, snatched at a moment's whim when the subject was unaware. There was one of Antuniet frowning over some problem. Another capturing a rare expression of tenderness that made you wonder what she'd been gazing at in that moment. There were several of Anna: laughing, studious, biting her lip over some perplexity, and one simply staring thoughtfully into space. The last was finished almost to the point of being a portrait, perhaps from the length of time available, though it was barely larger than thumb-sized. It had that captivating quality of Hankez's best work.

At a movement close behind her, Jeanne turned to find Efriturik examining the sketches over her shoulder.

"I hoped I'd see you here," she exclaimed. "Antuniet said you hadn't done your sitting yet. And no doubt you'll soon be off about your mother's business to Paris again!"

Efriturik grinned and bowed over her hand. She so loved his attention to old-fashioned courtesies, even if it was only for show.

"No more Paris for now," he said. "Not until matters either settle down or heat up. No, I have an entirely different commission for now. My unit will be overseeing a survey of the navigable waterways of Alpennia."

He said it with an air of exaggerated martyrdom and she could almost hear the phrase as the title of a thick and tedious report. A cavalry unit might be ideally suited to traveling throughout the country, but it was hard to imagine a group of bold young men taking enthusiastically to engineering surveys. But when she looked again, he had a sly expression and laid a finger across his lips. So. Gathering information, perhaps, but not on waterways.

"Then perhaps we will see more of you in the salles this winter."

"Of a certainty," he answered. "And perhaps I will win an even more treasured invitation—one I thought I'd been promised."

She raised an eyebrow.

"To the Vicomtesse de Cherdillac's salon, of course."

Once again she found her hand twitching for the movements of a fan. She really must try to make them fashionable in the daytime once again. "For that you must petition the mistress of my revels. Anna has the charge of invitations."

They both looked over to where the subject of their conversation was working and saw her quickly look down as if she didn't want to be known to have been listening.

"With your permission," he began, but then he was commanded into place by Maisetra Hankez, who once again was no respecter of persons.

Jeanne remained for a while, watching both artist and alchemists at work, but she wasn't free to dawdle the entire day away, and she would need to return home and change clothes before any of her other errands.

She took her leave of Anna with a brief embrace, and more discreetly of Antuniet with a touch of her fingers to her lips and then to the crimson amulet around Antuniet's throat, saying, "I look forward to seeing the painting. Perhaps I might try to commission one of you for myself."

"If you can manage that, it would be a wonder. Though I plan to ask for one or two of the studies, if Olimpia's willing to part with them."

Jeanne had been thinking the same thing. Particularly the small portrait of Anna that had captured her so well. She glanced at the easel one more time before leaving, but the little sketch was gone. She frowned. Efriturik had shown quite an interest in the same drawing. Had he…? There was no way to ask.

CHAPTER TWENTY-SIX

Serafina

February, 1825

Serafina recognized the small creature that nestled in the pit of her stomach. It was jealousy. She'd learned to recognize it long before she'd learned to ignore it. Who was she to be jealous of anyone? Just as she had no right to give herself wholly, she had no right to expect the same in return. She'd been the first to urge Luzie to draw others into the plans for *Tanfrit*. But it had been theirs—just the two of them—for so long. Now here was Jeanne, visiting or summoning Luzie to discuss the business of the performance. There were the regular letters from Maistir Ovimen that left Luzie glowing with a pride that no one else could have given her. And there was Iulien Fulpi.

"I was thinking," Luzie had said, as they rode back together from the academy at the end of one of the music days, sharing the fiacre with Doruzi Mailfrit and another of the Poor Scholars. "I was thinking I might ask Iulien to look at the libretto."

And when Serafina hadn't responded immediately, Luzie continued, "I know, she's dreadfully young. But you couldn't tell that from her poetry. And that's what we need: poetry. The libretto tells the story well enough, but we both know it isn't what it might be."

The lyrics of the two pieces Iulien played for the *depictio* class had seemed nothing special—perhaps she simply hadn't an ear for Alpennian verse—but the way they wove into Luzie's settings…There was a crispness, a definition.

Margerit had acquiesced with only a few rules. "She must be properly chaperoned. She isn't allowed to be wandering around the city by herself." With a wry smile, "She's already sweet-talked me into letting her go down to Urmai by boat in the mornings so she isn't tied to my schedule. It isn't that I don't consider Maisetra Valorin a proper chaperone, but…"

But trips to the academy were a simple matter of going back and forth from the private dock at Tiporsel House. Evidently it was less thinkable to let a girl like Iuli walk alone through the Nikuleplaiz, even with a maid for company.

"I'll ask my Aunt Pertinek if she can find time to bring her," Margerit concluded.

And so Serafina sat on the sofa with Maisetra Pertinek, while Iulien sat beside Luzie on the fortepiano bench and eagerly followed along in the libretto as they worked, part by part, through the score.

"Are you enjoying teaching at Margerit's school?" Maisetra Pertinek asked.

Serafina pulled her attention away from the music and its effects. It was always hard to remember that most people were blind to the visions.

"I'm not really teaching," she said. "Just helping at this and that. I'm there as a student." She was enough ahead of the other students in the philosophy and thaumaturgy classes to be frustrated at their progress. That would improve, Margerit promised, once enough students had learned the basics that they could hold advanced classes. But would she have that long? Every day she expected a letter that Paolo's duties in Paris were over.

"Oh," Maisetra Pertinek said. "I had thought from what Margerit said… Well, never mind. What do you know about this opera that Iuli will be helping with?"

What do I know? I was there when the seed was planted. I dug through Margerit's library to find every scrap of history we might use. I've sat by Luzie's side for months shaping it into being.

"It's a historic drama. One of your Alpennian philosophers. Did Maisetra Sovitre warn you that it's to be a surprise and we don't want it talked about before the performance?"

Maisetra Pertinek looked affronted. "I should hope that I know how to hold my tongue when asked. Margerit can tell you that."

Yes, that must be true. There were secrets enough at Tiporsel House to practice on.

They had progressed to the scene in the second act where Tanfrit was being tempted to accept the book of forbidden knowledge that would put her soul at risk. It was one that had never felt entirely right, and Iulien must have thought so as well, for she stopped Luzie after the first exchange between Tanfrit and Theodorus to ask, "Why would she do that?"

Luzie took her hands from the keyboard and the cessation of both sound and vision left Serafina blinking.

"Why would she do what?" Luzie asked.

"She's already a famous philosopher and you show in the first act that she and Gaudericus like each other. So why would she think she needs sorcery to win his love? It doesn't make sense."

Luzie smiled at her. "It's an opera. Not everything has to make sense."

Iulien frowned at the lyrics in her hand. "But it could. Look." She pointed to one of the lines. "Theodorus tells her that what he's offering her is forbidden. Instead he needs to make her think it's valuable. He either wants to win her or to destroy Gaudericus. It doesn't make sense that he'd tell Tanfrit something that might make her refuse the book outright. Once she accepts the gift, then either she'll be grateful to Theodorus or she'll share it with Gaudericus and so betray him. But why would she do something if she knows it's wrong? She's supposed to be the hero, isn't she?"

It made sense, Serafina thought. Luzie had convinced her that people would expect a broad gesture. But it made Tanfrit look weak rather than misled.

"What about something like this," Iulien said. Frowning, she sang the lines with only a few changes.

Luzie picked up a pen and made a few notes on a separate page, then set it beside her score on the fortepiano. She set her hands to the keys and began again.

The *fluctus* shifted, hummed, circled.

Serafina rose silently and headed for the stairs. She paused briefly at the doorway to the parlor and looked back. They didn't need her for this. She had her own work waiting up in her room.

* * *

It was hours later when footsteps on the stairs were followed by a quiet knock. Serafina called out, "Come in," and placed a marker where she'd been reading. The closed doors had muffled the sound of the music somewhat, but only concentration had blocked out awareness of the other currents it stirred. She rose and turned as Luzie closed the door behind her.

"Serafina, is there something wrong?"

She wanted to lie. That would be easier than to speak the truth aloud. Every time she reached for something, it seemed she managed to do nothing more than brush it with her fingertips before it slipped out of reach. That glimpse of welcome and belonging in the church in Palermo. Paolo's promise to teach her. Costanza's eager desire. Margerit's brilliant insight. Luzie's enfolding warmth and the music that tied them together, closer than sisters. Or so she had thought.

"I miss you. I want you." There, she'd said it. But that wasn't really the truth either.

Luzie stepped closer and wrapped her arms around her. "I do too. I wish—"

Serafina stopped the wish with her mouth. During the summer, the dark had hidden their embraces. Now she moved her lips across the pink blush of Luzie's cheek, the pale column of her neck and back to her mouth once more.

Luzie leaned into her arms with a small contented sound and then stiffened at the creak of a floorboard and moved away. "Serafina, we mustn't…"

There was no hint of guilt or shame in her voice, only an abundance of caution. The same caution that had driven Serafina back to her separate room when the boys returned to school. The caution that kept their touches only to what might be excused by chance or circumstance. Serafina remembered the bittersweet night after Fizeir's opera, holding Luzie until she slept. Even then, she had known the summer's closeness was already lost. But how could she say that? *I miss the dream that we might have reached for if we had both been free. I want the illusion you gave me that I might have found somewhere to belong, someone to belong to.*

"Will you play me my mother's song? The one you wrote for me?"

Luzie touched her cheek. "Of course. Anytime you ask."

They returned to the parlor. The air was beginning to fill with the aroma of Chisillic's cooking—a thick hot soup that would keep on the stove until Issibet straggled home after the performance. The score for Tanfrit was still propped up on the stand of the fortepiano but Luzie simply folded it away and began the strains of the other piece from memory.

Serafina closed her eyes and leaned against Luzie's back, her hands resting gently on her shoulders. She could feel the play of muscles in an echo of the pulse of the *fluctus*. The magic ran through her, holding her, stroking her. The brush of her mother's thin white gauze shawl. The deft touch of her hands twisting hair into tight curls that fell around her face and neck. The scent of garlic and cardamom and clove. It blended in with the real presence of Chisillic's cooking: onion and rosemary and basil. And even so, those were all just the threads that wove the cloth. She wrapped herself in the garment of light and felt it sink within her, reaching for that inner core that was always empty, always hungry, always searching.

How could anyone think that music like this could be created in imitation of another's work? If the *Tanfrit* could stir one tenth this response in its listeners…

Serafina's hands clamped onto Luzie's shoulders and the music stopped abruptly. "That's it!" she breathed.

"What is it? What's wrong?"

"Nothing! Nothing!" Serafina was laughing through the tears that the piece always drew from her. "We've had it sideways all along."

She slipped down onto the bench beside Luzie and opened out the opera score. "We've been using the *fluctus* to tune the music, but we should be using the music to tune the *fluctus*."

"I don't understand."

"Do you remember what people said about your setting of Pertulif?" Serafina asked. "That they could almost feel the chill of the mountain wind and the touch of the snow? That's what we need more of. We need to make them *feel* the story, not just listen to it. I've been using my visions as a way of understanding how the music works. But we could use them like…like what I've been doing for the archbishop. As a map to show the path."

Luzie sounded doubtful. "Do you mean to turn the opera into a true mystery?"

"I don't think we can do that. At least Margerit doesn't think so." But Margerit had been wrong sometimes. Serafina shook the thought away. "We aren't calling on God or the saints. But we can create *phasmata* the same way a mystery does. Not everyone will experience it, but enough will. No one will mistake your *Tanfrit* for Fizeir's!"

* * *

The winter had been marked by freezing rain but little snow even into the beginning of February. Serafina had no sense of what she should expect from the season. The longtime residents of Rotenek all grumbled. Grumbling was their natural state. The river still ran low, despite the rain, but that had become the least of Rotenek's concerns. A barge had run aground downriver at Iser, blocking the passage of other boats. A fever had started in the crowded tenements on the southern edge of the city. Serafina knew of the last for Celeste had come to her begging another candle to work into healing charms.

Kreiser had sent her a note after the New Year, asking for her help in another reading. She had meant to send a polite refusal, but Luzie's troubles had distracted her and the reply had never been penned. Once, she thought she saw him as she crossed the Nikuleplaiz to find a riverman. She'd changed her path, excusing it to herself that there was no time to talk. The rain made the trip to Urmai uncomfortable, but it was cheaper than hiring a ride except on Luzie's teaching days. Sometimes Margerit would come by and take her if they both had early classes. But there were days when Luzie was the only reason she didn't ask about taking up one of the dormitory beds at the school. The Poor Scholars were already making arrangements to inhabit an unused building on the grounds.

She saw Kreiser again, coming home a few days later. This time he was loitering on the bridge over the chanulez by Luzie's house. There was no excuse to take the long way around and no way to pass without acknowledging him.

"Good evening, Mesner Kreiser," she said with a polite nod as she tried to push on by.

He took her by the arm and looked up and down the street for witnesses. She would have been frightened, except that Luzie's house was in easy shouting distance and someone would be home.

"There's no need for that," she said sharply, but his grip only relaxed when she turned to face him.

"You've been avoiding me."

It was true enough, but no need to let him know how unsettled the last session had left her. "I've simply had other concerns. What is it you want?"

"I need you to scry for me again." The edge in his voice might have been anger or fear. "I'll be leaving for Paris soon. I need a better idea of what I'll find there."

At the mention of Paris, Serafina started. But there was no reason for the Austrian to know she had connections there. She and Paolo didn't share a surname as Alpennians would. Even if they met…

"You know something." Kreiser's voice was grim and urgent.

"No, nothing of importance. Why would I know anything about Paris, more than what anyone knows? I've never been there."

"That doesn't matter," he said. "I want to work backward from the mountain zauberwerk again. This time I want you to look specifically for connections to Paris. When can we meet?"

Serafina took a half step further away. "It really isn't convenient for me to meet with you at all. Furthermore, it isn't suitable for me to keep meeting with you." She tried for a tone of stiff hauteur to mask her unease.

He eyed her narrowly. The air between them thickened with anger and desperation. "You haven't always been averse to doing unsuitable things."

"If you mean the park at Urmai, there was nothing unsuitable about that."

"I was thinking more about Maisetra Pertrez."

Serafina's heart pounded. How did he know about her affair with Marianniz Pertrez? And why bring it up now? They had been discreet. No doubt there had been some talk—there was always talk. But why should he have taken the trouble to dig it up? She realized she'd taken far too long to answer.

"And I was thinking," he said with deliberate menace, "about your charming landlady."

"What do you mean?" Serafina whispered hoarsely.

"It seems you have a bit of a reputation. Oh, not as much of one as your dear friend de Cherdillac. You really might want to be more careful about your friends unless you plan to live a blameless life. And now your very dear friend Maisetra Valorin is also spending a great deal of time with de Cherdillac. One might wonder what else the two of you have in common. It would be a pity if Maisetra Valorin's reputation were—" He thought a moment, then finished with, "—questioned."

Did he know something or was he simply casting a net? It didn't matter. Luzie's name couldn't bear the weight of gossip, especially not now.

"What do you want."

Kreiser smiled. "All I ever wanted was for you to help me locate some men in Paris. It seems so little to ask."

"When?"

"Carnival is coming to a close in a few days."

Serafina nodded. Elinur and Charluz had been making their usual plans but she had been too busy to think of it.

"Meet me at the main carnival ground out past the east gate of the city. I'll be at the fishmongers' guild show. We'll find some place quiet to work. Be alone."

Without waiting for her assent, he strode off back toward the plaiz. Serafina found she was shivering and chafed her arms to get warm again. She mustn't let Luzie see her like this. She mustn't let anyone know. He could destroy Luzie on a whim, just for revenge, and even Margerit couldn't stop him. For a threat like this, Margerit in particular couldn't stop him.

CHAPTER TWENTY-SEVEN

Margerit

March, 1825

The chaos of the Mauriz term had settled into the grueling march of the second term. It seemed far too early to be planning for the next year already. Margerit hesitated with her pen over the ledger before writing Spring Term on a new page. She'd kept the traditional name for the first session—the one that began the week after the feast of Saint Mauriz in the fall—but the remainder of the year didn't align as easily with the university calendar.

A long term beginning after Easter wouldn't work. It was all very well for young men, living in lodgings or free to stay on in town when their families left Rotenek for the summer. But the girls in the upper town would be at the mercy of their families' plans.

She'd chosen instead a full ten-week term in the spring, ending in concert with the university's short Lenten Term, but one couldn't call it that, not when it began earlier. Nor did the name of Easter Term fit for the summer session when she'd chosen to begin it at the end of May, to be certain of falling well after floodtide, whenever that might be declared. That one would be for the Poor Scholars and whoever else was left in town over the summer. A full session, not a short one. Akezze had worked out a plan of classes that would make the best use of that difference. It would have more practical studies for those expecting to earn their bread by their brains.

Margerit sat back and rubbed at her eyes. Perhaps she should simply name all the terms after the seasons, despite being scheduled around the feasts. It seemed a silly thing to worry over when there was so much more to plan. By the fall term—yes, she would simply call it the fall term—she wanted to find someone able to lecture in law. Once, she'd hoped to come to an arrangement with the university regarding classes in law and medicine, but that door was closed. She'd cobbled together a few lectures on medical topics, but that wouldn't be enough for the Poor Scholars who hoped to license as midwives or apothecaries. Barbara and LeFevre might have ideas on someone willing to teach the history and principles of the law to a pack of girls who would never have the chance to practice. Margerit scribbled another note in the margin to remind herself of that question. To think she'd considered herself hardworking when she was a student!

There was still time for more disasters—school disasters. There were enough of the ordinary sort, but she had no responsibility for them. She didn't dare call the term a success yet. Soon, perhaps, if they could get to the end of March.

There was a soft knock on the door, though she'd left it open in invitation. She looked up to see Valeir Perneld waiting. Margerit glanced over at the clock. Was she late for the thaumaturgy lecture? The girl's expression combined excitement and trepidation.

"What is it, Valeir? You must have news to share. Come in."

She still remembered her first meeting with Valeir, during one of the summers spent at Saveze. Valeir had been a student then, at the Orisul convent, just about to launch into her dancing season. The two of them had helped Sister Marzina devise and work a mystery to heal a little boy deaf from a fever. It had been a revelation to her how differently Valeir's *sonitus* worked from her own visions. Now the girl was one of the strongest pupils in the thaumaturgy classes and a constant challenge to Margerit's understanding.

"Maisetra Sovitre?" Valeir said. The excitement in her voice was infectious. "He asked last night. Petro Perfrit. We're betrothed."

For only a moment, disappointment ruled. *No, I don't want to lose you!* But this was a time for congratulations and a wish for every joy. It would come to this more often than not. They would come to study and then move on to take up the roles of wives and mothers. It couldn't be a matter of one or the other. She wouldn't allow herself to think that education was a waste for girls who then chose the conventional path. That was the argument of those who saw no point to educating them at all beyond languages and the arts.

"We'll miss you," she said, as she released Valeir from a quick embrace.

"That's what I—that is, Petro and I—we wanted to ask about."

Margerit glanced at the clock once more. A quarter of an hour before her lecture. She gestured Valeir to the chair facing her own and sat.

"What's this about?"

"I was thinking," Valeir began. "And I asked Petro because I don't think I could have married him if he said no. I want to finish my studies first. Before the wedding. Petro agreed, but my papa doesn't like it. He's afraid Petro will change his mind if I put him off for two more years. I was wondering—would you speak to him? To my father, that is?"

Now that was unexpected. A fiancé who was willing to wait for a girl to complete her degree? Or at least as much of a degree as they'd be able to offer her. But… Petro Perfrit. She remembered that name now, though it had been years. He'd been part of the late lamented Guild of Saint Atelpirt, the student guild she'd joined that had ended in the disastrous *castellum* mystery. She searched in memory. A quiet man, not sensitive to *fluctus* but solid in his approach to theory. A partisan of the Dowager Princess, but so many of them had been and that was all in the past now. It was odd to think that her own example in that guild might have influenced his willingness to choose and champion a scholar-wife.

"Yes, of course I will," she answered. "You've made a good choice in Maistir Perfrit. I don't know that your father will listen to me, though."

"He will," Valeir said.

Such confidence! And what had she done to deserve it?

"I'll call on your parents in the next few days. I imagine they'll be at home for visitors with so many coming to wish you good fortune." Margerit rose and gave Valeir another quick hug. "And it sounds like good fortune indeed. Now we mustn't be late for the lecture."

* * *

Margerit scanned the row of students looking for a face that held the answer. She didn't care to treat class discussions as examinations. Teaching thaumaturgy wasn't simply a matter of mastering a skill. These young women might have a hand in renewing Alpennia's future, just as the namesake of her academy had helped Gaudericus renew it in ages past. For that, she must spark curiosity, not simply demand correct responses.

"So, Ailiz, what would be the consequence of incorporating ambiguous reference in the structure of your markein?"

The girl closed her eyes and recited, "Ambiguous reference is when a description may be equally applied to unrelated things. When it describes but does not define."

Margerit sighed inwardly. "And how might that affect the resulting mystery?"

Ailiz looked to either side, hoping someone else would answer. "If the markein describes but does not define the ambit of the mystery, then the effects might take hold in a different place than intended."

"For example?" Margerit prompted.

"For example, in the *castellum* mystery you were telling us about. When the leopard was used to refer to robbers and brigands, but it could also represent the Maunberg arms. That was why the mystery deflected from the protective intent and attacked Princess Anna back when she was Duchess Maunberg."

Was that how she'd explained it to them? "That might be an example if the ambiguity had been inadvertent. No, that one was a case of misdirection, when one symbol is used to conceal a different intent. Yes, Doruzi, do you have an example?"

"In the Mauriz mystery that you were showing us in *depictio* class, when the ceremony says—" She struggled to recall the word. "When it says *aedificium* and it could mean either the church as a building or the church as an institution."

"Yes," Margerit responded. "That's closer. Now, Mari, think of an example that doesn't come from the lectures."

She waited patiently. It would do no good if they could only repeat back what they'd learned in class.

"If…" Mari paused. "This isn't from an actual mystery, but if you were using something as a symbol and instead the mystery worked on the thing itself…I was thinking of a love charm we did at floodtide one year. In part of it, the words say, 'Bring his heart to me.' And I was thinking—"

Ailiz made a disgusted noise. "That would be horrible!"

"Yes," Margerit agreed. "If the charm actually had power and brought you the living heart of your sweetheart, that wouldn't do you much good! Fortunately, love charms rarely have that sort of power. Acting on matter is hard, especially on living matter. That's why healing mysteries are so uncertain. Love charms are usually more subtle, working on the emotions or the perceptions. They work through concrete symbols, but the *fluctus* follows the easier path through the immaterial rather than the material."

"Then what would you do if you wanted to heal a heart?" Valeir asked. "How could you define the markein to indicate that you meant the physical body and not the symbol?"

It was a good question, Margerit thought. "I don't know, I've never succeeded with healing mysteries that acted so directly. Only ones to cool fever or to heal wounds without infection—ones that work with the body's natural desires. If a soldier's leg is amputated, mysteries can save his life but they can't regrow his limb. Even miracles must work hand in hand with nature. And as you know—"

They repeated with her the familiar litany: "When a mystery works with nature and not against it, it's hard to distinguish truth from fraud."

"And what I never want you to do," Margerit concluded, closing her book, "is to take credit for something that would have happened by nature. Now for next time I want you to read Desanger and identify all the types of definitional fallacies that could affect a markein."

When the clatter of departing students had quieted and Margerit had finished putting away her books, she turned to see Serafina waiting patiently.

"Do you have questions? I think we covered all this last summer."

"Not about the lecture," Serafina answered. "I was wondering if I might ride back to the city with you."

"Of course, if you like. But I won't be leaving for hours yet. I think there's a wagon taking some of the Poor Scholars back soon. You might catch a ride with them."

"I don't mind waiting," Serafina said. "It's quieter here. Luzie's house is full of her family—for the opera rehearsals and all."

In the end, it was almost dusk before the carriage collected them at the drive before the main building. "You should have taken the earlier ride," Margerit apologized.

Serafina shrugged. "Then I'd have to walk from the Poor Scholars' house." But there was a touch of worry in her voice.

"Is that a problem?" Margerit asked in concern.

No direct answer was forthcoming. "Do you know if Mesner Kreiser has left the city yet?"

"I think so," Margerit said. "Barbara would know. Do you want me to ask?"

Serafina shook her head. "It isn't that important. It's only…I was doing some work for him and didn't know if he needed more."

"Then ask Barbara."

Serafina was silent and the dim lighting within the carriage made her face hard to read. Margerit thought it best to turn the subject.

"Since we have this time together, I hoped you might give me your thoughts on how the thaumaturgy classes are progressing."

"It's…different, having the formal classes."

"I didn't mean for you in particular," Margerit hastened to reassure her. "You're far beyond what we're covering. But do you think the girls are learning things in the right way? When I took lectures at the university, we studied theology first and then the principles of thaumaturgy. Nothing so practical as what we're doing now, mixing in logic and applied theory. Barbara and I studied that on our own. It was only later that Akezze made me go back and study the philosophers in depth. Do you think it works?"

Serafina nodded, though it might have been just the jouncing of the carriage. "I think it works well enough. Why did you omit theology?"

It was a sore point. Sister Petrunel had asked the same thing. "I would have needed to have a priest come in to give the classes. And then it would have been hard to draw the line. I wanted to teach thaumaturgy in my own way, not the way it's taught in the approved books."

"Do you think it's wise to study mysteries apart from theology?" Serafina asked. "Isn't that why your Gaudericus was banned?"

"He was never banned," Margerit countered. "Just discouraged. People thought his teaching would lead to heresy and sorcery but I don't think I believe in sorcery."

"Kreiser does." Serafina's eyes glinted sharply in the faint light from the carriage lamps. "At least he talks about sorcery like something entirely different from church mysteries."

Margerit frowned. "I think sorcery is just what people call it when they don't like the purpose of a mystery. Whether it's a charmwife telling your fortune or the great mysteries in the cathedral, it all comes from the same source. It's all by God's will."

"And what about all the evil things creeping in through the cracks in the Mauriz mystery?" Serafina asked. "Do you think that's God's will?"

"I think…" Margerit said slowly, picking her way around the theological traps. "…that people may act in God's name and still do evil, either by intent or inadvertence. I think that even the saints can't protect us from every unlucky circumstance. And—" She held up a hand to stop Serafina's objection. "—I think we can't always know what God's purpose is in granting a miracle."

"That seems to be no answer at all," Serafina said. "We just continue on as we please and if we succeed it must have been God's will."

Margerit sank back into the cushions. "I don't know. It's beyond me. I'm only sure of the how and not the why. But what I do know," she said, returning to the subject at hand, "is that we're teaching the how and not the why. The mechanics have been the secret province of a few guildmasters for too long. Who even knows whether they have the right talents? I want to change all that. Anyone who has talent should have a chance to learn. I only wish I had a better way to find them."

"It isn't enough to find them," Serafina said. There was a wistful tone as if she had someone in particular in mind.

"What do you mean?"

"You could walk through the streets of Rotenek looking for signs of mystic talent, but that doesn't mean that you could help them when you found them. There's a girl I know—just the sort who could have benefitted from being taught, if she'd started early. But your school won't help her."

"Why not?" Margerit demanded. "You know I've said I'll take charity students."

"But she's not the sort who would take charity. And she helps support her mother. She couldn't simply leave all that behind to come to school. She'll be a charm-wife and a good one, but even you can't offer her the chance to be a thaumaturgist."

Then they were arrived at Maisetra Valorin's house and Margerit had no chance to ask further.

* * *

In the last week of the term, in the midst of the scramble to finish in time, Margerit was startled in the middle of lecture to see Barbara's face framed in the doorway, with Anna Monterrez at her side. Barbara never came down to the academy unannounced! Her first thought was of some disaster, but both of them wore broad grins that could mean only one thing.

"Antuniet?" Margerit asked eagerly.

"Safely delivered," Barbara assured her to the cheers of the entire class. "A girl." She seemed almost surprised at that.

Margerit would have handed the class over to Serafina and been on her way in an instant, but Barbara laughed at her impatience.

"It will be days yet before she's receiving visitors. There's no hurry! But I thought you'd want to know."

It might have been days before other visitors were welcome, but their wait was shorter. The next evening Margerit's carriage had barely drawn to a stop before the steps of Tiporsel House when Barbara hurried out to join her saying, "We've been summoned."

Antuniet, true to form, had refused the physician's orders to lie abed for the first two weeks and received them in the new-furnished nursery under the watchful eye of its attendant. If Margerit had thought that motherhood might change Antuniet, she quickly discarded that notion. It was Jeanne who cooed and hovered over the baby and brought it carefully for their inspection. Antuniet, looking drawn but satisfied—almost smug—presided over the gathering with the air of a queen holding state.

"So you see you were wrong," she announced to Barbara. "My alchemical child will not be the next Baron Saveze."

"No," Barbara agreed. "The next Baroness Saveze. And quite a line she will have to live up to."

Unlike Antuniet, Barbara had gone quite soft and almost motherly in the presence of the baby. Margerit watched her and Jeanne with their heads together over the small bundle and nearly burst out laughing when she caught Antuniet's eye.

"Have you decided on a name?" she asked.

Jeanne looked up and said, "Yes, do draw it out of her. I've had no success. I suspect we're waiting on the mysterious messages coming and going to the palace all day." She glanced at Antuniet meaningfully.

"I had thought," Antuniet said, "to name her Anna. But Her Grace has indicated that her support falls short of being named godmother."

And that name might have been confusing, Margerit thought, her mind turning at first to the other Anna in their lives.

"And so," Antuniet continued, "I have settled on Iohanna, in honor of Her Grace's mother." She looked over at Jeanne with a smile. "Of course, it's a common name. I see no need to be a stickler for tradition, but I'm sure I can find a namesake to stand as sponsor."

Evidently the choice was a surprise even to Jeanne, for her eyes filled with sudden tears. "Iohanna Chazillen," she whispered to the baby. "Do you like that?"

"Do you still wish me to stand as well?" Barbara asked.

Antuniet nodded. "If you are willing. Both of you." She included Margerit in the nod. "With three such godmothers, what could stop her?"

CHAPTER TWENTY-EIGHT

Luzie

April, 1825

A ripple of laughter ran around the table as Chisillic carried in the moulded orange crème herself and placed on the sideboard for Gerta to serve.

"Now what's this I hear about a shortage of oranges, Maistir Ovimen?" the cook asked.

Luzie watched her father repeat the comic tale, gesturing with those familiar hands, the fingers now knobbed with age. His hands might have lost the ability to play, but not the ability to draw a performance from others, whether the small consort assembled for the *Tanfrit* or the diners around her close-crowded table. She exchanged a glance with her mother and smiled as the years melted away.

Issibet was now chiming in with a counterstory about the hard years during the French Wars, and the part a particular shipment of oranges had played in ensuring the success of a production they had both worked on. Luzie had been too young to understand the significance at the time, but she'd heard the story many times in years after and could almost convince herself she remembered that treasured sweetness.

She would remember this in the same way: how her brother Gauterd had made time from his contracted performances to join her production, how her parents had made the journey from Iuten not only to witness the debut of her opera, but to add to the preparations. Her father had stood listening to the rehearsals in an unused academy building for only five minutes before he'd bluntly suggested that the musical direction be put into his hands. And those hands had coaxed the oddly assorted group of musicians and singers into a partnership. Even Benedetta Cavalli had abandoned her demands and airs at hearing that Iannik Ovimen had taken the reins. Luzie had forgotten the respect her father had commanded in his time. And it had been that gesture—treating her work as worthy of his labor—that had meant the most.

Half of her wished the boys could have been here—and Gauterd's wife and children as well—but the other half was grateful to avoid that added distraction. And where would she have put them all? As it was she had surrendered her own room to her parents and imposed on Serafina to make space for her, while Gauterd commanded Alteburk's room leaving the housekeeper to crowd in with the maids for the duration of the visit. No doubt there had been grumbling where she couldn't hear it, but the atmosphere was more like a floodtide holiday where everyone laughingly made do for the sake of being together.

Though one might think there was enough music in their lives at the moment, with the performance only two days away, they gathered in the parlor in the evening, bringing in extra chairs from the dining room, and she accompanied Gauterd for violin concertos.

"You were very quiet all evening," Luzie said later as Serafina blew out the light and slipped under the covers beside her. "I hope that letter you received wasn't bad news. You've hardly spoken since it came."

She felt Serafina's arms go around her and moved closer.

"Luzie...do you love me?"

A small ripple of panic went through her. Every time her thoughts had brushed close to that question she had turned away. Why couldn't they simply continue on like this? Enjoying the comfort of each other's bodies in the dark? Sharing the wonder of the music? Knowing there was someone who would always be there for the joys and sorrows?

"Serafina, I—" They had never spoken the word "love," not for what lay between them. That word would make them more than friends. It would turn delight into something...something more frightening. Love belonged to another world entirely, another time, other people. "Oh, Serafina."

"Never mind," came the voice in the dark. "It doesn't matter."

But it did matter.

* * *

It had drizzled in the early morning when the entire household had walked together down to Saint Nikule's for Easter morning services. Luzie had been in agonies, thinking it would drive away the audience, but by the time they emerged, so had the sun. As the company gathered later in the shelter of the old guildhall arcade and the sounds of the celebrations at Saint Mauriz's echoed across the stones, those stones were dry once more.

The first crowds began drifting out and down the steps of the cathedral. Her father signaled the opening notes of the horns and Luzie clenched Serafina's hand tightly enough to hurt. But Serafina was already lost in her visions, looking around her in wonder at the colors of the music that Luzie could only imagine.

They had drawn out the overture to have more time to catch the crowd. It would have been far too long in a theater, but Jeanne had insisted—the one time she had commented on the music itself. From where she watched, at one side of the stage area but still under the arcade, Luzie saw the first fringe of curious listeners deepen until there was no light between the bodies. After that, there was no telling how many had gathered.

The crowd had not been left entirely to chance, of course. Jeanne had carefully planted hints and suggestions. And there were those who had been included in the secret. The horns shifted into the triumphal march and voices rose as the chorus emerged in a procession from behind the temporary curtains, wearing archaic university robes. The ancient stone arches formed the perfect backdrop for the story. And there was Madame Cavalli, commanding the stage with Tanfrit's opening aria.

Luzie had expected the performance to feel excruciatingly slow. It always felt that way in rehearsals. But now the music stood in time as a single whole. To begin was to exist in eternity and to conclude all at once. It seemed they had barely started when the first act finished with the duet between Tanfrit and Gaudericus, and then Theodorus adding his baritone counterpoint of jealousy under it all for the concluding trio. She held her breath. There was applause, only a scattering at first, as they hadn't the cue of a curtain to mark the interval, but then growing to a respectable noise. This was the test: would they stay? The opera house was as much a grand parlor for visiting and display as it was a performance venue. Here, they had nothing but the music to hold people's attention.

Perhaps not only the music. Calls started up from the edges of the crowd hawking food and drink. The audience shifted, loosened, drifted, but they didn't leave. Not most of them. Luzie saw Jeanne moving gracefully among the front ranks, chatting and smiling, a word here, a laugh there. If only she had the confidence to do the same! She turned to Serafina, realizing that their hands were still gripped so tightly her fingers had gone numb.

"What do you see?" Luzie whispered eagerly.

"I see a spell being woven," Serafina whispered back. Her face twisted in thought. "It needs— No, save that for later. Did you see when Gaudericus first appeared and he recognizes Tanfrit and sings about how their minds will join as one—I swear there were women in the audience who almost swooned. And then when Theodorus began to sing, they—"

"Shh," Luzie interrupted. "We'll be starting again soon." She had seen her father signal to the musicians. Had the interval been so short or had it, too, sped by without her noticing?

Later, she would find it hard to remember the second act. She remembered the shiver that ran through the crowd when Theodorus offered Tanfrit the forbidden book, singing of the joys of learning and knowledge in a sinister echo of the first act's love duet. She remembered the way Serafina's breath caught when the chorus of university dozzures lifted their voices up around Tanfrit, predicting her fame and glory in the song "No woman past or yet to come." She remembered the way the audience stood gathered, rapt, impatient throughout the second interval until she feared they would begin demanding the final act before the singers were ready.

It began with a stirring in the blood like a tide pulsing in her veins. Tanfrit's aria "I offer up to you," Gaudericus recoiling from the gift, proclaiming his dedication to the purity of learning, "I pledge myself to you alone." Tanfrit's echo of the theme, despairing at having lost his love along with his trust. Theodorus taunting her after she spurns him, joining the procession of dozzures, leaving her alone on the Pont Vezzen. And then the climactic aria as Tanfrit chooses to throw herself from the bridge, "Let the waters rise up and wash away my sorrow." Benedetta's voice soared above the crowd, not in a cry of despair but an anthem of triumph. As she raised her arms, calling on the Rotein to receive her, Luzie could feel the surge of the water, the pulse of waves, rising, demanding, taking her into their embrace.

The music washed over and through her. There was a hush, and then the lone voice of a bassoon taking up the processional music in a minor key as the chorus returned, lamenting the flood that had washed through the city. So many lost. The body of Tanfrit found floating in the waters. Gaudericus lifting her up and singing "I pledge myself to you alone," dedicating his scholarship to her memory, while in the background the chorus of dozzures, led by Theodorus, reversing the message of "No woman past or yet to come," into a lament for feminine weakness, tested past its limits by the rigors of intellectual life. They had argued over that until the last, she and Serafina. But the opera was a tragedy, in the end.

The strings, like the waters of the Rotein, rose up and covered the last notes of the singers to mark the finale. Applause, like a pattering of raindrops, scattered among the crowd, rising to a cloudburst of sound. Luzie found herself breathing heavily, as if she had run a race. Her father turned, signaling the singers to return for their bows. And there was Jeanne, dragging her by the hand out into their midst and cries acclaiming the author, and the bewildering knowledge that they were cheering for her. For her and *Tanfrit*. There was no need even to think of Fizeir and how people would compare the two. It didn't matter. Nothing could compare to her *Tanfrit*. Nothing.

* * *

Someone must have made arrangements. Someone must have seen that the sets were packed off and the music collected. Someone must have hired the upper rooms at the Café Chatuerd, and that must have been done well in advance. Jeanne, no doubt. Luzie moved in a daze as the crowd finally thinned out and they drifted in a small crowd across the Plaiz to the café. She had dined in the lower rooms on occasion, but never climbed those sweeping stairs to that chamber of crystal and gilt chandeliers, with the city spread out beneath the bowed windows.

There was champagne and tables of pastries and a circle of admiring and excited faces: the musicians and singers, the patrons and close friends, all her family, both of blood and residence. There were speeches. Luzie was content for others to make them. Her father went on at length about her talents. Count Chanturi—Jeanne hadn't told her before who her mysterious patron had been—proudly took credit for recognizing her genius. Madame Cavalli held forth on the honor of creating the role of Tanfrit, though it was hard to say whether she felt she was being honored or conferring that honor. And then Luzie could not escape being pulled into the center of the room while everyone raised their glasses in toast and she stammered a few incoherent thanks before retreating once more.

Then a stream of well-wishers. At every turn, a word of congratulations, a compliment. Jeanne had gathered a careful selection of the cream of society. She recognized Mesnera Arulik, the Marzulins, the Peniluks, Count and Countess Amituz, Lord and Lady Marzim, even—to her shock and surprise— Baron Razik, Efriturik Atilliet himself. At a slight cough behind her she turned…and froze. Maistir Fizeir stood paused at the top of the stairs, still in the sober black suit he must have worn for Easter services. His expression was fixed, like the smile painted on a puppet. He bowed stiffly.

"Maisetra Valorin."

Had he seen the opera? She didn't dare ask. But if not, why was he here? His eyes flicked briefly off to her left. She glanced over and saw Count Chanturi watching them. The count raised his fluted glass briefly in salute.

"Maisetra Valorin, I must—" He took a breath. "I must congratulate you on your success. You have a rare talent."

Before she could do more than dip a brief curtsey in acknowledgment, her father was there at her side, clapping him on the shoulder.

"Fizeir! Good to see you again! What have you been up to while I've been kicking my heels in the provinces?"

Luzie made her escape. Serafina found her by the pastries. Picking off the layers of a flaky mille-feuille gave her something to do with her hands, though she wasn't in the least hungry.

"Did you feel it?" Serafina asked.

"I…I think so," Luzie said. "In the last act, you mean?"

Serafina nodded. "I saw something in your face…"

"I felt the river. It was in the music, flowing through me. Is that what you see?"

Another nod. "Something like that. I think—" Now Serafina sounded worried. "I think we did something."

"What do you mean?"

"I wish Margerit had been here. She might know."

Luzie looked around. She hadn't noticed that Maisetra Sovitre had been absent. It was no surprise, for she had enough concerns of her own, but it was disappointing. "Do you mean that you think we did something like a mystery? But I thought you said—"

"I'm not sure. There was something—" She shook her head in confusion. "When you design a mystery, the individual parts—they each have a power you can see. And when you put them together, it builds something different. But when a guild or a congregation comes together to celebrate it, that adds a force that wasn't there before. When we wrote the music, I wanted it to reach out and touch the audience. To make them feel the story. But today, it was like they were part of the performance. Part of the celebration."

"And what have we done?" Luzie asked.

"I don't know."

* * *

In an ordinary year, no one might have noticed it. Floodtide might start with a difference in color in the middle of the Rotein, an odd calmness or ripple in the currents, but then would come the slow inexorable rise along the banks until the steps at Saint Nikule's were covered, and the chanulezes filled their channels until the rivermen, poling up them, might have to duck when passing the bridges, and the waters would turn muddy and rank as the banks were scoured of a year's accumulation of silt.

In an ordinary year, the streak of muddy water in the center of the current would not have been considered enough of a sign to sound the bell in the Nikuleplaiz. But it had been three years since there had been an ordinary year. The city was eager for any sign at all that their luck was changing and the world was returning to its course. In the week after Easter, when the rivermen called out that first sign of floodtide, the idlers in the Nikuleplaiz chalked up marks on the stones of the river steps and called them out as each mark was dampened and washed away. One mark, two, three, but not a fourth. Yet it was enough of a sign that the priests raised a bucket and wetted Nikule's feet, though it was early in the season to despair of a true flood.

The city gave a sigh of relief and told each other that soon all would be well.

* * *

Luzie watched her roster of students dwindle as families packed and made summer plans. That was the unfortunate part of attracting a higher class of student, for only the wealthiest of the burfroi families followed the custom of leaving Rotenek for the entire summer at floodtide. There would be no music classes in the college's summer term. Still, there would be a breathing space between the exodus of family from her house at the finish of the opera and before the boys arrived home from school. The lighter summer schedule would give her time to work on the full orchestration for *Tanfrit*. Count Chanturi had pledged himself to see that it was performed at the opera house in the fall. Each time she allowed herself to think of that, it was slightly less terrifying than the last.

Charluz broached the subject of holiday plans as they gathered in the parlor two evenings after the floodtide bells had rung. "We haven't made arrangements for a trip just now, but Elinur and I thought we might take the waters at Akolbin at the end of May. Issibet said she might be interested. We could make it a general outing. Hire a house for a week. What do you think?"

Luzie did a few calculations. A week in Akolbin and a week total in travel, plus the hire of a house, but it would be a chance for Alteburk to hire a few extra girls in to do the summer cleaning. And even if her sons turned their noses up at so stuffy a thing as "taking the waters," it would be a pleasant change.

"Yes, I like that idea. Serafina?"

There was a silence that drew all attention. Serafina looked around at them and then down at her hands. "No, I won't be here."

"Oh," Luzie said in disappointment. "Do you have plans with Maisetra Sovitre?"

"I'm going back to Rome." She stood and left the room.

Luzie gave the others a puzzled glance as Serafina's footsteps tapped up the stairs, but they only shrugged so she rose and followed.

The door was open, which seemed enough of an invitation.

"Serafina? Serafina, what's wrong?"

She was crying, sitting in the dark on the edge of the bed. Luzie sat down beside her but Serafina shrugged off her awkward embrace.

"That letter I received, back before Easter. It was from my husband, from Paolo. He's back in Rome. I didn't tell you because…" She shrugged.

"Oh." Luzie had found it easy to forget that there was a husband. "You could write to him. Tell him about the academy. He's managed without you for what, three years now you said? That's hardly a marriage."

Serafina sniffed and felt around for a handkerchief until Luzie pressed her own into her hand.

"It doesn't matter how long he's been gone. He expected me to be there when he came back. And I wasn't. He's told the bankers not to pass on my allowance. I have enough left to return to Rome, but no more."

Luzie bristled. "How dare he!"

"He's my husband. It's his money. And beyond that, I owe him obedience. For as long as he hadn't commanded my return, I could pretend he wouldn't care what I did. But now?" She shrugged again.

There was no answer to that.

"What if Maisetra Sovitre gave you a salary at the academy. You do some teaching, it would only be fair. And—" Before the impulse could pass, she added, "And your room, that is…I need the rent, but you could share with me and I could rent to someone else."

"Do you love me?" Serafina demanded.

It sounded like the plea of a drowning woman. Would it be so terrible a sin to say yes? To say whatever it was that Serafina needed so desperately?

"Does it matter that much?" Luzie searched Serafina's face. It gave nothing away. "No, I don't," she said at last. "Not that way. But every other way—"

"I don't belong here. I knew that when I saw you with your parents and your brother. You were all…I never belonged here. I've never belonged anywhere."

Now Luzie held her tightly despite her protests. "Hush, hush. When must you leave?"

A gulping breath. A stifled sob. "I've already talked to Mesnera Collfield. She's traveling south to Turin at the end of May, collecting samples. I can accompany her that far, then I only have to make it to Genoa and take a ship. I'm sorry I'm being so foolish. I always knew it would come to this."

Luzie rocked her gently. Knowing never made anything easier.

CHAPTER TWENTY-NINE

Barbara

Mid-May, 1825

The proclamation of floodtide had taken them by surprise at Tiporsel House, but few of their plans were so dependent on the social calendar as to be upset by it. Barbara wrote ahead to discuss her plans for Turinz; Saveze would need to wait for the end of summer this time. Margerit's summer would be little different from the spring. But there was one member of the household for whom the end of the Rotenek season drew a sharp line.

Barbara saw her from the library windows, looking out over the gardens sloping down toward the river. Another spring when there had been no need to repair water damage in the lower gardens. This time, the gardeners hadn't taken the trouble to move the more valuable plants. Iulien Fulpi was making use of the solitude at the bottom of the garden in company with her maid. They sat on the marble bench near the small private landing—the one Barbara had always thought of as her own. The rolling current of the river provided a soothing place for sorting out tangled thoughts.

From the way the maid—she pulled the name out of memory: Rozild, the one Tavit had mentioned—from the way she was passing a steady supply of handkerchiefs and hovering closely, it was easy to tell Iuli's thoughts were not happy ones. Iuli made a sharp gesture and Rozild pulled back hesitantly, then returned up the path toward the house.

Barbara had been even less delighted at Iuli's arrival last fall than Margerit had been, but it was undeniable that the girl had claimed all their hearts. She might be willful and a trifle too adventurous, but Barbara found it hard to fault anyone for that. Iuli had done her part. She'd followed Margerit's rules—as far as they knew. She'd studied hard, behaved herself when taken out into society and had been surprisingly cheerful when there had been no time to hold the promised ball in her honor. Margerit had planned it for the brief second season between Easter and floodtide, but in the end there had been none.

And now Chalanz demanded her return—Chalanz and the agreement with the Fulpis. Back to the summer season of a provincial resort. It hardly seemed reason for tears. Iulien wasn't another Margerit to disregard balls for books. She had arrived on their doorstep uncertain what she was seeking. Had she found it here at Tiporsel House? Barbara remembered the Fulpi household well, but not fondly, from that first season when she had come into Margerit's life. A perfectly respectable family, comfortably situated, well thought of by their neighbors. What dreams did Iulien have that couldn't be realized there?

Margerit had escaped Chalanz by the caprice of the old baron, when he used her as a means of diverting his fortune from Estefen's hands. Iuli had no similar key to the door. Not yet. If she were older and no longer on her father's purse, her undeniable talent for writing might possibly bring enough for a genteel poverty and the limited freedom that came with it. Was that what she wanted? It would be four more years until Iuli was of legal age. Four years before she could even think of petitioning a court to declare her to stand on her own purse, should she care to weather the talk that would cause. Barbara found it hard to imagine her taking that path. Iuli had slipped into the life of Rotenek like a hand into a glove, but it was an elegant kidskin glove, not the mended woolen mitts of an impoverished scribbler.

If the four "f"s were what gave one a foothold in society—family, fortune, friends or fame—only two of those mattered to an unmarried girl of good birth: family and fortune. Even fortune was no use if family stood in the way. It didn't matter that Iuli had become family here at Tiporsel, joining the tightly-knit group bound by kinship and love that Antuniet teasingly called her saliesin, after the ancient feudal households. It was so strange to think of having one. She had grown up believing herself an orphan and, even before she gave her heart to Margerit, she had accepted that her life was unlikely to include marriage and children. And now her saliesin had increased with Brandel and little Iohanna Chazillen. It could be large enough to include Iulien Fulpi as well.

The thought, when it struck her, seemed so obvious she wondered it hadn't occurred to Margerit as well. Barbara looked out the window to where Iuli still sat forlornly on the marble bench and pulled the bellcord. To the maid who answered, she said, "If Maisetra Sovitre is still in the house, please ask her to join me. Send in some tea and then see we're left alone."

* * *

They consulted with LeFevre first, of course. There was nothing worth knowing about inheritance law that he couldn't recite from memory, complete with volume and section number. Yes, it could be done, if Fulpi agreed. And then they took the risk of laying the matter before Iulien herself, knowing the heartbreak it would mean if her father said no.

"He may refuse," Margerit cautioned, seeing the hope leap in Iuli's eyes. "He may feel I have no business even proposing such a thing. But if you would like, I can make the offer."

Barbara had expected Iuli to agree immediately, to seize her chance to stay in Rotenek. She watched the girl's initial excitement slide sideways into thoughtfulness.

"Would this mean that you were adopting me?" Iuli asked. "That you would become my mother, and not—"

Margerit shook her head. "No, of course not. But I would take you on my purse. That means I'd support you and be responsible for you, and that certain legal rights over you would transfer from your parents to me. It would mean you could live here with me. And in exchange for that, I'd settle the Zortun estate on you as a pledge for your dowry. That means it would come into your hands if you marry and is fixed as an inheritance if you don't. That's not something I do lightly! Much of the food on our table comes from Zortun. And so," she teased, "I'd be quite strict about suitors."

Iuli didn't smile at the joke. "Do you think that's what my father would care about? The dowry?"

If he didn't, he was a fool, Barbara thought. That was the whole point of making the offer. Nothing else would be a strong enough temptation to overcome Fulpi's scruples. But it wouldn't be kind to say that to Iuli's face, even if she put the matter into the best light: that Fulpi's duty as her father was to see to her future. "You needn't decide immediately. Think about it. Your father won't be here to fetch you home until the end of the month."

"I want to," Iuli said solemnly. "Cousin Margerit, I want to so much. But I don't want my father to think I was unhappy. That is, I *was*, but it wasn't because of him. And I want…I want to be able to go home. I don't want him to cut me off like he did you." Her voice grew tight. "Do you think he might do that?"

Margerit hugged her. "Of course not. The only reason he forbade me from visiting was because he wanted to protect you. He'll do what's best for you. We just thought this might help him decide that staying in Rotenek was for the best."

"Then yes," Iuli said. "Yes. Ask him."

* * *

The road to Turinz was becoming more familiar: the long stretch along the woods at the border, the way Sain-Mihail kept peeking through the hills before the road curved to meet it, the scar of Mazuk's canal standing as a reproach. Water filled it now, and there were tracks along the towpath indicating use. So he'd found his investors. Perhaps that part of their past could be forgotten. Even so, she hoped to avoid any meeting with him on this trip.

There had been rumors of highwaymen in those wooded hills—a legacy of the recent crop failures. Tavit, in one of his too frequent moments of caution, had insisted that she ride inside the coach. Watching Tavit and Brandel enjoy the long miles of fine weather on horseback turned her mood sour when they encountered nothing to rouse any sort of alarm.

They arrived at the manor late in the evening, but Akermen had everything ready for their comfort. And in the morning he stood ready to ride the bounds with her. It would be a brief visit, little more than a survey and a few days of hearing petitions.

"Maistir Tuting tells me the rents are better than we'd hoped," Barbara noted as they took a path along the edge of the vineyards toward the first of the villages within the title-lands.

Akermen only nodded. He seemed on edge. Did he think she expected miracles?

"Don't push matters too quickly," she cautioned. "There's no benefit in the long term if the tenants don't share the gains, and we need to weather these current storms first." A poor joke, she realized as the words left her mouth.

"Yes, Mesnera."

It was difficult to know Akermen's opinions from so few words. Barbara knew how it must be: they hadn't yet had time to develop trust, and the power was all in her hands. But Tuting's praise hadn't been hollow. She'd seen the numbers and given them to Brandel to review as well. Now she encouraged Brandel's questions. Perhaps Akermen would open up more as an instructor.

The young estate manager visibly controlled his impatience with Brandel's quizzing, but he began to expound further on the state of the land. Perhaps next time she would send Brandel here on his own. Not to make decisions—he was not at all ready for that—but to observe and report back. She broke in on Brandel's questions to mention the possibility.

Akermen returned to a brief, "As you wish."

That was a habit she would need to break. She needed someone with opinions and the confidence to pursue them.

Barbara returned to her probing of Akermen in the quiet end of an afternoon when the villagers had exhausted the petitions and grievances they had a right to bring before her.

"What do you think needs to be done in the next year?" she asked. "What changes would you make?"

He eyed her closely, clearly still judging how much candor she desired. "You had mentioned repairs to the manor."

She nodded wordlessly, waiting to see where that thought took him.

"I think it might be done. There are men standing idle with half the harvest ruined. Since no miracles are in the offing, if you accepted labor in place of rent—"

"But I've forgiven that share of the rents." Barbara interrupted.

"I mentioned it only as a possibility," he said stiffly.

Barbara mulled it over briefly and shook her head. "Cheap labor, but stone is never cheap. And the warehouse fires in Rotenek have made seasoned lumber dear even this far away."

"There's lumber to be had from Terubirk where they're clearing for the ironworks."

Barbara looked at him sharply. Evidently his proposal was more than idle thought. But she had no interest in a project that would rely on Baron Mazuk's cooperation or would put money in his purse.

"I'll keep it in mind for the future, but not this year. There's time enough. I have no plans to do more than visit at the present," Barbara said. "Perhaps in another few years..." She looked over at where Brandel was frowning over the correspondence he'd been set.

Akermen followed her gaze and his face went bland once more.

With her neighbor on her mind, Barbara noted, "So Baron Mazuk is building at last, and I saw the canal is in operation. I hope you've had no trouble with him."

Her manager looked startled, almost guilty. "Why would I have any reason to have dealings with him?"

"No reason at all, that I know," Barbara returned. "But he's been out of temper with me for the last year. If he ever looks to interfere with Turinz affairs, let me know."

"As you wish."

There it was again, the closing down.

"Is there anything you need for yourself?" Barbara said impulsively. "Is your salary adequate? Do you have enough resources for travel? Does Tuting answer your needs promptly?"

"There is something," he said. From his expression it wasn't simply a whim of the moment.

"Yes?"

"Mairet—he was sent to the council of commons last fall but he's been suffering from dropsy and can't travel. They'll be holding a new election. I'd like to stand."

Yes, he'd hinted in that direction before. "I hadn't realized you were thinking of leaving my service."

He shook his head in denial. "Not at all. I was hoping...that is, it would mean a great deal to have your support."

Barbara frowned. "My support would suggest to the world that you were my man in the council."

He nodded.

"It wouldn't do."

Akermen went still. "Do you doubt my loyalty?"

"Rather the opposite," Barbara answered. "I fear your loyalty. I have my own voice in the council of nobles. Two voices, for that matter. I have no business dictating a vote in the commons as well."

"And what if I pledged to be my own man," he said slowly.

There was a peculiar edge in his voice—something close to desperation—as if he were searching for the path out of some tangle.

"It wouldn't matter. It wouldn't matter to what people thought. And could you truly make decisions without thinking what it would mean to my interests? No, I can't support it." She shook her head once more. "Besides, I need you here, not chasing off to Rotenek every season. A career in politics is a fine thing to aspire to, but not while you're on my salary. Let's get Turinz back on its feet. When that's accomplished, the votes will come of their own accord."

"I see," Akermen said. This time when he fell silent, there was a deep calm. Some unspoken matter had been settled. And in the remaining days of her visit, he never mentioned the matter again.

* * *

It was a dream—that much Barbara knew. Images came in snatches, one after another without connection. Bright sun and a spirited horse between her legs. Voices, talking somewhere out of sight.

"Have you sent word to Rotenek?"

She heard Tavit answering and her mind drifted off. If Tavit were there, he would manage things. There was something she'd meant to tell him. Something he needn't worry about. They were both riding out in front of the coach and she called to him but he didn't turn. They'd passed the bend where the road overlooked Mazuk's canal. Mazuk? Was that what she'd meant to tell him? He needn't worry about Baron Mazuk.

"What did she say?"

"Something about Baron Mazuk. She must have guessed somehow."

If she were riding with Tavit, where was Brandel? Now she remembered. He was riding up with the coachman. She'd borrowed his horse, for her own had gone lame. She tried to turn back to look at him but the sun was in her eyes and she closed them against the light.

They'd been riding such a long time, surely they'd come to the inn soon. She was tired and thirsty. They'd be there soon. She'd toss the reins to a stableboy and call out, "Ho, innkeeper, a drink!"

"What's that?"

"I think she asked for a drink."

The river water was cold and clear. She didn't remember dismounting but she dipped cupped hands in the current and raised them to her lips. The water slipped through her fingers, running red back down the bank.

"We have to go."

Tavit was urging her on. They were on the horses again, racing down the road with the coach on their heels, and beside her Tavit's voice shouting, "Go! Go!"

There was a sharp crack...the axle of the coach? She tried to turn her horse but Tavit was at her side, grabbing her arm and screaming, "Go! Go!"

And she would have obeyed, but he had her arm in a grip of iron, his fingers digging through to the bone. She cried out.

"More laudanum?"

"Not yet."

They'd been riding through the woods, but the woods were on fire. Where was Brandel? Had he been on the coach? Aunt Heniriz would never forgive her. Was Brandel caught in the fire? There was no fire, it was a dream. She knew it was a dream.

"Brandel."

"Shh, he's gone to Rotenek to fetch Maisetra Sovitre."

Margerit? But why would Margerit be coming here? She had her own duties…the college.

"No. Tell Margerit…don't come."

"Mesnera, it's worth more than my life not to send for her."

That was Tavit's voice. But why was Tavit still grabbing her arm? She tried to shake him loose but she couldn't move. It was a dream. These things happened in dreams.

"Arm…"

"The surgeon says you won't lose it."

That wasn't in her dream. She struggled to rise. "Tavit!"

"More laudanum now I think."

She must be in the coach now. The slow rocking lulled her to sleep. They must have fixed the axle. But where was Brandel? Brandel was in Rotenek, fetching Margerit. When Margerit came, everything would make sense.

* * *

Bed. She was in a bed, but she couldn't remember how she'd come there or where the bed was located. That was less important in the moment than the pressure in her bladder. It was dark, but there would be a chamber pot somewhere easily to hand.

Barbara tried to rise to a sitting position and cried out as agony stabbed through her right arm. There was a sound from the other side of the room and the flare of a lamp wick being turned up. Tavit was there at her side, his face pale and hollow.

"Don't try to get up, you'll only make it bleed again."

Bleed? What did he mean? "If I don't get up I'm going to piss the bed."

Tavit sighed. "It wouldn't be the first time. Here, let me help you."

An arm reached behind her and she was pulled upright but the roaring in her ears blotted out whatever else Tavit might have said. The room faded.

When she woke again, daylight streamed through an unfamiliar window. She moved more cautiously this time, reaching over with her left hand to examine the source of her pain. Thick bandages were wound around her upper arm. Beneath it a dull throbbing promised sharper agony for misbehavior. The trip north through Turinz. They'd passed Sain-Mihail and been skirting the edge of the woods between there and the border. Then what? Shouts and hoofbeats. Highwaymen. So the reports had been true. But the rest was a blur.

"Tavit?"

The figure in the chair by the window started from sleep. In what must have been reflex by now, he was at her side, lifting a cup to her lips, then dabbing at her forehead with a damp cloth. This time when he helped her to sit, she remained conscious.

"Tavit, what happened?"

"Don't you remember?"

Barbara began to shake her head and thought better of it. She felt oddly fragile. "I remember the robbers, but that's all."

"They weren't robbers. That is, I don't doubt they would have robbed us if there'd been a chance. But their instructions were murder."

"Murder? Why?"

She watched as Tavit pursed his lips in thought. He must be calculating how much she was ready to hear.

"Mesnera, your estate manager betrayed you."

"Akermen? Why?" She seemed to be saying that word a lot.

"Evidently to protect Turinz from sorcery, or so he claimed. Perhaps simply for his own profit. It seems Baron Mazuk promised him something that he couldn't get from you."

Couldn't get? But there hadn't been anything…the council seat? Was that what this was about? Sorcery! That was nonsense. Except…how must it look, this far from Rotenek? She had claimed the title of Turinz and mystical disasters began happening. She was close friends with the Royal Thaumaturgist yet refused any benefit of that bond to Turinz. Akermen couldn't know how helpless Margerit was against what was happening across the land. But how could Mazuk promise him anything? Akermen held no property from him. Unless Baron Mazuk convinced Akermen that he'd soon have a hand over Turinz.

Murder. And who would the title to Turinz go to if she were killed? There was no heir-default in the Arpik line, not one of noble rank. Not unless…but Akermen had guessed she had plans for Brandel. If she died before those plans were put in motion, the title would revert to the crown. Mazuk might petition for it, but there was no certainty he'd succeed. For Mazuk, the goal must have been simple revenge. Or was there more? The canal had not been the only venture he'd made into Turinz. She'd put a stop to some she knew of. Were there others he couldn't risk her discovering? And even if it were only revenge, Akermen might not know that.

Barbara's head was spinning. Tavit was waiting for something.

"Where's Akermen?" she asked.

"Dead. Along with the two outlaws he hired. But not before I learned enough from him to challenge Mazuk."

"Tavit, no! You haven't—"

"Not yet. Mazuk's yours to accuse. But Akermen was mine."

Barbara closed her eyes. "I wish you hadn't."

"Mesnera, you don't understand. It was my right and my duty. When I saw you fall…When I thought I'd failed to protect you…"

"Tavit, I chose to ride in the open."

"That doesn't change my duty. But this wasn't the chance of the road; they always meant to kill you. It wouldn't have mattered if you'd stayed in the coach. I was absolved of that, but not of failing the honor of Saveze. You're in my charge. You don't have the right to take that from me unless you dismiss me altogether."

He was breathing heavily at the end of the speech, as he might after a bout in the fencing salle.

Barbara opened her eyes again and met his. She saw no doubt in them, no self-reproach. His last words hadn't been a challenge but a simple statement of fact. She reached across with her left hand and grasped his.

"For the honor of Saveze," she said.

Distantly, somewhere outside the building there were hoofbeats and carriage wheels on a cobbled yard and the shouts of men. Then feet pounding on a staircase and a hurried exchange of voices as the door opened. Margerit rushed in with Brandel close on her heels.

"Dear God in heaven, Barbara, what happened?"

Barbara winced as she failed to stop the impulse to rise. "It seems that I've been shot."

CHAPTER THIRTY

Serafina

Late May, 1825

Summer shifted the wares in the Strangers' Market from the bright luxuries meant to tempt shoppers from the upper town to still rare but more practical goods offered to those unmoved by the seasons. One last errand brought Serafina's steps to a booth presided over by a white-haired and wizened man. He sat behind the counter clutching one of the strings of beads that made the bulk of his wares, slipping the counters through his fingers and muttering over them one by one. She hadn't come to view the rosaries, but she examined several of the more precious ones to distract from the object of her true interest. Coral and crystal, lapis and silver gilt. She hesitated, and reached for a more humble string of enameled beads whose pendant cross was made from a piece of rolled tin.

The man paused in his counting. "Not the one for a fine lady like you."

Serafina ignored the empty flattery. She was returning to Rome in the same worn blue pelisse she had arrived in. No one would mistake her for a fine lady. She had one thing of value remaining and it sat hidden in the reticule dangling from her wrist.

"No," she echoed. "That one's not for a fine lady. The cross holds a relic, save it for someone who needs help." It was a guess, but a faint glow of power leaked from the seams of the metal.

Now she turned her attention to her goal: a collection of small figures standing at one end of the counter. There was no time for long bargaining. She slid her choice to the center of the space.

"An excellent choice. Very fine workmanship. Said to be—"

"Do you take trade?" she interrupted.

His eyes narrowed.

Serafina loosened the strings on her reticule and pulled out the pearl necklace. She hadn't worn it since the Royal Guild dinner…it seemed so long ago. She thought of Marianniz. If it had been a gift of the heart, she wouldn't think of parting with it, but…

"An even trade. I think you will have the bargain of it."

The man fingered the pearls and peered closely at the clasp, then tapped one of the beads against his teeth and nodded. "Would you like it delivered?"

She shook her head and he swathed the statuette carefully in a clean rag. It was small enough to slip into her reticule in place of the pearls.

When she reached the dressmaker's shop, Serafina paused to gather her resolve. She had said her goodbyes to Luzie and the others, to Jeanne, and to Margerit who was to pass them along at the school. But there was one more and she had put it off until it could be delayed no longer.

She turned the handle and heard the jangle of the bell echoing into the back rooms. Mefro Dominique came out to the counter, dressed as always in advertisement of her skills, her sharply tailored walking dress of figured bronze muslin finished with a turban striped in the same with green. She smiled welcomingly.

"May I help you, Maisetra Talarico?"

"I was wondering if I might speak to Celeste. Just for a few moments. I won't interrupt her work very long."

"Yes of course," Dominique replied. "She's in the fitting room. You know the way?"

Serafina nodded.

Before she could head for the doorway, Dominique added, "I'm grateful for the friendship you've shown to my daughter. She speaks of you often."

"It's nothing really," Serafina said. They both knew it was more than that. It was the relief, for only a passing moment, of seeing yourself in another's face. Of knowing even just the kinship of being strangers together. She smiled uncertainly and went through to the crowded sewing room.

"Celeste?"

The girl looked up eagerly. "Maisetra Talarico! I've been hoping to see you. Everyone is talking about your friend Maisetra Valorin's mystery. Tell me about it."

Was it still on everyone's lips? Celeste and her friends among the charm-wives would have sensed some of what the opera set in motion. Margerit had had a great deal to say about it, though her *visio* had only taken in the most wide-spreading effects.

"It wasn't a mystery," she corrected. "Only an opera, but yes, Maisetra Valorin could be a great thaumaturgist if only she were a *vidator* as well as an *actor*."

"But she has you for that," Celeste said.

That brought Serafina back to the purpose of her visit. "No. I have to leave. I came to say goodbye."

Celeste's expression froze. Then the excitement drained away, leaving only the face she showed to customers. "Thank you for coming to bid farewell, Maisetra. That was kind of you."

"Oh Celeste, I wish I could stay, but I can't. I brought you something to remember me by."

She drew the small figure out of her reticule and unwrapped it, then placed the likeness of Saint Mauriz on the table between them. "For your—what do you call it?—your little shrine." She had been thinking of this gift since she first saw the intricacy of the carved ebony features, from the rivets on his armor to the small tight curls of his hair peeking around the gilt halo.

"Oh Maisetra!" Celeste's composure slipped at last. "I—"

Serafina held her arms out and embraced her tightly, tears starting in her eyes. "I want you to promise me something. If you ever need help with your… your talents. If you ever want to reach for something more. Go to Maisetra Sovitre and tell her I sent you. I know you're needed here, but if there's ever a chance…"

She broke away, knowing that to stay longer would do neither of them good. Frances Collfield would be waiting at the coaching inn by the Tupendor where the road set off southward. Her one valise had already been delivered there. They were to set out at noon.

* * *

Traveling with Frances was precisely what she needed, Serafina thought, for Frances was happy to fill the miles with explanations of her research, descriptions of what samples she hoped to find on this trip, and the constant refrain of her relief that the successful publication of her book had made it possible for her to return to England. She could finally distribute copies to her subscribers and mend fences with the engraver of the plates.

"For he's written several very unhappy letters to my brother on the matter, and Edward passed them on to me. Though really, it's uncharitable of me, but one might think that Edward could have dealt with the matter himself. It's his fault that I had to bring the plates here to Alpennia to be printed in the first place."

If, at any time, Serafina found her mind turning to melancholy, she had only to point through the window at some interesting feature of the landscape to have Frances expound on rocks and soils, alluvium and sediment, and to discourse on the plants native to each feature. Underneath it all, Serafina could see the muddled currents of errant sorcery flowing through the land. It wasn't the sharp-edged menace of a directed curse. More a waiting hazard, like a long-forgotten wellhead, overgrown with vines.

On the day they began climbing through the hills, winding on narrow roads below whitened peaks, they both fell silent. What should have been clear roads were treacherously slick as they passed through shadow, and the fields beside them showed close-cropped grass from sheep and cattle that should have been grazing higher up by now.

When they reached the inn at Almunt, the hired coachman unloaded their luggage into the hands of a grizzled muleteer who looked them up and down and joked that they'd do better to wear the contents of their wardrobes. It would save the mules the trouble of luggage and keep them from freezing. But the bitter weather had been in place long enough that the residents of Almunt had risen to the task of outfitting those hardy travelers who came their way. In addition to the pack animals and a guide, they were presented with heavy cloaks and fur rugs to tuck around them for the muleback ride.

"You'll be as comfy as a chair in your own parlor," the muleteer assured Serafina when she looked askance at the awkward sidesaddle. She'd never ridden before, and the lurching gait took all her attention in the first hour as they threaded the trail between banked snow that had been cleared where a carriage road should have run.

Further from the border, the reaching fingers of the weather mystery had seemed to flow aimlesly. Now it spilled down the valleys and crested over the peaks of the hills like drifts of malevolent fog, fraying out as it met with the edges of Alpennia's protections. Having seen those protections at their heart, in the cathedral of Saint Mauriz, she could distinguish them here. The bright pulsing glow of the saint's blessing should have been a sharp-edged spear and gleaming shield. Here it felt more like the faint flickering of a sanctuary lamp: a promise of the Presence, but no more than that. And with every flicker, shadows slipped closer, like moths drawn by that dim glow that would have been driven off by daylight.

The *castellum* was stronger. Serafina could feel the layers, the courses that had been laid down with each repetition of the ceremony. The mystery had been designed as a defense and she felt it all around, growing thicker and stronger as the air grew thinner and colder. But the foreign mystery filtered through it, seeping through cracks in the walls, working its way around the stones, seeking blind spots between the towers. She could feel the pressure of its presence on the other side in dark reds and purples, swirling around the mountain peaks like the storms it gathered.

Having opened her senses to the fullest, Serafina could see other mysteries at work. A pulse like a beacon shining from someplace ahead of them. A monastery, she guessed from the shape of it, and a mystery meant to draw lost travelers to safety. The mules in their train each carried a charm—local work, no doubt—keeping their feet sure on the path. And along the trace of the stream they paralleled, there was a strangely familiar thread. It lapped in waves against the tendrils of the weather sorcery, whispering rise up, flow, be a river once more.

Rise up. She craned her head around to look over her shoulder down into the ravine, though mortal eyes meant nothing to what she sought. Rise up. No, she hadn't imagined it. There in the ice-rimmed waters of the stream was an echo of Tanfrit's song. *Let the waters rise up.* It had cut through the frozen power in the mountains and freed some small portion of the stream to flow down toward the valleys and, in time, to the Rotein. Looking more closely, she saw how it had prevailed, how the fierce pride and passion channeled into that aria had drawn power from the listening crowd, and followed their love and fear of the great river up through its tributaries and their sources and here to where the lifeblood that fed the Rotein was held captive. It had called to the ice, *Rise up. Let the waters rise up.*

They were moving through the borders now, past the limits of Mauriz's grace, outside the ambit of Margerit's *castellum*. The full force of what they held at bay battered at her senses like a blinding storm and she cried out.

"Serafina, what's wrong?"

She heard Frances's voice at a distance. And then their guide calling back, "Keep moving. We can't stop here."

Her mount continued forward, oblivious to the mystic winds that howled about them. It had gone wild, Kreiser had agreed, like a mad dog unleashed. It had been one thing to trace those forces on a map, another to be inside it. Kreiser had traveled these roads and others a year past. Had it been like this? But his *visio* was much weaker, hence his need for her eyes. There was no way to compare.

She could see Kreiser's map in her mind and found their place in it and all the small traces they'd hunted together. They formed a pattern, even in their chaos. She saw the remnants of protections—not those of Alpennia alone—and how the assault was drawn to them, hungry for what was forbidden to it. Those structures still stood, but like the shape of a house eaten from within by rot and ready to crumble at a touch. Would Archbishop Fizeir's mending of the Mauriz *tutela* repair them? Could the Royal Guild master the changes in the *castellum* in time? How long would even such protections hold in the face of continued assault?

The image of the spreading petals of a rose no longer seemed apt. More like the spreading ripples in a pond from where a stone had been dropped. But not one stone alone. No, the image was leading her astray. She worked to focus on those spreading forces and then to follow them back to the core, to that one pass, far to the east, that had been the center and origin of the mystery. There. It drew her as a lodestone draws a compass needle. Her awareness sped across the miles like a bird in flight. This time she pushed aside the image of roots, of interwoven spiderwebs, and saw that center as a vortex, a whirlpool, a spinning wind, and this time she dove down through the center of it, seeking its source.

The *fluctus* spun around her and she felt her body clutch at the saddle to keep from falling. Down, in, through. A shade rose up before her: a dry empty husk of a soul lost to salvation. She passed through it and it crumbled to dust around her. Other dry shadows swirled around her, caught up in the storm. And now a circle of men, chanting, high walls and colored windows. A woman's cry—of pain or passion. The brief flash of a face, dark like her own, glimpsed in a clouded mirror. Other faces, more empty ghosts. She recognized the signs of a mystery being performed, but this was only an image of what had gone before. A fading echo of the ceremony that had created the catastrophe. Where? Who? Kreiser had thought Paris, but she'd never been there, she had no bearings. What she had was a taste of the celebrants, a scent, an image—not of their physical selves, but of their essences. She might not know them on the street, but she would know their work if she encountered it again. And she had seen the shape of their errant mystery—seen it as clearly as in a *depictio* laid out on the floor of the chamber of mysteries— and she knew how it could be defeated.

One of the ghostly figures turned, saw her, reached out. Serafina fled sideways into the darkness. He grasped at nothing. And she was lost—lost except for the gleam of a beacon shining faintly through a blizzard. A bell, calling to wandering travelers. A voice…

"Serafina! Serafina, wake up!"

Her eyes fluttered open and Frances was bending over her. Warmth and shelter.

"Serafina, are you well?"

She sat up and drew her hands across her eyes to clear away the traces of the vision. "I'm here. I was following the mystery."

"We didn't know what had happened to you. The guide wanted to go on, but I insisted we stop here."

Serafina looked around. Yes, it must be the monastery whose beacon-mystery she'd seen earlier.

"Frances, I need to go back."

"Back?"

"It's all bound up together—I see it now. The walls are crumbling, and when they fall— Margerit…she needs to know. I know how to break it." Would they believe her or think she had gone mad? Serafina lowered her voice and spoke as calmly as she could mange. "I must go back to Rotenek."

* * *

It wasn't as simple as turning around and returning. Serafina argued long with Frances before she would agree to continue on her own journey. And then there was the maddening wait in the monastery guesthouse until a party heading north through the mountains could be convinced to add a stranger to their midst. In Almunt, another wait until a ride could be begged as far as

Nofpunt for a fee of five teneirs—as much as she could spare and still leave the public coach fare from Nofpunt to Rotenek.

The coach deposited her just inside the city walls at the Tupendor late in the evening with an empty purse. Truly empty. There would be nothing more from Paolo. The money was the least of it. Her thoughts shied away from tracing the consequences of her decision to its final end. This would mean a complete break. She would never see him again—not unless he chose to pursue her here to Alpennia. If she never returned to Rome, she would never see her father or Michele either. Was it worth it, what she had come to do? What did she owe to Alpennia that could match that cost? But it wasn't Alpennia, she knew that. It was some vision of the rightness of the world that had gone out of balance. And above all else, it was Margerit and Luzie and Celeste and the rest. Two years past, she had come to Rotenek seeking something. And if she hadn't found it, she had found so much more.

But for now there was the question of where to go. It was late and she would need to walk. The innkeeper would hold her valise for now as a pledge. In this part of town she knew only which streets were safe to keep to. The university district was a half hour's walk up Market Street. A year before, she might have sought Akezze at her lodgings there, but now Akezze had rooms at the academy. It would take another half hour to walk to the upper part of town, but Luzie would…no. She counted up the days. Luzie and all the rest would be at Akolbin. It must be Margerit. Margerit needed to know what she'd discovered. Margerit would know what to do. In the Plaiz Vezek by the university, she lost her way in the dark and had to ask a passing student which street would take her to the Pont Ruip. From there she knew the way.

The knocker on the door at Tiporsel House echoed hollowly. What if they had left on holiday as well? She'd paid no mind to anyone else's summer plans, knowing they had nothing to do with her. But perhaps the darkness within the foyer and the long minutes before a sleepy footman unbarred the door were only the lateness of the hour.

"Maisetra Talarico!" he said in a startled voice.

"It's unforgiveable, I know," Serafina said. "The hour, and with no notice. But I've only just returned to town and I have nowhere to stay. And I hoped Maisetra Sovitre…"

He stared at her in confusion for a moment, then said, "You haven't heard? The Maisetra has gone down to Turinz."

Turinz? Serafina's heart fell. "When do you expect her back?"

"Maisetra…we don't know. The baroness has been shot."

In the end it was Margerit's cousin Iulien who was roused from her sleep to make some sort of decision. She came down wrapped in a pale yellow dressing gown, her face paler still, perhaps expecting worse news than what the house had already received.

"Oh, Serafina!" she exclaimed. "I thought you were in Rome! What's happened?"

"I'm well," Serafina hastened to reassure her. "I came back because…oh, it doesn't matter just now. What's this about Baroness Saveze?"

She took in the jumbled story of bandits and chases on horseback, mixed up with pistols and swords, and guessed that half of it was one of Iuli's fanciful inventions.

"And are you here by yourself?" she asked Iuli in concern.

"Only until Aunt Bertrut comes back. They're only off at Marzim and should be here by tomorrow. When I heard the knock I thought they might be early. And you mustn't tell anyone that Margerit left me here alone!"

It was a peculiar sort of alone that could be had in a house full of servants, but Serafina nodded reassurance. "I shouldn't stay, then. I've only just arrived back and had nowhere else to go. Even my valise is still at the coaching inn."

The frightened indecision left Iuli's face. She straightened and Serafina could see just what sort of woman she might someday become.

Iuli turned to the waiting footman. "Marzo, please ask someone to wake Mefro Charsintek. Tell her that Maisetra Talarico will be my guest tonight and will need a bed made up."

The man looked from one to the other of them, clearly judging whether Iulien had the authority to give such a command, but then he bowed, saying, "Yes, Maisetra Iulien," and went to make arrangements.

CHAPTER THIRTY-ONE

Margerit

July, 1825

Barbara should have been here. This was her world—the game she had played since her youth. It was hard not to feel like a green girl in Princess Annek's presence, surrounded by the lords of state on one side and Archbishop Fereir with the masters of the most powerful mystery guilds on the other. Margerit had last known this scrutiny when she had been approved—no, approved was wrong, admitted—as Royal Thaumaturgist. This time it was Serafina who laid out the pages of the *depictio* with shaking hands and led the watchers through what she had seen.

Barbara should have been here—no, *she* should be at Barbara's side. Cooling her brow through the fevers, lighting candles to run through every healing mystery she knew, helping to change the bandages that covered the torn flesh and bound to it an array of amulets delivered from Antuniet's workshop. It didn't matter that every member of the household clamored to keep that vigil for her. She should be there.

"This is an extraordinary claim." Setun, the guildmaster of Saint Benezet's had claimed the role of challenger. Convincing him might not be essential but it would make the rest easier.

"We face an extraordinary danger," Margerit answered. She would have continued but the archbishop waved her to silence.

"Let the foreign woman speak. It is her vision we must judge today."

Knowing Serafina's unease in public, Margerit expected her to stutter and stumble. But she had worked with Fereir before in the spring. Perhaps that eased the way.

"Here," Serafina said, pointing to the first of the diagrams, "is what I saw as we approached the mountains just north of Almunt."

Margerit had been led through the journey five times or more and it chilled her anew each time. Serafina's description had been honed and distilled through repetition.

"The fractures in the Mauriz *tutela* have not only weakened its protections but provided a path for this foreign—" She hesitated before using the word. "—this foreign sorcery to enter the land."

They had argued over that. But one could hardly call the weather mystery a miracle, and the spreading effects of its disruption were scarcely coherent enough for the word mystery. Even curse implied more intention than seemed accurate.

"The All Saints' Castellum was meant to provide a different type of protection. Not a replacement. If there had been time for it to become stronger and more...more settled, then it might have kept the sorcery somewhat at bay. Instead, it too provided cracks to draw it in. It's as if—" Serafina's gaze unfocused as it always did when she was trying to find the best description. "It's as if the sorcery pushed harder wherever it found resistance. On the Swiss side of the mountains, Mesner Kreiser said it only affected the weather, but in Alpennia, in Piedmont, and along the Dolomites it fought the mysteries it found there and became wilder."

That was what had cut to Margerit's heart: the fear that the imperfections in her mystery might have caused more damage than it prevented. The Mauriz was Fereir's responsibility, but the *castellum* was hers.

The debate lasted for three days, but Archbishop Fereir lent the deciding voice.

"We have already begun the restoration and revisions to the Great Mystery of Saint Mauriz. This revelation only adds urgency to implementing them this year. We have two months to complete the preparations. And two months—" He fixed the Benezet guildmaster with a commanding gaze. "Two months to assist Maisetra Sovitre in preparing the Royal Guild for their *castellum*."

They would perform both together, it was decided. Saint Mauriz on the morning of his feast day to cast his restored protection over the land. The All Saints' Castellum in the afternoon to raise walls and towers as a bulwark against what followed. The *castellum* wouldn't be as effective as on its proper day, but there was no help for that. And afterward, a new mystery was being devised that would be a spear in the heart of the sorcery. But for all Margerit's probing, the guildmasters declined to share those plans.

* * *

Iulien's concerns always seemed to intrude at the worst possible time. Margerit knew that if it had been left to her, she would have given in to all of

Uncle Fulpi's demands, simply to be able to focus her attention on Barbara and the *castellum*. Fortunately, she had LeFevre to serve as her patience. He'd made her swear to promise nothing in advance of the contract and to hold her tongue when they finally gathered for the signing.

Several days of truce preceded that signing. It might have been better to lodge Uncle Fulpi somewhere other than Tiporsel House, Margerit thought, too late to make any change. It was the first time he'd come to Rotenek since her first Advent season here, when she was still newly arrived in the city and under his guardianship. To be sure, they'd crossed paths in Chalanz in summers past, but that had been on his ground—his, in some sense, even at her house on Fonten Street. Here he was reminded at every turn that Rotenek was her domain and it made him stiff and prickly. The only saving grace was that injury kept Barbara confined to their room. She had no such escape. Uncle Fulpi sat opposite from her now, unspeaking, while his lawyer and LeFevre went over the contracts in minute detail with the air of seconds before a duel.

Iulien waited anxiously in the library, with Aunt Bertrut to keep her company. They'd both lectured her sternly in preparation for this visit: be pleasant and agreeable, not meek, but biddable, no pertness or impatience. It might have been easier to wait there with her.

"There is a question," Uncle Fulpi's lawyer said, "of the provisions regarding the property in the case of marriage." He exchanged glances with his employer and continued. "The current provision is that the property at Zortun is to be deeded to Iulien Fulpi at the time of her marriage. We wish to specify that the final deed is to be transferred only if she marries with her father's approval. If she marries without approval, the property is to be held in trust until she has attained thirty years of age."

Margerit stifled a protest but not before her uncle had seen the impulse. Be still, she told herself. Give nothing away.

LeFevre took up the gauntlet. "Maisetra Fulpi cannot marry without her father's consent until she is of age. That is already specified in the contract, even though she will be on Maisetra Sovitre's purse. After she is of age, he may retract his portion of her dowry if she chooses against his consent. That is the law and is separate from our contract. But it is not reasonable for Maistir Fulpi to control the portion of her dowry that Maisetra Sovitre has contracted for."

The lawyer once again exchanged glances with his employer. "We grant that. However we are concerned that Maisetra Iulien's dowry may come to the interest of fortune hunters. Maistir Fulpi is not entirely satisfied with the provisions for her...ah...protection."

It was a valid concern. A large dowry was a two-edged sword. Just as it tempted Iuli's father to agreement, it might tempt suitors to go to unfortunate means to secure her hand. In the previous season, there had only been her reputation to protect.

They wrangled politely for the next half hour over whether it was necessary or reasonable to specify a list of approved vizeinos who might provide chaperonage at formal events, and whether it was advisable to hire an armin for her protection.

"And I don't mean that boy," Uncle Fulpi said, interrupting the discussion.

LeFevre once more calmed the waters. Maistir Fulpi should be assured that this was a household that took seriously the hazards for a young woman with a tempting dowry. He need not be concerned regarding the training and qualifications of anyone entrusted with responsibility for his daughter. Somehow the question of Brandel's suitability was never directly addressed.

In the end, the papers were signed as originally drawn up. Margerit was to be Iulien's guardian in all matters except final consent to her marriage. Iulien was to become a comfortable heiress, though not in any way close to what Margerit's own prospects had been. It was a second benefit, Margerit thought, that she was slowly chipping away at those prospects, trading the mansion at Chalanz for the Tanfrit Academy, signing away the Zortun estate. There was still a considerable income from investments, but with only Tiporsel House remaining to her own name, perhaps there would be fewer misguided suitors of her own to discourage.

Iuli was brought in and admonished to be an obedient girl and behave herself and that in future she was to spend at least a portion of her summers in Chalanz, lest people think her own family were no longer good enough for her. But then there were embraces and at least a few tears. Uncle Fulpi wasn't a monster, Margerit thought. He never had been. But it was a new world that she and Iuli lived in. He was a man accustomed to being master in his own house, not a guest in hers.

The visitors from Chalanz left to see to other arrangements that could only be made in the city, but LeFevre lingered. "Is the baroness receiving?" he asked. "Or would my presence be an imposition?"

"As if you could ever be considered an imposition!" Margerit protested. "In truth, she's going a bit mad to be out and about. Every person who comes to see her helps keep her still a little longer."

"How is she recovering?"

Margerit shook her head. "Too slowly. At least it seems that way. I know it's barely been a month. The fevers have mostly gone. Antuniet and Anna have spent weeks trying to perfect amulets against bleeding and inflammation and to calm fevers. I think there's an entire jeweler's inventory wrapped up in Barbara's bandages: emeralds, jaspers, carnelian. Healing the muscle is harder. The surgeon is satisfied and I've been doing what I can, but it may be the only miracle I'll be granted is that she's still alive. I've had so little luck with healing mysteries." She smiled bleakly. "I want to believe that patience will do the rest."

"But it was her right arm."

Margerit knew what he meant. Her sword arm. "Go up and see her. And try to convince her that the world will wait on her recovery. And convince her that there's no use in hiring a company of shadows to hunt down Mazuk and drag him into the royal court to lay charges. September will be soon enough. After all, where else could he go?"

* * *

Leave the attack to the guildmasters, the archbishop had said, but for all that she tried, Margerit couldn't be complacent. The *castellum* needed little additional work on the structure of the mystery itself. She had been waiting impatiently for permission to add the accumulated refinements. It only required more intensive rehersal and the substitution of key roles. That left time for thoughts to turn constantly to the remaining problem. They were assembled once more at Tiporsel House rather than the mystery chamber at Urmai. Barbara had insisted. Or rather, Barbara had threatened to go down to Urmai herself if they tried to leave her out of the discussions, and Margerit believed her. Traipsing up and down stairs was as much as Barbara was to be allowed yet.

"One more time, from the beginning," Margerit suggested, and as she'd done at least once each day since they'd begun to tackle the question, Serafina closed her eyes and began to recount the visions she'd had on the road from Almunt to Sain-Perinerd. Margerit took up her pen and began adding notes to those already crowding the page before her.

The Tanfrit piece...she still didn't know how to understand that part. But there must be something in the descriptions of how the foreign mystery fought with the attenuated edges of the Mauriz *tutela*, that would give them a clue.

Antuniet interrupted the recitation when Serafina came to the point of plunging through the vortex. "We've been over this again and again. It hasn't brought us any closer to a way to break the weather mystery. The Mauriz and the Castellum, they're both meant at heart to be protections. I don't see how they could be turned to attack unless you propose to include the *turris* against invasions again?"

A unanimous rejection ran around the room. The invasion tower had been the serpent in the garden, the dagger aimed at Princess Annek and her sons, inserted into the original mystery by Estefen Chazillen's agents. Antuniet knew better than most how unwelcome its return would be, even if completely rewritten.

"By rights," Akezze said thoughtfully, "an attack *should* belong to Mauriz. He was a soldier and bears a soldier's symbols. If the archbishop is already willing to make changes to the *tutela*, why not suggest adding it there?"

Barbara shook her head. "The Mauriz is meant to stand for the ages, not to be adapted each season like an old dress with a new hat. We need a mystery intended to strike this one target."

"We already have one," Serafina said quietly. "The opera."

There was enough conviction in her voice that the other conversations all paused.

"Use the opera," she repeated. "It makes sense. We already know it can affect the weather mystery. It's already an attack of sorts. And there are already plans to stage it in the fall. It's one thing we could have full control over."

"Could we?" Akezze asked. "What would your Maisetra Valorin think of that?"

Barbara followed with, "Would it have enough power? You said yourself that there were only traces of the…I don't know what we should call it. The song-mystery? It might have raised the river, but only by inches. If an attack carried no more power than that, it wouldn't be enough."

"But it isn't a mystery!" Margerit protested. "There's nothing of ritual in it. It doesn't invoke the saints—"

Serafina turned on her impatiently. "It doesn't matter that the opera doesn't invoke any saints. If it works, it doesn't matter. Lots of market charms don't call on saints. Or they call on people who aren't saints, like Mama Rota."

"Every market charm I've ever examined intends to call on divine grace, even if the names are wrong." Even to her own ears Margerit's protest sounded weak.

"Then perhaps your precious Tanfrit should be canonized!" Serafina said in exasperation.

How many saints had been unknown before undeniable miracles brought them to official attention? If Tanfrit's opera worked… Now that could be rather awkward for the academy if it became a site of pilgrimage!

Antuniet picked up the threads. "The power is just a matter of amplification, like the size of a guild. Margerit, you remember the first time we saw the Rotein awash with *fluctus* a year back. That was only the fortepiano and it was little more than a pretty show of lights. A half-dozen musicians and a crowd in the Plaiz raised something strong enough to pull a flood, however small. Now imagine if it played to a full audience in the opera house with an orchestra and a dozen singers in the chorus behind the soprano. It would be the difference between what I can call in the chapel with a single candle and one of the Great Mysteries in the cathedral. The opera's power is already connected to the weather mystery through the river's flow. It's only a matter of using that to channel the *fluctus*."

"If it works the same way as a true mystery," Margerit protested.

"Kreiser thinks it does," Barbara offered.

Antuniet turned on her with a snarl. "I don't give a damn what Kreiser thinks!"

The two glared at each other. They were all on edge. The suggestion was a good excuse for a break. Margerit rose from the table and said, "There's certainly no harm in preparing a second weapon in case the work of the guildmasters fails. Serafina, ask Maisetra Valorin to join us tomorrow, if she can."

When the others had left, Barbara refused to be helped back to her room. "I don't care what Delacroix says, it does me no good to convalesce in bed this long. If I can't manage the stairs without assistance it's because you won't let me walk farther than one room to another."

Margerit would have protested the word "let," but it was true that between the surgeon Delacroix, Tavit and herself, they'd hemmed Barbara in with concern and love. It was hard not to, after those first weeks. She went to caress

Barbara's cheek and slipped an arm around her, careful to avoid jostling the sling that kept the wounded arm in place.

"I wouldn't fuss as much if you knew your own limits," Margerit said.

"How can I know my limits if I don't test them? I'm going to walk in the garden."

Margerit bit back her first response. "That's a good idea. But take someone—Tavit, a footman, I don't care. Someone who can help if you need it."

* * *

The opera frustrated all Margerit's skills. She could see how the story built the basic structures—the equivalent of a *markein* and *invitatio* and *concrescatio*. But there seemed no logic to the workings, more a shaping of the emotions through word and voice. Serafina seemed to have an instinct for it that she lacked, and so she left the reworking of the performace in Serafina's hands. Hers and Luzie Valorin's of course. And—somewhat to her surprise—Iuli's.

"Are there any other of your compositions I might want to know about?" Margerit asked over dinner after Iuli had explained that she'd spent the day working on the new aria.

Iuli flushed. "Should I have asked permission? But I told you when Maisetra Valorin asked for my help with the libretto back in February. And you didn't say anything about it then."

No, but in February she hadn't been thinking of *Tanfrit* as a mystery. That wasn't Iuli's fault.

"I'm sorry, I remember now. But what is it exactly that you're doing? Every time we've tested you, you've shown no talent for mysteries at all."

"It's just poetry," Iuli said. "Nothing magical."

Margerit had only begun to interrupt when Iuli anticipated her.

"I'm sorry, Cousin Margerit. I know you don't want me to call it magic. But you don't want me to call the opera a mystery either, so I'm never sure what to say. But it's just...just words. Maisetra Valorin says I have a way with words. And it's so much easier when she's already written out the ideas and I have the music. And then we put it all together and Serafina...I mean Maisetra Talarico, tells us where to fix it. And Maisetra Valorin's father is teaching her to conduct the rehearsals."

Bertrut commented, "That would set the traditionalists on their ears. Though Luzie Valorin should know her own music best, so why not?"

"No," Iuli said. "He's teaching Serafina to conduct! Because she can see what shape the music is supposed to be."

The image rose in Margerit's mind: Serafina raising her hands and drawing *fluctus* out of the air with the music. It would be the music that drew it, but for those who could see, how might it appear? Perhaps magic was the right word after all.

CHAPTER THIRTY-TWO

Luzie

Mid-September, 1825

Luzie bobbed her head—indeed, she moved her whole body—in time with the music. It was an odd sort of dress rehearsal. At Serafina's insistence they performed in fits and starts, to prevent the mystery from building before its time. Her father was doing his best but it was impossible to tell how the work would come together. Except that it had once before. She turned to where Serafina stood frowning at her side.

"Are you sure this is necessary? It isn't how they're used to working."

"I don't know," Serafina said slowly. "We've never done anything like this before. The effects will be different, that's as much as we know. We've tuned every part of it as precisely as Margerit's *castellum*, but in the end it comes down to performance just the same."

The singers, too, were frustrated with the constant pauses. Madame Cavalli had returned—indeed, insisted on claiming the part of Tanfrit—but the others were new to their parts. The staging for the larger cast was different. More powerful, Serafina had said, but she'd also made some quiet suggestions in choosing the performers, based on talents only she could recognize. Everything had needed to be worked out anew.

From behind them came Count Chanturi's lazy drawl. "Perhaps, Maisetra Valorin, the next time I'm engaged to finance one of your operas, you will inform me in advance that it's to be a charitable project."

Luzie turned and curtseyed to him in welcome. She was always flustered in the presence of her patron. One never knew how seriously he meant anything. Where was Jeanne? She could tease and banter with the man as easily as breathing.

"I didn't...that is, we hadn't intended..."

But he knew that. He must be teasing. The decision to distribute tickets without charge had been part of Margerit's plan, only recently decided.

Chanturi raised her hand to his lips in salute and smiled. "No, of course, forgive me. The performance is at Her Grace's command and I do it only for the glory. Is my dear friend de Cherdillac here?"

"She was here earlier," Luzie said. "I think she might have left."

She relaxed when Chanturi, too, left. Couldn't it be over already? By royal command—but it went beyond that. Maisetra Sovitre had spared her the arguments over including her *Tanfrit* in the ceremonies for the Feast of Saint Mauriz. She only knew the result: by royal command the opera would be performed tomorrow evening after the other rituals. She didn't know how she would survive until then. Serafina's hands were twitching in time with the music. The wait must be just as hard on her.

"Serafina, have you...?"

No, this was no time to ask about plans. It was clear what had brought her back to Rotenek. Luzie hadn't understood even half of the story of her mountain journey with her talk of visions and storms and sorcery. But the drive to solve the puzzle—to understand and, by understanding, to turn disaster back to order—that was plain in Serafina's every word and expression. It might not be from love of Alpennia—what concern could she have for this place? It was the same love of learning—of truth—that they had written into Tanfrit's character. That could be enough of a purpose.

The additions to the third act now hinged upon that love of truth to serve the needs of the mystery. It still felt strange to think of her music as a mystery. Who was it that Serafina had quoted? The one who said that every act of man can be a mystery if done for the love of God? If God is truth, then perhaps that was enough.

The scene where Gaudericus refused Tanfrit's gift of the forbidden book had been expanded and rewritten. Now they both came to realize it was learning, not power, they sought. And in a soaring duet they reject and refuse all sorcery, consigning the text to the fire and pledging themselves to seeking only wisdom and knowledge. That was the heart of the mystery, where the power of the music, amplified through the attention of the audience, would strike out against the...the whatever it was they were fighting. A blow that might be unneeded or might be their last hope of success. In the opera, the moment was Tanfrit's glorious triumph before her tragic fall, when Gaudericus refused to return her carnal love. And then, as before, the river, the flood, the remorse, the dedication.

She saw that finale differently now.

"Serafina?"

"Yes?" Serafina turned, her hands still trying silently to guide the musicians to her vision.

"It was a tragedy—that Gaudericus couldn't love her the way she wanted—but it wasn't wrong. It was only his nature. Serafina, promise me you'll never throw yourself in a river. Not for me. Not for anyone."

Serafina looked confused for only a moment, then said solemnly, "I promise I'll never throw myself in the river. But never forget that we wrote that story. We chose that ending. We don't know what was truly in their hearts. We don't even know that Tanfrit really did drown herself."

That wasn't what she'd meant. Luzie swallowed hard and tried once more. "I want you to find...to find what you're seeking. I wish I could have been it."

Serafina's mouth twitched, but the expression was too quickly controlled to read. "How could I wish you to be anything other than what you are?"

* * *

They had been invited to witness the cathedral mysteries in company with Margerit's household, but Luzie had let Serafina go without her thinking she would be too nervous to sit still. That had been a mistake. There was nothing for her to do until the evening. In truth, there was nothing for her to do at all except wait and watch. Her father had taken her to the lower rooms at the Café Chatuerd to sip tea and watch the activity out in the Plaiz. They could sometimes hear bits of the ceremony when the tables around them chanced to fall silent. Would it work? All her life she had thought of the mysteries as mere ceremony. Not meaningless—not at all! No more than the Mass was meaningless, or confession, or any other sacraments. But as something that involved the soul and not the body. If she allowed herself to think of all that depended...How she wished she had Serafina's vision so she could *know*. Her hands began shaking, causing the teacup to rattle against its saucer.

"Luzie, you've done well." Her father's gnarled hands encased her own and squeezed gently.

"I know, Papa." She smiled wanly at him. "Do you know? When I gave my first concert two years back, all I could think was that I wished you could be here to see it."

"My Luzie, the famous composer. Do you wish Henirik could have been here?"

She blushed at the praise and shook her head. When had she last thought of Henirik? He deserved better than that. "But if my husband were still alive, I would never have written anything."

The thought carried guilt with it. Would she have traded all this to have Henirik back again? The loss had faded. The emptiness was being filled with other things, other people. In those first years, yes, absolutely. But now? To lose the music now would be like losing her soul. Now there was a devil's bargain to drive a tragic plot. Perhaps...Her hand itched to scribble down ideas. And in that impulse was her answer.

The cathedral hummed like bees around a hive when the Mystery of Saint Mauriz gave way to preparations for the Royal Guild's ceremony. Luzie could bear to be still no longer and walked down the sloping road from the Plaiz to the edge of the river while her father went to the opera house to review the music one last time. She paced slowly upriver to the Pont Ruip and down to the Pont Vezzen and back to the Plaiz to wander aimlessly along the shops and arcades that lined the cobbled expanse. There were few stragglers like her. The cathedral was packed with every body that could find a space. Excitement had gripped the city—at least the upper city. She imagined the wharf district with its barges, the poorer eastern quarter, the dark factories south of the university…no doubt they went about their lives today as always.

Would any of this touch them at all? The foreign plots, the arguments over ancient ritual, the singers strutting on a stage? They'd notice when the river ran its usual course, but there had been dry years and wet before and would be again. Would the absence of disaster be seen as a blessing? It was too easy, caught up in the excitement at the Tanfrit Academy, to think that what they did was all the world. For Mefroi Iannik, sweating before a furnace, or his wife, peddling cabbages in the market, what use were the soaring lyrics of "Let the waters rise up?"

The distant chanting in the cathedral swelled to a rumbling babble as the doors opened and the celebrants spilled out. Luzie drifted over to watch for Serafina. There, in a cluster with Margerit and the rest of the small party from Tiporsel House. She made her way across the current of people to join them.

"Luzie! There you are!" Margerit called. "This way. The Benezets and the other guilds have cleared out the cathedral. We have a quiet dinner waiting to fill the time while they're working, if any of us can find an appetite."

She had expected them to work their way further toward the north side of the Plaiz where cafés clustered around the skirts of the opera house and the Grand Salle, but instead the armins cleared a path to take them past the fountain toward the western side and the gates of the palace.

When she realized where they were going, Luzie exclaimed, "Oh, I couldn't! I'm not dressed…"

But Margerit tucked a hand under her arm, saying, "Don't worry. There's nothing formal in it. Just a chance to discuss the results so far and breathe a little. There'll be plenty of time to go home for evening dress before the performance."

It was a blur of cryptic comments and obscure descriptions. At first Serafina and Margerit had their heads together talking in excited and hopeful tones but slowly they fell silent and Serafina stared with unfocused gaze in the direction of the cathedral. Luzie managed to eat a little: a buffet of pastries and little tarts. And then came a sudden hush and deep bows all around as a tall, elegant figure in russet silk swept in. Even without the glint of the jeweled gold band that adorned her head, there would have been no mistaking the Princess of Alpennia. Luzie felt the weight of those sharp, hooded eyes briefly, then was given a nod and the relief of being ignored.

"How goes the mystery? Can you tell?"

Margerit answered in subdued tones. "The Mauriz…there were some surprises but the *charis* worked outward as it should. The *castellum* was better than any previous celebration."

"I meant the present one," the princess said.

All eyes turned toward Serafina where she stood lost in her visions.

Luzie knew every expression, every response Serafina might make as she watched the flow of mystic currents. But now her face was still. Gradually the rest of the room fell silent until the only sound was the servants, carefully replacing dishes on the long serving tables.

When the outer doors swung open, Luzie jumped. With slow and solemn tread as if still celebrating their ritual, a procession of robed figures wearing the colors of their guilds entered the chamber. Luzie's eyes darted among them. These were not the public guilds whose ceremonies were performed openly. Membership might not be secret but was rarely advertised. A familiar face turned toward her in brief recognition. Maistir Fizeir's expression turned cold as he looked away again.

"Did you succeed?" Princess Anna's voice rang through the room.

A tall man stepped forward and bowed. "Your Grace, we believe the ceremony has acted as intended. It may be some days before a certain determination can be made."

Luzie looked to Serafina and then to Margerit. They gave no sign of relief. Surely they would know? The new arrivals were bidden to the feast and a low rumble of conversation rose again. Luzie felt a presence at her back and turned. It was Fizeir, still with that carefully neutral expression.

"So, Maisetra Valorin, you will have your triumph."

"I beg your pardon?"

"Your performance tonight. You will have your revenge over me."

His voice was pitched low—not meant for others to hear—and she replied in kind.

"Maistir Fizeir, I do not desire or need revenge. If there is a triumph tonight, it will belong to all of us. I—" What could she tell him? That she had idolized him? That if he had ever given her an ungrudging word of praise she would have cherished it as a treasure? "Maistir Fizeir, if there is a quarrel between us, it isn't my doing. The salles of Rotenek can hold us both."

"Indeed they can," said a soft drawling voice at her other side.

She saw Fizeir stiffen further at Count Chanturi's rebuke.

Chanturi took her hand and slipped it around his arm. "My dear, you have preparations to make. My carriage awaits."

* * *

The strangest part of the day was returning home to dress. Charluz and Elinur buzzed around her, taking the place of Gerta's more ordinary attentions. It felt strange that Serafina wasn't there. The question had not been raised.

Serafina was a guest at Tiporsel House. Soon, Luzie would find a stranger to fill her room, after her father no longer needed it.

She turned to the glass. "Do I look like a famous composer?"

Charluz checked the clasp of her necklace, and Elinur held out the long white gloves, a gift from the household.

"You look just as you ought," Elinur said. "You mustn't keep the count waiting."

When they arrived at the opera house, the crowd parted as Chanturi escorted her through the entrance and up the grand staircase to Margerit's box. For once, his courtesies were comforting instead of teasing. The faces were a blur: Margerit, Baroness Saveze still with her arm bound up, Jeanne and Mesnera Chazillen, shadowed by young Anna Monterrez, and Serafina of course, elegant in her crimson gown; others she barely knew. The box was filled to the edges, as all the others were. From the other levels she could hear a hum of bright, excited voices, but the mood in Margerit's box was tense and somber.

Serafina took her hand and squeezed it. "It all depends on us now."

And then it began.

How could one view one's own work and know if it were worthy? Her fingers knew the music as she knew her own face, but now it stood apart, like viewing a stranger in the mirror. Voices swelled as the chorus in academic robes entered from the left and parted to frame the entrance of Tanfrit, the welcome of the chancellor, the joyous greeting from Gaudericus, the cold and envious asides of Theodorus. Did she dare to feel proud?

Luzie turned to Serafina as the first act drew toward a close, hoping to see in her face some reflection of the visions that the music stirred.

Serafina was shaking her head slowly and muttering, "It isn't right."

Margerit leaned toward them both and whispered, "Will it work?"

"I don't know," Serafina said hollowly. "It's there, you see it? But it's just slightly...out of tune. Out of time. I don't know...It may not be strong enough."

Luzie tried to work out what she meant. The orchestra was perfectly in tempo. No discordant notes jangled in the ear. The singers met their cues.

"Can we do anything?" Margerit asked, as applause swelled around them. The audience seemed to feel no lack in the performance.

Serafina rose abruptly, before the others had begun to stir and stretch. "Luzie, come with me."

She led the way briskly through the corridors, now beginning to fill for the usual promenade during the interval. Comments followed them as they passed. That's her. Maisetra Valorin. Where are they going? Who's the dark one? Some foreign thaumaturgist, I hear. Maisetra Sovitre's student.

A staircase took them down to the wings of the stage and into the orchestra where the musicians were taking their brief ease. What did she plan? What more could be done at this point?

"Maistir Ovimen," Serafina demanded, "I must conduct."

Luzie saw her father start and look affronted, but he turned to her. "Luzie?"

It was in her hands. So much was in her hands: the success of the opera, everyone who had trusted in her, Margerit's mysteries and—if they were all to be believed—so much more. No, it was in Serafina's hands. She turned and echoed Margerit's question, "Will it work?"

This time Serafina answered with fierce conviction, "Yes."

Luzie nodded to her father. "She must conduct."

The orchestra were hanging on the exchange and looked to him. Serafina had led them in rehearsals, teasing out the visions that guided her as the last details of the arrangements were hammered out. This was a different matter.

He bowed formally. The baton was passed.

Luzie watched the second act from a chair at the side of the orchestra where she would be in no one's way. It took much of the first duet before Serafina and the musicians had each other's measure. It didn't take mystical vision to see that something had begun out of balance. But during Theodorus's solo, when he laid out the trap by which he would either win Tanfrit or destroy her, it began to feel that they were moving as one again. Serafina coaxed and commanded, roused and quieted, following a score that only she could see.

Luzie could feel when the music caught hold of something deeper. It wasn't in the sound, or the way the lyrics seemed to breathe life into the very air around them. It was more of a swelling feeling within her body, as if all her senses were on fire. She felt Tanfrit's ambition and desire within her bones. The music washed over her like the touch of a lover, caressing, demanding, bringing her to the edge of passion again and again.

When the cue for the second interval came, instead of thunderous applause there was an echoing silence. The audience held their breaths and all the world felt suspended. In an ordinary performance it would have been disastrous. Serafina looked back, almost wildly, at the ranks of spectators, the faces peering over the rails in box after box. The looming silence felt like the moment before a storm. It was a moment that must be seized. Frantically, Luzie scrambled up the steps at the edge of the stage and ducked behind the curtain.

The singers turned to stare. They'd heard the empty silence and had caught something of the tension.

"We need to finish it now," Luzie gasped. "Can you go on?"

They looked one to another. The sets were in place. There would be a missed costume change.

Benedetta Cavalli stepped forward and proclaimed, "Let the show continue!"

The orchestra slipped into the music for the curtain like a hand into a glove. There had been no sound from the house, not so much as a cough or the closing of a door. The tension that had begun to fray and fade stretched tight once more, like the hairs on a bow drawing the rich tones of the violins into the waiting silence. And then Tanfrit, bringing the gift of the forbidden book, like a lover offering her heart.

Luzie could almost hear hundreds of voices sigh as Gaudericus launched into "This I refuse." And then the rising crescendo of Tanfrit and Gaudericus, their voices twining in the counter messages of "I pledge myself to you alone."

Serafina seemed to call out with her whole body, turning the music end over end, as the two singers held up the black bound volume between them, singing, "I abjure thee, I dismiss thee." The chorus, standing almost in the shadows at the rear of the stage, chanted a slowly rising echo of the duet. The horns joined the strings and the kettledrums hammered a heartbeat, sounding, sounding, sounding, until Serafina—her eyes on some cue not of the world—brought her arms down with a violent jerk.

This time the audience erupted with a roar, a catharsis of voice and hands that filled and overflowed the hall. Whatever it was they had meant to do had been done. They had succeeded. Luzie could feel it as a bone-deep certainty.

A brief change of scene: a painted bridge of lath and canvas. Tanfrit and Gaudericus meeting on the arch. Gaudericus's rejection and then, as Tanfrit reprised "I pledge myself to you alone," the taunting by Theodorus as he left with the chorus of scholars.

The tension became palpable once more as Madame Cavalli cast off the mask of spurned sweetheart and drew herself up in pride and fury. *Let the waters rise up.* It swelled, just as the waters of the Rotein would swell when the spring rains cast themselves against the mountain peaks. *Let the waters rise up.* The orchestra rose, not in trumpets and drums this time, but with the nearly imperceptible crescendo of flowing water. *And wash away my sorrow.* As before, it was not the despair of an abandoned lover, nor even the fury of jealousy—for how could Tanfrit be jealous of Sophia, the same goddess to whom she was pledged? Madame Cavalli sang it as a paean of triumph. The final victory of Tanfrit's return. It was not sorrow that was washed away but shame, defeat, regret, all the things that had held her back in life. She didn't cast herself into the waters but demanded that they come to claim her.

Luzie could feel the power of the music, what Serafina might call the *fluctus*, pouring through her. In her imagination, she saw it flowing through the Plaiz and down to the Rotein to mingle with the waters and summon them.

It was done.

A soft gesture of Serafina's baton called to the bassoon, and then to Gaudericus's final aria. The soothing, mournful chorus brought the audience back to themselves. *No woman past or yet to come.*

It was a lie, in the end. Tanfrit's legacy might have lain forgotten, like her bones beneath the stone in Urmai, but her work lived on. It had spurred Gaudericus to defy those who would have dismissed his theories as heresy. It had inspired Margerit Sovitre to believe that a woman could become a great thaumaturgist, and to pledge herself to that same study. Perhaps she might consider rewriting that final chorus.

* * *

"What will you do now?" Luzie asked.

She and Serafina had slipped away, at last, from the celebratory reception and wandered down from the Plaiz to the Pont Vezzen. They'd crossed to the middle of the span and leaned on the stone railing to watch the river flow toward them, glinting in the moon's glow.

"We did it," she said softly. Even without Margerit's reassurance, without the palpable relief on the faces of the guildmasters, she would have been certain. There was a weight lifted from the city, like the calm after a storm has broken and passed, when the earth smells damp and fresh and new.

Serafina moved as in a daze, her eyes still full of visions. "I wish you could see it like I do," she whispered. "It's like a river of light."

A shiver ran down Luzie's spine. It was a curious sort of magic that Serafina had called when she took up the baton. Not a magic like the alchemist's fire that changed one substance for another. More a magic like what Jeanne achieved when she placed two people in conversation and created partnership, or the complex magic that a classroom could inspire, drawing in minds that would change themselves. Without the music, there would have been no magic, but without Serafina there would have been no music—at least none like what they had achieved tonight.

"What will you do now?" she repeated.

"I don't know. It isn't—" She fell silent and for a long time there was no sound but the faint splashes of the Rotein against the bridge abutments. "It isn't how I thought it would come. The magic. I've been trying for so long. Maybe nothing is what I thought it should be. I don't know."

The air was colder than either of them had dressed for, but Luzie didn't want to be the first to break the moment.

"Margerit asked me to teach," Serafina said suddenly. "A real teacher, not just a student filling in. She said it was ridiculous for me to pretend otherwise. I'll have a salary. A small one."

"Then you aren't going back to Rome?"

Briefly, Serafina's face looked bleak and worried. "I can't. Paolo would never forgive me now. Not for leaving him. Not for finding my magic without him." She shook her head, not in negation but like a bird settling its feathers. "I don't belong there. I don't know if I belong anywhere." She'd said something like that before, but this time there was no bitterness. "Maybe that doesn't matter. For now, I plan to stay."

CODA

Late September, 1825

High in the mountains to the east and south of Alpennia, a warm wind caressed the icy passes and kissed the snow-choked valleys. For three years winter had held dominion beyond its proper reach. Now silver threads tumbled down from the heights. The melt gathered in rivulets; rivulets turned to streams; streams fed rivers. The Esikon, the Tupe and the Innek fed the Rotein in turn. The tributaries of the great river swelled and grew as they flowed through Eskor and Chalanz and Rokefels. And in Rotenek, the water began to rise, climbing the steps at the Nikuleplaiz one by one.

Bella Books, Inc.

Women. Books. Even Better Together.

P.O. Box 10543
Tallahassee, FL 32302

Phone: 800-729-4992
www.bellabooks.com